SLOW MOTION
GHOSTS

www.penguin.co.uk

SLOW MOTION GHOSTS

Jeff Noon

doubleday

TRANSWORLD PUBLISHERS
61–63 Uxbridge Road, London W5 5SA
www.penguin.co.uk

Transworld is part of the Penguin Random House group of companies
whose addresses can be found at global.penguinrandomhouse.com

Penguin
Random House
UK

First published in Great Britain in 2019 by Doubleday
an imprint of Transworld Publishers

A CIP catalogue record for this book
is available from the British Library.

ISBNs
9780857525611 (hb)
9780857525628 (tpb)

Typeset in 12/15 pt Adobe Garamond Pro
by Integra Software Services Pvt. Ltd, Pondicherry

Printed and bound in Great Britain by Clays Ltd, Elcograf S.p.A.

Penguin Random House is committed to a sustainable future
for our business, our readers and our planet. This book is
made from Forest Stewardship Council® certified paper.

1 3 5 7 9 10 8 6 4 2

To Steve

SATURDAY

11 APRIL 1981

Blood and Petrol

Hobbes arrived at Brixton police station around eight thirty that night. He travelled in with four other officers in a patrol car, one of whom kept effing and blinding at what he was seeing through the windows. 'Jesus Christ! Can't we just let them kill each other?' Charlie Jenkes told him to shut the hell up, it was bad enough.

DI Hobbes sat there, squeezed on the back seat. He felt sick with nerves.

At the station yard they were quickly organized and issued with orders. Hobbes took charge of a group of nine uniformed constables.

Christ, he hadn't done anything like this, not for years.

A van drove them at speed to a drop-off point, spewed them out, into the mayhem. They had six plastic shields between them, their only defence against whatever waited for them out there on the frontline. No helmets, no proper riot gear. Hobbes's task was to drive the rioters off Shakespeare Road so a fire engine and an ambulance could get through. He got the line fixed and set the men marching in step, but the rank was quickly broken as they entered the fray. Youths were gathered further down the street, cutting it off. A police car was lying on its side. One rioter bent down to light a pool of petrol and the car burst into flames. The young men and women cheered and danced around the vehicle.

They looked like teenagers. Kids. Nothing more.

Most of them were black, but there were some white faces among them.

Hobbes shouted orders. He forced his squad to get back in line, to stand its ground, shields interlinked in front of them, centurion style, and then to move forward slowly, slowly, one step at a time. No heroics. 'No fucking heroics, do you hear me?' His words were blown aside by the night's craziness.

In a side street a fire engine was waiting to come through, an ambulance parked up behind it. The front window of the fire engine had been smashed in. Now Hobbes had his objective in sight, he urged his men on. They were moving well, already pushing some of the rioters back into a cross street, when a hail of missiles landed on them. Rocks, house bricks, bottles. They smashed and clattered against the shields. He tried to keep his men together but it was no good, more missiles came over and the line staggered, an officer lost his footing, and two of the shields broke apart. A beer bottle found its target, hitting a constable full in the face. He fell. His colleagues stumbled around him.

Hobbes ran to the fallen man and pulled him free of the scrum. The officer's nose was broken. Eyes glazed over, watery. No recognition in them.

'Pull back, pull back!'

By sheer force of will, Hobbes got the nine men back to the parked van, two of them dragging their injured colleague along. In the distance Hobbes could see even more burning cars, and beyond that a building on fire, a public house.

Kill the pigs! Kill the pigs!

Smoke stung his eyes. He was out of breath, his sides ached. In more than twenty years on the force he'd never faced anything like this, not even when he was on the beat himself, working streets as poor and deprived as these were. Something had changed in the passing years.

Hobbes screamed at his men to regroup, and they did so under his command, eight of them now. And he pushed them forward, putting himself in the frontline, glad for the shield he shared with the officer at his side, a man he had never seen before in his life.

The missiles hit like the force of God, worse than before, over and over.

He could hear cheering. Kids were running forward to lob their stones and bottles and then retreating back to their own lines. It was war, plain and simple.

But the cops were breaking through now, forcing the rioters back. And then a bottle hit a shield to Hobbes's left and exploded into flames. Ignited petrol splashed over the shield, turning it into a sheet of yellow fire. The bloody thing wasn't even fireproof. The plastic of the shield melted. The heat was intense.

The line broke, fell back.

Hobbes was left there, alone.

Half hidden in the shadows, someone was lying on the street ahead, groaning. Not a policeman, he saw that now. A civilian. A black woman. Caught in the crossfire. He had to help her, and so he ran forward, keeping low. Time slowed to a crawl, the sirens grew distant in his hearing. He glanced back.

His men had scattered to other positions, he was exposed.

No protection, no defence. Just himself.

The woman was unconscious. He couldn't move her.

A bottle broke into smithereens on the pavement next to him, followed by a scream of rage. Hobbes looked up to see a single youth running towards him, his features hooded: race, colour and identity hidden. In his hand a weapon of some kind, a stone or a brick. Hobbes staggered. He started to move away and then felt something thud against his head.

There was no pain, not at first.

His hand touched at his temple.

Sticky, red. What the fuck was that?

He stumbled, nearly fell. His legs were weak. And he knew by instinct that the rioter was almost upon him, coming in for a second attack.

Hobbes closed his eyes, his hands came up to protect his face.

And then he was being pulled back, away from the trouble. Somebody had hold of him, was dragging him off the street as two lines of shielded officers ran forward as one, straight into the maelstrom. The noise was overwhelming.

But now Hobbes had fallen into a side alley.

It was quieter here, secluded. He felt the wall at his back and slid down to the ground. Charlie Jenkes was there with him. His friend had saved him.

'Charlie,' he whispered, his mouth hardly working.

'Keep quiet,' Jenkes replied. 'You got hit.'

Yes, he saw the blood now and his eyes blurred over.

'The woman . . .'

'She's safe. Don't worry.'

Jenkes pressed his palm against Hobbes's head, against the cut. And they knelt together, the two of them, as close as they'd ever been as partners. It was a simple act of comradeship. But when he looked directly at Detective Inspector Jenkes's face – dirty, streaked with soot and sweat, teeth gritted – he saw only madness written there, a hatred that burned as wildly and fervently as any of the rioters they were facing that night.

Hobbes should've guessed right then that something was going to go wrong.

But he didn't guess. He couldn't. Days would pass before that hatred was played out to its full intensity, and by then it would be too late.

SUNDAY
23 AUGUST 1981

Examination of a Mask

He stood at the gate of the semi-detached house, peering along the short garden path to the front door, the downstairs windows, and the upper-storey window behind which he knew the dead person slept on, waiting for him. It was coming up on nine in the evening, the sky cloudy, but a street lamp's glow directly overhead gave off a clear yellow light. The other members of the squad were standing around chatting, leaning against their cars, or handling the small crowd of onlookers that had already gathered, waiting for Inspector Hobbes to finish whatever it was he had to do. He could hear laughter, one of the old lags mocking him, no doubt. But he had to be alone, that was his thing. He'd only been here a week since the transfer. And before that, four weeks off, paid leave. For his own protection. And now this.

He couldn't believe he had to prove himself all over again at the age of forty-four, but there it was.

He kept on looking, examining. It was a perfectly normal suburban house in a well-tended avenue lined with trees. The garden was overgrown compared with those on the two neighbouring sides. Perhaps the resident had been lazy, maybe he was away from home a lot. Perhaps the neighbours disliked him because of this, for bringing down the property values of the street. Hobbes had a mind that clicked through possibilities, one after another.

He opened the gate and walked down the path to the door. He knew that the woman who'd found the body had rung the bell a couple of times, and then walked around to the rear of the house. He wondered if she'd peered through the half-open curtains of the front window? He copied her imagined actions, seeing a sparsely furnished living room, part of a coffee table, and a television set.

Hobbes followed the woman's route down the side of the house. He wanted to trace her steps, to understand the moment of discovery.

There was enough light from the windows to view the back garden. It was even worse than the front: a scruffy lawn marred with patches of earth, dying flowers at the borders, and an old armchair close by, slowly decaying. There was a wooden fence and beyond that a line of trees, the night sky over South West London.

The back door of the house was ajar. Cautiously he pushed it further open and stepped inside. Unwashed pots in the sink, trays of half-eaten TV dinners, the waste bin overflowing. The stink of rotten food. Again, the state of the room contrasted with the street, the expected middle-class values. He walked along the corridor into the living room. The walls and the ceiling were painted white. One armchair, a settee, the coffee table. The new minimal look; he'd seen it in the Sunday supplements. Except that one entire wall of the room was lined floor to ceiling with shelves of vinyl records, with an expensive-looking hi-fi system fitted neatly among them. The only personal detail was a framed photograph showing a young man with an older couple: son and parents, smiling. Two cups on the table, each one half filled with cold tea. Stretched out between the cups were several sheets of paper, one next to the other, overlapping. Some were covered in typescript with handwritten additions; others entirely handwritten complete with many crossings-out. It looked like poetry, or song lyrics. The signature *Lucas Bell* had been added at the bottom of each sheet of paper. The name was vaguely familiar to Hobbes.

He walked back into the hall and paused at the foot of the stairs. A sound could be heard coming from the floor above. A voice. It was very quiet, requiring all his attention to hear it. He headed up the stairs, taking them slowly, and by the time he'd reached the landing his breath was held tight in his throat. His senses were perfectly alert. On the left he passed an open doorway and saw a room filled with musical instruments: guitars, keyboards, amplifiers, a drum kit. He thought briefly that this was a strange part of London for a rock musician to live: sleepy, leafy Richmond. There was a story there, Hobbes felt sure.

He moved on a few more steps along the landing and then stopped. Now he could hear it clearly, the music playing softly from a doorway ahead. The same line of a song repeated over and over, carried by a young male voice. He followed the sound into the front bedroom and stood in the doorway, studying the scene in front of him.

The moment. Take it in. Concentrate.

The room was lit only by the street lamp outside, shining through the partly open curtains, tinting the blue walls and the white sheets. A man was lying on the bed. The victim. He was fully clothed, dressed in a blue shirt and black trousers, his body twisted into a terrible shape.

Brendan Clarke. Twenty-six years old.

This much Hobbes knew. The name and age of the victim. But he resisted as yet the urge to examine the body. Instead he continued his careful search of the room. It had not been cleaned or vacuumed in a while; every surface was covered in dust. He saw a telephone on a small table against the far wall. An ashtray next to the phone contained the long stub of a cigarette, its white filter tip stained with lipstick. Hobbes thought about that; he noted the brand name written around the filter.

The song played on, coming from a music centre near the window. A few records were stacked against the wall, with the sleeve of one album lying on the floor beside the machine: *Backstreet Harlequin* by Lucas Bell. Now Hobbes remembered the name of the singer from early in the last decade, the glam rock era. The lid of the player was raised and the record album was circling. A lump of sticky blue putty, the kind used to fix posters to walls, had been placed on the vinyl, near the end of the first track. Because of this the stylus cartridge was held in place, so that the needle was trapped in the groove. The same musical phrase was repeating itself endlessly, marked by a click, a few bars of instrumental sound and the singer's voice, one half-line of lyrics.

Nothing left to lose . . . click.

Nothing left to lose . . . click.

Nothing left to lose . . . click.

Hobbes examined the surface of the record as it spun around, looking for prints. He could see none. But then he stared at the lump of putty and his eyes widened. A fingerprint was clearly visible in the soft blue material.

He looked out of the bedroom window, at the lamp-lit length of Westbrook Avenue. It had started to rain. That would make it worse for the officers who were still waiting down there. They all hated him. For his odd ways, his attitude, and most of all for what had happened to DI Jenkes. The stories travelled with him. He turned back to face the room. In doing so, he noticed in the uniform coat of dust on top of a cupboard, a clean circle, some few inches across. Something had been removed. This image was carefully stored away.

Now for the body.

Hobbes walked back to the bed and stared down at the victim's face. The blood had long dried. The doctor had given an estimated time of death: late last night or early this morning, call it midnight for ease. Christ, but that was a long time to wait, twenty-odd hours lying here alone. With the music playing for all that time, heard by nobody until that poor woman got here an hour ago and found the body.

He studied each wound in turn.

One of the eyes, the left one, was little more than an empty dark pool. The mouth had been slit at each corner a full inch, forming a cruel grin. A crude letter X had been carved into the forehead. Smaller injuries were visible on the cheeks and brow. Blood had also flowed from a jagged cut in the right-hand side of the neck, probably the injury that had killed him. It left a large dark red stain on the pillow beneath.

The victim's mouth was wide open, filled with some object, but Hobbes could not tell what it was because of the blood that had welled there. It might be a ball of crumpled paper. He guessed it had been placed in the mouth after death, and he felt a sudden urge to reach inside the mouth and pull the object loose. His fingers twitched with impatience.

He breathed easily, with intent, to steady himself.

The victim's shirt was also stained with blood around the neck and chest. He bent closer. There was something inside the breast pocket, the edge of it protruding. With a fingernail he nudged it free until it lay exposed on the shirt front. It was a playing card of some kind, a court card, but of a design he had never seen before: a young man was walking along happily, a dog at his side. One more step would lead him over the edge of a cliff. The card was marked with a zero at the top, and the designation *The Fool* at the bottom.

Hobbes leaned back upright. There was a second reason why he liked to be alone in these initial moments of an investigation, beyond the urge to concentrate; he needed to make the pledge without being stared at, or wondered about. He did so now, speaking in a cold whisper: 'Mr Clarke. I will find out why this was done to you. From that knowledge I will find out who did this to you. I will hunt the perpetrator down and bring them to justice.' He paused and then added, 'This I promise.'

Hobbes stepped back a few paces.

He had seen many crime scenes over the years, a few as bad as this or worse, but even given the circumstances and the state of the corpse, something about this room, this particular situation, was not right, not as it should be.

He was missing something.

The thought took him over completely.

DS Latimer found him five minutes later when she entered the room. He was still there, motionless, silently staring down at the body of the victim.

13

Twisting Green Pathways

The station's interview room was small and windowless, already hazy with cigarette smoke. A female constable was standing to attention near the door. There was a wooden table with three scuffed plastic chairs set around it, and nothing much else.

Here the woman waited.

Hobbes watched her through the glass.

Early thirties, wild blonde hair with red streaks, the whole thing barely tamed with some kind of shiny gel. Her clothes were a mismatch of colours and textures: scarlet, gold, black, a polka-dot collar seen above a striped waistcoat. Her face held a numbed expression.

Hobbes glanced through the pages of the woman's statement for a second time, noting a few items of interest.

He turned to DC Fairfax, who was standing nearby.

'There's not much here.'

'No, well. She's a bit stuck-up.'

Hobbes gave him a glance, nothing more. 'The woman's in shock.'

'Sure, I guess—'

'Bloody hell. Find me an office to work in. It's like a KGB cell in there.'

'We're a bit overrun. Actually. Sir.'

Now Hobbes gave him the full stare. Detective Fairfax kept up his surly grin for a moment more and then shook his head in displeasure, and left the room.

Hobbes entered the interview room. He nodded at the female officer and then said to the woman at the table, 'I'm sorry about the wait.'

She turned her face away.

Hobbes sat down and introduced himself. 'I'd take you to my office, but . . . well, I haven't got one. Not yet. I've only been here a short while.' He coughed. 'So then, let's get ourselves sorted out, room-wise. Then we'll talk.'

The woman sat in silence. She looked down at her fingertips, which were still grey from the print powder. Hobbes fished a packet of Embassy Red from his pocket. 'Will you join me?' She shook her head. But then reached for her own packet of Consulate on the table. He lit her cigarette with his lighter. Her hand was shaking. He looked at the ashtray: each stub had been marked by her lipstick.

'You smoke mentholated?'

A slight nod in answer.

'I'm trying to cut down, myself,' he said. 'But you know how it is.'

'Simone Paige. That's my name.'

Now her eyes were locked on his.

Hobbes drew deep on his cigarette. 'Have you thrown up yet? No. You should try. It helps.' He grimaced. 'I can remember my first ever sighting, plain as day.' He paused and then added, 'I was seventeen.'

Her eyes blinked. 'I don't intend to . . .'

'To what?'

'To see another dead body. Not for a long while.'

'Of course not.'

Hobbes scanned the woman's face, taking in all that he could. She was entirely at home with her age, her features showing their very first lines, the cheekbones sinking in rather than puffing out. The remains of the day's make-up was still evident. Her eyes were set wide apart on her face, the ends elongated and sharpened. There

15

was a fierce element of control both in her manners and her appearance – a tough nut to crack, Hobbes thought.

And then he was aware, intensely aware, of her gaze on his own face.

They were both examining each other.

Hobbes wasn't used to this, yet he didn't turn away.

Eye to eye, neither giving in. Until at last Fairfax returned. Hobbes stubbed out his cigarette and led Simone out into the corridor. Along the way he said to her, 'You're a writer? Is that correct?'

'A journalist. A music critic.'

He remembered the vinyl record with its repeated message.

They entered a much smaller room, an office. It was occupied by a police constable who was studying a large paperback book.

'Out of here.'

The fresh-faced PC tried to explain. 'Sir, I was looking something up in the police manual.'

Hobbes snorted. 'That thing? Nothing in there will help you when the fists start flying. Go on, give us some room.'

The uniformed officer left them. Hobbes sat down and gestured for Simone to do the same. 'This will do us.' He placed a cassette recorder on the desk. 'You must've done a fair few interviews yourself, I imagine, in your job?'

'Hundreds,' the woman said. 'Too many.'

Hobbes blew on the microphone. 'Please state your name one more time, for the sake of the tape.'

'Simone Paige.'

A smile came to Hobbes's face, nothing more than a slight crinkle of the mouth. Then he stood up. 'Excuse me for one moment.' And without explanation he left the room and closed the door behind him.

'Finished already, sir?'

It was the young constable who'd been using the office for study. He was standing in the corridor, clutching the volume of *Blackstone's Police Manual* in his hand.

'Not yet.'

The officer couldn't quite meet Hobbes's stare. He'd probably heard the rumours from the older guys.

'What's your name?'

'Police Constable Barlow, sir.'

He was in his early twenties, tall and stick thin, with extraordinarily neat hair. His skin looked like a razor would simply glide off it.

'Right, Barlow. Here's tonight's lesson, a little trick of mine . . .' He nodded towards the office door. 'I've left Miss Paige in there on her own.'

'The person who found the body tonight?' The young man looked overly excited at the news. 'Do you suspect her?'

Hobbes sighed. 'I don't know yet, but something's going on beyond the norm, that's for sure.'

'What makes you think that?'

'She smoked a cigarette, in the bedroom.'

'Did she?'

'Next to the phone.'

'And that means . . .'

'Think about it, Barlow. Come on, come on!'

'I am. I'm thinking, sir.' Barlow took out a notepad and pen and jotted something in it. He had to juggle with the police manual as he was doing so; it looked awkward.

'Anyway, so what I've done – and keep this quiet, won't you?'

'Yes, sir.' Barlow was whispering.

'I've left the tape recorder running. In there.' Hobbes nodded towards the office door.

'She doesn't know?'

'She might realize, eventually.'

The young man held a breath. 'I'm not sure. Is that legal, sir?'

'A simple mistake on my part.'

'So you think she might say something? She might talk to herself?'

17

'I hope so.'

'What if she turns the machine off?'

'Guilty. One hundred per cent.'

Barlow frowned. 'I don't think—'

'Lesson number two. Don't believe all the bullshit you hear from your superiors.'

The younger man searched for something to say in reply. His mouth opened and closed. Hobbes smiled to put him out of his misery.

'How are you on rock music?'

'Not bad, sir.'

'Good, good. Find out everything you can about a singer called Lucas Bell, big in the early seventies.'

'I know his records. Some of them—'

'By tomorrow.'

'Will do, sir. Any particular reason why?'

'I'm curious.'

Barlow's head lolled to one side as he looked at his notebook. Hobbes could practically see his brain thinking. Then the young man's eyes lit up. 'Oh, right . . .' He pointed to the door. 'You think she rang 999 from the bedroom?'

'I do. And then she lit a cigarette.'

'That is a bit strange, I guess.'

Hobbes rubbed a finger and thumb against his forehead. He mumbled to himself: 'And something else . . . the phone wasn't next to the bed. It was across the room.'

'I'm sorry, sir. I don't understand.'

'Oh, I'm just thinking aloud, Constable. Trying to work things out.'

Barlow put his notebook away. 'There's one thing I don't like, sir.'

'What's that?'

'There being no sign of a struggle. That's right, isn't it?'

'It is.'

Barlow shook his head. 'Now you see, I would struggle. If someone was coming for me with a knife, sir, I would struggle like all hell.'

'You would indeed.'

Hobbes walked back into the room. Simone Paige had lit another cigarette. She was staring at a wall calendar issued by the town council advertising the glories of Richmond upon Thames. The image for August 1981 showed Hampton Court Maze photographed from above. Hobbes sat down and checked to see if the cassette tape was still spinning in the machine. It was.

'I know you've given us a statement already, Miss Paige.' Hobbes browsed the file and recited in a dull tone: 'Arrived at the premises at such and such a time, went upstairs, found the deceased, Brendan Clarke, lying on the bed, called the police, and so on.' His own rather gruff voice returned. 'Yes. All very useful. But what I'd like you to do is to answer some questions of my own. Do you mind?'

Simone shook her head.

'Tell me about your relationship with the deceased.'

'My relationship?'

'Yes. Did you know him well?'

'We were . . .'

'Yes?'

'Friends.'

Hobbes's expression was quite cold by now. 'So, this is a man that you first met last night, I think that's correct?'

Simone nodded.

'And yet, as you say, already you're *friends* with him?'

She answered simply, 'That's how it is.'

Hobbes referred to the file. 'It says here that you met Mr Clarke at a concert. So let me see. You arrive at his house a day later, and you walk in without a door key, or anyone opening the door for you, and you walk upstairs and you go into the bedroom, and . . .'

Simone was silent. Hobbes leaned forward in his chair.

'I need you to concentrate, Miss Paige. This is very important. A man has been killed. Murdered in his own bed. You were the first person at the scene.'

She stubbed her cigarette out in a metal wastepaper basket. Her voice was steady. 'The door was already open.'

'Yes?'

'The back door of the house, it was open already.'

'Fully open?'

'No. Just a little way. That's why I went inside. I thought that Brendan must be in.'

'So you walked round to the back of the house, a house you'd never visited before, in the hope of what?'

'I thought . . . I thought that maybe he was in the back garden, or that he hadn't heard me ringing the bell.'

'I see.'

Hobbes's tone rattled her, he could sense that, but she kept her control well. 'I had an appointment at Brendan's house, at eight o'clock. The meeting was important to him. So, when he didn't answer the door, I was puzzled. It felt wrong.'

'And you investigated?'

'Well . . .'

'Go on.'

'Well, it's a good job I did.'

Their eyes locked.

Hobbes smiled, he spoke calmly. 'What was it that made you think Mr Clarke might be in trouble?'

'The television was on. I saw it through the front window.'

'But still, that's hardly a danger sign.'

She looked at him. 'It was enough.'

Hobbes nodded. He said, 'But I don't think the television was switched on, not when the police first arrived.'

'No. I turned it off.'

'Now why would you do that?'

'The set was boiling hot. It must've been on for ages.'

Hobbes rubbed at his eyes. This woman had disturbed his crime scene. He hated that. Why the hell can't people leave things alone?

Simone continued, 'And then, when I'd turned it off, that's when I heard the voice.'

'The voice?'

'Yes, from upstairs.'

'You mean the song? From the record player in the bedroom?'

'Yes. It was too loud.'

'It was? It didn't seem that loud to me.'

'I turned the volume down, after I found the body.'

'Why?'

'It was too loud,' she said again. 'It was disturbing me. And . . .'

'Yes?'

'It was disturbing Brendan.'

Hobbes looked at her. Those eyes, her whole attitude. Which planet had she beamed in from? 'And what about the song being played?' he asked.

'What about it?'

'Does it mean anything to you?'

'No. Nothing. It's just a song.'

Again, that cold tone. But Hobbes knew she was lying. 'I think it means something,' he said.

Still she wouldn't be drawn. Silence.

He leaned back in his seat. 'Tell me the story, please. From the beginning.'

'There is no story. I met Brendan at the Pleasure Palace. Boy meets Girl. Boy chats up Girl. Girl goes round to see him the next day. Boy dead. What else is there?'

'That's where the concert took place? The Pleasure Palace. I don't know it, I'm afraid.' He could see her surrender, if only a little. 'You must be tired, Simone.'

Her head twitched in response. She edged for the cigarette packet. Stopped herself. Her fingers drummed on the metal leg of the chair.

'Tell me about the gig.'

She forced herself to speak. 'The Pleasure Palace is a venue in Covent Garden. Brendan was the vocalist of the headliners who were playing last night. Monsoon Monsoon.'

'Monsoon?'

'Monsoon Monsoon. That's what they call themselves. After the gig, Brendan and I got talking. We went to the dressing room.'

'And what happened there?'

'We talked. Like I said.'

'About?'

'Music. The gig. Other things. The usual things. He gave me his telephone number, and told me to give him a ring when I got a chance. That we could maybe meet up. But instead of all that rigmarole, I just made a date for eight o'clock tonight. And that's it.'

'So you were attracted to each other?'

'To be honest, I'm not sure. My feelings were confused. But . . .'

'Yes?'

'We shared a common interest.'

'Which was?'

'Lucas Bell.'

Inspector Hobbes looked at her without speaking.

'You've heard of him?' she asked.

'A little. Tell me more.'

'He's a rock singer. Well, he was. He's dead now. But he had number one singles, a couple of them. And a number one album, all around the world.'

'And it was Lucas Bell's music that was playing in the victim's room?'

Simone was staring at him, nodding, and he realized that she was as curious about this matter as he was. He asked, 'What did you think when you heard the music playing?'

'I had other things on my mind.'

'And now? Having had time to think?'

22

'I haven't had time to think. Not about that. Not for one second.'

Hobbes coughed. 'And so the two of you, Brendan Clarke and yourself, you both, what, shared an interest in this singer?'

'A passion. We shared a passion. We both loved Lucas Bell intensely. His work, his life. What he stood for. His music, and his commitment. That's why we were all there.'

'At the club?'

She nodded. 'It was a tribute gig. Brendan and his band played a lot of Lucas Bell's old songs. Cover versions, you know? And the place was absolutely packed. Because, well, lots of people feel the same way. They all love Lucas. In fact, now more than ever. It's crazy.'

'You're referring to fans? Admirers?'

Her face darkened. 'Lucas killed himself for the sake of rock and roll. He was a martyr. That's why people love him so much.'

Hobbes felt vague memories stirring, of the story in the papers, and on the nine o'clock news. Suicide. Some years ago, the mid seventies.

'Simone?'

She looked at him. He could see that her eyes were glistening.

'Do you have any idea who might have killed Brendan Clarke? Any theories at all?'

She thought for a moment and then said, 'He wanted to show me something. At the house. A piece of memorabilia.'

'To do with Lucas Bell?'

She nodded. Breathed out, relaxed slightly. 'Some of the Lucas Bell fans . . . well, some of them go beyond normal adoration.'

'You're saying they're dangerous?'

'Yes. A few of them. Very much so. Vindictive. Cruel.'

Hobbes pursed his lips. The feelings came from deep within her, that was obvious. She'd been hurt in some way. But what was she telling him, really?

'What was this piece of memorabilia, as you call it?'

23

Simone could not look him in the eye as she answered. 'I don't know. I wish I knew.'

He glanced at the file and changed tack.

'Tell me. What state was Brendan Clarke in, when you found him?'

'What state? I'm sorry, I don't—'

'Well, you've already turned the TV off, and lowered the volume on the record player, so I'm wondering . . . Did you disturb the body in any way?'

'I tried to save him—'

'I'm sorry?'

'I thought he might be alive. I thought I saw him move. I lifted the sheet away from his face. But . . . but no. He was dead.'

Hobbes was suddenly very alert, jolted by electricity. 'You lifted the sheet away from the victim's face?'

'That's right—'

'The face was covered?'

'Yes. With the bed sheet.'

'You never mentioned this in your statement.'

'Well, I'd forgotten. I didn't think it was important.'

'Oh, it's very important. Very much so.'

'Why?'

Hobbes waved the question aside. 'What did you make of the card in the victim's shirt pocket?'

'I didn't see a card.'

He pulled an evidence bag from the case file and dropped it on the table. The strange playing card was nestled inside, plainly seen through the clear plastic. Simone looked at it for a moment, before saying, 'It's the Fool's card from the tarot.'

'Enlighten me.'

She studied him. 'Most people think the tarot pack is used to tell fortunes, but actually it's a medieval system of knowledge.'

'And this card represents?'

'The young man is setting out on his journey through life, full of confidence. So confident, he doesn't notice the chasm gaping at his feet.'

Hobbes nodded. 'And does this mean anything to you?'

'Not to me, no. But Lucas Bell was obsessed with the tarot.'

'I see.'

'And he always said that this . . .' She touched the evidence bag gently. 'That the Fool was his special card.'

'And why should it be in Brendan's pocket?'

'I don't know.' Her voice wavered. 'Maybe Brendan put it there himself? Maybe it was always there.'

'No. It has blood on it. It was placed there after the fact.'

She made a noise in response, a tiny cry of pain. Hobbes looked at her. She was biting her lip with her front teeth.

'Are you keeping information back from me?'

'No.' She glared at him, her eyes fierce and dark. 'Absolutely not.'

'Tell me about the telephone.'

'I'm sorry?'

'You rang the police at that point.'

'I did, yes.'

'From the bedroom?'

Now she hesitated, so he pushed the point. 'You've known this man for what, an hour in full, if that, and yet you're quite happy to ring from a phone a couple of yards from his body. His mutilated, bloody corpse. I don't buy it. I just don't. I think you'd walk downstairs, and ring from the hallway.' He shrugged before adding, 'Any *normal* person would do that.'

'Are you insulting me?'

'I'm wondering, that's all. What was going through your mind? As you sat there and waited, smoking a cigarette?'

And now she spoke simply and clearly: 'I didn't want to leave him alone.'

At last, Hobbes could see that she was telling the truth. He pictured her in Brendan Clarke's bedroom, keeping the dead man company, the music playing, the blue smoke from her cigarette drifting in the dimly lit air.

He clicked off the tape recorder. 'Thank you. I'll be in touch if I need anything else.'

Simone nodded in response, and made to leave. But at the door she stopped and turned.

Hobbes stared at her. 'Yes, what is it?'

'There was a piece of paper inside Brendan's mouth.'

So then, she had studied the corpse as closely as he had. Hobbes couldn't get this woman straight in his mind. What was her motivation?

He stared at her. 'I can't discuss that.'

Simone Paige left the room.

Hobbes gathered his thoughts. His eyes closed momentarily as he pondered the known facts. Then he rewound the cassette tape back to the beginning and listened to the opening moments of the recording, the witness stating her name, himself making his excuses and then leaving the room, the door closing behind him. And then silence. Simone shuffling in her seat, fingers tapping at the table. Her breath.

He leaned in closer to the machine's tiny speaker.

A cigarette taken from the packet, the rasp of a lighter flint. The smoke drawn into her lungs, and a sigh of pleasure. Silence once more. Moments going by. And then at last she spoke to herself, her voice rising quietly from the speaker grille.

He couldn't believe what he'd just heard.

The Face Illuminated

Hobbes saw the word as soon as he walked down the side passage towards the door of his flat. Four letters in red paint, scrawled across the panels of the door: *SCUM*. His mind clicked into working mode. The paint was sticky to the touch, but not wet. Probably an hour or less since it had been applied. He studied the ground below the door. The pathway was concrete, so there were no footprints. Drips of red paint spotted the surface. He could imagine that the person's shoes might also be marked. Possibly. He didn't like the word *possibly*, it tied a painful knot in his thoughts. Maybe Fairfax was to blame; the young detective had made his dislike plain, right from the start. But then again, Hobbes could easily imagine one of his former Charing Cross colleagues doing this; that would be more likely, given how much he was hated at the old station. He told himself to keep working. The edges of the letters were too sharp, not diffuse. The person had used a pot and a brush, not a spray can. Now that struck him as unusual. Someone older perhaps? It certainly explained why there were so many drops on the ground. He went inside and found the only paint he owned, a small can of blue acrylic he'd bought to touch up scratches on his car. He sprayed over each letter.

Back inside the flat, he tried to settle down. It was quiet, far too dark. Shadows hunched in the corners, ignoring any lights he switched on. Some animal was scratching away in the walls. It was there every night.

The place had been the best he could find at short notice. In truth, he'd been glad to get out of the family home, if it could still be called that. Any remaining love between himself and his wife had grown icy cold as the trouble started. And then there was his son, Martin. Still missing. One problem after another, building from Brixton and its terrible aftermath in that cellar in Soho.

Hobbes poured himself a whisky and sat down to watch the television. He listened for five minutes or more to a man in a mauve corduroy jacket explaining polynomial long division, before he realized he was watching *The Open University*. He leaned over and reached for a book from a shelf, a collection of English verse that had belonged to his mother. Inserted inside was a piece of paper, discoloured, the writing pale, almost lost. Lost, as its meaning was lost. This was the one mystery he could never solve. And sometimes he would frown at this fact, and at other times smile. But now his attention kept drifting away. He couldn't stop thinking about Brendan Clarke and the way the sheet had been pulled up over the face. He wished he'd known that earlier, when he'd examined the body . . .

Immediately he sat up in the chair. The book fell from his hands.

The murderer had hidden the face! The murderer had mutilated Brendan Clarke's face, made a terrifying artwork of it, an elaborate display, and then covered it up. All that work, the time spent, the mess, the blood flow, the details of the various cuts.

The thoughts had set in. The questions. Sparks in the brain, too many of them.

What had the murderer been thinking?

Hobbes finished the whisky and went to bed. He undressed, wrapped the loop of string around his ankle, and climbed under the sheets. It was a necessary precaution, the string. And against all his expectations, he was soon asleep. The form of Charlie Jenkes was the last thing he thought of, as he was in his youth, laughing and drinking and telling jokes. A ghost. The darkness of the room gathered, and settled. One hour passed, another, one more. And then Hobbes woke up suddenly with the image in his mind, perfectly formed.

The street lamp.

He got up immediately, forgetting the length of string in his haste; the other end of it was tied to a bedpost, and he was pulled back by it as he tried to walk away. He slipped the loop over his foot, put on some clean clothes and went out to his car. He drove the short distance to Richmond police station on Kew Road and picked up the keys to Brendan Clarke's house. Westbrook Avenue was quiet when he got there. He glanced at his watch; past four in the morning. Still dark. Good. He needed that. A patrol car drove slowly by, the two officers inside staring at him. He waved at them and nodded.

Hobbes entered the house and made his way upstairs. Not much had changed in the front bedroom. The body was gone, and the bed had been stripped of its sheets.

He went to the window and checked the curtains. They were coloured green and fawn, in an abstract pattern. He had the idea that men never changed curtains, or hardly ever, and that they never cleaned them. And Brendan Clarke had lived alone. In contemplation, Hobbes pulled the curtains together. They didn't quite meet in the middle, which made it even worse. And he noticed that a clothes peg was fixed to one side. Clarke had used this to hold them together. It was like something out of a T. S. Eliot poem, or Philip Larkin, something lonely. There was a sadness to it. He clipped the curtains together, and even now the light from the street lamp outside streamed through, right across the bed. Bloody hell. How could he have missed it? He cursed again, and recalled the words of DI Collingworth, his first proper teacher.

Always look elsewhere, Henry. Turn away from the corpse.

He switched on the overhead light and looked across the room to the telephone on its cabinet. His eyes narrowed. Such an odd place to put it, so far from the bed. It would mean the sleeper would have to get up if the phone rang. It didn't feel right, not at all. He studied the bed frame, and then searched the floor and soon found the four indentations in the carpet.

Now that was strange.

MONDAY

24 AUGUST 1981

X for Unknown

He would never get to sleep now, so Hobbes headed back to the station and read through the case file: the brief, typed-up interviews with the street's residents, those they could find last night; Simone Paige's initial statement to Fairfax; the doctor's notes. It would take a while for the forensic and autopsy reports to come in, but he'd asked for one piece of evidence – the fingerprint in the blue putty on the record player – to be quickly checked against the victim's prints. They matched. That set his mind working; it corresponded to what he'd worked out in his visit to the house.

He looked through the sheets of A4 paper found in the living room, and the one found in the victim's mouth, which had been removed and carefully unfolded. It was preserved in its own see-through plastic bag. The paper was creased and smeared with blood on the reverse, but the writing on the other side was clear enough. It was the lyric sheet of a song called 'Terminal Paradise', the words typed out, with later additions written in ballpoint pen. There was a composer's signature at the bottom of the sheet.

Lucas Bell.

At a quarter past six Hobbes ate a breakfast of fried eggs on toast in the canteen and then went to the incident room and prepared the board, ready for the morning meeting. For a moment he stood stock-still, clearing his mind of everything but the task ahead. He had to demonstrate his worth, now more than ever.

PC Barlow was the first in, looking even fresher and pinker than yesterday. Meg Latimer arrived on the dot at seven, looking like she'd not long fallen out of bed but with her usual smile in place; she was the only one who had welcomed Hobbes to the station. She'd had her own share of career troubles in the last couple of years, especially with her alcohol intake. She'd received a written warning apparently, so maybe it was just a mutual sense of despair that she felt with Hobbes.

DC Fairfax sauntered in ten minutes later. His hair was washed, brushed back, sticky with wet-look gel. He was dressed in a smart jacket and open-necked shirt over a pair of stone-washed jeans. The sleeves of his jacket had been pushed up at the cuffs to show off his tanned arms. No doubt he was heading for early promotion to detective sergeant, and beyond; the powers that be seemed to prefer these new young professional types. Fairfax made a muted excuse for being late and sat down at his desk. He took out a bacon sandwich and started to eat it, paying special attention so that none of the grease dripped on his clothes.

Such was the team.

Hobbes began. 'Sometime around midnight on Saturday, a young man was killed in his own house, in his own bed. His name was Brendan Clarke.' He pointed to a photograph of the victim on the board, one that showed his features unmarked. 'Mr Clarke was twenty-six years old. He lived alone, as far as we know. Meg, did you get a chance to talk to the parents last night?'

Latimer nodded. 'Briefly. They wanted to see the body.'

'They identified him?'

'The father did. He was shook up.'

'What did you gather? First impressions.'

'They're well off. Live in Maidstone. Devoted to their son, by all accounts. An only child. Brendan never wanted for anything, or so they say.'

'Little good it did him.'

Hobbes stared at Fairfax, who had spoken through a mouthful of sandwich.

'What? It's true.'

Hobbes shook his head. 'We'll talk to them properly, today. Now then . . .' He turned back to the board. 'The victim's face was mutilated, sliced in several places with a knife. One of the eyes, both sides of the mouth, the forehead.'

'But there's no sign of the knife,' Fairfax stated.

'No. It was taken away from the scene. Meg, can you make sure a search is made for any discarded weapons in the area?'

'Already on it.'

'Good. OK then. We're still waiting for the autopsy, but I'm inclined to agree with the doctor's best guess, that the stab to the neck killed him.' He looked around the room. 'Now the face is, I believe, very important in this case.'

'Because the murderer left the rest of the body undamaged?' Latimer asked.

'That's right. One area of attack. A focus.' Hobbes quickly moved on. 'Brendan was a musician. A singer in a band called Monsoon Monsoon. They weren't exactly famous. But music is a key element here.'

Fairfax smiled. 'Music? Really?'

'Yes, really.'

'I agree, sir.' This new voice came from the back of the room, where Barlow was standing. They were the first words he'd spoken.

'What's the plod doing here?' Fairfax asked.

'PC Barlow's helping us.'

'Helping? Hasn't he got some traffic to direct?' Fairfax looked around for the support of laughter; receiving none, his face settled into a smug grin.

Barlow dared to take a step forward. 'Music is very important,' he said. 'And the face, also.'

'You've got him well trained, sir,' Fairfax commented. 'He's repeating every little thing you say. Woof, woof!'

Barlow was holding a plastic shopping bag, which only added to his comical aspect, and Hobbes couldn't help feeling for him. But this was life in the snake pit. He'd have to get used to it.

Latimer said with a broad smile, 'Ignore him, love. I'll look after you.' The young man blushed.

Fairfax belched, far too loudly, and put his feet up on his desk. 'Sorry. Sir.' He grinned.

Every time Fairfax said the word *sir*, it sounded like an insult.

Hobbes took a step forward. His voice was purged of all emotion as he spoke: 'I'd like it, Fairfax, if you could use a civil tone.'

And now at last they were all looking at him.

'Do you hear me? Do you? Everyone?'

His question was met with answering murmurs, even from Fairfax.

'And while we're about it, Detective Constable, next time turn up on time.'

'I was delayed—'

'And take your bloody feet off the desk!'

Fairfax did as he was told.

'Thank you.' Hobbes took a breath. 'What I'd like us all to do is go through the events of the day, as far as we can construct them.'

Latimer started the ball rolling. 'There's not much from the residents. Nobody saw anything untoward, certainly not around midnight. But we do have a statement from the neighbour on the right, a Mrs Newley, who saw a woman leaving the victim's house around eight in the morning, via the back garden.'

'Do we have any idea who this is?'

'No. The woman in question was walking towards the back gate.'

'Description?'

'Young. Dressed in dark clothing. That's all.'

Hobbes looked at the witness interview. 'It says here that the neighbour saw her face.'

'Only briefly. The young woman glanced back, and then hurried through the gate when she realized that she'd been seen.'

'Anything? Anything about the face? Was she carrying anything?'

'It's all there, guv. I got what I could.'

He let it go for now. 'So then. Who is this woman? Any ideas? Come on. Quickly!'

'The murderer,' said Fairfax. 'Who else?'

'But she left in the morning, that's a long time after our time of death.'

Fairfax shrugged. 'Fair enough. So this woman, let's call her Miss X for now, right, she stayed the night.'

Latimer shook her head at this idea. 'The killer slept the night?'

'Sure. Why not?'

'Is that what you'd do?' she asked.

'Hey, I'm not a killer. Who knows what's going through her sick little head.'

'She'd have to be pretty crazy—'

'She's sliced a guy's face open, Meg, darling. How crazy do you want?'

Latimer stared at him. 'I don't think . . .'

'Let's hear it.'

'Well, I don't think a woman did this.'

Fairfax raised his hands in glee. 'Ah, here we go.'

'What? I just don't believe—'

'Oh, you don't *believe* it. And what about feminism, then, eh? Equal opportunities for murderers, men and women alike.'

Latimer laughed. 'You're a piece of shit, Tommy. You really are.'

Fairfax started on his protest, but Hobbes shouted them both down. 'That's enough!'

Latimer appealed to him. 'I'm serious. There aren't many cases, sir – to my knowledge, anyway – of female perpetrators who go to such lengths as this.'

'That's true,' Hobbes said.

'Sure,' Latimer added; 'we can give out as good as we get, when needed. But a knife to the eyes, no. Facial mutilation? Just no!'

It seemed like a final statement, and the room fell silent for a moment.

'We keep it all in mind,' Hobbes told them both. 'Every possibility, until only one remains.' He looked at Latimer. 'What did the neighbour mean by "young"?'

'I don't know.'

'Teens? Early twenties?'

'It was a glance. That's all.'

Hobbes bit his lip. Christ, despite all the trouble, he wished he was back at the Charing Cross nick. At least there, the coppers didn't have to be told what to do all the time.

'How did she get inside the house, this young woman? Any ideas?'

'I reckon the victim let Miss X in,' said Fairfax.

Latimer guffawed.

Hobbes studied the board for a moment and then said, 'Actually, I might agree with Fairfax on this.' He looked at each officer in turn. 'I do think the victim let the killer into the house, quite willingly. Brendan Clarke knew the killer. Or he was expecting the visit.'

He took a breath and pictured the scenario in his mind.

'It starts in the living room. The two of them are drinking tea. One of them is showing the other something. The lyric sheets. If it's a woman, maybe things get heated. Maybe they . . . maybe they kiss.'

Fairfax grunted, but then thought better of it.

Hobbes carried on. 'For now, let's say Brendan Clarke invites our Miss X upstairs. She gives her assent. She takes out the knife, or whatever it might be, from her bag or her coat.' He paused for a moment. 'Now she follows him upstairs. Brendan is lying on the bed, waiting for her . . .'

Hobbes was there himself, in the room, in the night. The victim lay before him.

'What happens next?' he asked.

'She joins him on the bed,' Fairfax offered.

Hobbes murmured. His hand had formed around an imaginary knife handle. 'Yes. Clarke's completely subdued by now. He doesn't see it coming.' Hobbes made a movement without realizing it, pushing the blade slowly into the side of the imagined victim's neck, copying the murderer. 'And then . . . and then she makes her strike. She kills him.'

He was whispering. Silence fell over the room.

'You see, there was no struggle.'

Moments passed. Hobbes seemed to come out of a trance. He broke the mood by calling out to the back of the room. 'Right, Barlow?'

'Correct, sir. No struggle.'

'This wasn't a fight. It was a seduction.'

Latimer shook her head in disbelief. 'So you really think our killer's a woman?'

'It's one possible scenario. But Clarke seems to have just given in.'

Latimer sighed. 'Sure, sure . . .'

Hobbes turned to her. 'Something on your mind, Meg?'

'I'm thinking about the early morning visitor,' she replied. 'Let's say that Miss X isn't the killer at all. She breaks in later on, in the morning. Maybe she's just a burglar, or even a fan of his band, what are they called?'

'Monsoon Monsoon.'

'Right. And she finds the dead body of Brendan Clarke. Gets scared, as you would, and scarpers through the back door. Leaving it open. At which point, the neighbour, Mrs Newley, sees her leave.'

'But there's no sign of a break-in,' Fairfax offered.

'I don't know. She picked the lock? A window was left open, maybe.' Her voice trailed off as the ideas petered out.

Hobbes nodded. 'Either way, it still leaves us knowing very little about our killer. The person, male or female, who murdered Brendan Clarke around midnight. So then, we need to find this Miss X. She might have seen something we've missed, or moved something, or even taken something away.' He thought for a moment of the clean circle on top of the dusty cupboard in the bedroom. 'And if Meg's theory is correct, then we have two sets of traces in the house: the murderer's and the burglar's.' He frowned. 'It's getting messy in there.'

Everyone fell quiet.

'There's another thing.' Hobbes hesitated. He didn't know how to say this properly, the idea was too strange. 'The victim seems to be completely under the killer's control.'

He let the idea sink in. All three of them were waiting for him to carry on. And as he looked at them, one by one, he felt a glimmer of the old power, the surge of adrenaline.

'This is a very different kind of seduction. This isn't sexual, at least I don't think so.' He took a breath. 'First of all, the lump of blue putty on the vinyl record.'

'It's called Blu-Tac,' Latimer told him.

'Yes. Thank you. There's a fingerprint in it, a very clear one. And we now know that it belongs to the victim.'

Fairfax sat forward. 'So that means, what, he set the record player up himself?'

'It looks that way. He either chose the track, the exact portion of music, himself, or the murderer made him do it.'

Latimer was puzzled. 'What are you saying?'

'I'm saying that the killer seems to be directing the victim. Clarke puts the record on, he sets up the Blu-Tac. This is the victim himself, preparing his own murder scene. And then . . . and then he moved the bed.'

Again, there was silence. They all stared at him.

Fairfax was the first to speak. 'He what?'

'The victim shoved the bed across the floor from its usual place, up against the opposite wall. Over to where we found it.'

'How the hell do you know that?'

'I thought it was strange, because where the bed currently is, it's bang in the path of the street lamp from the window. I went back, in the night, and I pulled the curtains across the window. Even with them closed, the light falls right across the pillow. I can't imagine anybody choosing such a position to sleep in. Can you?'

Nobody dared to answer.

'Also, the telephone wasn't next to the bed, which is where most people would place it, I'm sure, in a bedroom. So I looked at the bed frame. There are finger and palm prints visible. The powder found them. Here, and here . . .' He placed his hands in the air in front of him, and pretended to push the bed across the floor. 'Also, there are four indentations in the carpet where the bed used to sit, obviously for years. And there are tracks still visible in the carpet pile, showing where the bed was pushed. It happened very recently, I'm guessing right before the murder.'

He paused for a moment.

'Now, maybe the prints on the frame belong to the perpetrator, I don't yet know. But I believe the killer made Brendan Clarke do this himself. The bed had to be moved. It was all part of the night's seduction, the ritual.'

Fairfax groaned. 'But why? For what purpose?'

'I can think of two reasons. Anybody?'

There was no reply, so Hobbes took up the slack. 'One. To replicate some other scene, a bedroom from the past, for instance – from childhood, or from a former relationship – a scene that holds some kind of psychological importance.'

'Too bloody Freudian for me,' said Latimer.

'Or two, and this is more likely, I think: to show off the handi-work. The murderer wanted to present the face in a specific way, the cut face; they wanted to present it in the light.'

'Like a stage set.'

This came from Barlow. Hobbes had forgotten he was there. 'Exactly. Like a stage set. This is theatre. But then . . . and this is where it gets weird. The victim's face was covered, with the bed sheet.'

'I didn't know that,' said Latimer.

'No. Simone Paige admitted to me that she'd folded the sheet down, away from the face, when she'd first discovered the body.'

Latimer groaned. 'Fairfax, this wasn't in the statement that I read.'

'No . . .' The detective constable was looking mightily pissed off. 'Paige never mentioned it.'

'Bloody hell. You could put some effort in.'

Fairfax stood up and faced Latimer, his face creased in anger. 'Leave it out, will you, Meg! I did my job.'

'Half-heartedly, as always.'

He moved across the room towards her, his fists bunched.

'All right, all right!' Hobbes stepped between them. 'We're not here to fight. Fairfax, sit down.'

The DC was still fuming, but he went back to his desk and sat on the edge of it.

Hobbes let the mood settle before continuing.

'So you can see the problem. Why go to all that trouble with the bed, and then with the cutting of the face . . . and cover the work up? Does that make sense to anybody?'

Nobody spoke.

Fairfax shook his head in despair. 'It's a mess. We're getting nowhere.'

'No, no. Keep thinking! What about the face itself?' Hobbes asked. 'Why those specific wounds? They have to mean something. Come on.'

Barlow spoke up from the back of the room. 'I think I know, sir.'

Everyone turned to look at him.

'Let's hear it then, Constable.'

Barlow came forward. He spoke quickly before his nerves took over. 'I think the killer created a portrait.'

The team watched as the constable walked to the front of the room, his tatty shopping bag in hand. Latimer did her best to suppress a smile, while Fairfax laughed quietly. But Barlow seemed not to notice. He stood to attention and started to speak.

'The record playing in the room was by the pop star Lucas Bell.'

'Didn't he top himself?' Fairfax asked.

Barlow nodded. 'He did. In 1974. In fact, exactly seven years ago tomorrow. He put a gun to his head and shot himself.'

There was quiet in the room now.

'It was shocking at the time,' Latimer said. 'I was strictly a soul girl back then, but even so, I still remember it.'

Barlow continued, 'Over the years since, the singer's popularity has grown, especially among today's teenagers. They see him as some kind of hero figure.'

Hobbes added, 'On the night he was killed, Brendan Clarke's own band played a gig in honour of Bell.'

Fairfax lit a cigarette. 'I'm not getting this at all. I mean, do we seriously think this dead pop star is important to the case?'

'Well, the person who did the murder,' Hobbes explained, 'definitely had some need for that record to be playing. Lucas Bell meant something to them.'

'What, like a fan?'

'Yes, a fan. Maybe.'

'You're saying a fan of this old glam rock singer killed Brendan Clarke?'

'I don't know. It's a start.' And even as he said the words, Hobbes felt the idea flutter away, almost lost.

Fairfax went on, 'It could so easily have been somebody else, an acquaintance, a relative, a lover, or someone from Brendan's own band, even.'

'And all of those possibilities will be looked at, believe me.'

'Oh, I believe you, because it's me and Meg here who'll be doing all the legwork on it, while you and Mr Plod – begging your pardon and all – will be listening to bloody records, and generally pissing about. Sir.'

Hobbes closed his eyes. His hands gripped the edge of the desk he was leaning against.

Whatever expression there was on his face was enough to silence them all.

But still he waited. His grip tightened until his fingers were hurting, the only way he knew of staying in control. Without opening his eyes, he found himself speaking. Coldly, calmly. He ignored Fairfax.

'Constable Barlow.'

'Sir?'

'To the point, please. About the victim's face.'

There was a slight pause before Barlow started again on his story. Hobbes opened his eyes, taking in the scene. Latimer was concentrating fully, whilst Fairfax was staring directly at Hobbes, his facial expression set firmly in neutral. And beneath that, hatred, resentment. Hobbes could feel it from the young detective: he seemed to blame him personally for what had happened to DI Jenkes.

Would it never end?

PC Barlow reached into his plastic bag and pulled out a record album. He held this up for all the team to see its front cover, which featured a purple background with the title *KING LOST* printed in yellow across the top, and the name of the singer in smaller lettering across the bottom.

'This is Lucas Bell's third and final album, *King Lost*. As you can see, the front cover is plain.' He fumbled with the record sleeve. 'But on the inner sleeve, the singer has changed his appearance. He's wearing a mask.' Barlow opened the sleeve, displaying the full gatefold. Hobbes moved round to join Fairfax and Latimer, in order to view the image revealed.

The purple of the front cover was continued within, shown now to be a vibrant night sky. The moon was visible. A neon sign, matching the lettering of the front sleeve in colour, dominated the upper left-hand side of the sleeve. It was the name of a fish and chip restaurant, Duffy's. Below this was the torso of Lucas Bell, photographed against the restaurant's brightly lit window. The young man's chest and shoulders were bare, and his face was hidden behind a painted-on mask: the skin powdered all over white, the mouth smeared red with lipstick and extended at each side into a cruel clown-like grin. A large black teardrop was etched below the left eye, and the singer's forehead was decorated with a letter X in blue. It was a startling image, and it took Hobbes only a few seconds to realize what he was looking at: with the knife cuts on Brendan Clarke's face, the murderer had copied each element of the famous rock star's mask. It was, as the young constable had said, a portrait. A portrait in blood.

But then Barlow pointed out another feature of the image: one of the singer's hands was visible, holding a small rectangular object against his bare chest.

It was a tarot card. The Fool's card.

Dolls and Curses

Fairfax left the room first. Hobbes made an effort to follow him down the corridor, but then thought, *Why, why should I?* Bloody jumped-up little shit.

DS Latimer came up to him. 'That wasn't too bad, was it?' she asked.

He shook his head in dismay.

'Fairfax will come round.'

'Will he?'

'It's up to you, guv. But Tommy's a good policeman, I swear. He's young, headstrong. Give him a chance.'

'He blames me, Meg. I know what's going on.'

Latimer inclined her head. She was a couple of years younger than Hobbes, a striking dark-haired woman, a divorcee. He'd overheard stories in the locker room about her social life, but frankly he didn't believe it. Or he didn't want to. He looked at her now. Her eyes were quick and sharp, and her mind was always working overtime.

'Even over here, we knew about Charlie Jenkes,' she said. 'He was a legend in the Met.'

Hobbes had to admit it. 'He was.'

'And you know Fairfax and him are connected? Fairfax's dad grew up on the same estate as Jenkes.'

This unsettled Hobbes. 'I didn't know that, no.'

'This is why he's been so bloody obnoxious, of late. Charlie was a family friend. Bounced young Tommy on his knee, apparently.'

Hobbes reached for the cigarette that she offered. 'I really don't care. Fairfax has to pull along.'

'Actually, guv, I think you're best to let him run where he likes. He might well surprise you.'

'He pisses me off.'

'Well, sir . . . you piss us off. So that's fair.'

He stared at her. Her voice had taken on a slight edge.

'What did you say?'

Latimer learned in close. 'Don't think for one minute that I sympathize with what you're going through.' Her eyes narrowed. 'Because I don't. I think what you did to DI Jenkes was wrong. Very wrong.'

Hobbes couldn't believe what he was hearing, but he let her carry on.

'None of us wanted you here, but you know that already. You were foisted on us.'

'You think I actually want to be here?'

Latimer kept her face straight. 'I'll do whatever you ask of me, sir, because that's the kind of copper I am, but honestly . . .' She smiled. 'I don't give a monkey's arsehole.'

This last sentence was aimed right at his heart, and it cut through.

He gave his best hard stare, held it on her.

'Are you done, Detective Latimer?'

'Pretty much.'

'That will be the last time you'll talk to me like that, I swear.'

She gave a brief nod in reply, nothing more.

'Now, I'd like you to help me interviewing the parents.'

'The woman's touch?'

'Call it what you like.'

'Sure.' She gave her assent. 'I'll meet you outside.'

DS Latimer was already walking away.

The situation was worse than he'd thought, Hobbes realized. Working alone had always been a part of his nature, ever since he'd made inspector, but this was different. His wife and son wouldn't speak to him, he had very few friends left. Christ, he still didn't have an office. Only this morning, arriving early, the station's caretaker had looked at him like he was a pariah.

He went out to his car, not bothering to wait for Latimer. He was about to set off when PC Barlow knocked on his window. Hobbes wound down the glass.

'Yes? What?'

He could see the young man flinch at his words.

'I was just . . . I was wondering if you wanted me for anything else, sir?'

'No.'

He drove off, glancing at Barlow in the rear-view mirror as he reached the gate. Hobbes immediately felt guilty and even considered turning back for a second or two. But the feeling passed.

The Carlton Hotel was in the town centre. He found a parking space and made to leave the vehicle but stopped with his fingers on the door handle.

He couldn't move.

His body was shaking. He couldn't stop it from happening.

A panic attack. He cursed aloud at his colleagues, at the police force in general, his family, the times he was living in. England. Thatcher. The world. Himself. The whole fucking game. The murderer. The missing elements barely glimpsed, just out of reach.

And once more he was back in the cellar at Soho, on that night that ruined him. The man's blood splattering on the wall . . .

Hobbes banged his hands against the steering wheel as hard as he could bear. A dose of pain to shift his focus, to free his body from its spell.

Keep moving, keep looking. Remember the pledge that you made.
Brendan Clarke.
I will hunt your killer down and bring him to justice.

This I promise.

But right now it sounded like a hollow prayer.

He walked the short distance to the hotel and showed his warrant card at the reception desk and then took the lift up to the third floor. The victim's father opened the door to him and invited him into their room. His wife was sitting on the bed, wringing a handkerchief in her hands, tightening it into a long thin coil.

He introduced himself, and then said, 'I'm truly sorry for the loss of your son.'

Mr Clarke had no time for such sentiments. 'When can we have his body?'

'Not yet, I'm afraid.'

Mr Clarke walked to the window, where he stood in silence looking out. The sky was grey, flat, layered with haze.

Hobbes sensed that the victim's mother would be the more revealing.

'Mrs Clarke . . .'

She murmured something. He leaned in.

'I'm sorry?'

'My name is Annabelle. Have you any news for us?'

'Nothing solid.'

'We need to know who did this to our child.'

'Yes. Yes, I understand. I just need to ask a few questions.'

Mr Clarke came forward, saying, 'We'll do all that we can to help, rest assured.'

'Good. Thank you. First of all, who would want to hurt your son? Was he under threat in any way?'

Mr Clarke answered: 'No. Absolutely not.'

Hobbes rubbed a finger along his lips. 'Well, somebody hated him.'

Annabelle Clarke caught a breath. She made a high piercing cry.

The victim's father stared at Hobbes, his eyes never leaving their target. His mouth opened to speak once more, but then closed again. Hobbes watched as the fury left him, to be replaced by a look of sheer hopelessness. The man's body crumpled.

Hobbes said, 'I have to ask every question that needs to be asked.'

Mr Clarke turned back to his wife, who looked up and said to him in a trembling voice, 'Let's help him, Gerald. It's all we can do.'

Hobbes knew he had to take advantage of the moment. He sat in a chair and asked, 'When was the last time you saw Brendan?'

Annabelle Clarke spoke. 'It was last week. He would come home every few weeks or so. Usually once a month.'

'So this would be, what day?'

She thought back. 'Last Tuesday. Yes. He left on the Thursday morning.'

'Heading back to London?'

'I guess so.'

'Did you know about the concert in London, with his band?'

'No. He didn't keep us up to date with such things. We . . . well, naturally we've always encouraged him . . .'

Her voice trailed off. Her husband stepped in. 'We had different plans for Brendan. I wanted him to follow me into Law. I have my own partnership. He actually started to study, but then dropped out after six months. He's always had an artistic side.' He shook his head, as though art was the worst of all endeavours.

'He was searching for his role in life,' Mrs Clarke added. 'He spent some time studying theatre.'

'But that didn't work out, either?' Hobbes asked.

'We offered him help at every turn,' Mr Clarke insisted. 'Money. Education. Support, in whatever hare-brained scheme he had. However . . .'

Both parents fell into silence. Gerald sat next to his wife on the bed.

Hobbes was starting to see another side to the Clarke family's life.

'Was Brendan troubled?'

Mrs Clarke looked down at her handkerchief. 'Our son was a very passionate man,' she said.

'What do you mean by that, precisely?'

'He loved music. He loved it very much. I will go so far as to say that he lived for it.'

Her cut-glass vowels kept breaking apart as she spoke, revealing her origins. Hobbes thought that she'd probably had elocution lessons.

Mr Clarke put a hand on his wife's shoulder.

Hobbes saw something in the gesture; it wasn't entirely natural. It was born of necessity, of the current moment. He couldn't help wondering how much love there was between these two, and even between them and their son. And for a moment he allowed himself to think of Martin, out there in the world somewhere, unknown, lost . . .

'Was Brendan obsessed, would you say?'

'That's one way of putting it, yes,' Mrs Clarke said. 'His collection is quite extensive.'

'Collection?'

'He was crazy about Lucas Bell. Do you know him? The pop singer?'

Hobbes nodded.

'Brendan spent a lot of money on things belonging to Lucas, or associated with him. We even helped him purchase some of the more expensive ones.'

'Where did he keep these?'

'A few at his London place. But most of them at our house.'

Hobbes made a mental note.

'And there was his little magazine,' Mrs Clarke added.

'I'm sorry?'

'It was a fanzine – well, that's what he called it, anyway. All about Lucas Bell, and his songs, his life, and his death. He was always writing about it, talking about it, the suicide. It worried us, didn't it, Gerald?'

Her husband nodded. He looked uncomfortable.

'Did Brendan have any interest in tarot cards?' Hobbes asked.

They both looked at him blankly, until Mrs Clarke said, 'His interests changed all the time, I'm afraid. Only Lucas Bell was a constant.'

'Brendan was your only child, is that correct?'

Mr Clarke answered this one. 'Yes.'

'I'm required to ask . . . where were you both on the day that he was killed?'

Mrs Clarke's hand wound and wound at the handkerchief. But her husband answered the question calmly enough: 'We were at home, with friends.'

'Could you write the name and telephone numbers of the friends down for me?'

Mr Clarke nodded. He stood up and walked over to the desk, where he started to write on a hotel notepad. Hobbes leaned forwards in his chair. He kept his voice low and soft, as best he could, as he spoke to the grieving mother.

'Annabelle . . .'

She looked at him with expectant, hopeful eyes.

'I need to learn everything I can about your son, about his life, his friends, his love life, any enemies or rivals he may have had.'

She glanced over to her husband. 'Talk to Nikki.' It was the barest whisper.

'And who would that be?'

'Nikki Hauser. She played keyboards in his band.'

'Monsoon Monsoon?'

She nodded quickly. 'Also, she was his fiancée. At least, she used to be.'

'They split up?'

'Yes.'

Her husband came back to the bed, handing a slip of paper to the inspector. 'What are you talking about?'

'I'm telling him about Nikki.'

'You think that could be important?'

'It might be,' Hobbes said. 'At any rate, I will have to speak with her.'

'Good,' said Annabelle. Her voice rose in pitch. 'Ask her why she hurt my son so much. And why she kept on hurting him, even after she'd slept with that other man.'

The outburst seemed to exhaust her, for as soon as she'd stopped speaking, her face dropped again, her eyes hidden.

'Which other man?'

'We don't know his name, I'm afraid. But Brendan knew about him. He told me.'

'I know it's difficult . . .'

They both waited to hear what Hobbes had to say. But there was nothing good or useful he could add, not in this situation. He got to his feet.

Mrs Clarke stood up herself. 'Whatever happened to Brendan,' she said, 'I'm sure that Nikki will have had something to do with it.'

Hobbes nodded. An idea came to him. 'Would you mind looking round your son's house with me?'

She stared at him, her mouth slightly open.

'It would be useful,' he added, 'to know if anything's gone missing.'

'Oh, I've only been there a few times.'

'Still, if you could.'

'Actually . . .'

Mr Clarke came to her side, saying, 'Is this absolutely necessary, Inspector?'

'I think so, yes.'

'Actually,' his wife continued, 'I'd like to see the house.'

That settled it. Hobbes drove them in his car, the two of them in the back, not saying a word to each other or to him the whole journey.

It was past noon when they turned on to Westbrook Avenue. Normal suburban life had returned to the street: a man walking a dog, a young couple strolling along without a care in the world.

As he parked the car, Hobbes mused to himself: after the Soho trouble, the police disciplinary panel had recommended that he be posted to a new borough. Which was fair enough – for a few weeks in London Central, as his colleagues had turned against him, he'd actually felt that his life was in danger. So he'd been posted to Richmond upon Thames to get him out of the way, thinking nothing much of interest could happen in these quiet leafy streets. Surely, not too much blood could be spent, not here?

He got out of the car. At first Mrs Clarke would not look at her son's house; her eyes were downcast. Hobbes led the way to the front door. Once inside, he followed the parents from room to room. This was his third visit in the last twenty-four hours. Thankfully, the smell of death had dissipated. Mrs Clarke tutted and wrung her hands in shame as she saw the mess in the kitchen, the dirt on the carpet, the unwashed clothes dumped on the floor.

'Brendan was a very clean boy, usually,' she said. 'It was only in the last year or so that he let things slip. Ever since his love affair with Nikki fell apart.'

They moved into the living room. Mrs Clarke picked up the framed photograph of herself, her husband, and Brendan. She didn't move. Her eyes never left the image and she made a tiny murmuring sound.

'Annabelle?' Her husband put his hand on her arm. 'Are you sure you're up to this, dear?'

She pushed his hands away in irritation and set off once more, walking back into the hallway. She stared up towards the floor above, and then climbed the stairs. Hobbes and Mr Clarke followed after her, on to the landing. They paused at the music room.

'We bought him a lot of those instruments,' she said.

Hobbes followed her inside. 'Have you noticed anything missing yet, or out of place? Anything at all?'

'No. But like I said, we hardly came here. This is the fanzine I told you about.' She pointed to several piles of magazines stacked high against the near wall.

'Your son mentioned that he had an item here, something of great importance regarding Lucas Bell. Have you any idea what that might be?'

She thought for a moment. 'He had so many precious things, so many treasures, but like I said, most of them are stored at home, not here.'

They moved along the corridor towards the front of the house.

'I'd like to visit your home one day soon,' Hobbes said. 'To see Brendan's collection.'

Annabelle Clarke had stopped at the open door of the front bedroom, and was staring inside. 'Is this where . . . ?'

Hobbes nodded.

She grimaced. 'Is there any blood?'

'No. Well, a little, perhaps.'

They walked into the room. Mrs Clarke's eyes widened as she looked at the bed, the bare mattress. She gasped and held a hand to her throat. 'The bed's been moved,' she muttered. Her eyes darted about the room, taking it all in. 'And there is something missing.' Hobbes felt his pulse race. She had wandered over to the cupboard and was looking at the clean circle in the dust that he had noticed yesterday. She wiped her finger in the dirt.

'Mrs Clarke? What is it?'

'A doll,' she answered.

He was confused. 'What do you mean?'

She turned to face him. 'You know, a figurine. A model figure.'

'Of what?'

'The singer, Lucas Bell. The man he loved.'

Mr Clarke groaned. He was standing near the bed. His wife turned on him. 'Is there something wrong?'

'You know . . .'

'What? Gerald? Do you have something to say?'

'You shouldn't use that word. It's disgusting.'

'But he did *love* him. Brendan loved Lucas Bell. He loved him!'

Hobbes and Mr Clarke watched her in silence.

Teardrop

They stood in silence on the pavement outside the house. Each person was entirely alone, or at least that's how it felt to Hobbes, himself included. The minutes stretched by, until at last a squad car pulled up at the kerb. PC Barlow got out and immediately went up to Mrs Clarke and starting talking to her. He kept his voice low; Hobbes couldn't hear what was being said, not properly, but he saw that the poor woman responded well to the constable's words. Barlow led her to the squad car and guided her into the rear seat; her husband followed. They were both grateful to the young policeman.

Hobbes told him, 'They need to go back to the Carlton Hotel.'

'Will do, sir.'

'Listen, Barlow, I do want you to keep working on this.'

Barlow smiled at the prospect.

'When you get back to Kew Road, carry on with your research: Lucas Bell, his death, his girlfriends, colleagues, his songs. Anything at all that seems relevant. Oh, and look into Monsoon Monsoon. The victim's band. See how they're faring in the press, and sales, fans – anything like that.'

Barlow nodded and got into the car. Hobbes watched him drive away, then he went back inside the house and headed upstairs to the music room. He wanted to collect some of the fanzines. He took the top copy from the pile stacked against the wall. Brendan Clarke's magazine was called *100 Splinters*. The cover showed a black-and-white artist's sketch of Lucas Bell, and below it the legend: *Seven Years Since the Passing. Revelations, Memories, Interviews.* A good number of earlier editions were also available, going back years. Hobbes selected a few different issues and took them with him when he went downstairs. He put the fanzines in his car and then walked up the path of the next house along, number 49, and rang the bell. It was a Monday afternoon, but he was hopeful the neighbours would be in. He'd read through Latimer's interview report already, but over the years he'd come to realize that witnesses were often shocked, and would often hide things away for various personal reasons. Once again he heard the voice of DI Collingworth in his head.

Check. Check again. Check a third time.

And don't think for a moment that three times is enough.

Collingworth had taken Hobbes under his wing when he first made detective. He was a tough, smart, chain-smoking, Old Spice-wearing copper who shouted at Hobbes more than he spoke to him. *Do this, do that, never stop, never give up!* Then he'd grimace and cough his guts out. But my God, Hobbes had learned the ropes quickly, brutally sometimes. He remembered one incident when he'd been locked in a room with a week-old corpse and told to find out what was wrong with the scene. The stench had been overpowering, and the state of the dead body made him sick. It was the height of summer. Flies buzzing. Dead flesh crawling with life. Hobbes was in there for ten minutes before he found it: a few curls of pencil shaving on the tabletop. But no sign of any pencils elsewhere, and the room clean and tidy otherwise. He sat at the table. Without further movement he was now facing where the corpse was posed, propped up in the armchair. It seemed ridiculous, such a tiny detail. It might mean nothing at all. Yet he imagined himself sharpening a pencil, ready for . . . could it be: ready to draw a likeness of the victim?

Check and check again, and again. Never stop checking.

The door of number 49 was opened by an elderly man. He was thin, not very tall, with a beaky face, and greying hair parted low down on one side. His eyes were slightly magnified by a pair of National Health spectacles.

Hobbes showed his warrant card to him. 'Mr Newley?'

'Yes?' The man looked suspicious.

'Detective Inspector Hobbes. I'd like to speak with your wife.'

The man disappeared into the house and a minute later the witness herself came to the door. The same age as her husband, she was dressed in an emerald-green trouser suit, and her chestnut hair, vigorously dyed, was bound up in a matching green scarf. Once again, Hobbes introduced himself. She hesitated for a second and then said, 'Please, come inside.' He was led into the hallway and offered a cup of tea. Hobbes declined.

'I'd like you to take me through the events of yesterday morning, as closely as you can.'

'It's a terrible thing,' she said. 'Brendan was such a fine young man, I always thought. Despite . . .'

Her husband finished the sentence. 'Despite the noise, and all the filthy rock and rollers turning up there every week, playing that racket. And the state of the house. And all the girls, of course.'

'Oh yes, he was very popular.'

Hobbes nodded at this. 'Mr Clarke played a concert on Saturday night, in the centre of London. Did you see him coming home after that? It would have been quite late, I imagine.'

'No, I'm afraid not. We were in bed by half past ten. That's right, isn't it, Robert?'

Her husband nodded. 'Yes, we always are.'

Hobbes looked at them both in turn. 'You didn't hear anything in the night, any strange noises?'

'How do you mean?' Mrs Newley asked.

'Any cries, or shouts? Arguments. Anything like that?'

They both shook their heads.

'We're detached,' Mr Newley said. It took Hobbes a moment to work out what he meant.

'That's fine, don't worry. Now, what happened in the morning?'

Mrs Newley told her story. 'I got up at eight, as is usual for me. I went downstairs to the kitchen to start making breakfast, and that's when I saw her through the window, the young woman.'

'Show me, please.'

The three of them walked along the hallway into the kitchen at the back of the house.

'I was standing here at the sink, filling the kettle,' Mrs Newley said, 'when I saw a movement in the garden next door. At first I thought it was Brendan, but he never ever gets up that early. And then I realized it was a woman. Also . . .'

'Yes?'

'She was moving strangely.'

'How do you mean?'

'She was staggering a little.'

'Like she was drunk? Or on drugs? Or injured?'

'No, not like that.'

'How then?'

Mrs Newley was looking worried as Hobbes put the pressure on her. 'She was moving slowly, and swaying.'

'Was she scared? Nervous? In shock?'

'Yes, that was it! Scared. And I saw that clearly later.'

'When you went outside?'

'Yes.'

She opened the back door and walked outside. Hobbes and Mr Newley followed. The garden was immaculate, with well-ordered flower beds and a perfectly mown lawn.

'I usually come out here early on, anyway,' she said, 'to feed the birds.'

There was a wooden bird table in the centre of the lawn. Hobbes walked over to the fence that separated the two gardens; it was low enough to give a clear view.

'Where was the woman by then?'

'She was heading for the back gate. But then she stopped. I think she must've heard me.'

'So she turned round?'

'Yes.' Mrs Newley's face took on a troubled expression as she remembered the details. 'I was suddenly frightened.' Her husband took her hand in his and squeezed it.

'Why were you scared?' Hobbes asked. 'Anything in particular?'

She thought for a moment. 'No, not really. But she was there. And I was here, and she was looking at me, directly at me. And like I said, she looked scared herself.'

'Did you recognize her?'

'I would have to answer *no*. But Brendan did have a lot of people round. There were parties, and suchlike. And people often ended up in the back garden.'

'It could all get a bit rowdy,' her husband added.

Hobbes nodded. 'Was she carrying anything?'

'I'm not sure. A bag, maybe.'

'What kind of bag?'

She couldn't answer. Her eyes blinked repeatedly.

Hobbes paused, waiting for her to settle before putting the crucial question.

'Mrs Newley, you saw the young woman's face. What did she look like?'

She thought for a moment. 'Average height.' Her brows creased. 'I don't know what else to say.'

'What was she wearing?'

'A black coat.'

'What kind of coat?'

'A black one.'

Hobbes tensed up. Mrs Newley hurried on. 'A black coat and a black hat. There was talk of rain on the radio, so that seemed normal.'

'Could you see her hair at all?'

'A few strands hanging down, that's all.'

'Colour?'

Mrs Newley shook her head.

'How old was she?'

'Oh dear, I'm sixty-eight this year. So they all look young to me. A teenager, I would say.'

'What about her face?' Hobbes asked. 'Was there anything about her features, anything at all? You must remember something!'

Mr Newley drew close, saying, 'Excuse me. Please don't talk to my wife like that. We're trying to help.'

The vision of Brendan Clarke's sliced-up face came back to Hobbes. The mask of blood. It was a reoccurring dream in the daytime.

'This is serious,' he said. 'A serious crime. A murder.'

Nothing was said in return. The three of them were still standing around the wooden bird table. It seemed absurd, like a scene out of a play.

Mrs Newley relented. 'I only saw her for a glance, like I said. A few seconds.'

Hobbes sighed. Maybe there was nothing here, nothing of note.

Then he heard Mrs Newley whisper.

He stepped closer. 'I'm sorry, what did you say?'

'A mark.'

'How do you mean?'

'I'm trying to think.' Her eyes were scrunched up as she concentrated.

Hobbes pressed on. 'You have to tell me. Anything at all.'

She tried to relax. 'There was a mark on the woman's face.'

He felt a stab of hope. 'What do you mean by that? What kind of mark? What colour?'

'I don't know. Dark, maybe.'

'Blood?'

The thought obviously scared Mrs Newley. She shook her head vigorously.

'Show me where it was on your own face.'

Her hand came up slowly to touch at her left cheek, just below the eye.

Hobbes felt a surge of hope. 'Could it have a been a birthmark, or a tattoo? Or face paint?'

She nodded eagerly to all three options.

'Might it have been a teardrop? A painted teardrop? Mrs Newley . . .'

She spoke clearly. 'Yes. It could've been. Now that I think about it.'

Hobbes fell silent. His mind clicked through its paces, the machine reactivated.

A few spots of rain began to fall on the well-kept garden.

The Six Wounds

DS Latimer collared him as soon as he got back to the station.

'I was waiting for you.'

Hobbes shrugged off the remark. 'I prefer it that way. Working alone.' Before she could respond to this, he handed over the contact details for the parents' friends and asked her to ring them, to check the alibis. Looking around the incident room, he asked, 'Where's Fairfax?'

'Running down Brendan's band.'

'Good. I need to talk to them.'

'A lead?'

'Brendan's mum named the keyboard player of Monsoon Monsoon as a possible suspect. Nikki Hauser.'

'On what grounds?'

'Intense dislike.'

Latimer made a smacking sound with her lips. 'Mothers and sons. The usual story.'

'Apparently, they were engaged to be married.'

'Brendan and the keyboard player?'

'Yes. And it ended badly. And another man may be involved, a lover.' Hobbes looked over at the incident board.

Latimer nodded. 'I'll let Fairfax know about Miss Hauser, ask him to bring them both back here.'

'Both?'

'The band's a trio. Vocals, keyboards, drums.'

'I also called in on the neighbours,' Hobbes told her. 'Mr and Mrs Newley.'

'Oh yeah, you checking up on me?'

'You missed something.'

'Christ, you're really trying your best to be liked.'

'You missed something, Meg.' It was a fact, nothing more.

Latimer sighed. 'Let's hear it.'

'The young woman seen in the back garden had a mark below her left eye. Possibly a black teardrop shape.'

'Like the mask? The rock star's mask.' Latimer was excited.

'Exactly. Lucas Bell.'

'Well, this is no ordinary burglar then, if that's even what she is. She's a fan.'

Hobbes considered. 'I'll bet you a month's salary that Miss X was at the Monsoon Monsoon gig that night.'

Latimer thought about it. 'Maybe Nikki Hauser was the woman leaving the house in the morning?'

'Possibly. But wouldn't the Newleys know her by sight, if she was close to Clarke?'

'I can take a photo round to them, see if there's a match.'

'Thank you.'

'PC Barlow brought in material on the group.'

She showed Hobbes a few photographs of Monsoon Monsoon, the three musicians posing in a cemetery. Nikki Hauser looked to be older than the other two. She was dressed in dark clothes offset by a plethora of silver rings, brooches and necklaces. Her hair was cut in a short, feathery, manly style, and her eyes were enhanced by a fog of make-up. She was a mysterious presence, almost ghostlike, like a figure superimposed on the image. A thin young man, presumably the drummer, slouched next to her. Brendan Clarke stood to the side, one arm draped over a headstone. He was dressed like a beat poet: fifties-style jacket, white shirt, skinny black tie. He was the only person staring at the lens. His face, artfully devoid of any emotion, held the world at bay. And then

Hobbes saw the name and dates on the gravestone they were posing against: *LUCAS BELL 1948–1974*. And below that a carved inscription: *Fear no more the heat of the sun.*

Hobbes asked, 'What else have we got? Anything new?'

'No sign of a discarded weapon. We've searched dustbins, alleyways, the usual places.'

'So the perpetrator took it with them.'

'Looks that way. And here's the autopsy report. Just in.'

He took a grey folder off her, flicked through it. Latimer summed it up for him. 'A serrated blade, quite small. A steak knife would do it. The neck wound killed him, severed the jugular. But it wasn't a professional job. A lucky slice.'

'The facial cuts?'

'Straight after, we think. Before the blood had a chance to stop pumping.'

'Anything else?'

'Not much. The perpetrator's right-handed.'

'What order were the cuts made in?'

'Page five.'

Hobbes found the relevant section. *Left eye, left side of mouth, right side of mouth, the two cuts on the brow to make the cross.* It was a best estimate, he knew.

Six wounds altogether, including the one to the neck. The mask in place. But why? For what purpose?

'The eye was the vital wound,' he murmured. 'The main target.'

Latimer said, 'The killer really wanted to make him cry. I mean, that's one hell of a teardrop.'

He scanned the rest of the report. Time of death was confirmed as being somewhere between midnight and two. 'Anything else?' he asked.

'Fingerprints.' Latimer held up a sheaf of papers. 'The victim's. A few from Simone Paige. And plenty of unknowns. The band members, I imagine, in the main.'

Hobbes shook his head in worry. 'What about the bedstead?'

'Only Clarke's.'

'So he pushed the bed himself.'

'Yes, looks like you were right on that one, guv.'

He nodded. It was good to have the theory confirmed. 'So Clarke set up the bed, and the record player with the Blu-Tac, and everything. He set that fragment of song playing.'

Latimer nodded. 'What the hell was he doing?'

They were both silent for a moment.

Hobbes handed back the fingerprint file and stepped over to the board, where numerous photographs of the body and the crime scene were pinned. There was a cheap-looking record player on a table next to the board, with a bunch of albums and singles propped up beside it.

Latimer said drily, 'PC Barlow's been studying the songs.'

Hobbes looked at the sleeves. Most of them showed the real face of Lucas Bell, with the singer seen in various locations. The inner sleeve of the first album revealed a portrait of Bell in what looked to be a tiny bedsit. He was reading a copy of James Joyce's *Ulysses*.

'Makes you wonder, doesn't it?' Latimer said.

'What's that?'

'How come such a pretty boy needs to hide behind a mask?'

Hobbes shrugged in reply. The singer was certainly unique-looking. 'I wouldn't exactly call him handsome, Meg. I mean, if he wasn't famous, would you even look twice?'

'What's your point?'

'I'm trying to work out just why so many people idolize this guy, so many years after his death, and why one of them is now drawn to the act of murder.'

'The mad-fan theory?'

Hobbes's face creased up in thought as he studied the singer's face. 'There's something about Mr Bell, about his looks, his manner.

His eyes. It's easy to imagine that he'd been bullied, as a kid. Beaten, even. Maybe that's part of his appeal?'

'Spot on, I reckon.'

'And maybe that's why a certain kind of fan goes loopy for him. They're identifying with his weakness, not his strength. And . . .'

'And if we can identify that weakness in the fan, we'll have our killer?'

'Something like that, yes.'

He smiled. The mood had relaxed slightly. 'Tell me, Meg, do you recall seeing a doll in Brendan Clarke's house anywhere? A model figure of Lucas Bell – pop memorabilia. Mrs Clarke told me it was missing.'

'Nothing like that, no.'

Hobbes rubbed at his eyes. He fell silent. And then in a mumble, almost to himself, he said, 'I don't know. I just don't know.'

'Are you all right?'

Hobbes looked at her. 'Meg, listen . . . about earlier . . .'

'Save it. We have to get on, like it or not.'

'We do. I'm aware of that. But what happened back in Soho . . .'

She was looking at him. He felt the words were trapped in his mouth.

'Meg, I know you've heard the story . . .'

'Sure.' Latimer's gaze was unrelenting. 'A cop killed himself.'

'I didn't string him up.'

'You handed him the rope.'

'And what's that supposed to mean?'

'It means that you brought DI Jenkes down, you got him sacked.'

'Now look, I don't need to justify myself to you, or to anyone.'

Hobbes's raised voice cut through the babble of the incident room. The other officers present looked over at him.

He added in a softer voice, 'It pains me to say it, but Jenkes was a racist. And he paid for it.'

'Fucking hell,' Latimer whispered, close to him. 'The Brixton riot had just happened. We were all racist back then, for a couple of days at least.'

Hobbes didn't know how to answer that. He didn't like to think about it, but there was some truth in her statement. He remembered his own anger.

'It doesn't excuse what Jenkes did. Or the other two coppers.'

She glared at him. 'There were four officers in that room, weren't there?'

A pain cut through Hobbes's left temple, where he'd been bricked during the riot. It still played up, whenever he was pushed.

'Four people,' Latimer said again. 'And you joined in.'

'I didn't!'

'That's what the others said . . . It's common knowledge.'

'Common knowledge? Christ! You're meant to be a detective . . .'

'I am.'

'They lied.'

Latimer kept on: 'You joined in and then turned tail and rang the bell on them. Any way you measure it, that stinks.'

She glared at him. Hobbes held his tongue for a moment, and then said, 'I was there. I know what I saw.'

'And you didn't do anything?'

Now he couldn't speak at all. Latimer took a step back. She could see that he was troubled. 'Inspector,' she said, 'I'm sorry, but it's your word against the three other officers. You were attacked. You had to defend yourselves. You all did!'

Hobbes looked at her. What could he say against such an argument? It was useless. The ranks had closed up in support of each other. Only one thing came to mind, a fact that still filled him with anguish, even after these months had passed. He spoke quietly.

'Charlie Jenkes was my friend. My best friend.'

That was all. A simple statement. But even as he said it, he wondered at his own knowledge: why hadn't he seen the truth about Jenkes? Or perhaps he had, all along, and chosen to ignore it.

His voice softened. 'Right now, I can't trust anyone.'

There was a slight pause and then Latimer said, 'The thing is, sir, a number of our officers were shipped over to Brixton for the riot.'

'I can guess that. All the London stations were called upon.'

'One young constable was injured. Badly injured. Pete Gregson. He's still hasn't come back to work. He might never make it back, we don't know yet.'

Hobbes frowned. He was beginning to understand why there was such resentment towards him, here at Kew Road. 'So what are you saying, Meg, that an eye for an eye is a good thing?'

'It's a war.' She sighed. 'That's what it feels like.'

'I felt the same, on the night. But now, thinking back—'

Latimer's frustration overtook her. 'They're all against us. The press, the public, even our own top brass. We're figures of hate.'

Everyone in the room was now staring at the two of them. Hobbes was about to order them to get back to work, but instead he let the moment play out, the unease. He spoke clearly so they could all hear him:

'There's only one way forward, and that's to tell the truth. And that's what I did. It's painful. Yes. But what else can we do?'

'Right now, honestly, I feel like jacking it in.'

'Don't do that. Please, Meg. This is your job, your life.'

Latimer relented. 'Let's work this case together, find the killer.'

'And then?'

'And then we see how it feels.'

'What about Fairfax?'

'Oh, you'll never get him onside, you know that. It's too personal.'

Hobbes looked away for a moment, lost in thought. Then he turned back and asked, 'Where's that record cover? The last album.'

She handed him the *King Lost* sleeve. He opened up the gatefold and stared at the painted face. The teardrop, the X, the widened lips.

'What's your memory of all this,' he asked, 'from the time?'

'Well, like I said, I wasn't a massive fan. But I recall the mask, the character he'd invented. Lucas Bell actually started calling himself King Lost in interviews, I remember that much.'

'But what does it mean, in terms of the murderer's act, the desecration of the victim's face? What's the killer doing? What's he feeling?'

Seeing the autopsy report, Hobbes had automatically gone back to thinking of the perpetrator as male. The nature of the wounds swayed him.

Latimer pondered. 'This face, this mask . . . it means something to the killer.'

Hobbes tried turning the problem on its head. 'Maybe it's not an act of hatred?'

'What else can it be?'

'I don't know. An act of love.'

'You're losing me.'

'It's meticulous. The work of an artist.' Hobbes frowned. 'You see, that's what I keep coming back to. The deliberate nature of the work. The set-up of the room. The light through the window.'

'The staging.'

'Exactly. This isn't a madman. It's not sadistic.'

'I can buy that. Brendan was killed first.'

'A sadist would have kept the victim alive while he carved the mask. That's why I think it's love. But a twisted love.' He took a breath. 'This scares me. It really does.'

Third-Party Blues

DC Fairfax rang in with an update on the musicians in Monsoon Monsoon. 'I've found the drummer. But the keyboard player is proving tricky.'

'Nikki Hauser?'

'That's her. No sign at her flat. There's a flatmate, but she's claiming Nikki hasn't been home since the gig on Saturday. Suspicious, right?'

'It is.'

'I'll keep looking.'

'But you've got the drummer at least.'

'Yeah. A real piece of work. One of those peacock boys. And totally off his nut on God knows what. I'll bring him in.'

'Actually, no. I'll meet you.'

'Whereabouts?'

'The Pleasure Palace.'

Hobbes drove to Covent Garden. He found a place to park and then walked through the crowds until he reached the narrow back street where the club was situated. It wasn't much to look at: a scuffed green doorway, a painted sign, and a few posters advertising this month's events. Not much of a palace, and hardly any promise of pleasure. But even in the daytime a group of young women stood around, some of them with punk hairdos and ripped clothing, the others dressed up in more outlandish colours and styles. Fairfax was standing there, alongside an ill-looking young man. Fairfax was holding him by the back of his collar.

'Here is he. One Matthew Tate.'

The young man spluttered. 'Sputnik, man. You have to call me that. Everybody does.'

Hobbes recognized him from the photograph of the group. 'You play the drums in Monsoon Monsoon, is that correct?'

'Yeah, that's me. What of it?'

'We need a few words.'

'Yeah, well, tell Miss Piggy here to get his mitts off me. This is police harassment, this is.'

The drummer was in his early twenties. Jet-black hair, long on top, cropped at the side, gelled into a weird shape like something out of a science fiction movie. He wore a lilac shirt, a paisley silk scarf and close-fitting purple trousers, the bright colours set against the pallid grey of his face. He was fidgety, wound up, his eyes focused on an ever-moving dot some few feet ahead of him.

'You dirty little scumbag,' Fairfax was saying. 'You make me sick, you really do.'

'You keep your fucking hands off me, man. I'm warning you!'

Tate's voice was slurred. Hobbes knew that he would have trouble getting much out of him.

'Do we have a way in?'

'The owner's here,' Fairfax said. 'Mr Carlisle.'

'Good.'

Hobbes examined the posters beside the door and found the listing for the Monsoon Monsoon gig. It read, *The spirit of King Lost, resurrected on stage!*

Fairfax led the way inside. They passed a cloakroom and then came out on to the club floor. It was a medium-sized place with a low ceiling and a series of small alcoves around the side. A pair of cleaners were working away, mopping the dance floor, while a lone barmaid washed and stacked glasses behind the bar. Hobbes could smell the stench of stale beer and cigarette smoke even over the acrid pine scent of the floor cleaner. Despite that, the place did have a certain opulent grandeur, the ceilings hung with velvet cloths and brass lamps, and large cushions scattered here and there around the edges of the floor.

They found Mr Carlisle waiting for them near the stage. He was a cheerful-looking man dressed in plain black trousers and a white T-shirt which was stretched tightly across his chest. And he wasn't that old; maybe thirty. His hair hung down over his eyes, and a Freddie Mercury-style moustache dominated his face.

Hobbes ignored the outstretched hand. 'You're the owner?'

'Owner. General manager. All-round dogsbody and washer-up.' He laughed to himself. 'Andy Carlisle, at your service.'

'You were here for the concert on Saturday night?'

'It was a big night, the place was rammed. We had to turn punters away at the door, and I really don't like doing that.'

'Am I missing something?'

'In what way?'

'Monsoon Monsoon are hardly famous.'

'No, no, not at all. And to be honest we weren't expecting much, but then the tickets began selling like there was no tomorrow – you know, once the rumours started flying around.'

'Rumours?'

'About what the group were going to do. About what the singer had planned.'

Hobbes asked, 'And what was that?'

'He was going to conjure up the ghost. Like a séance.'

'You mean the ghost of Lucas Bell?'

'No. I mean the ghost of King Lost. That's two different people. Very different. Living in the same body.'

The manager's expression was entirely serious.

Hobbes scanned the space, picturing the empty club crowded with people. He saw Matthew Tate sitting on a cushion with his back against the wall, smoking a roll-up.

Carlisle asked, 'What do you need from me?'

'Are you aware that the singer of Monsoon Monsoon is dead? Murdered?'

'Yes, I heard that. Such a drag.'

'What do you remember of the concert that night?'

Carlisle thought for a moment. 'Not much, in detail. I tend to work the whole place, keep myself moving, checking on things. But the climax of the gig was amazing. I had to stop and stare. One of those nights where you think: is this going to be an orgy, or a riot?'

'Yeah, man!' This was Tate, piping up. 'It was a fucking magic spell. We filled the room with phantoms, believe me!'

'In yer box, sunshine,' Fairfax said. 'We'll come to you.'

Hobbes kept on at Carlisle. 'Are there any photos?'

'Well, there were a number of rock journos in, and a few photographers.'

'Any in particular?'

'The best of them is Neville Briggs.'

Fairfax took a note of the name.

Carlisle smiled. 'You know, without Lucas Bell there would be no Pleasure Palace.'

'Why's that?'

The manager looked thoughtful. 'My friends and I all hated punk. We hated its naff left-wing politics, and its so-called "authenticity". Absolute hypocritical bollocks. We thought that pop music was essentially about glamour, and romance. It's a fantasy. An escape from the daily toil. And we were old enough to remember the years of glam rock, so we were playing David Bowie records, T. Rex, Roxy Music, Sparks. And Lucas Bell. This was late 1979, when we started out, in a back-room club off Wardour Street, no bigger than a cupboard. But word spread and soon we found ourselves surrounded by like-minded people, many of them younger than us. The kids began dressing up in fancy outfits, following the lead of the glam rock singers. In fact, we only let people inside if they were dressed in some unique fashion. No punks, no hippies, no bores. You know, just how Lucas Bell sang it; the border blossoms.'

'What does that mean?'

'The outsiders, the people on the edges of society. The beautiful flowers that grow in ditches and concrete.'

Hobbes shifted his focus. 'Did anyone threaten Brendan Clarke that night?'

'There was some kind of incident outside, I believe.'

'After the gig?'

Carlisle nodded. 'I didn't see it myself, but apparently one of the Lucas Bell fans shouted at him, tried to hit him.'

'You've no idea who that was?'

'No. I only heard about it later on.'

Hobbes thanked Carlisle for his help, and gestured for Matthew Tate to get up and move to the centre of the floor. With a shock he realized that the young drummer was crying, tears streaming down his ashen face.

'What the hell?' Fairfax said, seeing this. 'What's up with him now?'

'He's distressed.'

'That's right,' Tate said, his eyes fixing on Hobbes momentarily with some kind of gratitude. 'That's it, see. I'm *distressed*. It's too much to take in. Way too much. What can I do? I mean, he's dead. Brendan is dead!' He spun round, crying out to the room. 'You see, what I'm saying is . . . I'm saying . . . who's going to do the singing now? That's my question, see. That is the question.'

Hobbes brought the young man under control. 'You liked Brendan, did you?'

'Oh yeah. A top geezer. Well, you know, a bit stuck-up and all that. But smart with it. And I thought he was going places, I really did.'

Hobbes could see that Fairfax was getting restless, shuffling around as the questions continued. He tried to ignore him, setting his sights on Matthew Tate alone.

'So Brendan was ambitious? He wanted to be successful?'

Tate scratched at his face idly. Hobbes noted that his fingernails were painted with a glossy purple lacquer.

'Successful? Nah, man. He was into the music, you know, just the tunes. Mind you, he was rolling in it, wasn't he, loaded parents and all, he never had no struggles. Not like me . . .'

The young man's voice trailed off as he lost track of his thoughts.

Fairfax prowled the floor. 'Ah, I've had enough of this.' He moved in on Tate. 'What the hell are you saying?'

Tate spun off in a new direction. 'You gotta keep playing, haven't you? Keep the beat going.' He banged out rhythms on an imagined drum kit, sending a pulse of energy around the room. 'Here we go. Wallop! Yes, sir. Very nice.'

Fairfax grabbed hold of Tate by the wrists, stopping his movement.

'Hey! That's persecution, that is.'

Fairfax laughed. 'You kids are all the same. Little pasty-faced rebels dressed up in yer mummy's blouses.'

Hobbes decided to let Fairfax carry on for a while, if only to see whether the heavy approach would lead to anything useful.

The detective constable asked, 'When was the last time you saw Brendan Clarke?'

'Right here, man. Where else? At the gig. Singing, like.'

'You didn't go round to his house?'

'We dropped him off, sure.'

'After the gig? You drove him home?'

'Nikki did that. Nikki always drives. She doesn't drink, see.'

'But you saw him go into the house?'

'Yeah, sure.'

'Was he alone?'

Tate wet his lips.

'Well?'

'Sure, he was alone. What else?' His eyes widened. 'Hey man, what're you saying? I never killed him! It wasn't me.'

76

Hobbes stepped forward, asking, 'How was the gig?'

'Ah, it was a riot, man, A fucking explosion! The crowd were loving it, crazy all the way.'

Fairfax grunted. 'This is a waste of time. He's a fuck-up.'

'You go on then. Find the photographer.'

The two detectives stared at each other. Hobbes waited for a rejoinder of some kind. But none came.

'Yeah, I can do that. But listen, guv . . .' Fairfax drew Hobbes to the side. 'I was out of order this morning, at the meeting. I was being a bit of a twat.'

Hobbes was surprised. He looked at his colleague with interest. 'That's all right. I get the same way, sometimes.'

'Yeah, we all do.'

Fairfax sauntered off towards the exit door, grinning at the barmaid on his way out, and getting a smile in return.

The cleaners and the manager had moved on. Hobbes sat down at a table and nudged a chair out for Tate, an invitation. They sat adjacent to each other. 'Here you go, have one of these.' He pushed his pack of Embassy across the tabletop.

'Oh right, cheers. Nice one.' Tate reached into the pack with trembling fingers. He lit the cigarette from the flame of Hobbes's lighter, and sucked in the smoke like this was his last day alive. His breath made a high whistling sound.

'That other copper's a bit heavy-handed, if you ask me.'

'He can be. I agree.'

Tate nodded. 'Sure. Yeah. Some people, normal people like, they just don't get what's at stake, see? It's important: how you do things, how you look, and how you fucking well compose yourself, you know what I'm saying?'

Hobbes nodded. 'At your own pace. Tell me what you remember about Saturday night.'

Tate smiled, the first gesture that came from within, rather than being an effect of the drugs. 'You're not a bad bloke, like, for a rozzer.' He breathed out smoke and collected his wits as best he could.

'It was all meant to be for Lucas,' he began. 'For Lucas Bell. The whole gig. It was a tribute to him.'

'And this was Brendan's idea?'

'Oh yeah. Bang on. He fucking loved Lucas. Sorry . . . for the swearing, like.'

'That's all right.'

Tate took two quick drags of the cigarette, one after another. Hobbes could see that he was starting to relax.

'Brendan was mad keen, and Nikki, she was well up for it as well.'

'How do you mean?'

'Oh man, they were talking up some shit together. To conjure up Luke's spirit.'

'That's how they put it?'

Tate nodded his head, and once started he couldn't stop the movement. He looked like a bird pecking at a seed and missing it every time. The young man's eyes had now taken on a feverish glow as he brought the gig to mind. Suddenly he stood up and walked on to the dance floor. He jumped up on to the stage. His eyes were open wide in wonder as he spoke.

'The lights go up, right? All crimson and gold, really spooky. And then Brendan comes out wearing the full mask, the full King Lost regalia.'

He looked down at Hobbes, who had stood up himself now.

'You mean he'd painted his face?'

Tate nodded. 'Man, it was scary to behold. White face, the lips extended and painted ruby red, the teardrop just here.' He touched his left cheek. 'The cross on the forehead. The whole shebang.'

'What was the crowd's reaction?'

'They went mental!' Tate began to sway from side to side. 'At first there was just shock. But then as Nikki started up the chords of the first song on her synth, and I came in with the drum lick . . .'

78

His hands tapped out a beat. 'I had them. I had them moving! And then Brendan started to sing. Man, it could've been Lucas Bell himself, I swear!'

'So it was going well?' Hobbes asked.

'Ah, it was incredible. Totally fucking incredible, the best gig ever.'

Tate fell silent, his body coming to a rest. He seemed to have gained focus. Hobbes pressed on.

'What happened next?'

'It just built and built. You see, after a few numbers people realized that we were copying the exact set list that Lucas did at the Rainbow all those years before, on his last ever gig. The exact same songs in the same order. Like I said, we were raising up spirits. This was our night and the ghost of Lucas Bell, I swear, he joined us there on the stage. And then it all took off, crazy like.'

'Yes?'

Tate stared down at Hobbes. 'We started up the final song. The last song from the very last album, where King Lost takes his overdose and rises into rock and roll heaven to be accepted by angels with electric guitars and day-glo wings.' The drummer suddenly stopped talking. He looked terrified.

'What's wrong?'

Tate shivered. 'At the end of the song, Brendan brought out a knife.'

'A knife?'

'It was there in his hand, I dunno where it came from.'

Tate's own hand was outstretched, as though the knife was there before him, held in his own grasp. Hobbes didn't need to urge him on, not now.

'We'd stopped playing, Nikki and I. Even she looked shocked. And a bit scared. There was silence in the club. Everyone was just standing there, staring ahead. And then . . . and then Brendan cut into his own face.' Tate's eyes fluttered. The imagined knife shuddered in his hand. 'He cut the mask away.' Tate paused for a second to gather his breath. The next words came in a series of gasps. 'It's all a daze . . . all a daze . . . I can't see . . . the mask . . . his face . . . all bloody . . . all red in the lights . . .'

Now he fell silent. His body was drained of energy.

Hobbes clambered up on to the stage to join him. 'Brendan did this for real?'

'No, no. It was a trick. A fake knife, fake blood. I don't know how he did it, but I saw him backstage, and he was all right again.'

'How did the audience react, when he did this?'

Tate looked directly at Hobbes. 'That was the thing, they fuckin' loved it. Because Brendan had copied exactly what Lucas Bell had done, seven years ago, when he'd destroyed the mask of King Lost, in front of the crowd at the Rainbow. Nobody knew it at the time, but that was Lucas killing off his own image, just weeks before he killed himself.' A spasm went through Tate's body. 'Brendan did the same. The exact same thing. And now . . .'

'Yes,' Hobbes said. 'And now he's dead.'

Tate shook his head in disbelief. His mood had changed. He looked like a fragile young man, someone genuinely saddened by his friend's death. 'How can it be?' he asked in a quiet voice. 'How can it be? It doesn't make sense.'

'Everything makes sense, eventually,' Hobbes replied. 'I'll find out.'

Tate sat down on the edge of the stage. Hobbes knelt beside him.

'So what happened after the gig? Did you see him speaking with Simone Paige?'

'Who's that?'

'A journalist.'

'Oh right, yeah. I know her. I saw them later on, outside. Brendan, Simone, and this other kid, a girl. There was some kind of argument.'

'Between Simone and Brendan?'

'No, man. This girl.'

'A teenage girl?'

'Yeah, yeah. She was shouting at Brendan, calling him a fake.'

'Why would she say that?'

'Who the hell knows? Crazy, maybe. She cried out, "There's only one Lucas Bell!" It was loud, man, everyone heard it. And then she reached out and slapped Brendan. Slapped him! Right across the face.' Tate shook his head in disbelief, reliving this moment.

'How did Brendan respond?' Hobbes asked.

'Super cool. As always.'

'Any idea who the teenager was?'

'I reckon that journalist woman knew her. That's all I can say.'

Hobbes thought for a moment, and then asked, 'Did Brendan and Simone Paige get together that night?'

'Yeah. I saw them a while later, didn't I? In the dressing room. I walked past the door and there they were, the two of them, real close.'

'Close?'

'Real close, you know what I'm saying?'

'No. Tell me.'

'They were kissing.'

A detail Miss Paige had failed to mention in last night's interview.

'Did you hear what they were talking about, Brendan and Simone?'

The young man wiped at his eyes. 'No, nothing. I moved on.'

Hobbes asked, 'Do you know where Nikki Hauser is?'

'Sure, man, She's probably down in Hastings already, for tomorrow's event. She never misses it. Not ever.'

'What's happening tomorrow?'

'It's the anniversary of Lucas Bell's suicide. The exact day. The fans meet up in Witch Haven. That's the name of the field, like, the place where Lucas did himself in. The crowds turn up there, every year.'

Hobbes processed the information. Then he asked, 'Why do they call you Sputnik?'

'Because most of the time I'm floating in space.'

'And the rest of the time?'

'Playing the drums. Jesus, when I think back . . .'

'On what?'

'The early days, you know? It was me, Brendan and Nikki, the three of us against the world. In fact, Brendan rescued me.'

'From where?'

'From the street, man. Oh, I did some bad things, some nasty things, to get by. You see what I'm saying?'

'I do, yes.'

'So when Brendan started chatting to me and we got to talking about music, and I told him how I used to play drums in the Boys' Brigade, back before everything went crazy bad for me, well that's when my life started afresh.'

Hobbes sat down on the stage edge. 'Tell me, Sputnik, was Brendan working on anything special that you know of?'

'Special how?'

'Something to do with Lucas Bell. Apart from the gig, I mean. Anything?'

Tate thought about it. 'There was the fanzine. That took up a lot of his time.'

'*100 Splinters*?'

'That's the one. You should read it. That's where Brendan showed his true self.'

Hobbes absorbed this and then asked, 'Anything else going on in his life?'

Tate grunted in dismissal. 'He was preoccupied, I know that.'

'With what?'

'Who knows? Maybe with Nikki, and the trouble they were having.'

'Right.' Hobbes handed his pack of cigarettes to Tate. 'Here. Save these for later.'

'Is this a bribe?'

Hobbes smiled. 'No. I'm trying to give up. Did Brendan have many girlfriends?'

'Brendan? No, I wouldn't say so.'

'What was the relationship like between Brendan and Nikki?'

The young man looked at him. 'Oh, they were all lovey-dovey to begin with, but then the hatred set in. Sheer bloody hatred.'

'But they were engaged, isn't that true?'

'Yeah, but only for a short while. It was a nightmare. One minute they were all over each other, kissing and that. Practically having it away in front of me. Pardon my existence. And the next second they were spitting blood, arguing. And there I was, hiding in the corner of the van.'

'I can imagine.'

'The third-party blues, man. There's none worse.'

'Who called off the wedding?'

'That would be Brendan.'

Hobbes leaned in. 'Why? Do you know?'

'He told me that he learned something about her, about Nikki. Something bad. Really bad.'

'Any idea what it was?'

Tate shook his head. 'Something to do with Lucas, I think.' He looked disappointed. 'You know Nikki did a session spot on *King Lost*. Assorted keyboards. "Extra texture", as it says in the credits. She did some touring with him. Truth is, they had an affair, of sorts.'

'Her and Lucas?'

'Spot on. And that's why Brendan asked her to form Monsoon Monsoon with him, because of that connection, And of course . . .'

'Of course?'

'You know what I'm saying, Mr Detective. Do your job.'

'And that's why he fell in love with her?'

'Bang on! Nikki's the direct line back to the source. She's spoken to Bell, which is something Brendan has never done. She's shared a stage with him, a tour bus, cheap hotel accommodation, the works. Sexola. Rumpy pumpy. So kissing Nikki is a bit like kissing Lucas! Creepy, isn't it?'

'Yes. Very.'

'And so when I saw him chatting up that Simone woman, the journalist, I thought, here we go again, Brendan's up to his old tricks.'

'How do you mean?'

'Simone Paige was another one of Lucas Bell's squeezes. In fact, she was probably the greatest of them.'

'I didn't know that.'

'The grand passion of his life, apparently. So no wonder Brendan fell for her.'

Hobbes nodded. 'You've been very helpful, Sputnik.'

'Yeah, yeah. Sure. Whatever, man.'

'Do you think Nikki could've killed Brendan?'

Tate stared into the distance. Hobbes thought he wasn't going to answer. But then he spoke in a low voice: 'She'd have to be roused.'

'Angry, you mean?'

'Yeah. Like really, truly pissed off.'

'And then? Would she be capable?'

Tate nodded gleefully. 'Easily, man. With great fucking pleasure.'

The Woman in the Car

Back at Kew Road station Hobbes spent an hour looking through the copies of *100 Splinters* he'd taken from Brendan Clarke's house. The homemade magazine was A4 format in size, with sixteen pages, the text typewritten, photocopied and held together with a couple of staples. The subject matter ranged across the whole of Bell's life and work, with nothing deemed too trivial for analysis. Simone Paige's name was mentioned in several issues. One article examined in detail her relationship with Bell: first meeting, falling in love, imagined sex life, the break-up. Brendan called her the 'last major passion in Bell's life'. Although the writer made no direct claim himself, he did note that Simone's '. . . cruel and selfish rejection of Lucas Bell's love was seen by many as a major factor in his subsequent decision to take his own life'. The piece ended with a look at Paige's drug problem, and the period she spent in a private clinic after Bell's death.

Reading all this, Hobbes couldn't help but think about the message Simone had left on his cassette tape, thinking she was talking to herself alone.

He would speak to her about that later today, if he got the chance.

Turning his attention to the most recent issue, the seventh-anniversary special, his eye was drawn immediately to an article entitled, 'Lucas Bell's Final Hours: Who was the Mystery Woman?' Here Brendan Clarke claimed to have located and interviewed a witness who had seen Bell on the night the singer killed himself. This witness was Danny Webster, a 'self-employed plumber' in his mid thirties, a resident of Hastings, who had known Lucas as a teenager. The article took the form of a verbatim interview. It began with Brendan Clarke asking about Webster's knowledge of Lucas Bell's life, and his music.

Danny Webster: I was never a massive fan, or anything like that. I was more into heavy metal. But I did buy that last album, the famous one.

100 Splinters: *King Lost*?

DW: Yeah. I listened to that a fair bit. It was good, some good tunes, but a bit over my head, most of it. The lyrics and such.

100S: It's a concept album. It tells a story, of a character called King Lost.

DW: Sure. I picked up on some of the references in the lyrics to Hastings, landmarks and all that. And then there's the cover. That fish and chip shop he's photographed outside? Duffy's? That's in Hastings.

100S: So you've lived there all your life?

DW: That I have. Yes.

100S: And did you know Lucas Bell at all, from when you were a kid?

DW: I knew him when he was younger, at school, like. We were the same age, in the same year.

100S: What was Lucas like at school?

DW: He always looked a bit weird, but maybe that's just me looking back, with what I know now, I mean. To be honest, he wasn't part of my crowd. He hung around with the outsider kids. The losers. Sorry, but that's how we thought of them.

100S: It reminds me of some of Bell's lyrical concerns. How King Lost isn't only a lost king, he's also the King of the Lost.

DW: Yeah, sure. I suppose.

100S: Let's talk about the night of Lucas's death. That would be August twenty-fifth, 1974. A Sunday. You claim that you saw Lucas that night?

DW: I did, yes.

100S: Tell me about that.

DW: Well, I was standing on Sedlescombe Road, to the north of the town, waiting to cross the road. I'd just come out of the pub. A car stopped up the road from me, and a man got out from the front passenger seat. He looked dazed, like he was drunk or something. He walked a few paces towards me and then stopped. And that's when I realized. It was Lucas Bell.

100S: You're sure it was him?

DW: Absolutely.

100S: Who was driving the vehicle?

DW: A woman.

100S: What happened next?

DW: Well, like I said, Lucas walked towards me and then stopped. He stared at me. Then the car moved forward a little way to catch up with him, and the driver shouted through the open window at him.

100S: What did she say?

DW: She told him to get back in the car.

100S: How did Lucas respond?

DW: He seemed not to hear her at first, but then . . . it was like he'd come out of a trance or a coma of some kind, and he reacted. He must've heard her because he got back inside.

100S: And then?

DW: The car carried on along Sedlescombe Road. That's it.

100S: In which direction was it travelling?

DW: Away from the town, northwards.

100S: Towards open country?

DW: Yes. Towards . . . where he was . . . where his body was found.

100S: Can you remember what kind of car it was?

DW: That's easy. It was a Ford Capri. I know my cars. Bit of a hobby of mine. Yes, a blue Ford Capri. Very nice.

100S: And what time of night would this be?

DW: After eleven, definitely. Hang on, you said it was a Sunday, right? So that would have been early closing. Maybe a bit earlier . . .

100S: Why didn't you mention all this to the police at the time?

DW: I did. Or at least I tried to. But they didn't seem that interested.

100S: Really? That's weird.

DW: I didn't think about it for a while. Lucas was buried by then. I wasn't a hundred per cent sure of what I'd seen at the actual time, because I was a bit drunk you know, but later, when the funeral was on the news and all that, with the crowds gathered, well that's when I started to put the pieces together. That's when I knew it was him. It was Lucas Bell. Because he'd stared directly at me.

100S: What else can you tell us about the driver, the woman?

DW: I didn't see much of her, but I caught a glimpse as the car passed by.

100S: Did you notice anything distinctive about her? Her age? The colour of her hair, maybe? You didn't recognize her?

DW: Sorry, no.

100S: You couldn't see her face?

DW: No. Not clearly.

100S: Let me ask again, to make sure. How certain are you that it was Lucas Bell that you saw?

DW: He stopped under a street lamp when he got out. I saw him clearly. Well, let me say this: if it wasn't him, I'd be severely surprised. I'd be gobsmacked.

100S: And by the time you came forward, what do you think, had the police already worked out all the details in their heads?

DW: Yeah. The coroner had made his verdict. 'Death by his own hand', and all that. I read it in the *Sun*. Everyone was so sure that he'd acted alone. After all, he'd tried it once before, right?

100S: Lucas Bell's previous suicide attempt?

DW: Yeah. And he'd acted alone that time, hadn't he?

100S: We think so, yes.

DW: So there it is. Cut and dried. I guess I was the only person to see this woman. What else can I say?

100S: One final question. You said that Lucas looked 'dazed'. Tell me, what did you mean by that?

DW: His eyes were all glazed over. And he was swaying a bit.

100S: Could he have been on drugs?

DW: I guess so.

100S: Do you have anything more to add?

DW: I will never forget that face, not now, not knowing who he was, and what he was about to do. It will stay with me. It will haunt me.

100S: Thank you for your help.

The interview ended there. A blurry photograph showed a man standing near a set of traffic lights at a road junction. A caption read, *Danny Webster on Sedlescombe Road, Hastings*. Brendan Clarke went on to ask the reader, 'Who was this woman? Was she an old friend or colleague, or somebody new in his life? A fan? A lover? A relative? What role did she play in his suicide, if any?' The article ended with the statement, 'Only by finding this mystery woman, the driver of the car, can the singer's final hours be pieced together. We may yet know the truth of that night and the reasons for Lucas ending his life.' To finish, he listed the more obvious candidates for the role, nine of them, with details of their relationship to Bell – guitarist, publicist, stylist, friend, and so on. Hobbes had heard of only two candidates.

Nikki Hauser (Keyboard Player, Lover)
Simone Paige (Journalist, Lover)

On the magazine's final pages, Clarke talked about his upcoming gig with Monsoon Monsoon, where he hoped to take on the spirit of King Lost. The final paragraph read:

The ghost of Lucas Bell hovers close by, ready to be called down as needed. And we surely need him now more than ever. Our times are dark, our country divided by riots and strikes, as our rulers tighten their grip. 1981 is splintered, torn to shreds. But Lucas was and always will be the torch that leads us forward. I pray that King Lost welcomes me, that he takes possession of my body. The mask awaits. Paradise awaits!

Hobbes couldn't help seeing Clarke's face as it was at the end, sliced up, bloodied, transformed.

The mask killed him.

Caught on Tape

Barlow talked as he drove, relating his findings about Lucas Bell: the singer's short life and career, his tragic demise. Dead by his own hand at the age of twenty-six. It was, Hobbes noted, the same age as Brendan Clarke.

Bell's story was a mystery in itself. He'd released two long-playing records to moderate success in the early seventies. And then for his third album he had suddenly appeared as a new character, King Lost. His appearance on *Top of the Pops* in October 1973, where he sang the album's first single dressed in full costume and mask, had electrified and shocked the living rooms of Great Britain. His louche, ambiguous sexuality held a new kind of appeal for a new generation. Parents were outraged, the kids rejoiced.

'King Lost was a tragic rock and roll clown, a Pierrot figure. Hence the white face and the teardrop. And the album tells of his adventures in life, in love, and so on. And in the last song on side two, his death.'

'Suicide?' Hobbes asked.

'It's not entirely clear. But that's how people have read it, in the light of subsequent events.'

The car moved on. Night was falling over London, softening the edges of houses, bus shelters, shops, phone boxes.

'And then at the peak of his worldwide success, Bell kills himself. Such a waste.'

Hobbes lit a cigarette. 'Do we have any clue why?'

'The story goes that Bell invented King Lost as a mask to hide behind. But he was messed up inside, drugs, booze, endless touring, the whole rock star curse. You know how it goes, sir – loved by millions, but lonely when the stage lights go dark.'

Hobbes glanced at the dashboard clock. It was past eight. The early morning visit to the victim's house was taking its toll. He felt grit rubbing at his eyes, and he promised himself a good night's sleep when he got home. It had been a long, long day, and not much to show for it. Latimer had checked out the Clarkes' alibis, and confirmed they were at home in Maidstone at the time of their son's murder. She'd also shown a photograph of Nikki Hauser to Mrs Newley: no definite recognition, but the witness couldn't be entirely sure. So Hauser could still be Miss X. Meanwhile, Fairfax had tracked down the address of the photographer, Neville Briggs, only to find no one at home.

The car stopped at a zebra crossing to allow a young couple to cross the road, arm in arm. Hobbes stared at them with a twinge of envy; they seemed to be utterly lost in love. It made him think of his wife. And his son. The old family home in Willesden. There might still be a chance, yes, perhaps. If he could just get his career back on track.

The car moved on, along Camden High Street. The warm evening air had brought them all out, the weird and wonderful, the damaged, the lost, the dreamers: mohicanned punks and dreadlocked rastas, drug addicts, dealers, gaudy boys and girls, all vying for attention in a clash of colours and styles. The littered pavements were stacked with all kinds of goods for sale. Every surface was covered in layers of fly posters: Steel Pulse at Dingwalls, Visage at the Electric Ballroom, Soft Cell at the Music Machine. On a personal level, Hobbes enjoyed the sights and sounds. But as a policeman, he saw it in an entirely different light. In fact, there was a heavy presence of uniformed officers on the streets that evening. They were stopping people, and searching them.

'Look at that,' he said to Barlow as they passed one group. 'The bloody idiots are having a go at young black men.'

'Aren't they the main culprits? For crime, I mean.'

'Christ. Have you been talking to Fairfax and the others? No, they are not the main culprits.'

'But we're catching them at it. Otherwise, how come so many of them are in prison?'

'Because we keep bloody well going after them. That's the problem, see? People resent it.' Hobbes clenched his teeth. 'And we never bloody learn. Four months ago, Brixton was in flames, the people rioting.' He fell quiet for a moment as he remembered the events of that terrible night, and his own involvement in them. 'And since then we've had riots in Handsworth, Chapeltown, Toxteth.'

'And coppers injured in every one.'

'Welcome to the frontline, PC Barlow.'

'It's not what I expected, sir, when I took on the job.'

'No. No. Of course not.'

Hobbes gave it a moment's thought, then added, 'It's going to happen again, believe me.' Barlow started to answer him, but Hobbes was on a roll. 'Meanwhile, our boys are lining up to protect the National Front on their marches. The bloody NF! I mean, can that be right?'

'I don't know, sir.'

'You don't know?'

'What about freedom of speech?'

'You mean the freedom to hate?'

Barlow didn't reply. Well, Hobbes knew it was best to keep your mouth shut these days, in the force; bow your head and say 'Yes, sir, straight away, sir', and get on with the task in hand. The police were under siege, that was the mentality. Hobbes hated it. But he also hated the idea the public carried around, of all coppers being thugs and racists. The Tory Party in uniform, that was the latest nickname. Maggie's Army.

'Bloody Thatcher,' he murmured.

He could hear Barlow hold back a gasp.

'What's wrong? Have I shocked you now?'

There was a slight pause before the constable spoke up. 'So you're really anti-Maggie? I never believed it.'

'It's the talk of the locker room, is it?'

Barlow's renewed silence was enough for him to know the truth. 'Well then?'

'Yes, sir. That's what they're saying.'

They had by now driven over Camden Lock, heading for a quieter part of the town. Barlow was fidgeting, his hands opening and closing on the steering wheel.

'Steady on. Let's not have a crash.'

'It's just that, well, Maggie gave us that big pay rise, didn't she?'

'She did. And God bless her for it.'

'So then?'

'So that doesn't mean that we're in her debt, and that we're supposed to do every last thing she bids. And does she have to use such a ruddy great hammer, knocking the people into shape?'

Barlow shook his head. 'I didn't have you down as a socialist, sir.'

Hobbes felt his blood boil. 'I'm not a bloody socialist!'

'But Fairfax called you a . . .' The constable hesitated.

'Yes?'

'A red, sir. A commie.' Barlow was suddenly nervous. 'Don't tell him I said any of this, will you?'

'Don't worry. I know I'm not liked.'

They drove on in silence for a while. They were nearly there.

Hobbes knew that Barlow had a good heart, he could sense that. But if Fairfax and his chums got their claws into him, he could see the constable going the way of so many others: the backroom deals, a nod and a wink, a blind eye being turned. It went on. Christ, he'd even given into temptation himself, once or twice, when he was younger. But what could you do? How could you fight it?

'Barlow?'

'Sir?'

He was going to explain everything to the young officer. His side of the Soho story, what had really happened down in the cellar of the drinking club. Get it out in the open. But his courage failed him. Or rather, the absurdity of the situation got to him. It was all so bloody desperate.

That stupid fucker, Charlie Jenkes, hanging from a beam in his garage.

And they were blaming Hobbes for all of it.

'You wanted to speak, sir?'

'What? Oh, no, never mind. It's nothing.'

'This is her road. What number is it?'

'Thirty-one.'

The car slowed as they searched for the house along the crescent-shaped avenue.

'I'm not sure I'll ever get on with DC Fairfax, though,' Barlow admitted. 'All those jokes, and that. And the way he talks to DS Latimer.'

Hobbes grinned. 'Actually, I think he's got other things on his mind, these days.' And then he asked, 'Are you on duty tomorrow?'

'It's my day off.'

'Good. How do you fancy spending it at the seaside?'

Barlow looked confused. 'Oh right, you mean Hastings? The Lucas Bell anniversary?'

'Exactly. I have it on good authority that one of our chief suspects will be there. Nikki Hauser. Along with a host of other crazy fans. Because I know Brendan Clarke's murder is all tied up with Lucas Bell in some way. And I need to be at the heart of it all. I need to get a feel for things.' He paused. 'What do you say? A day out, fish and chip supper on me. And meanwhile, you'll be doing some proper detective work. Digging deep.'

'Out of uniform?'

'Obviously. You'll stick out like a sore bloody thumb otherwise.'

Barlow answered immediately. 'Yes, sir. I can do that.'

'Excellent.' The car pulled to a halt. 'Now let's see what Simone Paige has to say for herself.'

They got out of the vehicle and walked towards the house. It was a ground-floor flat in a large and very smart Edwardian building. Hobbes rang the bell and they only had to wait a moment before the door opened. And there she was, dressed pretty much as she had been the night before, but grubbier, and more dishevelled. Her hair was mussed up even more than he remembered it.

'Oh fuck. You again.'

'A couple of questions, Miss Paige. That's all.'

'At this time of night?'

'I'm afraid so. If you don't mind.'

Finally, she invited them in and showed them into the living room. It was spacious, tidy, sweet-smelling. The walls were covered in framed posters, each one advertising a band or a famous concert, most of them dating from the sixties or early seventies – the Grateful Dead, Led Zeppelin, The Who.

'Sit down then, if you must.'

Hobbes remained on his feet. He could tell that Simone had been drinking: her face had taken on a reddish glow. He was about to start his questions when a man came in carrying a freshly opened bottle of wine. His face was finely boned, handsome, his body lean and fit for his age. And from nowhere at all Hobbes felt the bitter tang of jealousy.

'Everything all right, Simone?'

'Yes. It's the police.'

'I guessed that.'

Hobbes held back a retort. He immediately read the situation: the look in the man's eyes, his nervousness, his frustration. He'd come round in protective mode, the shoulder to cry on, the calming embrace. That old ploy.

'What do they want?'

'I don't know,' Simone answered. 'I really don't.' Her voice was edged with sadness, and something more: anger, steadily growing.

'Did you invite them?'

She shook her head in reply. The man drew himself to his full height: Hobbes had a couple of inches on him, but the other man didn't let this overwhelm him. 'I don't think this is very polite, officer.'

'This is a murder case.'

'What's that got to do with Simone?'

'I'm trying to find that out.'

'She's already talked to you.'

Hobbes kept his voice steady. 'Not adequately.'

Silence. The man glared at Hobbes and was about to say something he would almost certainly regret, but then Simone said, 'Leave it, Nev. Just bloody leave it.' And the moment passed. The man moved back a little, enough to allow Hobbes to breathe again.

Nev? He made a connection with the name given to him by the manager of the Pleasure Palace.

'Neville Briggs? You're a photographer, is that correct?'

There was no answer. Simone said, 'He is. Why?'

'I need to see some of your photographs, from the Monsoon Monsoon gig. Would that be possible?'

Again, Briggs didn't answer. Simone sighed. 'Of course it's all right. Do as they say, Neville.'

'I'm especially interested in any shots of the crowd, faces, people, that kind of thing.'

'I want this over with,' Simone added. 'Whatever it takes.'

Briggs nodded. He picked up on her mood. 'Sure. I can do that.'

'I think it's time for you to go,' she said.

He bit at his lip. 'Righty-oh. I'll see you around then.'

'Just bloody go, please. Christ.'

He picked up his jacket from the back of a chair. Hobbes said, 'We'll be coming round tomorrow morning, early on. Can you have things ready by then?'

'Yes. Sure. If it's necessary.'

Briggs left the room. Hobbes waited until he heard the front door close, and then he sat down on the settee.

'So. Miss Paige.'

'Yes?' She poured herself a glass of red wine.

'Will you be going to Hastings tomorrow?'

'I doubt it.'

'There's some kind of ritual down there, I believe? To mark the death of Lucas Bell.'

She shrugged. 'They'll only attack me.'

Hobbes coughed. 'By the way, I'm working on your theory.'

'Which theory?'

'The idea of a crazed fan.'

She frowned. 'I don't think Brendan or his band had that many fans.'

'No, but Lucas Bell did. And that's why I'm here.' He leaned forward. 'First of all, I hear that you witnessed an altercation on the night of the gig.'

'Did I? Between . . . ?'

'Between Brendan and a young woman, a teenager?'

'Oh, right. Yes.'

'This young fan wasn't keen on Brendan wearing the King Lost mask.'

'No, she wasn't. She was going crazy, shouting at Brendan.'

'Do you know her name?'

'She's called Morgan, and she's very active on the Lucas Bell scene. Morgan Yorke. A bit nuts. But she's just about the only one who bothers to see my side of the story.'

'Tell me what happened.'

'She came up to me after the gig. Outside, this was. She offered her support.'

'For what?'

'I'd received some nasty comments from people in the crowd.'

'Why do they hate you?'

'Because . . .'

'There must be a reason.'

'It's not important.'

'Because of your relationship with Lucas?'

She stared at him. Her eyes, those startling alien-type eyes, were filled with hatred. Hatred, aimed at him. It was unsettling.

'Oh, so you know everything, do you? About my private life?'

'No. Not yet.'

He let the statement hang in the air for a moment. Then he asked, 'So what happened after the gig?'

'Morgan and I were outside, chatting. And then Brendan Clarke came up, introduced himself, and said that he'd like to talk to me. And that's when Morgan got angry and started shouting.'

'Can you remember anything specific that she was saying?'

'She said that only Lucas had the right to wear the mask of King Lost. That's all I can remember, but she was horrible about it.'

'Did she threaten Brendan in any way?'

Simone thought for a moment. 'Well, she hit him. Does that count?'

'That's more than a threat.'

'It was only a slap.'

'Only?'

'Why are you asking this? You're not saying that Morgan Yorke killed him, are you?'

Hobbes smiled in answer. 'Can you tell us where she lives?'

She nodded. 'In Hastings. I don't know where, exactly.'

'That's good enough. We'll find out.'

Hobbes thought: another reason for the trip down to the south coast. He said, 'Actually, Simone, I'd like to talk about Lucas Bell, about your relationship with him.'

She made the barest gesture of compliance.

'You were going out with him in 1974. When he killed himself?'

'We'd split up before that. Two months before.'

'But still, you were close, by all accounts. Very close.'

Simone looked at the floor, muttering to herself.

'I'm sorry. I didn't hear you . . .'

'Yes, we were close.' She looked at him. '*Intimate* – as they call it in the press.'

'That's interesting.'

'Why?'

'Because, increasingly, I believe that Brendan Clarke's death is tied in with Lucas Bell's life in some way. All I need to do is work out the connection.'

'And you think I can help?'

'I do.'

'Why?'

'Because you knew them both . . .' He paused. 'Intimately.'

'I wasn't intimate with Brendan! What is this?'

'But you kissed him.'

Her expression passed into surprise. She shook her head.

'We have a witness,' Hobbes said. 'In the dressing room. You were kissing.'

'It wasn't like that.'

'It wasn't a kiss?'

'We nearly did. That's all. Almost. Our lips . . .'

He waited.

'Our lips brushed. That's all.'

He kept looking at her. 'Did that upset you? That nothing further happened?'

'The moment passed.' A quiet regret entered her voice. 'As so often.'

He nodded for her to carry on, encouraging.

'That was all. I was drawn to him.'

'Because?'

'He looked like Lucas.'

'On the stage, you mean? With the King Lost mask?'

'No, in real life. There was a resemblance between them. Brendan told me that when he was younger, his friends kept telling him that he resembled Lucas Bell. And he played on it over the years. He identified with Lucas because of this, he followed his career, copied him. The same clothes, hairstyle, and so on. It made him special, it made him stand out. Anyway, that's what he told me.'

Hobbes processed this.

'So your attraction was based on mimicry?'

Now she looked angry. 'I miss Lucas. I really do.' She finished her glass of wine in one last gulp, poured herself another straight away. 'And yes, that stupid fucking Brendan Clarke reminded me of those times, the good times. The golden years. Is that a crime?'

'What was stupid about him?'

'Sorry?'

'You described Brendan as being stupid.'

'Well, he was. A total idiot. You can't go round pretending to be someone else. You just can't. And now look . . . look what's happened to him. It's too fucking sad to even talk about.'

Hobbes nodded. He gave Simone a moment to calm down while he looked around the room. His eyes settled on something, an object on a shelf. He stood up, saying, 'Do you mind if I look at your books?' He walked over to the bookshelf, letting his fingers trace over a number of rock star biographies written by Paige herself.

'I'd appreciate it,' he said, 'if you didn't mention anything about Brendan's injuries in the press.'

'No problem. Oh, but I've already told Neville. Is that wrong?'

Hobbes smiled. 'I'll have a word with him tomorrow.' His hand stopped at the object he had noticed before. 'Is this yours?'

Simone nodded.

He picked up the figurine standing on the shelf. It was a plastic model of Lucas Bell, about ten inches tall. He was singing into a microphone, his body arched back in a rock star's characteristic pose. The face was painted in the full King Lost colours. Every detail was perfectly rendered: the stark white face with its blue cross and grinning lips. Even the tiny painted teardrop was visible. The figure was standing on a portion of stage floor, and the singer's name was written on the base, next to a serial number: 7/20. A very limited edition.

'Where did you get this?'

'From Morgan. She gave it to me as a present, a few months back.'

'The young woman who shouted at Brendan?'

'Yes. She makes them herself. Sells them mail-order.'

'I see.' Hobbes turned to her. 'Does Morgan wear a teardrop, here . . .' He touched at the skin below his left eye. 'Painted on?'

'Sure, on special occasions. But lots of the fans do. It's a mark of respect, of identity.'

Hobbes needed more. 'You didn't take this doll from Brendan's house, did you, from his bedroom?'

'No. Of course not.'

'Because a similar figure was taken. We know that now.'

Simone answered in a burst of irritation: 'Why are you here, why are you bothering me? I've said what I have to say.'

He looked at her. 'May I use your cassette player?'

She sighed. 'Over there, the music centre.'

'Thank you.'

He pulled a cassette tape from his pocket. He slotted this into the machine and pressed the play button. There was a quiet continuous hissing sound as the tape's wheels began to spin.

'What are you playing?' Simone asked. She stood up.

'It's the recording of our interview, last night. At the police station. I'd like your opinion on something you said. Is that all right?'

Simone nodded. She couldn't imagine what she was going to hear. But the tape rolled on in silence.

'I left it on by mistake,' Hobbes explained, 'when I left the room. It'll start soon.'

Simone moved closer to one of the loudspeakers, listening.

She could hear herself on the tape, shuffling about in the chair, mumbling to herself, lighting a cigarette. Hobbes watched her closely, studying her reaction. She was embarrassed at being recorded like this, unguarded, that much was obvious. She swayed from foot to foot. Her mouth was crooked with worry.

And then her voice was heard from the tape, speaking quietly, gruffly, to herself.

It's all my fault. It's always my fault.

Simone's eyes narrowed. Her fine cheekbones twitched, just a little.

'Wait,' Hobbes said. 'There's more.'

A second time her voice rose from the twin speakers, the words plainly spoken.

They both died. They died because of me.

Drawn in Blue Ink

Hobbes clicked off the cassette player. He looked at Simone, waiting for clarification. None came. 'Would you like to explain that statement?' he asked.

'That was . . .'

'Yes?'

'I was talking to myself.'

'You were indeed, Miss Paige.'

'You can't take any account of that. I was tired, scared, out of my mind.' She glared at him. 'Oh, for fuck's sake, I'd just seen a dead body!'

'Yes, and that's very upsetting. I understand completely.' But Hobbes didn't want her to settle, not quite yet. 'Still, it's something of note, I think. It implies a certain kind of feeling. A feeling beyond the norm, shall we say?'

Simone could not answer him. Could not even look at him. Hobbes and Barlow were taking up too much room; her eyes fluttered to escape them both.

Hobbes closed in. 'What were you thinking, when you said those words to yourself?'

Now she sighed. A deeply drawn breath. 'It's the truth,' she said. 'The truth. They both died because of me.'

Hobbes kept his voice as low as hers. 'Please tell me why.'

'Very well. But I need to go back, to the beginning.'

'That would be useful.'

She seemed to find strength from this simple request. She sat back down, topped up her wine glass and began to speak evenly and clearly.

'I met Lucas Bell in 1970 when I reviewed one of his early gigs for the *Melody Maker*. I was nineteen years old, almost twenty. He was twenty-two. I'd arrived in London earlier that year, seeking my fortune.'

'So you fell in love?' he asked.

'Not straight away. Oh, I was fascinated by him, without a doubt. But only as any young woman might be, with a man on stage, singing his heart out about things that seemed to be amazingly important.' Her face had taken on a gentler expression.

'But you got to know each other?'

'He came up to me after that first gig, I don't know why. I had the impression that he chose me in some way. His first words to me were, "You have the most extraordinary eyes." It sounds ridiculous, speaking of it now.'

'I can understand,' Hobbes said to her.

'We became friends. I was the first journalist to take his music seriously. I knew from the start that Lucas had something to offer, something new after the sixties' dream had failed. Something more dangerous, more tempting.'

'This would be glam rock.'

'Yes, it became known as that, after a time.'

Hobbes thought for a moment. 'So when did your relationship begin properly?'

'That would be late 1972. November. After Lucas's first suicide attempt.'

Hobbes recalled the article he'd read in the fanzine. 'Right. I've only recently heard of this.'

Simone nodded. 'He took an overdose after the second album and tour. He was a troubled young man. And that, I'm afraid, was very much part of his appeal. It still is. Because the fans love him for his scars, his pain, his passion.'

'Even to the point of death?'

'Exactly. Rather than live out an empty life following the mean-ingless laws of the music business, he took the noble way out, and ended it all.' She paused. 'Well, that's one story anyway.'

'And the other?'

'That he shot himself because I threw him aside.' She wiped at her eyes. 'Either way, the fans hate me. Either I broke his spirit, or I broke his heart. Fickle muse or ravenous groupie. Take your pick.'

Her voice took on a steely edge and she started to rant.

'They're fanatics. So many of them. You don't know what they're like. Crazy idiots. Sorry. I shouldn't . . . but they never stop. They never fucking stop! They send me notes, terrible messages, they threaten me. But all I ever did was love him. That's all I ever did. I loved him.'

Her voice quietened. She looked embarrassed.

Hobbes was scrutinizing her. 'So, out of his failed suicide, you fell in love?'

'I know it sounds strange. But I do think there was an element of me finally being able to love him, now that he was sick. It's dreadful, but there it is.'

'No, I can see that.'

'We met up at a restaurant. He was gaunt, even for him. And washed out. And more beautiful than ever. By which I mean, all his usual practised charm had disappeared. I felt I was seeing him for the first time. The real face.'

She stopped. Hobbes waited.

'Is there something wrong?'

She spoke to herself alone. 'I was thinking . . .'

'Please, out loud.'

'Lucas had given up on so many things, including music. Basically, he'd had enough. He could no longer face the public. He wanted to disappear, that was his only desire. But the people at the record company were pushing for him to start recording the third album.

He told me all this. And I said to him, "Why don't you wear a mask?" It was said in jest, or half jest. Truly. But he looked at me, and smiled. And there and then at the table he started to sketch out a face. He invented a character, a persona, right in front of my eyes. It was the birth of King Lost, although he didn't have a name until later.' Simone's face brightened. 'It was amazing to watch. Something changed between us at that moment.' Now her eyes sparkled as the memories took over. 'That night we came back here, and we made love for the first time. It was . . . it was wonderful.'

She stopped, as though suddenly aware she had an audience. Both Hobbes and Barlow were staring at her, totally fascinated by the tale she was weaving.

'Let me show you something.'

Simone left the room. Hobbes turned to Barlow and said, 'What do you think?'

'Of Miss Paige?'

'Yes.'

The constable hesitated. 'I get the impression . . .'

'Yes?'

'That she's lived more in one year than I have in my life.'

Hobbes grinned. 'You're probably right.'

Simone came back in carrying a small suitcase. It was battered and scuffed, marked with a few travel stickers of foreign cities. She placed this on the coffee table and clicked it open. Neither Hobbes nor Barlow could see inside. She rummaged around for a moment and then pulled out a piece of cloth. This she unfolded so the two officers could view it.

It was a large table napkin, the kind favoured by restaurants.

'This is King Lost,' she said. 'His very first incarnation, as drawn by Lucas that night.'

Hobbes stared at it.

Here was the mask. The adopted persona of the pop star drawn in blue ink. A rough sketch only, but with the familiar split grin, the X on the brow and the falling teardrop all in place. Hobbes was astounded. He knew very little of rock stars and their lives, but this felt to him to be a true artefact, the relic of a saint. For the first time he got an inkling of the singer's true power, of why so many worshipped him. And most of all he couldn't help thinking of poor Brendan Clarke, marked in the same way, the famous mask copied on to his face with a few cuts of a knife.

Barlow whistled. 'That's got to be worth something, hasn't it? It's like viewing one of Hendrix's guitars.'

'Oh, it's more than that,' Simone said. 'Far more. This face would soon be adored by millions of people around the world. Lucas was filled with energy, after he invented King Lost. The whole album was written, recorded and released within four months. It made him famous and because he could hide behind the mask, it enabled him to get on stage again, to face his audience, to sing. For a while anyway, a year or so.'

'So what happened?' Hobbes asked. 'Why did he stop?'

Simone took a gulp of wine, swirled it around her mouth and swallowed. 'I don't know. I honestly don't. He got tired maybe, tired of the pretence. I'm only guessing.'

'You grew apart?'

'Yes, as his fame spread.' She frowned. 'I had given myself to this man completely, following him into places I should never have gone. I was fearful of addiction, of illness. Of dying, even. I had to withdraw.'

'He was a drug addict?'

'He was. And he very nearly pulled me under with him.'

'Was that why you split up?'

'Partly. I don't want to go into it, if you don't mind.'

'So how did Lucas take the break-up?'

'He had other worries on his mind by then. But we both knew that we would always be friends. He was a reclusive person, which was part of the problem. There was me, and his manager. We were the only two people that he ever really trusted, I think.'

'What happened to his manager?'

Simone pursed her lips. 'Toby Lear? God knows. Rotting in hell, I hope. You know, it was Toby who bought the gun for Lucas. The stupid bastard.' Her face bristled with anger. 'Toby played up to every whim Lucas had, pampering his cash cow, no matter the consequences. I hate him. Even now.'

Barlow was scribbling away at his notebook throughout all this, doing his best to keep up with the story and the memories as they streamed out.

Hobbes thanked Simone for showing them the napkin. Then he asked as gently as he could, 'So what happened in the final weeks of his life?'

'It was the end of the tour. The last gig was taking place at the Rainbow in Finsbury Park. I went along. I hadn't seen him for a while. And he played the entire concert in the King Lost mask, beginning to end.'

'And then he destroyed the mask? On stage?'

Simone's face showed no emotion. 'He did, yes. He sliced into it. Or at least pretended to. People were screaming. Some of them were crying. I've never seen anything like it. Not before, not since. It was a public offering, a ritual scaring.'

She fell silent, before dismissing the memory with a shake of her head.

'Of course it was all fake. A special knife, a blood capsule.'

Barlow asked a question, his first of the session: 'I understand that Lucas went missing after the gig.'

She nodded. 'For three weeks. Nobody knew where he was, not at the time.'

Hobbes frowned at this. 'Nobody?'

She met his gaze and held it for a second or two before answering: 'Nobody at the time. But we now know that he rented a place outside of Hastings, in the countryside, close to Witch Haven field. A small cottage.'

She stopped speaking. Her eyes closed, suddenly overcome by tears. The fingers of one hand traced over the lid of the suitcase.

And when she continued with her account, Hobbes had to lean in close to hear her properly.

'The next thing I knew was when my editor rang me up, to tell me about Lucas's body being found. He'd shot himself.'

She paused and drew a breath.

'I wasn't that surprised, to be honest. I'd always known that such an outcome was on the cards.' She brushed off the feelings. 'Anyway, that's the end of the story. I went into a private clinic to get cleaned up. I didn't even go to the funeral. Which is one more black mark against me, in the fans' minds. But I'd had enough. Enough of the pain, the love. The fucked-up, twisted pain of love. Everything. It was over.'

The room was quiet.

Hobbes and Barlow were both staring at Simone. Her eyes were downcast. One hand still clutched at the now empty wine glass. Hobbes felt it might crack in her grasp.

She said, 'But the worst thing is, thinking back . . .'

Hobbes waited. She had not yet looked up.

'It was my idea, the mask. In some way, I can't help feeling that I painted his face for him. I placed the mask on his face.'

Hobbes asked, 'I can understand why you might think you were responsible for Lucas Bell killing himself. After all, enough people have told you so, over the years. But what about Brendan Clarke? You said on the tape that you were to blame for both deaths.'

She came back to the present moment. Her eyes were dark, glistening.

'I have the kiss of the devil.' The phrase cut the room into silence. 'That's what one fan said about me. She wrote it in a letter and shoved it through my letter box, the paper smeared with blood. And yes, they know where I live.'

'In that case, you should report the threats.'

'But maybe they're right, the fans? The things I love, or reach out for . . . they die.'

Hobbes didn't know what to say.

Simone spoke quietly now. 'Finding him like that, seeing Brendan's face like that, the cuts, the blood . . .' She frowned. 'It was the mask, wasn't it? A copy?' She looked at Hobbes directly. 'The King Lost mask?'

'Yes. I believe so.'

The wine glass fell to the carpet. 'Oh God.' Her head dropped into her hands.

She was closing up, still holding secrets. Hobbes couldn't let that happen.

'Simone, we're having trouble with certain aspects of the case, specifically to do with music.' He nodded at Barlow. 'Neither of us are experts.' Her body showed no response, so he carried on. 'What can you tell us about the record that was playing in the victim's room, the repeated phrase? Simone?'

At last she gathered herself together. Her hands came away from her face and she breathed in heavily. Then she rose and walked over to a record rack. She chose one. 'It's from Luke's debut album,' she said. '*Backstreet Harlequin*.' She spun the vinyl disc in her hands to bring side two uppermost, and slipped it on to the spindle of the music centre's turntable. Carefully she placed the stylus on the record. 'The song that was playing is the title track.'

Music filled the room. Lucas Bell's singing voice was vibrant, full of life and love and yearning.

'He wrote this when he first came to London,' Simone explained. 'A young man's vision of the big city.'

Hobbes tried to concentrate on the lyrics. One particular line in the chorus jumped out at him – *Lost in the Soho blues* – and he knew precisely what was being said. His own arrival in London came to mind, when he'd driven down from Lancashire as a young man: that sense of being adrift, helpless against the current, fearful, and yet filled with such excitement at the prospects of a life that was just starting to unfold. He looked over at Simone. She was moving gently from side to side. Her eyes were closed and her face had taken on a peaceful, faraway expression. For these few moments she was free from her troubles, whatever they might be, however deep they might travel.

And then she opened her eyes and gestured to them both: 'Listen. Listen!'

The final chorus began, taking off on a different tangent than before. Lucas Bell's voice rose to its highest, most urgent level:

Just another backstreet harlequin,
Lost in the Soho blues.
I've given just about all I can give,
Now there's nothing left to lose.

Hobbes was drawn immediately back to the victim's bedroom, the body lying on the bed, and that one phrase, 'nothing left to lose', repeating over and over in the trapped, humid air.

A few more emphatic, defiant chords and the song came to an end. Simone removed the needle from the record. 'There it is,' she said. 'The song as it was originally recorded. Three and a half years later, when he wrote his suicide note, Lucas used this same song as his model. But he changed the final words of the song slightly.'

Hobbes was fascinated. 'What did he put?'

'He wrote, "I've loved just about all I can love. There's nowhere else to go."'

Hobbes envisioned how this woman must've felt at the time; surely this was a message to her alone, a curse almost. And the fans would definitely take it as that; it would be read as Lucas Bell blaming Simone directly for his actions.

He looked at her. 'So Brendan Clarke's killer must've known of this history?' he asked.

She nodded. 'It's common knowledge, a major part of the Lucas Bell mythology.'

'Which means the murderer was making a point. By playing that record, and that particular phrase, he was drawing a direct connection between this current death, and the one that took place seven years before?'

'That's it,' Simone replied. 'That's all I can think.'

'And what is the connection? Do you know?'

She looked at him, hesitating.

'Simone, I need to know. Only you can tell me.'

'Very well. Brendan Clarke told me, in the dressing room after the gig, that he had proof.'

'Proof of what?'

'That Lucas Bell's death wasn't an act of suicide. In fact, he was murdered.'

Hobbes sat back in the chair. He could hear Barlow's pen nib scratching feverishly at the notebook.

The Brendan Clarke case was expanding and reaching out to merge with another case, another young man's death from years before.

'I've read a few articles in the *100 Splinters* fanzine,' he said at last. 'And yet nowhere did Brendan mention the possibility of Lucas Bell being a victim of murder.'

Simone grimaced at this. 'No, well, he wouldn't. Because he knew how the fans would feel about that. That they'd hate it, completely and utterly. Because as it stands, the story is perfect.'

'Explain this.'

'A number of the fans, I'm sure, are actually glad that Lucas Bell is dead, because their fantasy is set free by the act. And if he *has* to die, let it at least be for a good reason.'

'You make him out to be some kind of sacrificial lamb.'

'Well, yes. His suicide is a valiant act. Self-sacrifice. But if Lucas was in fact murdered, then he's just another victim. The myth dies.'

Hobbes thought for a moment. 'The thing that Brendan Clarke wanted to show you, the item of memorabilia . . .'

'He wanted to show me the evidence. The proof that Lucas had been murdered.'

'And what was the proof?'

'I don't know. How can I know? I arrived too late.'

'He gave no indication of what it might be?'

She shook her head.

An obvious motive came to Hobbes. 'So maybe Brendan was killed because of what he knew?'

'Yes. That's what I've been thinking recently,' said Simone. 'The murderer has got away with it for seven years. Now someone was closing in, and they had to be killed.'

'But why carve the mask on his face?'

She frowned at this. 'I'm not sure. A punishment. A warning. Probably for some crazy messed-up personal reason that we can't yet work out.'

He wasn't happy with the words 'we' and 'yet'. But in truth, Hobbes was no nearer an answer than she was; he simply didn't know.

He signalled to Barlow, who came over and handed him a clear plastic wallet containing a single piece of A4 paper. Hobbes held this out towards Simone. 'This is the sheet of paper found crumpled up in the victim's mouth. There's blood on it, I'm afraid.'

She took the plastic wallet off him.

Hobbes explained, 'Most of it is typewritten, with some handwritten corrections added here and there, probably at a later date.' He nodded at her. 'Simone, I was wondering if you could shed some light on it for me.'

'I'll try.' She examined the paper through the plastic. 'Yes, this is definitely Lucas's handwriting. That's his signature at the bottom.'

'Good.'

'When we talked after the gig, Brendan told me that he'd bought some of his personal belongings. This must be one of them.'

'But we now know that this is a photocopy.'

'That makes sense, actually,' she said. 'Serious collectors often make copies for their everyday use, and keep the originals in a safe place.'

Hobbes leaned closer. 'What can you tell me about the song itself?'

'How do you mean?'

'Is there any particular reason why this one was chosen?'

'Let's see.' Simone studied the lyrics. 'The song is called "Terminal Paradise". It's from the *King Lost* album. But it's curious.'

'Why?'

'Well, this is an earlier version of the song. The words are not quite the same as the recorded version.' She looked up. 'Lucas showed me some of his songs in draft form, but not this one. Most of the lines are the same as later on, but a few are different.'

'Do you have any idea at all why this ended up inside Mr Clarke's mouth?'

Simone shook her head.

'No.'

She looked back to the paper in her hand and this time her eye was drawn directly to a certain word. Hobbes saw a shiver come over her.

'What is it? Something of interest?'

'Yes.' Now she looked surprised. 'But I don't know what it means.'

Hobbes stood up and walked over to her. Barlow followed.

'What can you tell us?'

She indicated the lyric sheet. 'You see the changes here, that Lucas made in biro? Well, those are the lines that were actually used in the song, as later recorded. But the typed words, here, these are his first thoughts. Now, you see this verse, the edited version, here . . .' She pointed to a group of four lines and sang them quietly, almost to herself.

There's no escaping it:
Every sin has its price.
Let's hope that moonlight triggers
A password for Paradise.

'These are the words as recorded on the album.'

Hobbes nodded, 'Why is this important?'

'Well, now look at what Lucas originally wrote for that verse. Here. Do you see?'

He studied the original typed-out words as Simone read them aloud:

There's no escaping it:
We love what we cannot kill.
Let's hope that moonlight triggers
A doorway to Edenville.

Hobbes looked at Simone. 'Well, I prefer the official version, definitely.'

'Oh, so do I. But these were his first thoughts.'

'And this means something to you?'

'Not to me. But to Lucas. That one word: Edenville.'

'Let me see.' Hobbes took the lyric sheet from her hand and studied it. He saw the typed word *Edenville* crossed out with a blue line and the word *Paradise* scrawled above it.

Simone explained: 'Brendan Clarke mentioned it to me after the gig, in the dressing room. He asked me, "Have you ever heard of Edenville?" And I said no. I asked him what it meant, but he wouldn't tell me. And that was when he told me that he had proof of Lucas being murdered.'

Hobbes said, 'Are you getting all this, Barlow? It's important.'

'Yes, sir. Every word.'

Simone carried on. 'But later on, travelling home, I vaguely remembered Lucas saying this word to me once.'

'You can't remember precisely?'

'No, not clearly. Not at first. But I started to read through my old journals of the years when we first met. And there it was. *Edenville.* The word seemed to jump out at me after I'd skimmed a few pages, as though I subconsciously knew where it would be.'

'And?'

'Luke said it to me a couple of days after we'd first got together. Our relationship was very intense. He was, I truly thought, the love of my life. We shared secrets, lots of them. But this one he wouldn't share. He just said, "One day, if the time is ever right, I'll tell you the story of Edenville." And that's all I recorded from the conversation.'

'So he never told you. And you still don't know what the word means?'

'No. I have no idea.'

'It might be a place? A real place?'

'Or imaginary,' said Barlow.

Simone thought about this. 'All we know is that the word seems to be important to Lucas, to his life, his work.' She referred to the lyric sheet again. 'But here he's scrubbed it out, changed it. He won't sing it out loud. He doesn't want anyone to know about it, not directly. He's ashamed, or scared. Maybe it's something from his past, from his days growing up in Hastings. You see, Lucas often took ideas, feelings, or even actual events from his life, and twisted them, exaggerated them, to form the subject matter of his songs. But he always hid the truth behind poetry, metaphors, symbolism, and the like.' She thought for a moment, and then added, 'Once we were talking about the popularity of King Lost, and he told me how everyone thinks they know the secret of King Lost, fans and critics alike, but the fact is, not one person's got it right, nobody's broken the code.'

Her voice trailed off.

Hobbes resisted the urge to prompt her, waiting until she was ready to speak again.

'And the truth is, I've always suspected that Lucas didn't kill himself.'

'And why do you think that?'

She looked at him. 'On the last night I ever saw him alive, face to face, Lucas made a promise to me. This was just before he disappeared, after the final gig. The promise wasn't made directly, not then, it was more a feeling shared between us. But later on he did put it into words. In a letter that he sent to me on the morning of the day he died.'

Hobbes waited. Gently, he urged her on. 'And what did he promise?'

Simone searched inside the old suitcase and pulled out an envelope. She handed this to him. It was already open, slit along the top edge, and addressed to Simone Paige at this, her Camden address. 'He posted this on the day that he died, you say?' She nodded. He checked the postmark. *Hastings, 25 Aug 74*. He pulled out the letter inside and unfolded it. It held a single line of handwritten text.

Simone explained, 'He'd been away for three weeks, no one knew where. And then he sends me this.' She hesitated. 'I've never shown it to anyone before.'

'Why not?'

'I don't know. I suppose I could never quite unravel its meaning. But not just that. I was scared. That I actually knew the meaning too well. And the truth of it was too scary to contemplate. And then later . . .'

'Go on.'

'Well, the message contrasted so much with his suicide note.'

'Yes, I can see that.'

Hobbes read the brief message a second time.

I'll come back for you. Keep waiting, my love. Luke X

Simone made a sound. He looked up at her. 'Are you all right?'

She wiped at her eyes and looked away, embarrassed. 'It's so full of promise,' she murmured. 'And the kiss at the end. It's too much to bear.'

He had to agree with her.

This didn't sound at all like a man who was about to kill himself.

119

The Silhouette

Hobbes dropped Barlow off at Camden Town tube station and then drove on towards the West End. He had one last job to do before he could even think about sleep, one last place to visit, and he wasn't looking forward to it. Along the way, he thought about the case as it currently stood. The first full day had now passed, and what did they know? Two nights ago, Brendan Clarke and his band Monsoon Monsoon performed a gig in honour of Lucas Bell. Clarke took on the late singer's King Lost alter ego for the night. After the gig he introduced himself to Simone Paige, one-time girlfriend of Bell. Brendan told Simone that Lucas had not committed suicide; rather, he'd been murdered. Brendan said he had proof of this. A few hours after the gig, he himself was murdered by person or persons unknown. Early the next morning a young woman was seen leaving the victim's house. And then some twelve hours after that, Simone Paige arrived and found Brendan dead, his face sliced into a cruel version of the King Lost mask.

Those were the facts. Beyond that, everything melted away into fog.

Edenville. It was important, he knew that. And according to Simone Paige, Brendan Clarke seemed to link it to the idea of Bell's murder.

Hobbes managed to find a space in the multi-storey car park on Brewer Street, and from there made his way on foot to his destination. The streets of Soho were packed with revellers. He could sense the excitement in the air, the fear, the joy, the lust. Though he was aware the square mile was a sink pit, a dark maze of streets, and a hellhole if you took the wrong turning at the wrong time of night, my God, how he missed it.

He walked past posters offering support for the IRA hunger strikers and grafitti calling for Maggie's demise, and then slipped down an alleyway at the far end of Wardour Street. It was off the main drag, this place, hidden away in the shadows. La Silhouette. A members-only club. The French name always made him smile; this couldn't be any further from the romantic boulevards of Paris. He tapped on the door and was greeted by a face he knew from the past, one of the cloakroom attendants, Karen. She looked surprised to see him, but thought about it, and shrugged and let him in. 'It's your funeral, Detective.' He followed the sound of jazz along the corridor into the lounge. This was an after-hours drinking den, a leftover from the old Soho scene of the fifties, when failed, dirt-poor, alcoholic artists and poets sat around the alcoves arguing about their latest masterpieces. Now the place was frequented by off-duty coppers, the hard nuts of the Met, plain-clothes bruisers, a good number of them as corrupt as shit in a blocked-up toilet. And two or three of them, Hobbes had to admit, were bloody good at their job, and more or less fair with it.

The last time he'd been here had been two nights after the Brixton riot.

Heads turned as he entered the place, and one by one conversations fell silent. All eyes were on him.

'Christ, Hobbes!' a rough-sounding voice spat out. 'Are you looking for trouble?'

It was Leonard Mawley, a punch-drunk detective sergeant approaching the age of fifty. He'd been turned down so many times for promotion he was now riding out the days till his thirty years' service was up, not giving a nun's fart about anything but his own back.

The music was cut off.

'No, I'm not.' Hobbes kept his voice cold, stating the truth. 'I'm looking for whoever it was wrote the word "scum" on my front door last night.'

He heard a chair scrape across the floor. Another. Someone behind his back said, 'Fucking hell.' A voice filled with hate. Hobbes didn't turn round.

Mawley stepped close to him. 'Now what makes you think it's anything to do with one of us?'

'An educated guess.'

'Oh, is it now? So you're showing off, are you?' Laughter. 'You've got an *education*?'

'I just need—'

'Yes?'

Mawley's ruddy face was inches from his own. Hobbes could smell the booze on his breath, mixed in with the stench of a recently consumed chicken chow mein.

'I need to see the room, Len.'

Mawley guffawed. A couple of the other men joined in.

'Fuck me, but you've got some balls on you.'

Flecks of spittle landed on Hobbes's face. He fought the urge to wipe his skin clean. Mawley grinned, wired for a fight. His mouth opened and closed. But then another man stepped into the light.

'That's enough, Leonard. Back down.'

Mawley immediately followed orders. Hobbes turned to the newcomer. It was Chief Superintendent Lockhart, Hobbes's old boss. His eyes glared for a moment in the smoke-filled room, like those of a wild animal. Then he smiled and clasped his hand around Hobbes's shoulder. He laughed out loud.

'Here he is. The prodigal returns.'

The voice was so full of charm and good humour that Hobbes was tempted to relax. But he knew better than to be pulled into the game.

'I need to see the cellar.'

'Still looking for evidence, is that it?'

'No. Not at all.' Hobbes shook his head. 'I know what happened down there.'

'Of course you do. You being a witness and all. Well, more than a witness, I think.'

Before Hobbes could answer this remark, Lockhart summoned the club's barman: 'Joseph, fetch us the key, there's a good man. You know the one I mean.'

Joseph did. He walked around the bar, a lumbering hulk in a white shirt, a purple velvet bow tie and matching cummerbund. He handed over a brass key ring.

'Go on,' Lockhart called out to the room. 'Get your snouts back in the trough.'

His underlings all did as they were told, quite happy to be insulted by their leader, and the hubbub of conversation started up again. Lockhart led Hobbes along a corridor and down a flight of steps into the cellar. He opened a heavy wooden door with the key and went through. Hobbes followed.

It was a small room, far smaller than Hobbes remembered it on his previous visit. Bare plaster walls, windowless, almost airless, a single vent clogged with dust. A bulb on a frayed brown flex. And when the door was shut behind him, as it was now by Lockhart, the walls seemed to close in even further. Hobbes felt his throat constricting.

Lockhart came close. He seemed unaffected by any kind of claustrophobia. 'Maybe you're not the prodigal son, Hobbes. Maybe you're Daniel returning to the lion's den.' He didn't wait for a response. 'So then. How does it feel, being back down here?'

The chief inspector hadn't changed a fraction in the last four months: skeleton thin, his bones clearly visible under the tight skin of his face. His grey-blue eyes stared at Hobbes without a hint of compassion in them.

'How does it feel?' Lockhart repeated.

'Bad.' It was a simple answer, hardly adequate. But what else could he say? 'They've cleaned up the place,' he added.

'That they have. Washed the blood off the walls.'

The remark hit Hobbes like a blow to the stomach, and without a moment's thought he was cast back to the night when his life changed irretrievably, and everything he knew and loved about being a policeman was tainted by sin.

Nearly three hundred policemen had been injured on the Friday and Saturday of the Brixton riot, back in April. About sixty civilians also received injuries. It was sheer bloody luck that no one had died, on either side of the battle lines. Yet in the press the coppers were being openly blamed for the disturbance, painted as the villains. And then, on the Monday night, when some kind of normality had returned at last to the London streets, Detective Charlie Jenkes and one of his old Vice Squad cronies, Paddy Boyle, had rounded up a young black man and dragged him into La Silhouette. It was a quiet night in the club, coming on for half past ten. Hobbes had been drinking there for a couple of hours along with Len Mawley and a few other officers, all of them well pissed up by then. Hobbes shouldn't have mixed the beer with the painkillers he was taking for the cut on his head, but there it was. With the riot still buzzing in his skull, he'd watched in a daze as his two colleagues had dragged their captive down the stairs into the cellar. He and Mawley had followed, curious as to what was happening.

The man was in his twenties, and obviously on drugs. His eyes were looking ahead without focus. He was pressed back against the far wall of the room, held in place by Paddy Boyle as Jenkes paced the room, his hands bunched into fists.

'What's he done?' Hobbes asked.

'The bastard was mouthing off to one of ours on the street,' Jenkes answered. 'Paddy here saw the whole thing. He called us cunts. The whole lot of us. Pigs and cunts. Blamed us for attacking Brixton.' He turned back to the young man. 'Isn't that right, boy?'

The black man stared back at him, suddenly defiant. He didn't have the look of an agitator.

'Charlie, he's just some Soho dropout, a junkie. Look at him.'

'He spat at the officer,' Boyle said. 'I saw it. Right in the face.'

'Fuck,' Hobbes said. He couldn't think of anything else to say.

Jenkes grimaced. 'Well now it's his turn.' He rasped his throat and drew up a gob of saliva which he spat out directly in the black man's face.

'How do you like that?'

Hobbes had begun to feel worried. Sick inside. He'd never seen his colleague acting this out of control before, and he knew the situation could only turn out bad. He'd started to say something, but then Jenkes yelled, 'Come on, we can all take turns!'

At that point, instantly, Hobbes lost all his feeling for Jenkes. He didn't know who this man was, but it wasn't his friend of the last few years. Another man had taken over, another personality. That night in Brixton had been the trigger.

Hobbes glanced over at Len Mawley and saw the look of horror on his face. Jenkes shouted, 'Mawley, come on! Walk the bloody line for once.' And that was enough, the words a spark to an oily rag. Mawley moved over to help Jenkes and Boyle with the now struggling and screaming black man.

And then the fists had rained down, the kicks came in.

Their victim fell halfway to the floor.

The assault continued.

Hobbes couldn't move. His lips parted but nothing came out, no words.

The black man cried. The wailing sound filled the tiny stone cell.

Blood splattered against a wall.

Hobbes's vision blurred.

'Stop.' That one word. And then, louder: 'Charlie, for fuck's sake. Stop it!'

Jenkes turned to him, smiled, and asked if he wanted to join in.

Hobbes moved forward, his fist already swinging, but aimed at his partner's face. The blow was countered easily, caught in an iron grip. Hobbes was bent over backwards. His spine crackled with pain.

Jenkes grinned. 'Oh, you really don't want to do that, Henry.'

The use of Hobbes's first name sounded like an insult.

Jenkes threw him aside. He staggered and fell against the wall.

The black man was staring at Hobbes now, a silent pleading. But what could he do? He was outnumbered.

He backed away. He turned and ran up the stairs of the now empty club. Only the barman Joseph was still there. He looked at Hobbes with dead eyes, knowing full well what his establishment was being used for. Hobbes stumbled out into the darkened alleyway, and from there on to Wardour Street. He gulped for clean air.

He ran to the phone box on the corner and dialled 999 and called in the assault. 'Hurry. It's an emergency.' He replaced the handset without giving his name. Then he stepped to the gutter and threw up.

Slowly, he made his way back to his car, past glowing neon signs, all-night coffee bars, people out enjoying themselves.

For Detective Inspector Henry Hobbes, the night was over.

The young black man, whose name was Michael Hennessey, suffered two broken ribs, severe bruising to the face, stomach and thighs, and a ruptured eyeball. He came to in hospital the next day to find himself blind in that eye.

Hobbes was pained by guilt. But he'd made the call at least. He had probably saved the man's life. Yes, he could tell himself that.

Keep saying that. Don't stop saying it. But . . .

A week or so later he woke up early one morning without a single thought in his head. He walked into the Charing Cross police station and wrote up and signed a report describing what he'd seen that night, naming the three officers involved, everything, his own presence there, the attacks, the words said, everything he could remember.

Then the shit came down.

Two months later the internal affairs unit had made their results known. DS Mawley tried to take the blame on himself, as some kind of protective gesture, but the investigating officers quickly saw through that. He was let off with a slapped wrist, because his role in the actual physical assault had been minimal, but DI Jenkes and DS Boyle were found guilty of 'unnecessary use of force in an arrest'. Hobbes wasn't surprised at all by the phrasing. He'd expected a whitewash. But the national press, both left- and right-wing, turned on the officers; they were seen as shaming examples of a racist police force. Four days later, even before any official punishment had been doled out, Detective Inspector Charles Jenkes had slung a rope over a steel beam in his garage and hanged himself by the neck.

His daughter, twelve years old, had found the body.

Chief Superintendent Lockhart tapped Hobbes on the shoulder, saying, 'Come on then. Tell me what's on your mind.'

Hobbes was back in the tiny cellar room once more, looking at the cleaned walls, the spotless floor. He saw the superintendent's shoes, polished a shiny black. He always was the neatest of them all, a stickler for the details, the regulations. And yet. Hobbes bent down.

'You looking to grovel, Henry?'

'You know what I'm looking for.'

'I think I do. A spot of red paint, perhaps?' Lockhart smiled coldly. 'But you know I wouldn't be that lax. I gave them a clean afterwards.'

Hobbes came back up. He looked Lockhart in the eye. 'You wrote that word on my door?'

'That I did.'

'Why?'

Lockhart stared back at him.

Hobbes worked it out. 'You goaded me. You knew I'd come here.'

'Aye. I wanted to see if you still had it in you. If you still had the guts. And it seems that you do.'

Hobbes shook his head to clear it. He could hardly breathe.

'What do you want from me?'

Lockhart's face set into a hard, fierce look.

'I want you to find out who killed Charlie Jenkes.'

Tethered

Hobbes woke up shocked by a feeling or an event he couldn't remember one second later, as he sat up in the clammy sheets. The dream slipped away from his grasp. In this desolate bedroom, silence reigned. Not a thing moved. He became aware of his own laboured breathing.

He thought about his wife, Glenda. The days they'd spent together, the nights. The child they'd made together, a son, Martin. Current whereabouts unknown. And even when love's fire had dimmed, still the idea that he and Glenda would be there for each other into old age seemed as strong as ever. But it turned out that was too much to ask; being a copper's wife was a specialist job. The constant fear was one thing, the crazy messed-up hours another, but worst of all was the hatred sent a family's way when things went wrong.

Hobbes was to blame for a fellow officer's death, for his suicide.

Not just a fellow officer, but his long-time partner. His supposed friend.

That's all his colleagues believed.

Close up the ranks, support the team. No matter what. That was the rule. And Hobbes had broken it. He'd gone his own way. It was stupid. His was a single voice in the dark, in the cold heartless night. And he knew more than anything it was his own guilt that had caused him to speak out; guilt for not doing enough that night.

And then the chief superintendent's words came back to him, hinting at some other truth that he'd never even considered before. Lockhart wanted Hobbes to work on the case in secret, in his own time. 'For the sake of the force, Hobbes. And if not for Charlie's sake, then for his family's sake. For the sake of that poor kid who found him strung up like that.' What else could Hobbes do, but agree to look into it? He was from the Central London squad after all; he was used to crimes coming at him from all directions, all at once.

And then Hobbes heard the voice. It came from the next room, the box room. The place where he'd stored all the things he couldn't bring himself to get rid of when he'd moved. Personal things. Things that stirred memories.

Slowly, he moved his legs and sat up on the side of the bed. He got to his feet.

Listened.

Nothing. Had he been mistaken? No, there it was again. Quiet, persistent. A cry. It sounded plaintive, almost in pain.

He stepped forward, moving slowly, carefully, holding his breath. He could feel the carpet under his bare feet.

Another step. One more. And then he stopped. Something was wrong. He couldn't move any further. Was it fear? His heart pounded.

He tried again. No, it was no good, he was trapped, held in place.

Then he looked down and saw the string tied around his ankle.

Damn it. Not again.

He was awake now, properly, fully.

There was nobody in the house, only himself. Himself and his fears, his loneliness. A police officer – trained, experienced on the street, supposedly in charge – who had to take this stupid precaution every single night against sleepwalking. Tethered like a dog. It had started after the riot. And had grown even worse after his wife had asked him to leave. A few times he'd woken up to find his hand on the front door of his flat, struggling to get it open, to escape. Once, at three in the morning, he'd actually come awake standing on the pavement outside, pyjama-clad, staring down the empty lamp-lit road.

Where the hell did he think he was going?

What would he find when he got there?

TUESDAY

25 AUGUST 1981

Available Light

Neville Briggs lived in a mews cottage in Notting Hill. In a spotless, immaculately furnished living room, surrounded by framed prints of his own works on the walls, he showed Hobbes and Barlow photographs taken at the Monsoon Monsoon gig on Saturday night. The members of the audience were young on the whole, too young to have been into Lucas Bell when he was alive. But they were true fans, that was obvious; many were dressed as their hero, in shiny fabrics, long silk scarves, velvet jackets, their features speckled with glitter. A good number of them had decorated their faces with the King Lost mask.

Hobbes saw Simone Paige among the crowd.

Briggs had framed her slightly off-centre, illuminated by a yellow glow from above. She looked different from those around her: unadorned, without a costume or a mask other than her own style. Her eyes, which looked even stranger under the club lights, were hooded, creased with worry. It was impossible to know what she was thinking or feeling, but it wasn't anything good, that was for sure. A girl nearby was staring at Simone with a look of obvious hatred on her face.

The photographer smiled. 'Simone is a fascinating subject.'

'What do you have of the band on stage?'

Briggs showed them a series of shots, each from a different time of the night: Sputnik at the rear of the stage behind his drum kit, Nikki Hauser at the keyboards, and Brendan Clarke standing centre stage, spotlit, the King Lost mask resplendent on his face.

In subsequent photographs the singer's make-up had started to run as the place heated up. The sweat was dripping down his features.

The crowd was going wild with passion. One image showed a teenage girl clambering on to the stage to embrace the singer. It made Hobbes wonder just who she thought she was embracing: Brendan Clarke or Lucas Bell? A man or a ghost?

The final photographs depicted the climax of the gig: the first showed Brendan Clarke with a knife in his hand, holding it against his painted face. And then the face itself in close-up, dripping with red. The make-up, the sweat, the fake blood. The stark white of the stage lights.

'It truly was remarkable,' Briggs said. 'I felt that I was being dragged back in time, back to 1974.'

'To Lucas Bell's final concert?' PC Barlow said.

'I was Bell's unofficial photographer. Tobias employed me.'

'You mean Toby Lear?' Hobbes asked.

'Yeah. Bell's manager. He used me on a good number of occasions.'

'So you were friends with Lucas?'

Briggs smiled. It wavered on his lips. 'Oh yes, we were close. Well, as close as you can get to a rock star on the rise.'

He seemed to lose himself in the act of contemplation as he looked over the images of Brendan Clarke in the damaged mask. Then he cleared his throat and said, 'It's a terrible affliction, to be someone who can't stop taking photographs, who can't stop recording the thing that's happening right in front of their eyes.' Briggs shook his head in despair. 'There's no stopping it. The camera has to click away, no matter the pain on view. The subject *has* to be captured.' His mouth was set in a fierce line. 'Oh yes, I'm a voyeur. That's my burden.'

Hobbes asked, 'What did you do after the gig on Saturday?'

'I went home alone, as per usual. I suppose that puts me under suspicion?'

'What about immediately after the gig?'

'I went outside to talk to Simone. And then Brendan Clarke turned up.'

'Did that make you jealous?'

The photographer looked at Hobbes. 'No, why should it?'

'But you like Simone, I take it?'

'She's a friend, nothing more.'

Hobbes looked at him. Was he lying?

'To be honest, she got in the way.'

'Of what?'

Now he looked at both Hobbes and Barlow, one to the other, without speaking.

'You mean,' Hobbes said, 'that she got in the way between you and Lucas Bell?'

Briggs nodded. 'She ruined it for me. She took him from me. She stole him. And Lucas was never the same afterwards.'

'You mean he went straight?'

The remark brought a look of anger to Briggs's face. His lips moved to form a rebuff, but none came. Instead, his eyes closed for a second. Some distant memory stirred in his mind. And then he said, 'Ah well, I've forgiven her now.'

'And you think that Lucas had love for you?'

He smiled. 'Oh yes. He travelled both ways.'

Barlow made a noise. Hobbes raised a hand to quieten him.

Briggs, emboldened by his confession, carried on. 'I have always liked, and loved, boys and girls equally. And a few years after Lucas died, we had a bit of a fling. But—'

'You and Simone?'

'Yes. We clung to each other in the night. It was a melodramatic episode. But she's always been hung up on Lucas, far more than is good for her. He's never . . . well, Lucas has never really died for her.'

'I see.' Hobbes thought for a moment. 'Simone told you, I believe, about the state of Brendan's face. The cuts.' Briggs nodded. 'What do you think about that?'

'It's terrible. That mask always brings bad luck with it.'

'How do you mean?'

'It's cursed, isn't it? I wish Luke had never invented it. He'd still be alive today if he hadn't, I'm certain of it.'

Hobbes made Briggs promise not to tell anyone about the wounds to the victim's face. Then he asked, 'Did you see anyone threaten Brendan on the night?'

'Sure. That super weirdo bitch, Morgan. She slapped him across the face, pure fifties style.' He pointed to a figure in one of the photographs of the audience. 'This is her.'

Morgan Yorke looked young, her face still soft with puppy fat. The painted teardrop under her eye glistened, caught in a beam of silver light. Her whole face was screwed up in distaste as she stared at Monsoon Monsoon on stage. It was strange to see such an expression among those who surrounded her, all the other revellers clearly enjoying themselves, giving themselves to the night, to the blissful moment. Morgan's hatred shone through.

'It's sad, really,' Briggs said. 'She and Brendan were both idiots, both of them fighting over who loves Lucas Bell the best, who knew the most about him, down to the tiniest morsel. Fucking hell! The guy's been dead for seven years, can't they let him lie in peace?' He paused, sighed, and then asked, 'Do you know the song "Slow Motion Ghosts" by any chance?'

Barlow spoke up. 'I do. It's off the second album. It's a good song.'

'It's a very good song. And I always think that was Lucas predicting the after-effects of his own death.' The photographer fell silent. Then he made a rueful laugh. 'Don't you see? Lucas is still here. His ghost is still affecting us.'

Hobbes held his stare.

'Tell me, Mr Briggs, what do you make of Lucas Bell's suicide?'

'What do I make of it?'

Hobbes didn't want to give too much away, so he simply said, 'You knew him fairly well. Why do you think he did it?'

'Well, that's the big question.'

'And what's your answer?'

Briggs took a moment to reflect. 'Lucas rang me a few days prior . . . well, before it happened.'

'He telephoned you?'

'Yes. He sounded terrible. Obviously upset about something. In fact, he wanted me to come down there, and save him.'

'And what did he mean by that?'

'I wish I knew.'

'So he told you where he was staying?'

Briggs shook his head. 'No. Not exactly. But he did say he was in his home town.'

'Hastings?'

'Yes. The dark was closing in.'

Hobbes looked him in the eye. 'Why do you say that?'

'That's what Lucas said to me, Inspector. *The dark is closing in.* His exact words.'

Hobbes's mind worked at the information. 'Did you think someone was threatening him?'

'No. I knew he was suffering. After all, he'd only recently killed off King Lost, live on stage. So I took it to mean he was getting his act together. Facing up to things, to his troubles, whatever they might be.'

'Yet you didn't go down to see him.'

'Oh, but I did. A couple of days later. I was feeling terribly guilty.'

'You said you didn't have an address.'

Briggs shook his head. 'I didn't. I thought I'd have a look around, ask some people, see if I could find him. I booked into a bed and breakfast, stayed overnight. Hastings isn't that big a town. It was a pretty conservative place back then. And Lucas was a very distinctive-looking man, and he was famous, so I thought he'd stand out. No luck. No one had seen him. I even tried his family home. He'd shown it to me when we did the cover shoot for the *King Lost* album. But the woman who answered the door wouldn't even give me the time of day. And anyway . . .'

'You were too late?'

Briggs couldn't answer. He looked down and spoke quietly. 'There was a place.'

'A place?'

'Lucas would sometimes talk about his childhood, when his guard was down. Once he told me about a field in the hills outside the town that he and his friends used to go to in the summer holidays. He called it Witch Haven. It was a magical zone.' Briggs looked up at the inspector. 'A place he'd go to, for escape. To escape his troubles. And so, I put two and two together.'

Hobbes waited a moment for further information. When none came, he asked, 'So you had a feeling he might've gone there? Is that it?'

'I got up very early the next morning, ready to drive back to London for a fashion shoot. And I thought, well it's on the way, maybe it's worth a chance. So I drove there, I drove out to the field.'

Hobbes made a guess. 'Were you the one who discovered the body? Mr Briggs?'

The photographer nodded, quickly, fiercely. 'I found . . . I found his car. You couldn't mistake it. It was a Ford Capri and he'd had the bodywork painted in a special shade of eggshell blue. Lucas always kept it shiny and polished.' He smiled briefly at the memory. But then his mood darkened once more. 'It was parked in the middle of the field. Everything was still, and so quiet. I remember it all, quite clearly. I was the only person visible for miles around. There was a crow resting on a fence pole, a few sheep. That's all. And the car just resting there, stark blue set against the grass and the hills and sky, the distant sea.' His hands were clenched together on his lap. 'The driver's door was open.'

His voice broke and he paused.

Hobbes let him have a moment of quiet, before asking, 'What did you see? What did you see inside the car?'

Briggs didn't respond, at least not verbally. Instead, his whole body tightened up within itself. His eyes screwed shut, his arms folded themselves around his chest. He rocked back and forth, back and forth, and his head slowly tilted forward, hiding his face from view.

Hobbes and Barlow waited. They looked at each other. PC Barlow had the look of a man severely out of his depth. He opened his mouth to speak, but then decided against it.

'Mr Briggs?'

There was no response to Hobbes's voice. None, except a low moan that escaped the huddled mass.

Hobbes stood up. He gestured to Barlow that they should make their exit.

'Sir, we can't leave him like this.'

'There's not much we can do here, not now.'

He thanked the photographer again for his help, again receiving no reply. They made their way outside and walked to the car. But Hobbes stopped as Barlow made to get in. 'Hang on. I don't think Briggs has finished with us quite yet.'

'I don't understand.'

Hobbes smiled. 'What's your real name, Constable?'

'My what?'

'What does your mother call you?'

'James. Well, Jimmy, actually.'

'Well then, Jimmy, our Mr Briggs has got more to say, I'm sure of it. He just needs a moment alone.'

Barlow looked confused. 'Is this . . . is this lesson number three, sir?'

'What's that?'

'Lesson number three?'

'Aye, if you like. Sometimes it's best to move away. Give them room.'

A minute passed. Barlow looked up and down the narrow mews. He coughed politely, and stamped his feet on the cobbled pavement. Another thirty seconds went by. Still, Hobbes waited. And then, as if on cue, the front door of the house opened and Briggs came out. He was holding a large white envelope in his hand.

'I haven't shown these to anyone, not in all the years since.'

'What are they?'

'Just . . . just take them off me, will you. They're eating up my soul. God help me!'

He hurried back to his house.

Hobbes opened the envelope. Inside was a series of photographs. He flicked through the first few, a couple more, and even before he'd reached the last one in the batch, a thought struck him like a flash of lightning.

He was looking at a murder scene.

The Gallery

They came off the ring road and hit the A21, which would take them down to the south coast. PC Barlow turned on the radio. Pop music, aimless chatter, squeaky jingles. 'There's one thing I don't understand,' he said. 'Briggs told us that Lucas Bell said "the dark was closing in". But I can't equate that with the letter he sent to Simone Paige on the day he died. There, he seemed hopeful.'

Hobbes agreed. 'He did. I think the young man was torn, in two minds, so to speak. He was scared of something, something bad. Either in his mind, or in the world. Maybe he was reaching out to Simone, as that final day dawned.'

'But it went wrong?'

'By his own hand, or another's – it all went wrong.'

They drove on and Barlow told him what little he knew about Monsoon Monsoon's career. 'They never caught on, sir. Two albums out, both sold next to nothing. Dropped by the label.'

'So adopting the Lucas Bell myth gave them a boost?'

'It did. It's funny, but their final gig was the biggest of their career.'

They stopped for petrol and refreshments at a service station. Barlow bit into his ham and pickle sandwich and asked, 'So what are we looking for, sir, when we get there?'

'Number one job is to find Nikki Hauser. She's mixed up in this, I'm sure, and I'm hoping she'll be in Hastings. And then there's the young woman who threatened Lucas Bell after the gig. You found her name and address?'

'Yes, sir. Morgan Yorke.'

'That's the one.' Hobbes added another sugar to his tea. 'I've already chatted to the Hastings police, and they'll have a small force at Witch Haven field, just to keep the peace. Our liaison there is . . .' He found a scrap of paper in his pocket. '. . . DC Jan Palmer.'

Barlow grinned. 'And what about Simone Paige?'

'What about her?'

'Do you think she'll be there? You've got your eye on her, I reckon.'

'She's a suspect. Everybody is.'

'Really?'

'Every single person, no matter how slight the association. You must always doubt. Doubt everything, do you hear me? And everyone. Even the innocent.'

Barlow frowned. 'Don't you trust anybody?'

Hobbes fell quiet.

'Sorry, sir. I've overstepped the mark.'

'Never mind. I know how I appear.'

Barlow looked embarrassed. Hobbes finished his tea in one gulp. 'But what the hell, here I am. Still standing.'

The constable didn't respond, not at first. He brushed crumbs off his Harrington jacket and looked around the cafeteria. It was past midday, and the place was filling up with travellers. Music played over the sound system.

'What happened, sir?'

Hobbes looked up, straight into the younger man's eyes. He knew what was coming.

'What really happened in Soho? There are so many rumours flying around, it's difficult to know what to think. Did they really beat up that black guy?'

'They did. Viciously, too.' Hobbes reeled off the names: 'Detective sergeants Len Mawley and Patrick Boyle. And Detective Inspector Charles Jenkes.'

'You saw it happen?'

'That I did. As close as you are to me now.'

Barlow gave a low whistle. 'Bloody hell.' It was the first time Hobbes had heard him swear. 'That's terrible, if it's true.'

'Oh, it's true.'

'I hate it. I hate the fact that policemen have to act like this.'

'You think they *have* to?'

'Circumstances—'

'No!' Hobbes said. 'Fuck the circumstances.'

'But, sir—'

'There is *no* excuse. No matter the provocation.'

Barlow started to speak. And then bit his tongue. Hobbes lit a cigarette and drew on it deep for comfort. For some reason he was able to lower his guard slightly in the constable's presence; he was reminded of the conversations he used to have with DI Collingworth on stake-outs, sharing knowledge and jokes, in lieu of secrets. The old way, the old codes. Body armour. And every now and then a glimmer of light, a single word. The hint of a painful truth. And then silence.

Hobbes took another drag. He said, 'The worst thing is, I should've got in there, pulled them off. But I was scared. I was shaking, I couldn't move. Until that is, I turned and ran.' His hands lost their tremble. 'I ran. And that's it.'

Barlow sat there opposite him, saying nothing.

Hobbes shook his head, 'Oh, I don't expect you to understand. How can you? You're too young, too green. This job . . .'

'What of it?'

Hobbes thought carefully before continuing. 'Policing changes you. And mostly for the worse. But all that matters in the end is that the small part, the tiniest part that's changed for the good, that's the part you let grow.' Barlow nodded at this. 'Will you do that? Will you promise me you'll try your very best to do that?'

The constable spoke quietly, but firmly. 'I will. I'll try.'

Hobbes was glad to hear this. It was a start. But the conversation had set his mind on the troubles he now faced with his family. His son had left home. He was only seventeen, for Christ's sake. A runaway. That was the outcome of all this.

When he first got married and Glenda fell pregnant, he'd promised himself that he would be a good father, different than his own; that he would be there for his child, no matter what. But the job had taken over, the extreme nature of it, the constant battle against the dark. It was a kind of sickness. And without Hobbes realizing, the balance had shifted. And then one afternoon, when the press had gathered outside his house, and the photographers closed in, his son, Martin, had slipped away, climbing the locked gate of the back garden. Hobbes had been at work at the time, and it was only later that night that the teenager's absence became a concern. The boy had not been seen since. An absurd notion came to Hobbes: *I have to prove myself. I have to! For Martin's sake.* Only by doing this, could he tempt his son back home.

The meal done and cleared away by a waitress, the inspector took out the envelope given him by Neville Briggs. There were a dozen photographs inside, as well as a strip of negatives. 'So this is Witch Haven field,' Hobbes said as he looked at the first image. 'The place where Lucas Bell killed himself. Or was murdered, depending on which story you believe.'

Hobbes went through the photographs, uncovering each one in turn.

Early morning. The light grey-cast, slanted, a thin mist still hanging around in patches.

A dirt roadway, a portion of a stone wall, and a gate.

Witch Haven field beyond, with a lone blue car parked in the middle, where the gentle roll of the hill sloped away. The vastness of the sky arching over, the sea barely visible in the distance, between two hills.

Each shot took them closer to the vehicle.

In one or two photographs, the image was blurred. The photographer's hands shaking, perhaps?

'I don't get it, sir,' Barlow said. 'Why would Briggs take photos as he's approaching the vehicle? Is he expecting the worst? And wants to record it as it happens?'

'Maybe. You've seen how pent-up he is. A crazy artistic type.'

They moved on to the next image, which showed the Ford Capri in close-up. One of the doors hung open.

'But there's another explanation. Briggs has already seen what's inside, and has gone back to record the car from different places, different angles. He's making a project of it.'

'That's a bit cold-hearted, isn't it?'

'It is. Very much so.'

'Christ!'

Hobbes had already glimpsed the offending photograph when Briggs had handed them to him.

'Calm yourself. You'll have to get used to it one day.'

Barlow was looking a bit pale around the cheeks. But now he reached over and picked up the final photograph in the sequence. He stared at it, his eyes unblinking.

Hobbes watched him.

The young man drew in a breath. 'I wasn't expecting it to look this bad.'

'No. No, it's a hell of a way to go. A messy end.'

Hobbes looked at the photograph himself, searching for clues. It was taken through the open front passenger door of the car. It showed a clear view of the victim's face. It wasn't the worst bullet-to-the-head job Hobbes had ever seen. The weapon must've been small, a pistol, low calibre. Still, most of the right-hand side of the temple had gone, obliterated in a mire of blood and bone.

Barlow said, 'I don't understand why he's sitting in the passenger seat.'

'This was mentioned in an interview I read yesterday, by a witness who claimed he saw Bell on the night of his death, being driven up to Witch Haven by a woman.'

'And we don't know who this woman is?'

'We don't. Or even if the story is true.'

Hobbes shook his head. 'You know, Barlow, when I first took these out of the envelope and flicked through them, the first thing I thought was: murder scene.' He let the idea simmer. 'Not suicide. Murder.'

'What made you think that, sir?'

'I don't rightly know. It just came to me, unbidden.'

Barlow looked worried. 'I don't know, sir.' He pointed to the final image. 'Maybe this is Lucas Bell killing off King Lost, for real.'

'So you still think it's self-inflicted?'

'Yes. Or no. It's murder. In the sense that he's killing King Lost.' He hesitated. 'I'm only speculating.'

'Good, keep going.'

Barlow smiled. 'OK. Maybe the last performance on stage was just the rehearsal for this, a final and much more personal act.'

'And what about the murder of Brendan Clarke?'

'A crazed fan doing exactly what Lucas did? Killing off King Lost a second time. I mean, what greater homage could a fan offer?'

Hobbes thought about it. It sounded extreme, but he'd learned enough over the years to know that the human heart had no restrictions.

'Maybe. Yes, maybe.'

But something still puzzled him. He went back through the photos, studying the first couple as they came up. The feeling of viewing a murder scene had arisen before he'd reached the bloodied face. What had he seen? He turned his attention to the third photograph, the fourth. It suddenly struck him that the images he was looking at had been taken exactly seven years ago, to the very day. He searched on. The next picture showed the vehicle from the front, head on, the windscreen too dark to show the horror that lay behind it, the car's long bonnet.

A tingle ran along the detective's neck. 'Do you see that, Jimmy?'
Barlow scanned the image and then nodded.

A card was lodged on top of the dashboard, pressed up against
the inside of the window like a talisman. Its colours and imagery
were easily recognizable to Hobbes by now: the young man walking,
the little dog, the chasm beckoning.

The Fool's card.

The very same tarot card that had been left on Brendan Clarke's
body.

A Field in England

In the end they didn't need the map that Hobbes had bought at the service station; they didn't even need to follow any road signs.

It was Barlow who first spotted them. 'Look, sir.'

Hobbes looked through the windscreen. Five or six people were walking along the road ahead, all of them dressed in black from head to foot. They stood out like a murder of crows against the green fields all around.

Barlow steered the car to follow the fans on to a wide dirt roadway that wound upwards between two ragged stone walls. Other people could be seen, dressed either in black, or in fancy, colourful clothing. A few cars, bicycles and motorbikes joined them on the trek, all taking the gentle rise towards the peak of a hill. The higher they climbed, the more crowded the road became. Now the car had to nudge its way through a throng of gatherers spreading out across the pathway. The road narrowed. Finally they pulled into a designated parking field that was already crowded with vehicles. A young woman asked them to pay for the privilege of leaving their car there.

They walked on. 'Let's keep it close, Barlow, shall we? We're fellow worshippers, nothing more.'

They filed up to where an older man, a farmer, was standing by a closed gate. The fans congregated here as they paid their entrance fee. Hobbes and Barlow joined them.

'This your first time?' the farmer asked.

Hobbes nodded. He handed over two one-pound notes, one for himself, one for Barlow. 'What's the drill?'

'No littering, no drink or drugs, no riotous behaviour. And most importantly of all, no scaring the livestock. On you go.'

They moved through the gate and started to descend the slope of the hill, following the other fans into Witch Haven field. Hobbes did a quick reckoning. There were about five hundred people in the field, all told, with more arriving all the time. The vast majority were young. Some preferred the more Gothic all-black look, while others mixed the older glam rock style with the current romantic look to create their own hybrid. Men looked like women, and women looked like men, and many of the revellers seemed to enjoy life in a hinterland between the genders. Hobbes couldn't help feeling conspicious, in shirtsleeves and an old pair of ill-fitting jeans.

They passed a hotdog wagon and an ice-cream van, both doing a roaring trade. A flock of sheep nibbled at the grass nearby, unperturbed by the human presence. A number of police constables were standing here and there in pairs, keeping their distance from the revellers, or mourners, whichever they were. But everything looked peaceful enough; there seemed no threat of violence. The sea was visible in the distance and the afternoon sun was edging its way homeward through a blue sky tinged with a ruffle of purple over the water. Possible rain. Hobbes had heard it on the weather forecast driving down. But the day was still warm. A small television crew followed some of the fans, the reporter engaging them in conversation.

Hobbes frowned. 'Brendan Clarke's murderer is here. I know it.'

'You think so?'

'If they're as mad about Lucas Bell as we think, then yes.'

Barlow's eyes widened. 'Incredible.'

Hobbes followed the constable's gesture. 'What is it?'

'The car, sir. The Ford Capri. It's still here.'

The vehicle was parked halfway down the field's slope, directly facing the sea. They moved closer to join the crowd of fans bunched around it. Barlow whispered, 'Actually, it's not a Capri. It's a Cortina.'

'The farmer must've bought it and parked it here. Good for trade, I suppose. A place of worship.'

The blue paintwork was marked all over with graffiti, a tangle of names and dates. The driver's window was open and the front and back seats were littered with hundreds of messages written on postcards and scraps of paper. Hobbes had never known such fervour himself, not for any person, object or god, and he couldn't help feeling a twinge of envy.

They walked on through the crowd. Hobbes had fixed Nikki Hauser's features in his mind. But there were so many people here: the numerous faces blurred together. He was pressed in on all sides.

Surely they could tell he was an unbeliever? Painted, glowering eyes stared at him, and at Barlow. In a field of self-appointed rebels and freaks they were the true outsiders. He steeled himself against the stares and returned them. Sweat made his shirt clammy against his back. The temperature seemed to go up a few notches and the crowd surged forward suddenly. There was a tussle. Hobbes almost fell as someone banged against him. His anger flared and he reached out to admonish the culprit. Barlow held him back.

Eventually, out of the push and shove an orderly queue formed and the two officers took their place in it, without any clue as to where it might lead.

The fields darkened slightly as the clouds crept forward and the atmosphere turned muggy. There was a peculiar tension in the air, a tightening of the skin. Fanzine sellers touted their wares along the line. Two lovers, each wearing a King Lost mask, kissed passionately as someone else, a friend or a stranger, took a photograph of them. This was a site of elemental passion.

The queue shifted along and at last Hobbes and Barlow reached their goal. Before them stood a homemade shrine fashioned from stones, bottles, nails, string and a few lengths of wood. Fans were kneeling in front of it, in attitudes of prayer.

A collection of votive offerings lay around the base of the shrine: a plastic necklace, dandelions in vases, a lace handkerchief, plectrums, guitar strings, locks of hair, and even what looked like slivers of fingernail. Candles flickered inside glass jars. An inscription had been carved into the central panel.

LUCAS BELL
9 March 1948 – 25 August 1974

Hobbes stared at the epitaph. All around him a silence had fallen. People were holding their breaths. Somebody coughed, and the silence broke. There was nervous laughter, sobs of pain: something held captive, something else released.

The two officers moved on. The heady smell of marijuana drifted over the scene and a gang of rowdy lads passed around a bottle of vodka and a joint, both acts in defiance of the farmer's wishes. Hobbes thought back to the last time he'd been part of a mass of people: Brixton, four months ago. How different the passions of the crowd had been that night, anger driven by fear, poverty, racism. And yet to his surprise he felt more connection to the black teenagers and disaffected white youths he had fought against that night than he did for the people around him today.

Just then Barlow tugged on his arm, saying, 'Do you hear that?'

Music was playing, an older fan singing a mid-tempo rock song accompanied by an acoustic guitar. There was no microphone or amplifier, yet the singer's nicotine-wrecked baritone rang out like a priest's at a service.

Barlow whispered, 'Do you see who that is? The singer? It's Johnny Valentine.'

'The old pop star?'

'That's the one. His name turns up in Lucas Bell's life story. They were good friends, in the early days. In fact, when Lucas first arrived in London he got a job playing guitar in Johnny's band. His first break, before he went solo and his own career took off.'

Hobbes had indeed heard of Johnny Valentine, and recalled seeing him on television a few times in the late sixties.

'He's changed a fair bit, since his heyday.'

'Yes. There was a scandal,' Barlow said. 'Caught in possession of drugs, alongside a high-society debutante. Pretty much a major offence, back then, for a working-class lad. The judge made an example of him, talking about his foul influence over the youth of the day. He was locked up for half a year. Which made him all the more popular.' Barlow shook his head. 'But these days, well, as you can see . . .'

Hobbes joined the edge of the small crowd assembled around the vocalist, who stood on a tiny makeshift stage made of wooden boxes. The image he had in mind of Valentine – a lively young rock star singing his heart out – was very different from the man present today. His brow was ridged with deep furrows and his greying hair sprayed with so much lacquer it looked like a warrior's helmet. Part of his face was covered in a sticking plaster. Life had eaten away at him. Still, he sang well, and the people were certainly appreciative of him being here. They clapped wildly as the song ended. Valentine spoke to them: 'Next up is one of Luke's ballads. "Border Blossoms".' He paused and took a breath. 'And this one's in honour of our recently departed troubadour, Brendan Clarke.'

The guitarist played the first notes of a riff. She was sitting on a stool beside the singer, her fingers skilfully picking out the chords and melodic runs. The rain started to fall, softly at first, and the song held the day in its minor-key mood. And then through the throng Hobbes saw the guitarist's face clearly for the first time, and he recognized her.

It was Nikki Hauser.

'Barlow. Quickly!'

The crowd bustled as the rain slanted down across the field, harsh now, fiercely driven. A late-summer storm. It flattened the flowers in the vases on the shrine and snuffed out the candles with a hiss. People scattered, some of them shrieking in surprise or glee. Only the truly faithful remained in place, hair flattened, make-up melting on their wet faces, one or two still defiantly singing. But the guitarist was already moving away towards the farm gate, with Valentine at her side. Hobbes pushed his way through the crowd and followed as best he could. His shirt was wet, the rain battered at him. He watched as Barlow caught up with Hauser and Valentine in the lane. There was an argument of some kind. Hobbes couldn't hear, but he saw that Valentine was shouting, waving his arms in the air. Hobbes put on a sprint, battling the downpour. He was out of breath and soaked to the bone as he reached the trio, and he saw that Barlow had his warrant card out and was holding it at arm's length to stop Valentine coming for him.

The singer spat on the ground. His elaborate hairdo had collapsed, pink skull on view through the now exposed thinning patches. He looked more than a little drunk. The sticking plaster on his face had slid away and Hobbes saw that the scar beneath was recently made. The blood had dried, scabbing over. 'I didn't know you was a cop, did I?' Valentine's voice had a thick Liverpudlian edge to it. 'Sorry, mate. I thought you were going for Nikki here.'

Hobbes ignored him. He turned to the woman, saying her name: 'Nikki Hauser?'

She looked at him with utter contempt on her face.

'We need to talk, that's all. It won't take long. About Brendan Clarke.'

There was still no reply. Hobbes stared at her. But her face was set, painted stark white, a black teardrop smeared on her cheek as the rain fell on her. Her eyeshadow gave the effect of a soft blue mist around her eyes, and her short spiky black hair made her painted features stand out even more. She had the look of a magical creature, something you might glimpse in a forest at twilight.

And then she spoke at last, venting her anger. 'Brendan? He's dead. I'm well shot of him!'

They stood there in the rain, the four of them.

Valentine grimaced. 'Look, Nikki love, I'm getting soaked through here. I'll wait in the car, all right?' He went off before she could reply.

Hobbes and Barlow led Hauser across the lane to where their own car was parked. They all got inside, Barlow in the driver's seat, Nikki and Hobbes in the back. He got right into it.

'What happened after the concert on Saturday night?'

'I went home.'

'One of my officers spoke to your flatmate, and apparently you never turned up.'

She smiled. 'I can explain that.'

'Please do.'

'I have a number of homes. Crash pads, you know? Places I can stay without asking. And Johnny always looks after me, when I'm upset.'

'So you stayed the night at Mr Valentine's house?'

'Yes, at his flat, after I'd dropped Brendan and Sputnik off at their places. I don't drink, you see, so I always get the driving job.'

'You didn't go into the house with Brendan?'

'No.' For the first time, a stab of regret entered her voice. 'That was the last time I saw him.'

Hobbes gave her space to breathe. The rain drummed on the roof of the car, splattered against the windows.

'Did you go back to see Brendan later that night, or in the morning?'

'No. Why would I do that?'

He tried his luck. 'What if I told you that you'd been seen, leaving the house in the early morning.'

'What? That's crazy! Who said that?'

'But you were close to Brendan, were you not? Engaged, I believe?'

'Oh, you know what they say in the fairy tales. Once upon a time, and all that.'

He looked at her intently, searching for insight. Hauser was, he now saw, older than she first appeared; she must be thirty or more. Beneath the rain-streaked make-up and the boyish haircut lived a woman slowly growing tired. Of what, he could not yet say. Her skin was peppered with tiny marks, a vestige of some long-ago disease, and her lips were thin, almost bloodless where the lipstick had been washed away. She'd travelled a long journey in life, Hobbes imagined, leaving her exposed now, and raw.

'Poor stupid Johnny,' she remarked, looking out through the side window. Hobbes followed her gaze and saw Valentine struggling to get inside a blue Hillman Avenger. The singer had dropped the car keys and was scrabbling in the mud looking for them.

'Barlow. Go and help the poor bugger.'

The constable set about his task, leaving Hobbes and Nikki alone on the back seat.

'What happened to Valentine's face?' he asked. 'The scar?'

'Oh Johnny. He's always in the wars.'

'Someone attacked him?'

'Yes, his worst enemy.'

Hobbes could see a genuine love in her eyes. 'How do you know Valentine?' he asked.

'We go back. I play keyboards in his band, when he can be bothered touring, that is. He's always hoping for one final hit.' She gave a little laugh. 'Aren't we all.' Her eyes closed. A few drops of rain fell from her hair, down her face. They looked like tears as they travelled the sharp ridge of her nose.

Hobbes decided to level with her. 'Nikki, I'm having trouble with the murder of Brendan Clarke, and I believe you can help me.'

'You think so?'

'Do you know of anyone who might have wanted to hurt him, to kill him?'

155

Now she looked his way, and whispered, 'I wanted to. I surely did. I wanted to punish Brendan. I thought often of stabbing him through the heart.'

'For what he did to you?'

'Yes.'

'And what was that?'

She smiled but refused to speak.

'His mother thinks that you had an affair with another man.'

'Oh, but Johnny hardly counts. I don't think he's got it up, not properly, since his last number one. It's comfort, that's all it is. Against the night, the demons, the old despairs. Still, Brendan was jealous, he wanted me all for himself.'

Hobbes frowned. 'Yes, fiancés tend to think that way.'

Her eyes narrowed within their halos of mascara and blue shadow. 'You're as lonely as the rest of us, whatever your name is.'

'Hobbes. Detective Inspector.'

'We all need something to help us through the night – isn't that true? Booze, drugs, sex. If we're fortunate, a loving companion.'

'Had you found that in Brendan?'

'Yes. I believe I loved him, for a while, at least. Until he . . .'

'Go on.'

For a moment he thought she was going to speak, but her mouth trembled, and closed. Hobbes watched her. She looked away from his stare.

The rain stopped as suddenly as it had started: summer turning itself off and on. The car's windows had steamed up. A dark shape appeared at one. It was Barlow. Hobbes wound down the glass to speak to him.

'How's Mr Valentine doing?'

Barlow had pulled his blouson jacket up over his head to create a makeshift hood.

'Drunk. Pissed off at God knows what. Picking at the scab on his face. Drawing blood. He's in no fit state to drive, that's for sure.'

'Good. I might have a word with him.'

Barlow put a hand on the door handle. 'I'm drenched.'

'No. Stay with him. Don't let him drive away.'

Nikki was stricken with worry. 'Johnny's in trouble. He needs my help. I have to look after him!'

'We'll be done soon enough,' Hobbes told her.

Barlow frowned but moved away, back to Valentine's car.

The inspector turned to Hauser. 'I can't find out who murdered Brendan unless I have all the details. Whatever's necessary for a true understanding. Do you see that?'

She nodded.

'I was talking to your drummer, Sputnik. And he told me that Brendan was upset because he'd found something out about you. Something bad. And that's why he'd broken off the engagement.'

She drew a pattern in the condensation on the window. An oval shape.

'Nikki? Do you have any idea what Sputnik was talking about?'

She smiled. 'He can barely keep a steady beat. He has no truth in him.'

Hobbes was getting frustrated. She was hiding herself away, behind the words, and her cleverness.

'Nikki, I'm afraid you will have to answer me.'

'Oh, it's quite simple. I told Brendan the truth about his dear, beloved Lucas, about the kind of man Lucas really was.' Once started on this track she could not stop, and the words tumbled out. 'I told him about the pain Lucas had caused. And the stupid, stupid things he'd done. The people he'd hurt, stepped on, cast aside to get where he was.'

'I thought you liked Lucas Bell?'

'I did. I do. But my love is based on the truth, not a fantasy. Whereas Brendan . . .'

'Brendan couldn't take the truth?'

'Brendan wanted the dream, the make-believe. He loved King Lost, above all else. Not Lucas.' She made a dismissive sound. 'You

157

know he was crying when he came off stage after the gig on Saturday. Brendan was crying because he'd damaged the precious mask. How ridiculous is that?'

'And all this was enough to make you split up? To call off a wedding? I don't get it.'

'Well, you don't know what I told him. And what's more, you never will.'

'I'm afraid—'

'Lucas revealed certain truths to me, about his past. But he swore me to secrecy.'

'Nikki—'

'Oh fuck off. I've already caused enough trouble as it is.'

It was hot inside the car now that the rain had stopped. Hobbes was sweltering; he was too close to the woman. He wished that he'd taken the front seat instead.

'And what about the Fool card?' he asked.

She turned to him, a curious look on her face. 'What about it?'

'We found one placed on Brendan's body.'

Her eyes fluttered. She was nervous, he could see that. Her hands twitched on her lap.

He insisted: 'What's the meaning of the card?'

'Lucas held one on the *King Lost* sleeve.'

'Yes, I've seen that. But why do you think the murderer marked his victim with it?'

Nikki didn't answer. Hobbes tried pushing her further: 'How certain are you that Lucas Bell killed himself?'

'As opposed to?'

'Someone else killing him.'

A cruel twist came to her lips. With a quick gesture she wiped the last of the painted black tear off her cheek.

'I need to get out of this car. Please. The walls are closing in. Also, you're starting to smell.'

'Yes,' Hobbes said. 'I'm aware of that. Thank you.'

She looked at him, and smiled despite her animosity, and for the first time a trace of simple human kindness was seen in her face.

'I can't let you go yet, Nikki. I might even have to take you into the station – is that what you want?'

She shook her head and whispered, 'No.'

'I thought not. None of us want that. So why don't you tell me what you know.'

'I don't know everything. Only what Lucas told me.'

'That's enough.'

She looked sideways at him and said, 'I believe the Fool has something to do with Edenville.' A pause. 'They used tarot symbols, to identify themselves.'

The inspector's mind raced ahead, as though a needle had entered a vein and shot him full of a drug. Here, here was the flicker of light!

He turned on the seat to face Hauser full on. 'What is Edenville?'

'It goes back to Hastings, to when Lucas was young, a teenager. A number of them got together and formed a group.'

'You mean a band? Musicians?'

'No. A group of . . . of outsiders. Some kind of secret society. Almost like a coven.'

'And Edenville?'

'That's where they lived.'

'The name of a house, you mean? Or a meeting place?'

Nikki's eyes narrowed. 'Maybe. Something like that.'

Hobbes tried to think; what did this mean in terms of the murder investigation? 'Tell me, was Brendan Clarke connected to Edenville in some way?'

'No. He wasn't. He had nothing to do with Luke's youth.'

'So what's the connection? Why was he killed?'

'I truly don't know.'

Her denial was simply stated. He was on the edge of believing her.

'But I do know that something terrible happened to the members of Edenville. Lucas started to tell me about it one day, when we were on tour.'

'You became close?'

She nodded. A slight smile. 'Yes. Very close, for a night or two. It was after Simone Paige had split up with him. I guess you could say he fell into my arms.'

She looked out through the window.

'He wanted to admit something to me, a crime. But I could see he was scared. He backed away from revelation.'

'You've really no idea what this crime was?'

'Sorry. No. And a few weeks later, he was dead.'

He had the impression that Hauser was still holding back from the truth, but could see no way of prising the information from her, not yet.

'How many people were in this Edenville club?' he asked.

'I've told enough already. Too much. Lucas made me promise.'

'I believe you know more. Why won't you tell me?'

'Because . . .' She hesitated. 'Because it would destroy all this.' She gestured towards the fans taking shelter in their parked cars, and the pilgrims walking back up to Witch Haven field now the rain had stopped. 'Everything these people believe in. The love they feel for Lucas. The truth would destroy it all.'

'Miss Hauser. I'm afraid that's not good enough.'

Now she stared at him with a terrified look in her eyes, and she whispered, 'They killed somebody. The Edenville group . . .'

Hobbes spoke urgently: 'Who? Nikki, who did they kill?'

There was no answer. Her head moved rapidly from side to side. He touched her hand, and she reacted against it violently, pulling away.

'Leave me alone! I need to get out of here. Let me out!'

Suddenly there was a commotion outside. A pair of hands banged against the window on Nikki's side of the vehicle, and Johnny

Valentine's face loomed at the glass. He was shouting madly: 'Nikki! Nikki, darling! He's trying to arrest me!'

'What?'

Her hand was on the door handle, pushing it down. Hobbes reached for her but he was too late. She was out of the car in a flash, pulling Valentine away with her.

Hobbes got out of his side door and tried to follow.

Barlow was rushing towards them. Nikki hurled abuse at him. 'Leave him alone, you fucker. He's innocent. He's a good man.'

'I didn't do anything, sir!' Barlow shouted. 'He went crazy on me.'

Nikki had pulled Valentine to her. They stood together, defiant against the police. Nikki spat and shrieked. 'Fucking pigs!'

Throughout all this, Valentine was silent. His facial scar glistened with fresh blood from the picked scabs.

Hobbes had to try one last time. 'Nikki? Think carefully. Think about Brendan, and what he meant to you. The love you had.'

She wouldn't even look at him. 'Come on, Johnny. Let's go home.'

'Tell me what you know!' Hobbes was almost shouting.

A group of fans gathered. They formed a rough semicircle around the scene.

'They're coppers!' Nikki spat. 'Stinking coppers! Spies.'

Murmurs travelled from one worshipper to another. Their faces showed a fierce anger, a shared emotion.

The sun beat down. The greenery all around sparkled with raindrops. Shining jewels. Across the hills a rainbow painted the air with its diffuse colours. Rock music drifted from an open car door. Another Lucas Bell song, a call to action. The fans listened, and responded as one. Hobbes and Barlow stood their ground, waiting.

The crowd moved in.

The Haunted Ones

Hobbes lay on the bed fully clothed, watching the smoke from his cigarette rise and flutter in the breeze from the partly open window. He brought his watch close to his face. Ten to six. Early evening and still light outside. He'd been asleep for a couple of hours, that's all. It felt longer. His stomach was empty and he suddenly remembered that he'd promised PC Barlow a fish and chip supper. Well, it would have to wait. Barlow had taken the car; he'd be back in Richmond by now, passing on his orders that Nikki Hauser had to be found.

The inspector stubbed out his cigarette and swung his feet to the floor. Thank God he hadn't walked in his sleep. That would've scared his hosts no end. He thought again of Chief Superintendent Lockhart's request. Hobbes recalled Charlie Jenkes's last words to him. They'd bumped into each other at the shadowy end of Berwick Street in Soho one Saturday afternoon a couple of days after the sentence had been passed. Charlie stepped out of the doorway of a private members' club, his breath stinking of beer, his eyes fogged over. Hobbes couldn't believe how different he looked to his old self, when he'd made the bullpen roar with laughter at the joy of life, and when he'd led them all into action, not caring about his own safety. Now despair flickered on his face at the sight of Hobbes, then anger. He swore, more to himself than anyone. Then he said, 'I thought we were mates.'

It pierced Hobbes to the core.

'We were,' he answered.

Hobbes stared past Jenkes to look through the doorway. A set of dusty, unlit stairs led downwards towards God knows what iniquities: one of those dives the police had shut down countless times, only for another set of lowlifes to reopen it.

He couldn't help commenting, 'You're keeping good company, I see.'

Jenkes showed his teeth, stained yellow from his Silk Cut intake, thirty or more a day. He was on the edge of saying something bad when Hobbes cut in, 'I hope you'll be all right, Charlie.' It sounded ridiculous, cruel almost. But he added, 'I really do.'

Jenkes laughed. 'Don't you worry about me, Henry. I'm well out of it. Fucking cops. Bunch of useless bastards, the whole damn lot of them.' He spat tobacco-coloured phlegm into a waste bin on a lamp post. A woman walking past looked at him in disgust. He grinned at her and then said to Hobbes, 'I've got my friends, people to turn to, and they don't care how dirty I am. I've got my plans.' And then in an instant his drunken bravado fell away and the old Charlie came into view. He said, 'I cocked up, good and proper.' His voice was full of regret. 'I'm sorry, Henry. I'm just so fuckin' sorry.'

And with that he stumbled away.

Hobbes thought back on it now. What had Charlie meant when he'd said 'people to turn to'? What plans? Had those plans gone awry in some way?

He found the bathroom and splashed some water on his face and then made his way downstairs. Mr Palmer was serving dinner to his family. Hobbes nodded at his greeting, and took his invitation to sit down. A plate of food was put in front of him: a lamb chop, boiled spuds, garden peas. Detective Constable Palmer came into the room, her hair shiny and clean from the shower. It made Hobbes aware of his own sorry state, his torn lapel and unshaven face. But no one paid him any mind except to urge him to eat and be merry. The food was divine. He ate gratefully. Husband, wife and child – a boy of five called Kevin – chatted of this and that, and Hobbes joined in where he could.

'How's your head, sir?' DC Palmer asked.

'It's fine. And thanks again for pulling them off.'

'Those effin' bastards need banging up.'

Her husband, William, covered the child's ears in a mocking manner.

'What? I said *effin*'! That's Queen's English, ain't it?'

Palmer certainly had a rough tongue on her, but Hobbes liked her, and her family.

'And anyway, it's true,' she continued. 'Just because they walk round like an orgy in a fancy-dress shop, doesn't mean they can't be nasty little sods.'

In truth, he didn't want to talk about it. He had handled the situation badly from the start. He should've taken Hauser and Valentine away from the scene, towards neutral ground. Witch Haven was charged with too many memories, and too much spilt blood. The fans were in the grip of stronger emotions than would ever govern them in normal circumstances.

Palmer grinned. 'Mind you, they scarpered like rats, once we laid in.'

Hobbes tried to remember the exact details. A blur of painted faces, the tribe of King Lost. And then a pair of officers arriving, DC Palmer and a male colleague. Barlow was laid out on the wet ground by then, his stone-washed jeans covered in mud.

Palmer laughed when he mentioned this. 'That young copper was well pissed off, when you sent him back to London. He wanted to get back out there and arrest a few teenagers.'

'Aye, Barlow's keen. I'll give him that.'

'You can stay the night, sir, if your case needs it. No worries.'

Hobbes nodded. 'That's kind of you.'

The dinner was finished and cleared away and the television was switched on. Family life. Palmer invited him to have a look at the back garden. They stood side by side at the edge of the small, well-kept lawn. The smell of the sea was in the air.

'Fancy a smoke, sir?'

'Aye, but drop the *sir*, will you? We're not on duty now.'

'Deal, if you call me Jan.'

A bird twittered from the neighbour's apple tree. Hobbes looked at Palmer. There was a subject which had not yet arisen. Hobbes had grown wary of other police officers over the last few months.

At last he spoke. 'You do know of my history?'

Jan Palmer didn't look his way. 'A little. From the news. Most of us do.' She blew smoke into the darkening air.

'And you don't mind me being here?'

Now she turned to him. Her eyes were sharp, unblinking. 'You put a fellow officer in the firing line. He took the easy way out.'

Hobbes wasn't quite sure what the detective constable was going to say.

'By all accounts, Jenkes had it coming. For what he did in that cellar.'

Hobbes felt gratitude welling up.

'I'm proud to have you in our home, Detective Hobbes. And also . . .'

'Yes?'

'I'm not just saying that because of, well, you know . . . ?'

'Of course not.' He grinned. 'It never crossed my mind.'

Jan Palmer's black face shone under the patio light.

He wanted to say *thank you*, but his throat tightened. Palmer saw his discomfort and broke off eye contact. They went back inside, and Hobbes asked for a street map.

Palmer laughed. 'You're not going out, are you?'

'I want to talk to a suspect.'

Hobbes set off. The streets were crowded with both fans and holidaymakers. Hastings was a seaside resort, small enough to walk around. He followed the directions he'd been given and soon enough arrived at the house. He wasn't expecting much because, from all he'd heard of Morgan Yorke, he assumed she'd be out tonight on some Lucas Bell-related jaunt. Yet the downstairs light was on behind the heavy curtains and he could hear music.

He rang the bell. There was no answer.

The house was a narrow two-up, two-down in the middle of a terrace. He checked the address one more time against the slip of paper Barlow had given him.

He knocked on the door with his fist.

'Police. Open up!'

Only a moment passed before the light went out and the music stopped. He banged on the door continuously, until at last it opened a crack and a single eye peeped out at him. A brass chain hung across the gap.

'I'm looking for Morgan Yorke. Are you her mother?'

'I am.'

'And your name is?'

'Violet Yorke.'

The woman took the chain off the catch but kept the door half closed.

Hobbes introduced himself and showed her his warrant card, saying, 'Do you know why I need to talk to Morgan?'

Mrs Yorke was in her late thirties, with a starved look about her. Yet her hair was dark and abundant, arranged in a tumble of curls around her brow. She looked nervous as she answered.

'Yes, I think so.'

'Good. I'm glad that you understand.'

Hobbes placed a hand against the panelling and the door opened completely, and he walked inside.

'Morgan's in her room.'

He followed her up the stairs. A bedroom door was open at the end of the landing. But Mrs Yorke stopped Hobbes before they reached the doorway.

'I'm very worried about my daughter.'

'Why is that?'

'She hasn't spoken to me, nor shown me her face – the face she was born with – not for days now.'

Hobbes looked through the doorway but the room beyond was very dimly lit. He could barely make out the figure sitting on a chair in the corner.

Mrs Yorke stepped forward, speaking quietly. 'It's a policeman, Morgan. He wishes to speak with you.'

A hand reached out to click on a lamp and by its shaded bulb Hobbes saw Morgan Yorke for the first time. He was shocked. The teenager had transformed herself as completely into Lucas Bell as Brendan Clarke had done on the night of the gig. But on her the make-up looked frightening, a true death mask. She had overdone the face paint, using far too much colour. The cross on the brow and the split lips were roughly applied. The black teardrop stood out against skin the hue of a week-old corpse. And her eye . . .

She leaned directly into the light to show off her handiwork.

Her left eye was ringed with red paint. And Hobbes knew then that this woman had seen the lifeless body of Brendan Clarke as he lay on the crumpled bed sheets. She had copied the face with all its cuts and incisions. He saw, as she deliberately turned her head for him, that her neck carried the crimson mark of the blade, mirroring the point where Brendan's jugular had been severed.

'Morgan? Can we talk?'

She scowled at him in response, and said, 'Pardon my rudeness, but I don't often have guests.' Her lips split further into a smile. Her teeth were stained from the make-up.

Hobbes rocked on his feet as he gathered his bearings. The bedroom was hot and stuffy. The smoke from an incense stick didn't help. The walls and ceiling were covered in purple wallpaper. Shelves of books and record albums climbed towards the ceiling on two sides. A wall clock was decorated with the brooding face of a well-known serial killer. The atmosphere was dark and oppressive. He tapped at the pane of a glass tank where a bulbous spider moved amid leaves and twigs. 'That's Octavia,' Morgan said proudly.

'She's eaten two male suitors up to now.' The arachnid's rounded belly glowed like a bulb filled with black ink.

Fixed to the wall above the single bed was a poster of Lucas Bell wearing the King Lost mask. He was dressed for a glam rock funeral, his dark jacket edged with gold piping and epaulettes, his hair feathered and layered, his thin body held at a precisely chosen angle to the camera's lens.

Hobbes picked up a pack of tarot cards from the bedside cabinet. The Fool's card was visible on the top of the deck. But this image was of a more elaborate design than the one found on Brendan Clarke's body.

'That pack was designed by Aleister Crowley,' Morgan told him. 'You have heard of him, I presume?'

'The mad wizard?'

She frowned at this. 'He was a magus, a true practitioner.'

'And Lucas Bell was interested in him, I suppose?'

Before Morgan could answer, Mrs Yorke came back into the room, carrying a tray with cups and a teapot on it. She placed this on the dressing table and started to arrange things, saying, 'I've made you some refreshments.'

'Thank you.' He waited until Mrs Yorke had left the room. Then he turned back to the girl, asking, 'How old are you, Morgan?'

'I'm seventeen.'

'And do you really believe in all this stuff?' He gestured to the nearest bookshelf with its collection of extreme art books and true-crime studies.

Morgan blinked. 'Truth is found in the night, more often than in daylight.'

Was she quoting something? He thought for a moment about answering back but he knew that her doctrine was firmly entrenched.

'I want to talk about Brendan Clarke, and what you found in his house.'

'Do you think I killed him?'

'I'm not sure, to be honest.'

She nodded. A mist of talcum powder rose from her fiercely dyed red-and-black hair.

'I am sure,' she answered. 'Because he was dead when I got there.'

Well then, here was Miss X.

Hobbes took a seat. The serial killer whispered from his clock face. *Tick, tick, tick, tick, tick.* Nine o'clock was a few minutes away. Morgan settled back into the shadows and began her story without any prompting.

'I stayed at a friend's place in London after the gig. But I couldn't sleep. I kept having these terrible thoughts. So I got up very early and took the tube over to Brendan's house. I wanted to talk to him, that's all. I hated him for what he'd done at the gig, taking on the spirit of King Lost like that. It's not fair. It shouldn't be allowed.'

'But you're wearing the mask yourself.'

'That's different.' She spoke with utter commitment. 'I wear it with love, with true understanding.'

Hobbes knew that the further she sank into her own world view, her own mindset, the more easily she would speak.

'How did you know where Brendan lived?'

'His address is printed in his fanzine. It was simple.' She paused, one hand coming up to worry at a long strand of hair. Then her voice hardened. 'I wanted to teach him a lesson.' Her expression widened, allowing the whites of her eyes to be fully seen. The face paint cracked. 'Not to kill him. But to teach him the proper ways of belief.'

Hobbes felt the truth of what she was saying. She could no more escape her calling than a Catholic priest could give up his creed.

'I rang the bell, but there was no answer.'

'So you broke in? That's it?'

'No.'

'No? How then . . .'

'I followed the instructions on the piece of paper.'

'I'm sorry?'

'It was stuck to the front door with a drawing pin. It was addressed to Simone Paige. Actually it just said *Simone*.'

'You read this note?'

'Of course. I pulled it loose from the pin, unfolded it. It read, *I'm in the back garden.* So I walked down the side alley, into the garden. Brendan wasn't there. But the kitchen door was ajar. I saw it straight away. So I went inside. I thought it was a sign, that the house wanted me to enter.'

Hobbes's mind reeled. He couldn't put it together. Why was the door open like that? Who left the note?

'Do you have this note?' he asked.

'No, I threw it away.'

'And what did you plan to do, once inside?'

'If Brendan was in, confront him. If he was out, leave a message for him, something he would never forget.'

'Such as?'

Now she looked at Hobbes directly, and he saw in her gaze an emotion capable of causing great pain, if it wanted to. 'I was going to shit on his floor. I would tear his clothes to shreds, scratch his albums. Pour treacle and baked beans on the carpet or chairs. Whatever I could.'

Hobbes had the feeling he was watching a piece of theatre, a drama many years in the making.

'But then I heard the music from upstairs, so I knew he was in.'

'And you found him dead?'

She breathed deeply, and her face settled back into that of a teenage girl, with traces of innocence still evident.

'Yes. Dead.' Her voice a whisper now. 'Just lying there in the pale light.'

'Was the face covered?'

'No. He was on view.' A tremble ran all the way through her. 'Poor, poor Brendan. All cut up like that.' A hint of a smile grew around her lips. 'Now, at last, the mask was applied properly.'

'Is that what you think the murderer was doing, Morgan?'

'I believe so.'

A moment of silence went by. Then Hobbes asked, 'And why was he killed?'

'Because he wore the mask in vain.'

She laughed, loudly enough for Mrs Yorke to appear at the door and ask, 'Is there anything you need?'

Morgan smiled at her. 'No, we're fine here, thank you, Mother.'

Mrs Yorke nodded. 'Are you telling him the truth?'

'I am. The whole truth.'

The mother turned to the inspector. 'She's done nothing wrong, you do know that, Inspector? Nothing serious.'

Hobbes didn't bother replying. Instead he asked, 'What did you do next, Morgan?'

'I covered the face with the sheet.'

'Why?'

'Isn't that what you do with dead bodies? Did I do wrong?'

He didn't answer.

'Then I went downstairs. I sat around for a while, thinking.'

'About?'

'About whether to call the police, or not.'

'You decided not to?'

'How could I? They would think I was the killer. Isn't that obvious? And also . . .'

'Yes?'

'I wanted to let him rot a while longer.'

Hobbes gathered his thoughts. The more this case progressed, the stranger the people became. He was aware that a number of women were clustered around the ghost of Lucas Bell, and by extension around Brendan Clarke. Not least the woman seen in the car on the night Lucas died, whoever she might be. These were the protective guardians of the pop star's eternal spirit, and Hobbes was cast as the infiltrator of the circle. But did this mean the murderer was female, too?

'What happened then, Morgan?'

'I was suddenly scared. I left the house. I went out through the back door.'

'You left it open?'

'Probably. I wasn't thinking straight. And then that stupid next-door-neighbour woman saw me, and I panicked. I just ran, and kept on running.'

Hobbes leaned forward in the chair. 'Did you take anything from the bedroom?'

Morgan nodded over towards a nearby shelf, and it took him a moment to spot the Lucas Bell figurine among all the other objects cluttered there. It was a similar height and style to the one he'd seen in Simone's house, again wearing the King Lost mask.

'Why did you steal it?'

'I didn't steal it. I took it back. I made it, it's mine. Brendan Clarke only bought it off me, mail order, and he no longer deserved it.'

'Morgan, did you take anything else from the house, any papers, lyric sheets, anything like that?'

She didn't reply. Her eyes blinked. The left one, with its circle of fake blood, twitched slightly, perhaps from irritation.

'If there's anything at all, please tell me.'

She started to shiver. Hobbes wondered if she was all right, if she was in charge of her feelings, her thoughts. Her mother fidgeted in the background, obviously scared for her daughter's well-being. But then Morgan brought herself into a sudden focus.

'I would like to keep it.'

'That might be possible. I don't know. It all depends on what it is.'

She sighed deeply and a terrible sadness crossed her face. He moved closer still, giving her no room to breathe, no time to consider.

'Do I need to search your room?'

The girl's head shook frantically. Her mother hovered near, saying, 'Darling, please do as the officer asks.'

At this, Morgan reached to a nearby shelf and picked up a white envelope. 'This. It was lying on the bed, near Brendan's hand.'

Before he did anything else, Hobbes asked Mrs Yorke to fetch him a clean plastic bag from the kitchen. Then he took the envelope from the girl's hand, holding it by the edges only. There was a single tiny smear of blood visible. By now, he wasn't too surprised to see the name of the addressee: Simone Paige. He turned the envelope over; the seal had been ripped open.

'You opened it?' Morgan nodded. Carefully, he took out the letter from inside. 'And read it?'

'What else could I do? It was such a precious object.'

Hobbes scanned the letter quickly – it was only one line long, written in capitals – and immediately he knew that Clarke had not written it. This was a message from the killer.

He said to Morgan, 'The note is signed. Does the name mean anything to you?'

'No. Nothing.'

He took her on trust; he had no alternative.

'Morgan, is your father around?'

She answered simply. 'I've never seen my father, not ever.'

Hobbes had suspected as much; there was something about this house, as though the entire place was sealed in a plastic bubble in order to keep the world at bay.

Mrs Yorke came back into the room carrying a clear plastic food bag. Hobbes took this and wrapped the letter and envelope in it.

She said, 'Haven't you upset my daughter enough, Inspector?'

Hobbes nodded. Indeed, he wondered how much more he could get out of this strange, lonely teenage girl, but decided it might be worth asking one last question, given her obsession and knowledge of Lucas Bell.

'Morgan, can you tell me how to get to Edenville?'

A thoughtful expression settled on the girl's painted features. 'Nobody knows.'

'But you've heard of it?'

A quick nod. 'Lucas mentioned it once, and only once, in a radio interview. It was early on, before he was famous.'

'What did he say?'

'I can remember exactly.' Her eyes gazed into the distance. '*All my songs come from the same place . . .*' The young woman had changed her voice for the quotation, giving herself a slightly deeper tone. Her face tightened with concentration as she tried to recall the rest of the words.

Her mother nodded. 'Morgan has a mind of silver. She can bring anything to mind about Lucas Bell, no matter how tiny or how far away.'

She looked on with love as her daughter started again on her task.

'*All my songs come from the same place. Let's call it Edenville.*' Morgan stopped again, and said in her own voice, 'And then the interviewer asks, "Where is Edenville?" And Lucas replies, *Nobody knows. Not any more, they've closed the gate.* That's it, I'm afraid. They moved on to other stuff.'

'You have this recorded?'

'No. But I heard it. In my bed, with my transistor radio under the sheets. It was the first time I'd heard his speaking voice. I was seven years old.' Morgan's eyes kept their brightness as she recalled the moment, and she smiled.

Hobbes thanked her. 'That was very useful.' And then he asked, 'Do you have any idea who killed Brendan Clarke?'

The girl answered in a grim voice: 'I do. I know for sure who killed him.'

The room was quiet, the clock seemingly suspended between ticks. Morgan's words barely disturbed the air. 'King Lost did it.'

Mrs Yorke gasped, hearing this. 'Please, child, don't go on now. We've spoken about this so many times!'

Morgan ignored her mother's wishes. 'King Lost came back. He is a vengeful ghost.' The girl's eyes glinted. 'He's haunting us. He always has done, and he always will.'

Hobbes remembered Neville Briggs saying something similar, about slow motion ghosts. Why were people so taken by this dead singer and his fictional persona? He was about to tell the young woman off when Mrs Yorke spoke again, her voice filled with pleading: 'Please don't say such things. You're upsetting me.' But the girl would not stop. Her voice rose in pitch to a near scream and then dropped down low.

'We are the haunted ones.'

Her mother came to her. She knelt at her daughter's feet, her thin legs curled under her. 'Oh, darling. Darling.' Instead of a mother, she looked like a maidservant paying homage at the throne of her dark queen.

Hobbes left them there.

Morgan's masked face stared ahead, the paint smeared across it.

Fair Harbour

Out of curiosity Hobbes followed a group of fans who were walking through the streets. Other people joined with them along the way, either alone or in groups. They moved with a single purpose. And then he saw why: they were all heading for a fish and chip restaurant called Duffy's, the name written out in gold neon, its glass-fronted interior brightly lit. In almost every way it was a perfectly average seaside restaurant, but tonight the owner was doing a roaring trade; a long line of people were queueing to be served and many others were gathered outside, about forty or fifty of them. They were all Lucas Bell devotees.

Hobbes watched the proceedings. One after another the fans stood before the cafe's window, all in identical poses, as friends took photographs of them. Their faces all held the same expression: wistful, infinitely sad, or at least their own approximation of the famous rock star's look. And then one young man took his place dressed in the full King Lost mask and adopted the exact pose that Lucas Bell held on the cover of the album, bare chest and all. When his hand came up to hold the Fool's card of the tarot in its appropriate position, the illusion was complete: here was the iconic record sleeve brought to life.

An older and rather shabby-looking photographer, obviously not a fan, was also taking pictures. Hobbes went up to him. 'Does this happen a lot?' he asked.

'A trickle all year round, and then it's like this every Lucas Bell day.' He spoke the phrase as though naming an official holiday.

Hobbes had to admit: 'It's incredible.'

'Isn't it just?'

The man had lived a life: it showed in his bloodshot eyes, in the slack folds of skin on his face. Hobbes had seen the type enough times: down-at-heel reporters, always hungry for a big story that never arrives. Small-town dreams.

A startled look took over the photographer's face. 'Oh my sweet Lord.'

'What is it?'

'Now this is more like it!'

He started to move, camera at the ready. Hobbes followed his path and saw the reason for his interest. A woman was standing at the far edge of the throng, her face set in a scowl as though she might well strangle someone. Even with her collar pulled up and the brim of her black floppy hat tilted down over her eyes, Hobbes recognized her.

It was Simone Paige. The photographer moved towards her. Hobbes grabbed his arm and pulled him to a stop.

'Hey. Let me go!'

'We don't need any trouble.'

The photographer explained: 'If the fans see her, they'll attack. I've seen it happen before.'

'Exactly.'

'And I need to get it on film.'

He tried to pull away. Hobbes held on tight. 'No you don't!'

'What's it to you?'

'I'm a police officer.'

But the photographer ignored this threat. Instead, he shouted out so that all could hear, 'Simone! Simone Paige! Over here!'

She turned in his direction. Others turned as well. The photographer took a quick shot of her, his flashbulb burning the night air.

'There she is,' he cried. 'It's her! It's Simone!'

Now the fans had seen her. A terrible noise rose from them, a loud chittering sound. Hobbes likened it to the noise a swarm of locusts might make.

Two of the more robust devotees walked towards Simone. But she stood her ground, she didn't back away. Hobbes thought she was brazening it out, or even worse, goading them. She removed her hat and threw it to the pavement. Her features were fully exposed under a street lamp's glare. Now some of the female fans approached. They hissed at her.

The photographer snapped away, capturing the whole scene.

Hobbes moved quickly. He put himself between Simone and the fans and shouted, 'Stay back. Police!'

The two closest lads glowered at him, their mascaraed eyes alive with aggression. An older female fan stood behind them, her face if anything filled with even more hatred. She pushed the younger lads forward, like a general urging her troops into battle.

Hobbes used his most authoritative voice. 'No more! Leave her alone!'

The fans stopped where they were.

'Go on. Back off! Or else I'll start making arrests.'

Hobbes felt his heart pounding in his chest, but he held his position. And then the fans started to relax; they bowed their heads and shuffled away. He turned to find the reason for their sudden compliance.

Simone had vanished.

Immediately he set off after her, rushing to the end of an alley-way, on to a dimly lit street. A figure was moving away in the distance.

The shadows took her as their own.

He hurried along, and then saw her again, standing perfectly still under an archway. Was she waiting for him?

He followed as she set off once more, from street to street. At one point he thought he could hear footsteps behind him, and he stopped and turned to look.

But the street appeared empty.

Hobbes moved on again. Simone seemed to know this part of town well. She led him around corners, past closed-down shops, through a marketplace, its stalls all covered over with plastic sheets for the night. He could never quite catch her. Until eventually they emerged on to a quiet, well-lit street. Simone was standing at the gate of a house. And this time, when Hobbes marched up to her, she remained where she was.

'What the hell were you doing back there?'

She shrugged. 'Don't you ever want to walk into the fire, just to get it over with?'

He didn't answer her.

'I'll take your silence as a *yes*, shall I?'

'As you like.'

He noticed a few soggy flowers and greeting cards fixed to the fence of the house, and a printed notice pinned to the gate reading, *No Lucas Bell fans. Thank you.*

Another site of devotion.

Simone said, 'They have to put that up every year. They don't like being bothered.'

Hobbes looked at the house: the pebble-dashed front, flowery curtains, plaster gnomes in the garden. The windows were all dark.

Hobbes made a guess. 'Is this Lucas Bell's family home?'

She smiled. 'This is the place. He was born here, and spent all of his youth here.'

There was a pokerwork sign fixed to the house front, illuminated by its own lamp: *Fair Harbour.*

'What is it, a boarding house?' he asked.

'It used to be. But it's just a family home now.' She smiled. 'Can you imagine, a boy like Lucas, growing up in such a place.' She smiled. 'He told me a little about his early life. He had to help out during the holiday season, with new people staying here every week. Kids running amok. And never mind the sleazy unmarried couples. He hated it.'

179

'Do his parents still live here?'

'No. They divorced shortly after Lucas set off for London as a young man. And I think his dad died a few years ago. There's another couple living here now. And I imagine they're sick and tired of the fans knocking on the door. Hence the notice. And the reason why they're out for the night. Very wise.'

'Why did you lead me here?' Hobbes asked.

'I was walking along, you followed.'

'Simone?'

'Oh, I always come here. It's the wellspring.' Her face took on a pensive expression as she thought back in time. 'Lucas first brought me here just before the *King Lost* cover shoot. We went to the fish and chip shop first, took some practice shots. Neville Briggs was the photographer. There was a small entourage: me, Toby Lear, a make-up artist, and I seem to remember that Johnny Valentine was there. He was a friend of Luke's. Oh, and that publicist woman, what was she called? Laura something. Laura Townes. Christ, but that woman hated me. I think she had her eye on Lucas.' Simone frowned. 'I'm trying to remember. Yes, Lucas drew me aside from all the bloody fuss, as he called it, and we slipped away. He brought me here and we stood outside, just like we are now, and he told me more about his life than he'd ever done before.' She pointed to the side of the house. 'You see the lean-to garage there?'

Hobbes nodded.

'That's where he practised with his very first band, the Purple Flames. This would have been the late sixties. He talked about saving up every penny of spare change to buy his first guitar, and about writing his first songs. He told me that he'd made a den for himself in the attic, and he and a few friends would sneak up there to hold secret meetings. And then . . .' Her voice faltered.

'What is it, Simone?'

'And then he started to cry. Right in the middle of his story.'

'Do you know why?'

180

She nodded. 'I believe so. I touched his arm, and asked him: "What are you crying for?" And he answered, "Nothing much." He spoke as quietly as I'm doing to you now. "Nothing much. The things lost on the way." That's it.'

She turned to face Hobbes as she repeated the phrase.

'Only the things lost on the way.'

And without anything specific being mentioned, Hobbes knew precisely what Lucas Bell had meant.

'And what happened then, after he'd started crying?'

Simone shrugged. 'And then we kissed, and walked back through the town to Duffy's fish and chip shop. Night was falling. The King Lost mask was painted on his face, Neville took his pictures, the manager and the publicist woman fussed around some more, and a gaggle of local girls gathered to watch. One of them even tried to make a grab for Lucas. And I remember thinking, *Oh my God, it's started already*. Because one look at him in the mask told me: this will make him famous.' She breathed heavily. 'It scared me, to be honest.'

A car passed by. Hobbes waited until the street was quiet once more. 'Simone?'

'Yes?'

'Would you mind telling me why you split up with Lucas? I ask only because I fear it might have something to do with the death of Brendan Clarke.'

Her eyes closed momentarily.

'I fell pregnant. And then lost the baby. It was . . . what can I say, it was too much for us.'

'I see. I'm sorry to hear—'

'Oh please!' She spat the words at him. 'Those days are gone, and all the people in them. And those of us sad enough to still be alive – well, we've changed in so many ways, it doesn't bear thinking about.' Now she breathed evenly, seeking balance. 'I left myself – my fundamental being, if you will – back there, in a room at a private clinic, a few weeks after Lucas died.'

Hobbes stood in silence as thoughts of his own past played in his mind.

He said, 'My mother killed herself.'

Simone Paige looked at him, and then away. 'What are you expecting? Pity?'

He found his self-control. 'Simone, I believe your life is in danger.' She didn't respond, so he carried on. 'The murderer of Brendan Clarke wanted you to discover the body.'

'How did he know I was coming?'

'I imagine Brendan told him. Or her.'

'Right. So they were having a nice little chat?'

'Seems that way, until it turned nasty.'

'Oh Christ.'

Hobbes watched her face carefully, as he explained: 'And once the murderer found out that you'd be arriving later that day, they left a note on the front door of the house, directing you to the back door, which was left open.'

'I didn't see any note.'

'No, it had been removed before you got there. As was this . . .'

He took the plastic bag containing the letter and envelope from his pocket, and handed it to her. 'This was left on the bed, right next to Brendan's body.'

She looked at the envelope first, at her own name written there. Then her eyes moved to the letter and she read the contents quietly to herself.

SIMONE, YOU'RE TO BLAME FOR THE KILLING.
LADY MINERVA.

'What does it mean?' she asked. 'The killing of whom? Of Brendan? Or Lucas? Tell me!' Her voice cracked, her hands were shaking. 'I don't understand.'

'Neither do I, not yet. But this worries me. I want to offer you police protection.'

'No.'

'Simone . . . you're at risk.'

'I'm not letting this take over my life. And who the hell is Lady Minerva, anyway?'

'You've never heard the name before?'

'Minerva is the Ancient Roman goddess of wisdom and poetry. But beyond that, I don't know, I'm not sure.' Her eyes narrowed as she tried to recall. 'Somewhere, somewhere . . . I've heard it before, I'm sure. Perhaps Lucas mentioned the name.'

Hobbes stepped closer to her. 'Simone, are you staying overnight?'

'I've got a room, but I don't know . . . I might drive back to London.'

'Just give us the word, and we'll do everything we can to keep you safe.'

The street around them was utterly quiet and still.

Her eyes, with all their otherworldly beauty, blinked and then locked on his in the glow of the nearest street lamp. He was drawn to her, he couldn't help himself. And yet, once again, he sensed on the deepest level that she knew more than she was telling, a lot more.

And then her hand grasped at his, the fingers curling around.

Was it fear, written there in her expression? Or guilt?

He could not tell.

WEDNESDAY

26 AUGUST 1981

Taken by the Tide

Hobbes and Palmer set off walking uphill, away from the sea. It was a fair slog but the air was crisp and clean, and he felt invigorated as his body settled into a new rhythm. Finally they reached their destination, a pub called the Crown and Anchor. The place had opened at eleven and it was barely twenty past, but already there were a number of drinkers in the place. Cigarette smoke drifted below the beamed ceiling.

Hobbes scanned the room. The clientele looked to be serious drinkers, older men in the main, a couple of middle-aged women. They looked his way as he stood by the doorway, a stranger in their midst. He was suddenly aware that DC Palmer was the only black person in there. But the expected reaction never came, as two of the men welcomed her with smiles and offers of drinks.

'Just a Coke, thanks, Alf,' she replied. 'Ice and lemon. And some crisps, if you're feeling generous.'

'Coming up, love. Cheese and onion, isn't it?'

'You know me so well.'

Palmer led Hobbes over to a table near the window, giving them a good view of the door. 'He's not here yet,' she said. 'But this is his watering hole, this time of day.'

'So then, we wait?'

'We wait.'

The pub livened up around noon and more people joined the flock. Palmer was on her second packet of crisps by then.

'Presto! Action stations.'

Hobbes followed her gesture, over towards the door of the pub, where a robust, thick-bellied man had wandered in. He sported a crew cut and a ruddy face.

'Now that fair specimen of British manhood is Danny Webster.'

'Good. But I think we'll let him settle in a bit.'

Webster went over to talk with two other men at a table in the corner. Then he crossed to the bar, chatted to the barmaid for a minute or two, before returning to the table with a tray of drinks.

'What do we know about him?' Hobbes asked.

'Nothing too bad. He likes a fight after closing time. Usually loses, because he's well plastered by then. He once threw a brick through a shop window, no one knows why. Recently divorced. And permanently unemployed since his plumbing business collapsed, but I suspect he's working anyway, cash in hand.'

'I know the sort,' Hobbes replied. 'Nursing his wounded pride.'

'Sticking a finger in the wound, more like. Do you want me to introduce you?'

'I don't think so, Jan. But I'll call you over if needed.'

'Fair enough.'

Hobbes went over to Webster's table and tapped him on the shoulder. Webster turned round and stared blankly at Hobbes.

'Danny Webster?'

'That's me.' He had a suspicious look on his face.

'Can I have a word?'

'Look, if you're another bloody Lucas Bell fan, then the answer's *No*. I've said my piece, and that's it.'

'Actually, I'm a police inspector.' He nodded at Webster's two friends. 'Give us a minute, will you, lads?'

The pair picked up their pint glasses without a word and went over to join another set of drinkers at an adjacent table. Hobbes sat down opposite Webster, who took a quick sip of beer and then asked, 'Have I done something wrong?'

Hobbes smiled. 'I read your interview in *100 Splinters*, about the night Lucas Bell died. I thought it was very interesting.'

Webster breathed out, obviously relieved. His features relaxed. Parts of his face were the shade of an unripe plum, evidence of years of serious imbibing.

'Yeah, well, I wasn't too pleased with it, myself.'

His voice was already slurry; this wasn't his first drink of the day.

'Why's that?'

'That idiot chopped a lot of it out, a lot of my words. I talked to him for ages, I did. Bloody hours!'

Hobbes nodded at this, as though in agreement. 'I have a few questions. Do you mind?'

'What's this about then?'

'You do know Brendan Clarke is dead?'

'What?' Webster looked genuinely shocked. 'No, I didn't know that.'

'He was murdered on Saturday night.'

'Jesus Christ. You don't think that I had anything to do with it, do you?'

Hobbes let him squirm a moment longer, before asking, 'Did you meet him in person?'

'Yeah, sure. He came down to see me, special like.'

'When was this?'

'About a month ago, something like that. We spent a good few hours chatting, then he went away. That's all. Honest.'

'Actually, I want to ask about Lucas Bell's schooldays.'

'Why?'

'You were in the same year, I believe?'

'The same form, actually, so I saw a fair bit of him.'

'Did Lucas have many friends?'

'Well, he wasn't one of the cool kids, you know.'

'Anything you can tell me, Danny, it would really help.'

Webster's eyes were suddenly focused. He finished his drink and placed the empty glass on the table. 'What's this about?'

'Just answer, if you could.'

Webster licked his lips. 'My throat's parched, I can hardly speak.'

Hobbes sighed, and then held up Webster's pint glass for DC Palmer to see.

Webster grinned. 'Now then, let me think back for you.' He angled his head slightly, the better to make his brain work. 'Yeah, Lucas had a small group of friends. The usual nutters and weaklings. They all hung around together. For protection, I suppose – not that it did them much good. There were some right bullies in that school. It all got pretty cruel at times.'

Hobbes got the impression that Webster might well have been one of the bullies; his face was shadowed by regret.

'Can you remember any of his friends' names?'

'God, no. I didn't speak to them that much.'

Palmer came over and placed a fresh pint in front of Webster. 'Cheers, love.'

She sat down next to Hobbes, and listened in as he asked his questions: 'Carry on, Danny, you were saying . . .'

'Maybe a Gavin somebody? Gavin Richards? Something like that.'

Hobbes made a note of the name. 'That's good. What about Edenville?'

Webster's pint pot stopped halfway to his lips, but he didn't speak.

Hobbes insisted: 'Does the word mean something to you?'

'To me, no.'

Hobbes was getting frustrated, and Webster saw this in his face. 'It's a shame you can't talk to Miss Dylan,' he said. 'She was very close to Lucas. And I'm sure she'd have had all the answers you need.'

'Who was she? A teacher?'

'Hell, no. It was a boys' school. The only woman there was old Mrs Prendergast, the dreaded matron. But Miss Dylan worked at the Brassey Institute.'

'What's that?'

DC Palmer answered this one: 'It's the town's library.'

Webster nodded. 'Miss Dylan came into school a few times a year, to talk about books and all that. And she also gave us elocution lessons, or tried to. In truth, she was a bit crazy. Always surrounded by a gang of weirdos, chatting to them about God knows what, stories and stuff. Poetry and what have you.'

'And Lucas was part of this group?'

'Right at the centre. They had a side room at the library where they used to meet, or you might see them walking along the promenade together, staring out over the water. Or even hanging out at the cemetery, studying the gravestones.'

'How many of them were there?'

'About half a dozen. Boys and girls. And Miss Dylan presiding over them like a head witch.'

'You can't remember any of the other people in this club?'

He shook his head. 'Sorry. I think I've drunk too much booze over the years. It's all a blur. Fact is, if Lucas hadn't become famous, I wouldn't even remember him.'

Hobbes asked, 'I suppose Miss Dylan isn't still here, is she? I mean, in Hastings?'

'She's dead. Didn't I say that?'

'No. No, you didn't.'

'Oh, it was a big thing. A tragedy, the local paper called it. They painted her as a lonely spinster, unmarried, you know. A sad woman.'

Palmer butted in. 'I think I remember this. It wasn't that long ago, was it?'

'About three years ago – 1978, I think.'

'What happened to her?' Hobbes asked.

'She was taken by the tide,' Webster answered.

The phrase caught the inspector by surprise. 'You mean she drowned?'

191

Palmer explained: 'It's a saying we use round here, going back to the old fishing days. It's the idea of a sacrifice to the sea: we take, and we give back.'

Webster nodded. 'There was a bad storm that winter, the waves coming right over on to the prom.' His eyes blinked as he brought the details to mind. 'And nobody knows why Miss Dylan was out in it, nor why she'd stepped so close to the front. There were whispers that she'd been drunk or on drugs. That she was shouting at the waves to take her. Or daring them to. And then whoosh! She was gone. A few seconds is all the sea needs.'

He put down his beer glass, already half empty.

'What was her first name?'

'Christ almighty. Her first name? Who do you think I am, Mr Memory?'

'DC Palmer? Any ideas?'

'No, sorry, but I can find out easily enough.'

'But she had a nickname,' Webster added. 'I remember now. This was just within her little group.'

'Go on?'

'It wasn't a horrible name or anything. At least, I think it wasn't. They called her Lady Minerva.'

Hobbes's heart missed a beat. He asked, 'Do you know why they called her that?'

Webster shook his head. 'Beyond me.' He took a long sup of beer.

'Was Miss Dylan's body found?'

'No. No, I don't think it was.'

DC Palmer agreed with him: 'She was washed out to sea.'

Hobbes let the thoughts stir in his brain. Then he asked, 'Tell me, Danny, did Brendan Clarke ask you about Lucas Bell's friends, and the librarian?'

'He did, yes.'

'And what about Edenville?'

'Well, that's why I hesitated, because he was really keen on finding out whether it meant anything to me. Really keen . . .' He hesitated.

Hobbes pushed him. 'Let's hear it then.'

They stared at each other. The lights, noise and constant chatter of the pub seemed to fade into the distance.

'It's a word I saw once, on the blackboard at school.'

'You mean a teacher wrote it there?'

Webster shook his head. 'No. Just the kids, this was, the boys of the gang. Lucas, the others. But they rubbed the word out as soon as I came in.'

'What did it represent?'

Webster looked confused. Hobbes spoke quickly, urging him on: 'What does the word mean?'

'It was a place. A town. That's all I know. I think Miss Dylan came up with the idea.'

'What was it? Was it Hastings? Did it represent Hastings? Or London, or some other place?'

Webster tapped at the side of his head. 'In here. Inside here. It's where they lived.'

'How do you mean?'

Webster's eyes were staring wild. 'An imaginary town. Edenville. It's a refuge. A place where they could feel safe. Paradise.' He laughed. 'For all the good it did them. They were mad, all of them. Complete loonies. I hated them! I just wanted to . . . I wanted to hurt them.'

He stopped speaking as though suddenly ashamed. His face was damp and his lips were flecked with spittle. Pain radiated from him.

'I was one of the worst. I never said in the interview, but I was a right bully back then, I was. A nasty piece of work.'

'Did you hit Lucas?'

'No. But his friends were fair game. Easy pickings.' He chewed on his lower lip. 'I'm not proud of it. Don't think I am.'

'I know you're not, Danny. I can see that.'

'I'm not proud of it,' he repeated, like an obsession. 'Not at all.'

Webster raised his pint glass to his lips before realizing it was empty. He was drunk, and it showed on his face, in the glazed, hateful look in his eyes.

Hobbes was losing him. 'Danny, listen to me, this is very important. Did this group of friends kill anybody?'

Webster looked shocked. 'What?'

'Lucas and his friends, did they kill someone, by accident maybe? Or did they harm somebody?'

'What? No. They were weaklings, the whole lot of them. Piss-poor specimens, they wouldn't dare squash a fly.'

Hobbes sat back in his chair. He shared a look with Palmer, and then spoke in a calmer voice. 'And you told Brendan Clarke about all this, Danny? About Edenville?'

'Yeah, I did. But I was surprised when I read the interview, because there was nothing about that mentioned. And he seemed so interested, you know?'

Hobbes thought aloud for a moment: 'He was gathering evidence.'

'For what?'

'That Lucas Bell had been murdered.'

Webster's eyes widened, hearing this. 'You mean . . . Bloody hell, by the woman in the car? The woman I saw that night?' The anger came back. 'Oh fuck. Have I thrown this away? I mean, look at me. I'm the prime witness! This should be my pot of gold.'

'Danny . . .'

'Get off me!' He stood up and pushed away from Hobbes.

'Danny, sit down.'

'I've been done over.' Webster jerked about like a puppet. His empty glass fell to the carpet. 'Oh shit. Oh fuck!'

Other people were looking round as Webster raised his voice. His two friends were looking concerned. One of them got to his feet. 'Danny? You all right?'

'Fuck off!'

'Hey, I'm trying to help.'

But he didn't want any help. The two men grappled; it was halfway between a fight and a hug. Hobbes's chair scraped across the floor as he tried to get out of the way of the two heavy-set men. The table was pushed aside. A woman nearby cried out in alarm. Someone else shouted out, 'Sit down, Danny! For fuck's sake.' Obviously, this was not an unusual occurrence. DC Palmer was on her feet, trying to separate the two men. But the fight ended as quickly as it had begun. Webster stood in the middle of the floor. The other drinkers were laughing at him by now. More disparaging remarks were made, none of which seemed to reach his ears. For one moment it looked as though he was going to bolt or rather stumble for the door. Instead he rallied and turned on Hobbes for one last time. He said to him, 'There's one thing I never told that stupid Brendan Clarke man. One thing!'

Hobbes kept his gaze steady. 'What was it?'

Webster snarled. 'He shagged her.' For some reason, he was speaking to the entire pub now. 'That's right, your ever so precious Lucas Bell, he shagged the librarian. It was fuckin' horrible, even thinking about it! She was so old. Horrible!'

This said, he collapsed back into his chair. His friend touched him on his shoulder and this time Webster let the hand remain there.

The interview over, Hobbes and Palmer made for the door. They walked back along the streets, towards the police station. Along the way, Palmer said, 'Why did you ask Danny if the group had killed someone?'

Hobbes thought back to what Nikki Hauser had said to him in the car, how Lucas Bell had almost confessed to her. He said to Palmer, 'A witness I was talking to at Witch Haven told me a story. I don't know if it's true or not, but there's a possibility that the Edenville kids, whoever they were, might've been involved in a crime of some kind.'

'Right. I'll look into Bell's schooldays, see what I can dig up.'

They moved on. It took them fifteen minutes to reach the police station on Bohemia Road, and as soon as they walked through the entrance, it was obvious something was wrong. Police officers were hurrying around, nervously chatting to each other. The desk sergeant was shouting into a telephone receiver: 'I don't care about that. I just need you to find DI Bailey for me. Now!' He banged down the phone.

Palmer went over to him. 'What's happening, Fred?'

'There's been a killing. I'm trying to find—'

'What?'

'I'm trying to find Detective Bailey. Nobody seems to know where he is.'

'Who's died?'

He looked at her. 'One of the Lucas Bell girls. One of the fans. That's all I know.'

Hobbes heard this and immediately thought of Morgan Yorke, he wasn't sure why. He stepped closer to the counter, saying, 'Tell me where. I'll take over.'

'I'm not sure DI Bailey would like—'

The telephone rang, cutting off the desk sergeant's protest. 'Yes, yes . . . OK, yes, I see, right.' He jotted something down on a notepad. 'No, I'm still looking for him.'

'What is it, Fred?'

The sergeant put the telephone handset down. 'An ID on the victim.' He squinted at the notepad. 'Her name's Paige.'

A fierce painful light blinked at the edge of Hobbes's vision as the name was read out.

'Simone Paige.'

Living in the Dark

Hobbes and Palmer walked up to the open front door of Fair Harbour. A constable moved aside to let them enter. In the crowded living room, Hobbes demanded, 'Who's in charge here?' Several heads turned at his voice, but no one answered.

Palmer said, 'I think we're still waiting for DI Bailey.'

'Has the doctor had his go?'

This time a plain-clothes officer spoke up. 'Yes, sir. He's been and gone.'

'Good.'

He looked round. An older woman, sitting on the settee, made a whimpering sound. She was trembling badly and her head was lowered into her chest, hiding her face.

'And this is?'

'The owner of the house, sir.'

Hobbes scowled. 'OK, everybody out. Now! Come on. Give me some room, for Christ's sake.' His command had sufficient intensity to force them all to move. 'Palmer, could you clear the crime scene for me?'

'Clear it?'

'Everyone out of there. Everyone!'

She seemed confused, hesitating before making her way out of the room. Hobbes bent down to speak to the woman on the settee.

'Can I have your name, please?'

She peered up at him. 'Mrs Saunders. Or . . . Vera. Whichever you prefer.'

'Vera. I'm Detective Inspector Hobbes.'

She nodded. Smiled briefly.

'Now then . . .'

Hobbes took a step back. He was suddenly at a loss. On the way over here he'd tried to keep his head free of all emotions, to empty it completely, so that the details of what he saw – of the body and its situation – everything would be clean in his mind. No distractions, no personal feelings.

Keep the heart at bay, Henry. Think like a razor.

DI Collingworth again. Always that insistent voice in his head. But how could he use the razor this time? He'd messed up. He'd messed up and a woman had died, someone he knew was in danger.

Hobbes looked around, to gather himself. The room was a fairy grotto of pastel shades, with a lawn of cream-coloured shagpile carpet underfoot. He imagined Mrs Saunders vacuumed daily. And dusted each of the many ornaments and vases at least once a week. His own mother did the same.

DC Palmer came back into the room. 'All sorted, sir.'

He nodded his thanks and turned back to the owner of the house.

'Mrs Saunders, I know this is difficult for you, but could you tell me what happened this morning?'

'Yes. I can try.'

'I believe Simone Paige came to see you?'

'Yes, it was around ten o'clock, after I'd finished putting the laundry on, when the doorbell rang. I get scared around this time of year, because of all the Lucas Bell admirers. Sometimes they pester me. But I peeked through the window and I saw that it was a woman – well, not a teenager, I mean. So I felt safe enough.'

'Do you live alone?'

'No. I have my husband, Trevor. But he's out at the moment, playing golf.' Her brows tightened.

Hobbes was drawn to a photograph lying on the coffee table, a snapshot of Simone Paige as a younger woman. What was it doing here?

'So you answered the door?'

'I did. And Miss Paige was standing there.'

'Did you recognize her?'

'Not at first, no. Not until she said her name, and then I had to check. So I came back inside, and found the photograph.'

Hobbes pointed to the photograph on the table. 'This one?'

'Yes. Lucas left that for me, you see.'

'Lucas Bell?'

'That's right. He used to live in this house, in Fair Harbour, when he was young.'

Hobbes nodded. 'And why did Lucas leave the photograph for you?'

'He said that I should never let anyone in the house, not any of the fans, I mean, unless it was Simone Paige. And he left this for me.' She picked up the photograph and stared at it, her eyes watering. 'He left me this so I would be able to recognize her.'

Hobbes thought about what he was hearing. 'Can we go back a bit. When did Lucas Bell come to see you?'

'Oh, he used to visit every now and then, you know? After he became famous. Yes, he paid me a handsome fee. Really, a silly amount of money, each and every time. How could I refuse?'

'And what was this money for?'

'Payment. To store his things here. In the attic.'

'I see. And when was the last time you saw Mr Bell?'

Mrs Saunders hesitated. 'A few days before . . . well, before he killed himself.'

Her hands were in the busy unnoticed process of crumpling the photograph.

'And he left something in the attic, that time?'

'Oh yes. Lucas would always bring something or other with him.'

'Do you have any idea what it might've been?'

She shook her head. 'That time, a cardboard box. I don't know what was in it. I've never looked at any of his things. He would phone me up, come round, take something up into the attic. Stay there for a while, and then come back down again, empty-handed. That's what happened every time.'

'Did you speak to him on these occasions?'

'Oh, well we chatted, of this and that. The weather, and so on. He was always very pleasant. Except . . .'

'Yes?'

'That very last time, I could see he was troubled by something. But I didn't like to ask. That was the time he told me about Simone Paige, and when he gave me the photograph. He told me that she, and she alone, was allowed to see what was stored in the attic.'

Hobbes considered. It sounded like Bell knew he was going to kill himself, or be killed, and he'd left something behind, here in his childhood home, for Simone Paige to find.

'And so, when Simone came to see you . . .'

'I told her everything, of course. She was very surprised. And excited.'

'Do you know why she visited you?'

'She said that she'd like to chat, about Lucas, his family, the house, and so on. But when I told her about the attic, nothing else mattered to her. She only wanted to see whatever it might be up there.'

Hobbes leaned forward. 'And then what happened?'

'We went upstairs.'

'Could you show me? Take me through the exact steps.'

Mrs Saunders hesitated, and then got to her feet and led the way out of the living room, into the hallway. A number of officers were waiting by the open front door, staring at this latest development. Hobbes ignored them; he followed DC Palmer and

Mrs Saunders up the stairs to the landing. Everything was spotlessly clean, every surface, except for a red mark on the wall: a partial handprint in blood.

'This is it.' Mrs Saunders had stopped at the foot of a metal fold-out ladder which led up to an open attic door in the ceiling.

Hobbes nodded. 'So you brought Simone here?'

'That's right. I pulled down the ladder, and she climbed up.'

'Did you stay here?'

'No, I went back to the living room.'

'Could you hear anything?'

'Nothing. Nothing at all. Not at first. But then . . .'

'Yes?'

'Well, Miss Paige was up there for a few minutes, and then I heard voices, loud voices, and a terrible scream. Something was knocked over, I think. It made a noise. So I called up the stairs, thinking she'd had an accident.'

'Did she answer?'

'No. But I could still hear sounds from up there, and then another scream, or rather, a cry. A cry of pain.' Mrs Saunders pressed her hands to her chest. 'Oh Lord, it frightened me.'

'And then?'

She'd stopped speaking. Hobbes looked at her, waiting.

'Mrs Saunders, what happened next?'

'I climbed the stairs to the landing, right where we are now, and I listened. It was quiet. Not a sound.' She took a deep breath. 'After a moment I found the courage to climb up, into the attic. I put my head through the gap, and I saw . . . I saw Miss Paige, just lying there. I thought she must've had an accident. So I was about to climb up further, and that's when I was attacked.'

'You mean somebody hit you?'

She nodded, and touched at the back of her head.

'Then what? You fell down the stairs, I imagine?'

'Yes. I did. It wasn't a particularly nasty blow, but it was enough to shock me, and I sort of fell or slid down the ladder to the floor, and I collapsed there. And that's when the person, whoever it was, climbed down after me.'

'You didn't recognize the person?'

'I hardly saw them. I was cowering, and covering my head with my hands.'

'Did he hurt you?'

'Oh, it wasn't a man. At least, I don't think it was.'

'A woman?'

'Yes, I think so.'

'You think so?'

Hobbes could see he was scaring her. 'Age? Appearance?' he asked.

Mrs Saunders looked distraught. 'Dressed in black, I know that. But really, she was just a blur. Maybe she wore a hat of some kind, or a balaclava.'

'Yet you knew it was a woman?'

'It felt like a woman. I mean . . . the *sense* of her, if you know what I mean?'

Hobbes prompted, 'And what did she do?'

'I thought she was going to attack me again, but no, she ran downstairs at full pelt, and out through the front door.'

'That's fine, that's fine.' Hobbes nodded to Mrs Saunders. 'Thank you, please go back to the living room now.'

She followed his orders gratefully. Hobbes started to climb up towards the attic, but DC Palmer said to him, 'Sir, you'll need these.' She handed him a pair of thin plastic gloves, which he pulled on to his fingers.

He said, 'Follow me up, but just look inside, leave it all to me.'

Palmer gave her assent. Hobbes reached the attic doorway and poked his head through the gap. The light was on, a bare bulb hanging from a flex at the centre of the room. The glow reached only so far, the rest of the space was in shadow. The usual array of unwanted household items could be seen: a pair of dining chairs, tea chests, an ironing board, pots and pans, and so on. A metal hat stand had fallen over.

The body of Simone Paige was lying half in darkness and half in light.

The face was visible.

Her eyes were open, staring ahead.

One of her hands was outstretched, as though reaching out towards Hobbes.

Splashes of blood spotted the floorboards around her.

Hobbes climbed over the lip of the doorway to enter the attic. He had to stoop to clear the eaves. He edged across to the body, feeling sick inside and furious at himself. *Observe. Observe.* There was a rough bed in one corner, consisting of a blanket arranged on some cushions. Nearby was a cup, a tin plate, a torch, a few tins of corned beef and a bag of apples. Was it possible that someone actually lived up here, in the dark? Or more likely, did the woman only visit every so often, when she knew Mr and Mrs Saunders were out?

He looked down at Simone. There was a deep wound in her stomach, and many other shallower cuts on the chest area. It looked like a frenzied attack. Her arms and hands were covered in defensive cuts. He searched around the body and saw a steak knife lying on the floor nearby, the blade covered in blood. He could see that it had been taken from a hinged wooden box containing other items of cutlery. Simone must've realized that she wasn't alone, that someone was up here with her. Hiding in the shadows, waiting, knife at the ready.

Panic. Fear. On both sides, probably.

Hobbes tried to imagine every emotion of victim and killer.

This wasn't in any way a planned attack, more a desperate act, driven by the urge to escape.

Perhaps driven by a fan's hatred of Simone Paige?

He stood up straight and waited for a moment, his body held still.

Then he whispered, 'Simone. Simone, I'm sorry. I will find out who did this to you. I will track them down, I will bring them to justice.' The usual pledge caught in his throat. 'This I promise.'

It was useless, useless. So many empty words.

'Did you say something?'

It was Palmer's voice. She was looking over the brim of the door.

'No, no. Nothing.'

Anger burned inside him. He tried to think about the killer's intentions. What the hell was so important up here? What was being protected? His eyes scanned the shadows. Beyond Simone's body he could see a collection of large cardboard boxes, three of them: presumably Lucas Bell's belongings. They were guarded by a tailor's dummy dressed in one of Bell's stage costumes, alongside a couple of guitars. A few other smaller items filled the spaces in between. Cobwebs, dust and mildew covered everything.

Hobbes stepped over the corpse as carefully as he could manage. He looked at the first of the boxes. It was marked in black felt-tip with the words *EARLY SONGS*. He pulled a few sheets of paper from inside, and recognized Lucas Bell's scrawl from the other lyric sheets he'd seen at Brendan Clarke's house. Presumably these were his teenage attempts at writing music. The second box was marked *ARTWORKS*. This too was packed tight with sheets of paper, but he left it for now and moved on to the third and last of the boxes, which was hidden behind the others. Unlike the first two, this last box was sealed with wrapping tape. At first he couldn't see any markings on the box but when he shifted it around he saw a single word written on the side in black letters:

EDENVILLE.

Dust caught in his throat. He felt he was staring at a treasure chest. Lucas Bell had left this box here for Simone to find, he was sure of it. He remembered Bell's words as she'd quoted them from her journals: *One day, if the time is ever right, I'll tell you the story of Edenville.* Well, that day had finally arrived.

Sadly, Simone would never get to see inside the box, never get to understand the secret.

Hobbes found an old fountain pen in a box of knick-knacks. He poked the nib through the wrapping tape and pulled it towards him. The box lid cracked open. He peered inside. It was stuffed front to back with paper: single sheets, exercise books, notebooks of various kinds. So many of them. He pulled out a few items at random. One sketchbook was titled 'Maps of Edenville'. Another smaller book was called 'Secret Passwords'. Another: 'The Complete Index of Edenville Museum'. There was an overwhelming amount of material. He pushed the contents forward to reach for the very first item, a sheet of paper with a few lines of text on it. The top line read, 'Edenville – Founding Members'. It was dated 12 September 1963. Below this it said, 'Let it be known: the following are deemed the true and worthy first citizens of the parish of Edenville.' A list of names followed. Not real names, but nicknames. Or rather, code names. Six of them. Four he didn't recognize, two of them he did:

Bo Dazzle
King Lost
Lady Minerva
Luna Bloom
Miss Caliban
Mood Indigo

It struck Hobbes with a force he could barely comprehend: the murderer of both Brendan Clarke and Simone Paige lay hidden behind one of those names.

Through Unreal Streets

The Hastings CID team took over the case. Hobbes asked only that he be allowed to take the Edenville box from the attic. He went back to DC Palmer's house, empty at this time of day, and he lost himself in work, trying not to think about Simone Paige and his failure to protect her. He spent a good few hours going through the material: fake biographies, designs for fictional buildings, accounts of political factions, religious cults, failed revolutions, battles, and many other items from the imagined town's history. Much of it was handwritten in differing styles; not the work of a single person but of a group, in all likelihood the six founding members working together. It was an incredible feat. Lucas Bell would've been fifteen years old in 1963, the date given on the first sheet of paper. Hobbes imagined the other members would be of similar age, apart from Miss Dylan. Here was an entire world conjured up from the depths of the adolescent mind. What made them create and describe in such detail this fantasy realm? He thought back on his own youth, the hours spent alone in his bedroom, listening to his parents arguing. He'd lost himself in books, in war stories, westerns, adventures in space. Perhaps Edenville came from a similar impulse to escape, but magnified beyond all sense of reality.

The level of detail was mind-boggling. Bus timetables, designs for flags and coats of arms, descriptions of books in the town's library, street maps, match reports for football games played by

Edenville United, recipes, poems, folk song notations, graffiti, mottos, news items and reviews from the local newspaper, and on and on and on. The sketchbooks contained paintings and drawings of prominent buildings, extensive parks and tree-lined avenues, winding pathways through a labyrinth of narrow streets. Many images showed the darker aspects of the town: broken windows, shadowy men and women peering from unlit doorways, smoking guns, knives, dead bodies in alleyways. This wasn't any normal idea of paradise.

The real mystery was Miss Dylan's part in this creative process. He could just about picture a group of adolescents producing such a work, but a fully grown woman, a librarian, a part-time teacher? It didn't seem right, somehow. Didn't she have enough in her adult life, without having to invent such fantasies? And of course, the most important question of all remained: how did this imaginary village from nearly twenty years ago connect to the deaths of Lucas Bell and Brendan Clarke?

He had already found a drawing of King Lost in one sketchpad. The picture was dated October 1963. So that moment in the restaurant which Simone Paige had described, when Bell first invented King Lost, all that was a lie: Bell was in fact remembering a mask and a character he'd invented, and adopted, ten years before.

Hobbes started to feel light-headed, thinking about it all. Every so often Simone's face would intrude, the look of surprise still caught in her features, frozen in death. He had to fight down the impulse to feel shame, or guilt, or indeed sadness; he had to keep working, investigating.

DC Palmer came in at three o'clock, with an update on the murder. She'd interviewed Mrs Saunders, and found out that there had been no break-ins at Fair Harbour, as far as she could recall. 'I thought that maybe someone had broken in,' Palmer said, 'and stolen a key, or made an impression of the key. But now, I don't know.'

Hobbes thought about this. 'Actually, I think the woman in the attic had a house key all along. Probably the back-door key, to make it easier to come and go as she pleased.'

'Where did she get it from?'

'From Lucas Bell himself, on the day he died. I think she took it off his key ring.'

Palmer whistled. 'Bloody hell.'

'I'll bet the locks on Fair Harbour have never been changed in all this time.' He pinched at the bridge of his nose with two fingers. 'Did Mrs Saunders remember anything more about the intruder?'

'No. Though she did say that she and her husband sometimes heard noises from the attic, but they'd put it down to mice, or pigeons.'

'I imagine the intruder's been paying visits for a number of years. Waiting until the Saunders are out, sneaking in, heading for the attic, pulling the ladder up after her.'

'She'd stay there a few days, do you think?'

'An hour, a day, long enough to do whatever had to be done. And then she'd sneak out again when the house was empty.'

Palmer groaned. 'But why?'

'Because of this.' Hobbes pointed to the cardboard box and its contents, spilled out over the table. 'Edenville.' He explained to her, as best he could understand it, about the imaginary village.

Palmer took it all in. 'Maybe the woman in the attic was protecting Edenville in some way, that's all I can think.'

Hobbes agreed. 'The attic itself must have some personal or psychological significance. In fact, Simone Paige told me that Lucas used the attic as a den, when he was young. He and his friends would hold secret meetings up there. So maybe that's where Edenville was founded.'

'The centre of the world.'

'So the material has to remain there.'

'It's like keeping the Crown Jewels in the Tower of London.'

Hobbes nodded at this. 'Yes, that's good. They're symbolic objects.'

'Otherwise Edenville will fall.'

They both stared in wonder at the array of material on the tabletop. 'So where does this take us?' Palmer asked.

'There are six founding members. I believe that one of them is our killer – responsible not only for the murder of Simone Paige, but also Lucas Bell, and Brendan Clarke back in London.' He showed her half a dozen sheets of paper. 'These are potted biographies on each member, taken from the box. Here, read the one for King Lost. It's very similar to the persona that Bell sang about on his final album.' Hobbes pointed out several passages. '*The ragged outsider figure who comes into town a stranger, and changes everyone's lives. The doomed hero struggling to withstand the cruelties of the world.* Some of these passages actually end up as lyrics in his songs. It's all here, this is the starting point.'

'Who else have we got?'

He pointed to another sheet. 'The only other name I know is this one. Lady Minerva.'

'Danny Webster told us about her. The name that the kids gave to the leader of their group, Miss Dylan.'

'There was also a letter found at the Brendan Clarke crime scene, signed by the same name.'

'But Miss Dylan died a few years ago, we know that. Drowned.'

'Well, either she survived and was washed ashore elsewhere. Or someone has taken over her persona.'

Palmer read out loud a few lines from Lady Minerva's biography: '*Through unreal streets she wanders, our goddess of wisdom, seeking companions for the dream. The five waifs come to her.*'

Hobbes said, 'There's a lot of stuff like that. Real adolescent outpourings.'

'What about the other kids involved?'

He shuffled through the remaining papers. 'Bo Dazzle, Miss Caliban, Luna Bloom and Mood Indigo.'

Palmer sighed. 'Well, Miss Caliban and Lady Minerva are female. And Luna Bloom as well, from the sound of it. So any of those could be our perpetrator. Mood Indigo could be either a boy or girl, I guess.'

'What about Bo?'

'It's usually a boy's name, isn't it? Like Bo Diddley.' She thought for a moment. 'I take it that no real names are given for these people?'

'None that I've encountered yet. But there's a lot of material to go through.'

Together they gathered up all the Edenville papers and notebooks and placed them in the cardboard box. Hobbes stored it in the cupboard under the stairs, and then left the house. He needed some air. He walked along Braybrooke Road, eventually heading down towards the seafront. After staring at the sea for a few minutes he turned back inshore and walked up Claremont Road until he reached the Brassey Institute, the building which housed the town's library. Hobbes asked at the desk for help, and then made his way over to the photocopying machine, where he made copies of all six Edenville biographies. After that, he found a seat in front of a microfiche viewer. A librarian brought him a set of folders holding scanned pages of the *Hastings and St Leonards Observer*. He started on the 1974 editions first, zipping through the pages on the screen until he found those relating to the discovery of Lucas Bell's body. The very first mention was brief: the corpse of an unknown man had been found in the early morning, in a field six miles outside of town, not far from the village of Westfield. Police were investigating.

The national press quickly picked up on the story, once the dead man's identity had become known, but Hobbes was more interested in how the local press had viewed the death. He went on to the next week's edition of the *Hastings Observer*. They made a big show of it, giving it full coverage on the front page. It was the kind of event that hardly ever happened in the town, that was obvious.

Inside, pages four and five contained photographs of Witch Haven field, with the original Ford Capri still in place. The shots were taken over a stone wall and the barred gate. A few policemen stood around. It was eerie, seeing it like this in shades of grey on the microfiche, as though covered in a mist. Hobbes looked for the name of the photographer, in case he needed to look at the originals for any reason; he was called Jack Lyndhurst. A photograph of Lucas Bell was placed to one side. The paper's editor had chosen the most brooding image possible.

Hobbes skimmed through the various articles, but there was nothing he didn't know already. Mention was made of Neville Briggs, the 'fashion and rock music photographer' who had found the body. The following week's edition told of the coroner's verdict: 'Death by his own hand.' And that was that. Hobbes leaned back in his chair and stretched his arms over his head. His eyes were starting to ache, but he had to keep going. He moved on to another folder, which held the newspaper's editions for 1978. He recalled Danny Webster mentioning that Miss Dylan had died in that year. It took a while to find what he was looking for, because Webster had got the date wrong; she'd died in late 1977.

The front page of the relevant issue displayed a photograph of a massive wave crashing over the town's promenade. The headline read, 'Woman Missing as Storms Batter Hastings'. The date of publication was 11 December 1977. The article related how, 'On Tuesday evening at approximately nine o'clock, 51-year-old former librarian Miss Eve Dylan was washed out to sea during the terrible storms that lashed the town throughout the night.' Miss Dylan's body was never found, only the remnants of her red sequinned evening gown tangled in a moored fishing boat's cables. It was a strange thing to be wearing, Hobbes thought, in the dead of winter. Had she been to a dance or a formal event of some kind? He found an article published a week later which offered a portrait of the drowned woman. Mention was made of a difficult, isolated life. Twice in the same article she was called a 'spinster'.

Eve had lost her job as a librarian a few years earlier, dismissed, it said, for 'conduct unbecoming', which made Hastings library sound more like the British Army. But there was no indication as to the nature of the conduct that led to her dismissal.

Hobbes wondered if she might be the mystery woman seen driving Lucas Bell out of town on the night of his death? It was certainly possible. And he remembered Webster's claim that the librarian had slept with Bell when he was younger. What dark, twisted passions had been stirred up over the years?

The only photograph of her had been taken a year or two before her disappearance into the sea. It was a grainy newspaper image, showing a woman of brooding aspect, with a severe haircut and angular cheekbones. Her eyes were circled by black rings, either from lack of sleep, or age, or some natural colouring. And a blemish of some kind marred the left-hand side of the chin, just below the edge of the lips. A large mole, or even a birthmark. It was an identifying mark that the eye was drawn towards.

Hobbes stood up from the desk and looked around until he spotted the oldest employee in the place. He went over to her and introduced himself as a police officer, and asked about Eve Dylan, and whether anyone here remembered working with her. The librarian's name was Doreen. Her rheumy eyes peered over a pair of bifocal spectacles. At the mention of her former colleague's name she immediately stopped what she was doing, and said, 'That woman! It was disgusting.'

'What did she do?'

Her voice lowered: 'Eve was found in one of the study rooms, interfering with a young man.'

'You mean engaged in sexual contact?'

'Whatever you want to call it. Anyway, we were all glad to see the back of her.'

'Do you know anything about Edenville?'

'What is it, a novel? A film? I've never heard of it, I'm afraid.'

'What about Minerva? Lady Minerva?'

The librarian's eyes blinked rapidly. 'That was the name of the literary and arts society that Miss Dylan started. The Minerva Club. We thought it was a splendid endeavour at first, a way of introducing young people to higher culture. Of course, as we now know, it was all a ruse to get herself close to her prey.' She roused herself to a higher pitch. 'And they were involved in occult practices.'

'What do you mean?'

'Tarot cards. Fortune telling. Aleister Crowley. All kinds of witchcraft.'

'Crowley?' Hobbes remembered Morgan Yorke mentioning the magician's name.

'I'm afraid so,' Doreen continued. 'In fact, that wicked man lived out the final years of his life in Hastings, in a house called Netherwood. That area's been developed into a housing estate now, but for years people would visit, to pick up on the supposed magical energies of the place. Can you believe such nonsense?'

'What kind of thing was Miss Dylan teaching the kids, do you know?'

'The doctrine of the True Will.'

'Which is?'

The librarian's face lit up at the prospect of sharing knowledge. 'Crowley's central idea was that each individual possesses a "true will", their destiny, the one desire they were born to express. Society, habit, tradition, the law, and so on, all these combine to suppress such feelings. But, according to the doctrine, we must all strive to uncover our true will, and give it expression in the world.'

'And if this true will turns out to be of evil intent?'

'Well, there's the rub, Inspector. Can you imagine those poor young people being taught such irresponsible ideas.'

Hobbes nodded to let her know he was taking it seriously. 'Tell me, Doreen, do you have any records of the club, membership, minutes of meetings. Anything like that?'

'No. Everything was destroyed after the scandal. It was all hushed up, I'm afraid.'

'No charges were brought against her?'

'How do you mean?'

'Was the young man a teenager? Over the age of consent, I mean?'

'Oh yes. If barely. But that's not the point, is it?'

Hobbes thought about Lucas Bell's confession to Nikki Hauser. 'Tell me, was the Minerva Club involved in any other trouble?'

'Of what kind?'

'They didn't attack people, injure them? Or worse?'

'No, nothing like that, not that I remember.'

Hobbes thanked the librarian and headed for the exit. He was thinking about the relationship between Bell and Miss Dylan. He wondered about the power this woman might have held over the teenager. Was it as simple and as nasty as molestation, or some other form of abuse? Or did she have real feelings for him? At any rate, Eve was a perfect name for someone who would invent and set up Edenville. Maybe, in some perverted way, Lucas Bell had acted as her Adam?

And between them, had they concocted something evil, had they killed together?

And was that impulse continuing, down the years?

A Talk on the A229

He got back to the Palmer household around half past five. Jan opened the door for him, and said, 'A friend's come to see you.'

Straight away, Hobbes thought of PC Barlow. He was gladdened by the idea, but a very different face greeted him as he entered the living room. Detective Constable Fairfax was sitting in an armchair, bouncing young Kevin Palmer on his knees.

'All right, guv? You look like you're in need of help.'

The five-year-old laughed wildly as Fairfax started to tickle him. Mr and Mrs Palmer looked on, smiling at the scene.

'Fairfax. It's good to see you.'

'I'll bet. I hear those Lucas Bell girls gave you a walloping.'

'It wasn't—'

'Never mind, we all have to take a punch now and then, in the line of duty. Don't we, Kevin? Yes, we do!'

The boy squealed with delight.

Hobbes started to gather his things together. He handed the photocopied biographies of the Edenville founders over to Jan. 'If you get a chance, could you study these, and see if it brings up any connections to people currently living in Hastings?'

'Will do.'

In return, she handed him a set of keys. 'House keys, in Miss Paige's possession.'

He made a quick call to Richmond police station, to get an address he needed. They said their goodbyes to the Palmer family and made their way to Fairfax's car. Hobbes placed the Edenville box in the boot. 'I have to thank you,' he said. 'For coming all this way.'

'Look, it's the least I could do, after the way I've been treating you.'

Hobbes couldn't get the measure of the man.

'Anyway, sir, maybe you'll pay me back one day.'

Fairfax pulled the car away from the kerb. 'I was sorry to hear about Simone Paige. She was a hell of a woman. A real doll. Mind, a bit too serious for my liking.'

Hobbes watched the brightly painted fronts of the houses pass by. He had the feeling he wasn't yet finished with Hastings, and its inhabitants.

'I'll bet you're missing the Smoke,' Fairfax said. 'The dust and the grime. The bright lights.'

'I am, it's true, but we're not going back to London.'

'No? Why's that, then?'

'A slight detour. I want you to take the A229.'

'Where the hell does that lead us?'

'Maidstone. Where the Clarke family live.'

'I thought we'd dismissed them?'

'Not quite yet.'

They drove on, leaving the built-up area behind them. Soon enough they had green fields on both sides, and a line of cars on the opposite side of the road; commuters making their way back home from London. Hobbes brought his colleague up to date on the Clarke case. Fairfax was mesmerized when he heard about Edenville, and the complexity of the teenagers' collective undertaking. He laughed and said, 'Actually, when I was that age, I had a made-up persona.'

'Really?'

'Well, you need something, don't you, something to hide behind? We all do.'

'Funny, I'd pictured you as being the leader of the gang.'

Fairfax grinned. 'Me? Jesus, no. I was a runt. Youngest of five lads. Living off scraps and hand-me-downs on a Dagenham housing estate. By the time I was eleven, I was a mess. Spent most of my time in my room – which, by the way, I had to share with my brother, Melvin. Hell on earth.'

'So, what, you made up a new image for yourself?'

'Well, see, I loved American comics. Spiderman, Daredevil, Batman and Robin, the Human Torch. In my mind, I was Spiral Man.'

'Spiral Man?'

'I know, it sounds daft, but that was me. I was Spiral Man. My superpower was the ability to jump through time, as I pleased. I was always using it to jump back ten minutes, say, and then coming up with the perfect reply to an insult. Or this time, you know, I'd dodge the blow.'

'Someone was hitting you?'

'Brother Alan, usually. Like I said, I was the youngest. The punching bag.'

Hobbes started to get a clearer idea of Fairfax's character. He'd known enough tough guys and macho types to know that weakness or pain often lay at the heart of their constant struggle to assert themselves.

Fairfax stopped at a roundabout, waiting for an opening in the flow of traffic. He put on a smile, held it in place. 'Now don't go telling any of this to Meg. She thinks I'm idiotic enough as it is.'

Hobbes kept it light. 'Your secret identity is safe with me.'

A few miles outside Maidstone, the talk turned to Fairfax's dad once again.

'What was his job?' Hobbes asked.

'Steelworker. Then unemployed when the factory went bust. After that a layabout and drunkard. I swore to myself – eleven, twelve years old – that I would never get my hands dirty for some other bastard's profit.'

'A cop's hands get dirty enough.'

'That was Uncle Charlie's doing. Me joining up, I mean.'

'Charlie Jenkes?'

'The one and only.'

'I think Meg mentioned that he was friends with your dad.'

'Best friends. The very best. That's why we all called him Uncle Charlie. They were like brothers, you know? Oh God, I loved him so much, as a kid. Whenever my brothers were having a go at me, I'd run off to Charlie's house. That was my getaway.' A sudden edge came into his voice. 'I mean, that man was my hero.'

There was an awkward silence. Hobbes spoke at last: 'You have to believe me, Tommy, I'm as sad as you are about what happened to him.'

'Sure. Sure you are.'

The mood had changed in an instant. Hobbes could practically hear Fairfax's teeth grinding together as he spoke. Perhaps he'd come down to Hastings for one purpose only: to confront him, out of sight of the other officers, away from prying eyes. The jokes and stories were a front, to get his superior's guard down.

The car started to slow down. Hobbes felt his heart tighten.

'What are you doing, Fairfax?'

There was no reply. He looked out of the window and saw a lay-by coming up. The car swung into it and came to an easy stop. Now everything was quiet. The sky had started to darken. An embankment on one side, the road on the other, a few cars passing by. Ahead, a wooden kiosk selling drinks and burgers to a trio of bikers.

Hobbes could see no easy way out of this. If it came to a fight, the younger man would beat him easily; he was fitter, stronger, and driven by anger. Hobbes turned to face him. The detective constable was staring through the windscreen. One hand tapped impatiently at the steering wheel.

Hobbes breathed in and out rapidly. 'Now look, Fairfax, what're you playing at? Is this some kind of game?'

'No games. I promise you.' He turned in the seat and stared directly at his superior. 'This is about Charlie, and about why he had to die.'

'It was fear. Don't you see that? He'd made a mistake and now he was afraid for his job, his standing. His dignity. He'd lost everything. There was no other way out.'

'Sure. He did a bad thing. According to you.'

'Did you really worship him that much, that you can't see the truth?'

'I don't think it's worship. But he stood for everything that was good, everything I loved about being a copper.'

'I agree, in the early days. But then he ruined it.'

Fairfax looked at him without blinking. And Hobbes saw something different in his face, a kind of surrender. His mouth trembled as he spoke.

'I hear that Charlie didn't kill himself.'

Hobbes started to reply, but then stopped himself. He hadn't expected this, not at all.

Fairfax was still staring at him. 'There's this story going round, see? That he was strung up.' His hand came up to rub at his face. The young man was sweating. 'He was murdered.'

'Who told you that?'

'I think one of those black bastards did it.'

'Fairfax—'

'Revenge. What else could it be?'

'Fairfax, where did you hear about this? Tell me!'

'Unless . . . unless it was a cop.' His hand bunched into a fist. 'Jesus. I hope not. Christ, no.' He was losing control. His face was bright red.

'Let's get some air. Come on.'

Hobbes opened the door and stepped out, hoping that DC Fairfax would follow him. He did. They stood together near the embankment. A breeze ruffled the wildflowers that grew along the edge of the concrete. Music was coming from the kiosk, a rock and roll number. It sounded like Chuck Berry.

Hobbes stood to attention. 'If you've heard rumours, Tommy, you have to put them aside. Charlie Jenkes hanged himself, that's all we know.' He could sense Lockhart over his shoulder as he said this. The mission was meant to be secret, he'd sworn to keep it that way. And Fairfax was too volatile, easily riled.

Still, he had to know something. 'Tommy. Can you tell me who started this story?'

Fairfax nodded. 'I called in on Charlie's wife last night.'

'Lisa?'

'She's scared out of her wits. Chief Superintendent Lockhart paid her a visit, a couple of weeks back. He's stirring up trouble.'

'What did he want, did she say?'

'He's looking for reasons, motives. Personal stuff, you know.' Fairfax blinked. 'That whole family is going crazy, breaking apart. I wish I could do something to help them.'

Hobbes nodded. 'Don't worry. I'll talk to Lisa.'

'Really?'

'Yes. Tomorrow. I'll sort this out, whatever the truth is.'

Fairfax gave him a weak smile. He looked defenceless and ill at ease.

'It's true then?'

'What is?'

'The story. That Charlie was murdered.'

'I'm not saying—'

'And that Lockhart has asked you to look into it.'

Hobbes felt sick. The smell of burning onions and fried meat wafted over from the kiosk. A car sped by, spewing out carbon monoxide.

'I don't know what you're talking about.'

The younger detective looked him right in the eye, and said, 'I want in.'

'Fairfax—'

'I need to be in on this. I need to find out what happened, for certain.'

'And then what? Retribution?'

Fairfax didn't reply, but his eyes held a pure glint of madness. It scared Hobbes. He considered carefully before speaking. 'It's easier to be a bad cop than a good one. Which way do you want to go?'

'Whichever's necessary.'

It was hopeless. 'I'll do what I can.'

'Thank you.' Fairfax's mouth twisted in a crooked line.

'Come on. Let's get on our way.' Hobbes led the younger man back to the car. They got in and set off, pulling out on to the main road.

'Look, Tommy, keep all this to yourself, will you? About Charlie.'

Fairfax drove on in silence.

A Cabinet of Curiosities

Mr and Mrs Clarke lived in a village called Holcombe St Mary some five miles outside Maidstone. A narrow winding road took them into open country. An enormous house stood alone at the edge of a field. Fairfax whistled his appreciation.

'This is it.'

The Clarke residence was a rambling three-storey property called Oulton Grange. The next house was some miles away across the flat landscape. Nearby was a smaller building, a barn or a stables of some kind. Hobbes and Fairfax walked through the extensive garden to the front door, which opened before they got there. Annabelle Clarke was waiting for them.

'I'm glad you could see us, Mrs Clarke.'

'Your detective Lattner rang, to arrange it. Is that her name?'

'Latimer.'

They moved along a central corridor. Hobbes heard murmured voices from a living room as they passed, and glimpsed a group of people through a doorway. Mr Clarke was among them, serving drinks.

'We have a few friends and relatives over tonight. They've all been very supportive.'

'Good. I believe your son's body has now been released?'

'Yes, thank you. We will bury him early next week.'

She stopped at the foot of the stairs. Hobbes could see that she was struggling to hold her emotions at bay. She dabbed at her eyes with her fingers.

'Forgive me.'

'That's all right. Whenever you're ready.'

She smiled. 'One tries to be strong, of course, for the sake of the family.' Her hand tightened on the banister. 'Sometimes, I'm absolutely certain that I've screamed out loud, but then I look around and nobody's paying any attention to me. Or hardly anybody. Just my husband. He'll be gazing at me so intently, so kindly . . .' Her thoughts drifted into silence.

They followed her upstairs. On the landing she turned to them and said, 'Dear Gerald threw all the money in the world at Brendan. Oh my, did he! You wouldn't believe the things we've bought for him over the years.'

Hobbes thanked her again. He felt at a loss.

'Is there anything in particular you're looking for?' she asked.

Carefully he said, 'There might be something in Brendan's collection that connects to his murder, but I won't know it until I see it.'

They entered a spacious bedroom at the back of the house, which was overly neat and very clean. It smelled of furniture polish. There were a good many cupboards and shelves, a writing desk, and a single bed with tightly tucked sheets. The walls were bare except for a few framed posters, one of them showing the *Backstreet Harlequin* album cover. Mrs Clarke lifted the lid of a large chest that stood on the floor beneath the window.

'This is his collection of relics,' she announced. 'Oh God, that's horrible isn't it, using such a word? It's just that Gerald and I always referred to it as that. The *relics*.'

Hobbes bent down to look through the contents of the chest. It was filled to the brim with objects: demo cassettes; dozens of plectrums; candid photographs of the rock star and his entourage (Simone Paige was seen in quite a few of them); autographed beer mats; a snapped guitar string stored safely in a box; set lists in Lucas's handwriting; a weird-looking pull-on King Lost mask made out of rubber; cigarette butts carefully sealed in plastic bags; even a handkerchief smudged with lipstick. Hobbes couldn't help wondering if the scarlet impressions were the markings of Simone's lips. It was astonishing.

'I did warn you,' Mrs Clarke said. 'There are wonders here.'

'How did he get hold of this stuff?' Fairfax asked.

'Brendan was voracious when it came to his passion. He would spend weeks or even months researching, making phone calls, going off to meet with strange people in strange places.' She pointed to a shelf which contained a number of cardboard folders. 'These, for instance, contain many of Lucas Bell's original lyric sheets. A particular obsession.'

Hobbes took one folder down and flicked through it. It made him think of the sheets of paper found in Brendan Clarke's London house: they were photocopies, but these were the originals, page after page of them. So many treasured objects. He had to admit: there was evidence of madness in the room.

As if in reply to his unspoken thoughts, Mrs Clarke said, 'This is only a small selection of items, Inspector. We have more in storage.'

Fairfax shook his head. 'This is crazy. I'm sorry. But it is.'

'I know. I do know. Dear Brendan had his problems.'

Her breath quickened. She was getting upset again. Hobbes watched her as her gaze darted this way and that, reluctant to settle.

Fairfax gestured for Hobbes to step outside, on to the landing.

'Look, what the hell are we doing in this place?' He spoke in a whisper, although it was doubtful that Mrs Clarke was paying them any heed.

'I know, it's tricky. I thought there might be something here, a clue of some kind.'

He walked back into the room and was about to speak when Mrs Clarke held up a hand to quieten him. She was standing near the bed where her son used to sleep, whenever he came visiting.

The sheets were freshly laundered from the looks of it. She ran a hand over the pillow, smoothing out a crease. Then she pointed to a small framed picture on the wall above the bed. 'This, I'm afraid, was the last thing Brendan stared at, before going to sleep.'

Hobbes moved closer.

'It was his most treasured possession.'

The inspector unhooked the frame from the wall. At its centre, sealed under glass, was a small piece of paper. He read the few words scrawled on it:

I've loved just about all I can love,
There's nowhere else to go.

Below this was Lucas Bell's signature.

'Do you know what it is?' she asked.

'I do. It's a suicide note.'

'I can assure you, it's genuine.' The very idea made her shudder. But then she turned to Hobbes and said, 'I suppose you think my son was mad, as your colleague does?'

He didn't answer. He couldn't, not truthfully.

'Inspector Hobbes?'

'Yes?'

'Do you have any idea who might have killed Brendan?'

'It's only been a few days. We're still—'

'Do you? Or don't you?'

Hobbes looked to the doorway for support, but Fairfax had vanished. He decided to tell the grieving woman the truth, such as it was. 'I believe that Brendan was murdered by somebody close to Lucas Bell, a friend from his youth. A woman.'

'A woman?'

'As I said, we're still investigating. But this person has killed at least one other person, maybe two, and they may well do so again. Until I understand the killer's obsession, the exact reasons for her actions, there's very little I can be certain of.'

Mrs Clarke frowned. 'Will you do one last thing for me?'

'If I can.'

'Tell me what Brendan looked like. When he was found, I mean. His face . . .'

'I'm not sure that—'

'I need to know.' Her eyes locked on his. 'I *need* to know. Everything, no matter how painful.'

And so he found himself relating the story of how he first entered the bedroom at 47 Westbrook Avenue, to view the corpse on the bed. Every detail was given. Annabelle Clarke listened with intent, with unblinking eyes, her face seemingly devoid of emotion. Afterwards, when it was done, she stood in silence. Then she nodded her head in thanks and said, somewhat matter-of-factly, 'That will help me.' She turned to the door. 'Now can we get out of here, please?'

By sheer force of will, she brightened her mood.

'There's one more thing I wish to show you.'

They walked downstairs, along the main corridor and past the room where friends and family were now talking. Gerald Clarke looked up but said nothing. They went out through the front door, into the garden. It was fully dark by now and the stars were clearly visible in the sky, so many of them. Hobbes looked to Fairfax's car as he passed, and saw his colleague sitting inside, listening to the radio. They moved on along another pathway that led to the smaller building Hobbes had noticed earlier. It was an old stables. Mrs Clarke unlocked the door and gestured for him to enter. It was dark inside until a light was clicked on. And then he stood where he was, frozen, staring ahead without saying a word. At last he managed to take a step forward, towards the lone vehicle that was parked in the middle of the floor.

It was an eggshell-blue Ford Capri.

Lucas Bell's car. The original. Hobbes knew that instantly.

'My husband bought this for Brendan, for his twenty-fifth birthday.'

The inspector walked around the vehicle. He peered in through the side window, almost expecting to see the front seats splattered with blood. But they were clean. And there was no tarot card on the dashboard; that was long gone.

'This is incredible,' he said at last.

'You really think so?'

'Where did you get it?'

'It's been on quite a journey, I gather. Nobody claimed it from the police car pound, so they sent it off to be crushed at the scrapyard. I'm guessing that somebody recognized its worth and saved it. What happened to it after that, I haven't a clue. Gerald bought it from a man in London. I don't know his name.'

'Did Brendan ever drive it?'

'A few times, when it was first restored. But after that, no, not really. But he would come out here to sit in it. Often for hours at an end.'

'Would you mind if I . . . ?'

'Please do.'

Hobbes opened the door and settled in behind the steering wheel. It felt like he was climbing into a time machine. It was easy to imagine how Brendan Clarke must've felt, sitting here. The vehicle was a temple, a zone of contemplation. Mrs Clarke stood some way off, almost out of sight. Nothing disturbed the sacred atmosphere. Dust motes moved in the plush interior, the plastic of the seat creaked under his weight. Hobbes closed his eyes. Colours flickered inside his head. He could almost hear music playing, a faraway song.

'Are you all right?' Mrs Clarke asked, knocking on the side window.

'Yes. Sorry. I was miles away.'

He looked around, overcome by a deep sadness. Terrible passions reached out from long ago, to claim their present-day victims.

Hobbes pressed at the glove box to open it. He knew that the suicide note had been found in there, the one he had seen upstairs, in the bedroom. But another piece of paper was now lodged in the compartment. This whole car was a shrine to Bell's final moments, replicating each detail perfectly. He unfolded the paper and looked at the words it held. It took him only a few seconds to realize what he was holding in his hands.

Here was the proof, at last.

The proof that Lucas Bell had been murdered.

THURSDAY
27 AUGUST 1981

Secret Lives

Hobbes woke early. He had a quick breakfast and then went outside to look for his car. As promised, Barlow had parked it close to the house. It was a strange feeling, to be driving out towards Ilford, a journey he used to make regularly whenever he visited the Jenkes household. He and Glenda would go round for dinner. They would often stay late, playing cards or watching home movies. Charlie always had to have the latest gadgets, aspirational to his core. He was the first of his circle to own a videocassette player.

'To have and to hold, and I intend to hold everything.'

The two men had become friends when Jenkes had transferred to the Charing Cross nick, back when Hobbes had first been made detective constable. They were a year apart in age and both on the way up, both aiming for detective sergeant. Jenkes was hot-headed, easily triggered, but fiercely loyal to the cause, dogged in pursuit of bad guys, and the very best man to have beside you in a show-down. As he'd proved in the Brixton riot.

It was impossible not to think of that night, and its consequences.

Hobbes turned into Waverly Road. In these large redbrick houses lived the successful refugees from the East End, the working class made good. Jenkes had put down his deposit on the semi-detached house and garden the day after being made sergeant, keen to escape the Dagenham estate where he'd been born and bred. Margaret Thatcher's arrival as Prime Minister in 1979 put the seal on his ambitions: nothing was going to hold him back now, he had as much right to the riches as any toffee-nosed bastard, that was his motto. In fact more so, because he'd worked so bloody hard to get his hands on the prize.

Hobbes rang the bell and waited. It was just shy of half seven, and he knew that Lisa would be getting the kids ready for school. She opened the door and looked at him through her tortoise-shell-framed spectacles, her eyes unblinking. Despite rehearsing a few lines on the journey over, Hobbes didn't know what to say. She shook her head in dismay and then turned on her heel. He followed, closing the door behind him and walking through into the kitchen. Lisa Jenkes fussed over her two children, giving out orders, and shooing them to get their school bags ready. Hobbes waited, not daring to get in the way. A transistor radio on the counter belted out the hits.

'Come on, you two, out of the house, now.'

Lisa bundled her son towards the front door. Then she gave her daughter a peck on the cheek, and told her to have a good day.

Hobbes and Lisa were alone.

She turned off the radio. The quiet lay between them. Lisa stood against the counter, wiping a cup with the tea towel, over and over.

Hobbes said, 'I'll put the kettle on, shall I?'

He opened the cupboard and saw three of every item, one of Charlie's old habits passed on from his father's time as an engineer in the Royal Air Force: one for use, one for spare, one in case the spare goes missing, or breaks. The sight of the three packets of Typhoo tea, one opened and the other two next to it, made Hobbes shiver with a sudden emotion.

He had always felt so at home here.

Lisa asked, 'How's Glenda? And Martin?' There was a tremor in her voice.

'They're fine. Hanging on.' He couldn't bear to tell her the truth, not just now. She had enough troubles as it was. 'Martin's learning guitar.'

Lisa touched his arm. 'I never thought I'd see you again,' she said.
'No, well. I've been a bit . . .'

'Here, I'll do that.'

She turned to face the sink and began filling the kettle with water. Hobbes could see her shoulders trembling. He wanted to offer comfort but didn't know what was appropriate. All the visits to deliver the worst kind of news to parents and spouses – none of it helped him now.

'I was talking to Tom Fairfax last night.'

'Oh yes.'

'He's worried about you, and the kids.'

'He was right to be worried.'

'Lisa . . .'

She turned to face him, her eyes unseeing.

'Lisa, I'm sorry.' It was as quiet as anything he'd ever said in his whole life, as quiet and as gentle and as useless, but there it was.

A great sob went through her body, forcing her to sit down at the kitchen table.

'Stupid, stupid bastard.'

The words were spat out. It took Hobbes a moment to realize that she wasn't referring to him, or to Fairfax.

'What did he do, Lisa?'

Her fingers gripped his, tight enough to hurt. 'It wasn't Charlie's fault, not really. I had an affair. Last year.' Now the words were out, her hand relaxed slightly. 'It was nothing, honestly. A silly fling. Well, you know how it gets, Henry. Don't you?' She looked at him, her eyes wet with tears, as she repeated her line: 'You know how it gets sometimes.'

Her hand moved away.

'Oh don't look at me like that, Henry.'

'I'm not—'

'Don't you dare judge me!' Her voice was a spike, cutting into him. 'I'll bet Charlie's had his affairs. Many of them, I imagine.'

'I don't think so . . .'

'It was just the once, that's all. But he found out, Charlie found out who it was.'

'A fellow cop?'

She dismissed the idea with a shake of her head. 'Charlie beat the guy up. Really badly. This was just before the riot, the night before. He was all pent-up. Crazy. Like a beast.'

Hobbes remembered the look in Jenkes's eyes that night in the alleyway in Brixton.

'Oh God, he scared me so, when he came home . . .'

'He didn't hurt you, Lisa?'

'No. He wouldn't do that. But his face was horrible to look at, like he'd . . . like he'd been in a war, and just about survived.'

She took a deep breath.

'Only, see . . . the man I slept with . . . well . . .'

'What about him?'

'He wasn't a white man.'

'You mean . . .'

'Yes.'

Hobbes was shocked. He tried to work through the implications.

Lisa looked down at the table. 'He's a teacher, at Beth's school. Oh. Nothing much happened, not really, but, well . . .'

Her voice trailed off.

Hobbes kept on at her. 'And your friend didn't report it, when Charlie attacked him?'

She shook her head. 'No. No, I persuaded him not to. But then . . .'

'Go on.'

'I'm worried sick, Henry.'

'Why? What is it?'

Now she looked up at Hobbes. 'I'm scared that Lloyd – that's the teacher's name – I'm scared that he did something to Charlie, in retaliation. He made threats.'

'After Charlie attacked him, you mean?'

'No, no, later. After Charlie did that horrible thing, at the drinking den, to that poor black man.'

Hobbes looked at her. He didn't know what to say, not yet. The whole incident in the cellar of the Silhouette club was taking on another aspect, a much more personal one. The terrible experience of the riot, on top of Lisa's affair, had tipped DI Jenkes over into madness, into a blinding desire for revenge, against any representative of the race. And the victim at the club – Michael Hennessey – with the simple act of spitting in a policeman's face, had walked right into the centre of Charlie's madness.

'Do you know what you're saying, Lisa? This is a serious accusation.'

'Yes. I know. I know that.' Her hands fluttered against each other on the tabletop. 'But lately, he's been pestering me, Lloyd has. He won't leave me alone! The other night he came round, knocking on the door, and the kids were in, eating their tea, and I . . . I only just managed to get rid of him.'

She wiped tears from her eyes.

'Beth wanted to know what her English teacher was doing here. I had to make some excuse to her.'

Hobbes could see that she was near to breakdown.

'What does he want?'

'He's saying that now Charlie's out of the way, we can get together. But that's never going to happen. I mean, how can it?'

'No.'

She stared at him intently. 'I don't want anything to do with him, Henry. Nothing! Not any more.'

He let her settle for a moment and then asked, 'What is Lloyd's surname?'

'Patterson.'

'Lloyd Patterson. And his address?'

She told him and he wrote it down on a scrap of paper.

'The thing is, Lloyd's married as well.'

Hobbes tried to keep her focused. 'And so you're saying . . .
Lisa, look at me . . .'

'Yes?'

'You're claiming that Patterson killed Charlie? Are you really
saying that?'

She didn't reply. Her fingers tapped nervously at the tabletop.
And then her head made the tiniest of gestures, a nod.

'And do you have any proof of this?'

'No. No, of course not. But he was making threats, saying
that I deserved so much more, and that Charlie was a
hindrance.'

'A hindrance?'

'That's the word he used.'

Hobbes felt he was seeing Lisa Jenkes for the first time; her
husband's death had let loose the truth about the marriage, a truth
that even he as a close friend had been unaware of.

The kettle was whistling madly. She got up and turned it off.

'Lockhart's been coming round,' she said. 'Asking all these
questions.'

'I know.'

'He knows something's wrong.'

'Don't worry, I'll take care of it.'

'Will you, Henry?'

'I promise.'

A glimmer of hope flickered in her eyes.

He asked, 'Lisa, do you still own the garage?'

'Yes, but I can't go in there, not any more. I've been parking
the car out-front.'

'Do you have the key?'

She nodded, searched through a cabinet drawer and handed him
the fob. There seemed little more to say, and indeed Hobbes was
keen to escape the house; the atmosphere unnerved him.

'All I want to know is the truth,' Lisa said. 'The truth of how
he died.'

Hobbes left. He went back to his car first, to collect the report from the back seat, and then walked the short distance to a row of garages. The report had been waiting behind the door for him when he'd got home late last night, a present from Lockhart, and he'd skimmed through it before falling into bed. Strangely, its disturbing images had not taken root in his dreams, and he'd slept soundly. But he was now facing a very different level of apprehension.

There were ten garages altogether, their doors painted a uniform green. He'd been here a few times, with Charlie, when he'd helped with repairs to the car. Along the way he passed a back garden, and looked over to see a new clothes line hanging between two posts. He knew that the rope had been taken from there, an improvised noose.

Charlie had died late at night. When Hobbes had first heard about the suicide, he'd pictured his friend creeping into the garden under cover of darkness to steal the clothes line; the domestic nature of the act added another layer of sadness. But now he imagined a very different scenario: somebody taking the rope with the express purpose of wrapping it around Charlie's neck and pulling it tight, and then using it to string his body up. If this was the case, then the murder had been planned, or at least semi-planned: it was premeditated.

Hobbes reached the garage door and bent down to put the key in the padlock. For a second he hesitated, and then he pulled the door upwards.

Immediately, he knew that someone had searched the place, and thoroughly.

Charlie was a man who set great store by order and cleanliness. Whenever Hobbes had helped out here, every tool was replaced on its rightful peg after being used; each nut, bolt and screw was stored with others of similar size and shape in clear plastic boxes. Even the oily rags had their own compartment under the workbench. Rolls of black tape were stacked neatly on a shelf. And of

237

course there was at least three of everything. But now all these objects seemed to be slightly askew, as though somebody had inspected each one, and put them back in the wrong position. This wasn't the work of the police team who had first investigated the death. There would be very little reason to search for anything, nor to replace things. No, somebody else had done this. He imagined the killer in a panic, after the murder had taken place, searching, searching, desperately.

What had they been looking for? And more importantly, had they found it?

Hobbes skimmed the report's findings: ' . . . occlusion of blood vessels . . . asphyxiation . . . bruising on the neck . . . torn jacket . . . oil on the fingertips . . .' He didn't like that torn jacket, the detail disturbed him. Had anyone looked into this properly? It seemed unlikely. To those high up, Jenkes was a guilty copper, a disgrace to the service, and bloody good riddance to him. Case closed.

He looked at the photographs again: the dead body hanging from the crossbeam, the workbench from which, it was assumed, DI Jenkes had stepped forward and fallen into oblivion.

Hobbes started to search and found a bottle of whisky hidden away, and a collection of pornographic magazines at the bottom of the box of rags, and he thought: Charlie would've thrown those away before he hanged himself. It was a simple fact: he wouldn't have wanted his wife or kids to have found them. No, Jenkes would've taken care of such things. So now Hobbes set to work diligently. He spent a good twenty minutes going through everything, but nothing further was revealed, nothing found. The place was clean.

He looked up at the crossbeam, and wondered about the car. Why wasn't it in the garage, on the night . . .

'What're you doing?'

He looked round to see Elizabeth Jenkes standing in the garage doorway.

'Shouldn't you be at school?'

She groaned. 'Oh please. It's boring. Everyone keeps looking at me, and talking behind my back, like I'm the one who beats up black guys.'

Her anger seethed behind her studied expression.

'Does your mother know how you're feeling?'

Beth smiled. 'What the fuck does she care? Stupid old tart.'

Hobbes couldn't believe the language the twelve-year-old was coming out with.

'Beth—'

'What? Is it lecture time?'

'I was going to say, "Your mother needs you now", but I can see it won't make any difference.'

'You're right.'

He knew precisely what she was going through. He knew how she'd felt when she'd arrived at the garage to find her father's dead body suspended by a length of rope from the ceiling. He knew every emotion. He'd felt them himself.

He said, 'I believe your father acted with the best intentions, but those intentions . . .'

'They were fucked up, right? Piss-poor, fucked-up, evil, twisted intentions.'

'Well . . .'

'Well, you still haven't told me why you're here.'

'Your mother asked me to sort the garage out for her. She can't face it.'

He regretted the lie, but she took it in good faith and looked up to the crossbeam. For a moment the surliness left her face. Her eyes blinked and glistened. And he thought: soon, if this investigation pans out, the poor kid will have to swap one form of pain for another; from thinking her father took his own life, that sense of abandonment, to thinking instead of his final moments as he struggled against his killer.

Now her eyes had returned to his, and he saw her hands clench tightly and her body steady herself; she was fighting it, with the swear words, the spit, the nastiness. Some kind of control against the chaos, against darkness.

His own life was governed by a similar balance: seeking clues, fingerprints in the dust, blood samples, the damning lies, droplets of sweat on the skin of a suspect – and using them all as protection against the nightmares. Weak, fragile, necessary protection.

And so he told her. It just came out. It was the first time he had admitted this to anyone, in so many years.

He said, 'Beth, I found my mother, just like you found your father. I came home from football and I saw her lying on the kitchen floor. The whole place . . .' His voice cracked. 'The place stank. She'd turned on the gas and stuck her head in the oven.'

He paused. She was staring at him.

'I was seventeen.'

He was going to say more, but his mind was suddenly empty.

Beth seemed to be holding her breath. Then she asked, 'Why did she do it?'

'Because . . . well, because my dad had left home. She'd kicked him out. He wasn't . . . he wasn't the best of men. And then, it was two days before her divorce was going to be made final . . . that's when . . . that's when she did it.' He paused. 'She took her own life. I guess she couldn't face it, being alone. That's all I can think.'

They looked at each other across a few feet of space.

'She left a note, tucked in a book of poems. I still have it, and I read it now and then. I'm still trying to understand it, I guess.'

Beth drew a sigh. The sneer came back to her face. 'I hope to God you're not going to tell me that you know how I feel. Because . . .'

'No.'

'Because I swear, I'll lamp you one.'

'I'm thinking you would as well.' He nodded. 'Anyway, that's all I wanted to say.'

She nodded in turn. Recognition. A barely seen movement.

Quietly he said, 'Come on, let's go.' He closed the garage door, locked it, and started to walk along with the girl at his side. After a few steps, she said, 'I don't think I'll ever get over it, the sight of Daddy, like he was . . .'

He said simply, 'If you ever need someone to talk to, I'll always be available.'

She didn't reply. He could only hope it meant something to her.

They walked on a little way and he said, 'Can I ask, was the car in the garage, when you found him?'

'No, Mum had taken it for the night, visiting Grandma and Grandpa. Me and Junior went with her. We stayed overnight. When we came back in the morning, we drove up to the garage and I jumped out to open the door for her. And that's when . . .'

'OK. That makes sense—'

He stopped walking. A sudden thought irritated him.

Oil on the fingertips . . .

'What's wrong?'

He didn't answer; his mind was entirely elsewhere.

'What is it?'

'Go on, Beth, get to school. There's still time.'

She laughed at the absurdity of the idea. And with that she was gone, jumping over the nearest garden wall and disappearing down the side alley of a house.

Hobbes turned back towards the garage.

No car in the garage, no tools set out, yet oil on the fingertips . . .

What had Charlie been working on?

He unlocked the garage door and entered for a second time. He went over to the shelf where the cans of motoring oil were kept, all the same brand. The first two were full to the brim and the third half-empty, from the weight of it in his hand. He started with this one, pouring the thick black contents into a metal bucket. His hands were soon covered in the stuff, and his suit was speckled with stains. But when the can was nearly empty, he could hear something rattling around inside. It took him a while to ease it

241

through the opening, using a screwdriver. The object was small, wrapped in black electrician's tape for protection. He pulled this loose, revealing a plastic evidence bag sealed with even more tape. And inside the bag was a small cellophane packet containing a single strip of photographic negatives.

He held the strip up to the overhead light.

The images were blurred, and too small to see clearly; but he could make out enough to know it was a sex scene.

Seven Years Apart

Hobbes needed to get the photographs developed. He didn't want anyone in the police force to see them, not until he was sure of the contents, and he certainly couldn't take them into the local chemist. But there was one person he could ask, so he took the North Circular Road and drove to Notting Hill. Neville Briggs was willing to do the job for him, but he was still reeling from the news of Simone Paige's death.

'I should've gone down to Hastings with her.'

'I doubt it would've done any good.'

'How do you know? How can you possibly know?'

'I talked to her outside the house where she was killed. Lucas Bell's old house. I think she'd already made her mind up to go inside.'

Briggs closed his eyes, as though picturing the scene.

'Nothing would've stopped her.'

It was enough. Hobbes left the strip of negatives with the photographer and went on his way. He arrived at the station to find the team already working. He brought everyone together and went through yesterday's findings. 'OK then, let's see where we are,' he said. 'Meg, is there a match?'

'I'll show you.'

Latimer had copied the two items Fairfax had brought in that morning, and now she projected them, blown up, on to a screen. She explained, 'This is Lucas Bell's suicide note, borrowed from Mr and Mrs Clarke.'

Hobbes looked on as a slip of paper appeared on the screen, with its scrawled signature and final message to the world.

'As far as we know, it's authentic,' Latimer said. 'This is the actual piece of paper found in Bell's car, at the end of his life.'

Fairfax grunted. 'It's not much of a suicide note. A slip of paper? Someone should've questioned that at the time.'

Hobbes looked across. Fairfax wasn't his usual self; he slouched at his desk and his lips barely moved when he spoke. And instead of his usual immaculate appearance, he was dressed in the same outfit as last night, which was looking decidedly tatty.

'Let's not get bogged down in what should've been done in the past.' Hobbes turned back to the screen. 'Carry on, Meg.'

'OK. You can see here' – she pointed to the top edge of the slip of paper on the screen – 'the edge is torn. Now then . . .' She clicked a button and another, larger sheet of paper appeared on the screen. 'This is the paper the guv found yesterday, in the glove compartment of Lucas Bell's car.'

'It's a lyric sheet for the song "Backstreet Harlequin",' Hobbes explained. 'The same song that was playing on the record player in Clarke's bedroom.'

'That's right. PC Barlow has compared these lyrics with the ones on the album, and they are different. So we believe this sheet contains the original version of the song, as written by Lucas Bell.'

'He often changed lyrics,' Hobbes said. 'It was part of his creative process.'

Latimer nodded. 'And if you go to the last two lines, here . . .' She spoke the words of the song out loud: '*I'm just another backstreet harlequin, lost in the afterglow.* The line ends abruptly, as you can see.'

'And the paper's too short.'

Latimer smiled. 'And the paper's too bloody short.'

She clicked again and now both papers appeared one below the other, the lyric sheet and the suicide note. Together they made one A4 sheet.

'Put simply, the slip of paper was ripped off the bottom of the lyric sheet. So now the complete final verse reads . . . *I'm just another backstreet harlequin, lost in the afterglow. I've loved just about all I can love, there's nowhere else to go.*' She paused to let Hobbes and Fairfax take this in. 'And here we have the two pieces of paper magnified, and you can see they fit together exactly.'

Blown-up images of the papers filled the screen, the two items closely aligned to show that every tiny valley and peak of the torn edges corresponded.

The three police officers stared at the screen.

Hobbes took command. 'OK. So here's what I think happened. Lucas Bell's murderer knew where he was living outside Hastings, when he went missing. They met there, in his cottage retreat, and talked. Bell most probably had some of his old lyric sheets with him. The murderer chose an appropriate song and tore the paper in two, using the bottom two lines of the song and the signature to serve as a fake suicide note.' Hobbes let this sink in. 'The two pieces of paper then go on their separate journeys, passed from hand to hand, possibly for large amounts of money, we don't know. Eventually our Lucas Bell obsessive, Brendan Clarke, finds them. First one, then the other. And when he found this second item . . .' The inspector touched at the lyric sheet on the screen. 'He realized that the two pieces belonged together. This, in Clarke's eyes, is proof that Bell didn't kill himself, that he was killed, and his suicide faked.' Hobbes paused. 'And then a short time later he meets Simone Paige, and tells her he has proof of murder. He invites her round to see the two pieces of paper.'

'But only photocopies,' Latimer explained.

'Yes. Copies, only. The originals are kept in safekeeping in the family home. But then his murderer turns up, another woman who, I believe, was also very close to Bell. Now, given Clarke's obsession, he was probably fascinated by this woman, as he was by Nikki Hauser, as he was by Simone Paige. Clarke explains to her about the fake suicide note, and he mentions that Simone

Paige is coming to see him later on. At which point the murderer seduces him, and they go upstairs to the bedroom. She asks him to set up the song on the record player and to move the bed across the room, into the light. Clarke by this point is totally in her power. He probably thinks this is some kind of sex game . . .'

He stopped speaking. They all knew what happened next.

Latimer spelt it out: 'And then she kills him.'

Hobbes carried on: 'When it's over, the murderer leaves a note for Simone Paige to find, a taunt, a message across the years. And she leaves Brendan Clarke there for Simone to find, his mutilated face on view, the song playing on the music centre. Hours later, young Morgan Yorke turns up, covers Brendan's face with the bed sheet and steals the note left for Simone. And later still, Simone arrives and discovers the body.'

Hobbes turned back to the screen and pointed at the two pieces of paper. 'And now, after seven years apart, the two halves of the song are finally joined together.'

He looked at his two colleagues. Latimer was keen-eyed, happy to be in the middle of a case. But Fairfax had said very little, and it was almost impossible to read his expression.

'What's next, guv?'

'We keep looking, Meg. The same person killed Bell, Clarke and Simone Paige. But the Paige case is different, it's an act of desperation. Whereas the two men were killed as part of a ritual. Something to do with the King Lost mask.'

'But we don't know what the ritual is,' Latimer added. 'And there was no attempt to cover up Brendan Clarke's murder, no attempt to make it look like suicide.'

'Something has changed over the years, in the murderer's thinking. The second murder was planned. Clues were left. A definite point was being made.' Hobbes turned to Fairfax. 'Tommy, I want you to continue looking for Nikki Hauser. She knows more than she's told us up to now, about this secret society.'

The detective constable didn't reply to the request.

'Fairfax. I need you to concentrate on this case, and this case alone.'

Fairfax grunted and looked away.

'He's been like this all morning,' Latimer said. 'Acting like a complete moron.'

Fairfax rose to his feet and walked out of the room without another word. DS Latimer shook her head in despair and said, 'Wanker.'

Hobbes watched the retreating figure. 'I agree. But he's got his problems.'

They walked out into the corridor. Along the way, Hobbes looked in on PC Barlow, who was sorting through the Edenville box. Every inch of wall space was covered in sheets of paper, some of them typewritten, others handwritten, and even more showing drawings or photographs of people and places. Barlow sat at a cramped table, which was also covered in notebooks, sketchpads and yet more papers.

'Making progress, Constable?'

'Yes, sir, but it's a long job.'

'All I want is the names of the real people behind the nicknames.'

Hobbes rejoined Latimer. They walked outside, where they spotted Fairfax leaning against the bonnet of his car. He was staring at Hobbes as he smoked a cigarette.

'Give us a second, Meg.'

He walked over to Fairfax. 'Now look—'

'What did you find out?'

'Fairfax . . .'

'You went to see Lisa, right? Did she give you any clues?'

'It isn't like that.'

'So what is it like? Did Charlie kill himself? Or not?'

Hobbes didn't answer. Fairfax was too close to anger – he could so easily go crazy and hurt somebody. That terrible look was back in his eyes; it was almost evil in its intent.

A Woman's Journal

Hobbes used Simone Paige's house keys to enter the ground-floor flat. DS Latimer followed him inside. She said, 'I hate entering dead people's homes – when they've just died, I mean.'

'I know. They still seem present, somehow.'

Their voices echoed in the empty flat.

Hobbes led the way into the bedroom. It was well appointed, with burgundy walls and spherical paper lanterns and a great stretch of white gauze forming a lowered ceiling. The smell of perfume and cigarette smoke was still evident, a ghost in the air.

'What are we looking for, exactly?'

Latimer explained her idea. 'I read Barlow's notes of your interview with Simone, where she told you that she kept journals from the early seventies. They might well have details of Lucas Bell, the things he said to her, the things he did.'

'Clues to Edenville?'

'Let's hope so.'

It didn't take them long to find the battered suitcase under the bed. Hobbes clicked open the two latches.

'Here we are.'

Inside were a number of journals, each one marked with the year: 1970, 1971, 1972 and 1974. Latimer sat on the bed and started on the earliest one, while Hobbes began with the final volume. These words were never meant for anyone else's eyes, that was obvious, yet here and there a strange turn of phrase would appear, as though Simone could never quite stop being a professional writer, a journalist reporting on her own life.

Lucas came round. He looked bad. Drinking again. Me and him, I wonder now why we ever got together. We met one day on a narrow ledge, and had nowhere else to go, no one else to fall in love with. Yet another argument. I wonder how long now, before we fall apart? And who will tumble first?

'How are you getting on?' Hobbes asked.

Latimer didn't take her eyes off the journal in her hands. 'She's nineteen, just arrived in London, started work at the *Melody Maker*. Her first job.' Now she looked at him. 'She's full of life, but nervous, scared of messing up. It's painful, seeing this, and thinking of what will happen to her and Lucas later.'

'I know. I'm reading about just that.'

Hobbes had skipped to the later pages of the 1974 journal, the part that related to Lucas Bell's death. Here the writing broke down completely, the handwriting a barely readable scrawl in places, the images fragmented.

Can't sleep. His face, always there. Why? WHY? No answer, there's no answer. Only the dark outside. A little light in a window opposite, a life. I feel numb, words frozen. Days now. Days. Endless . . .

The final pages were written in the private clinic where Simone Paige ended up, after Bell's suicide. They detailed her attempts at becoming clean, the return to some kind of normal life, if such a thing was possible.

I have spoken to the doctor. Neville will pick me up later today. My only friend, now. I'm suddenly afraid of what he might think of me, of how I look. Will he see the same person as before, or will he look upon a stranger?

These were the last words. A return to a certain style, a coherent language. Yet nothing more was said, the journals abandoned. No more talking to herself.

The two officers read on. The room was quiet around them: the turning of the pages, a sigh, an occasional comment. Hobbes read Simone's description of the meeting with Bell where he first drew the King Lost mask for her. It was very close to how she'd told it at the interview, and there was nothing at all in the recollected language that implied that Lucas Bell had already created King Lost, years and years before. Why did he delude her about the mask's origins?

He skipped on a few pages to find a mention of Edenville.

Lucas doesn't usually speak of his childhood. There's a door, and it closed, it's locked. But we'd been drinking and smoking, and out of the blue, he said, 'One day, Simone, if the time is ever right, I'll tell you the story of Edenville. That will surprise everyone.' He laughed (bitterly, I think) and said it would make me famous, as a writer. 'It's a crazy, fucked-up story.' Of course, I asked what he meant. But he would say no more. And his eyes, when he looked at me, held such darkness within them, such sadness.

Hobbes read the passage a second time. He'd been hoping for more of a revelation and couldn't help feeling disappointed. He turned to the other items in the suitcase. The linen napkin was there, with its painted face. He found a batch of photographs: Lucas alone; Simone and Lucas at the seaside, smiling at each other; Simone standing with a group of other young people, the staff of the *Melody Maker* – long hair, hippie clothes, everybody smoking and drinking. One set of snapshots fascinated Hobbes.

They were taken at the *King Lost* album cover shoot. There was no sign of Simone Paige in any of these, so he assumed that she'd taken the photographs herself. But he recognized Neville Briggs in the background of one image, camera in hand; and Lucas Bell, of course, in many of the shots, the mask already painted on his face. The singer wasn't posing, he was just hanging around with his friends and colleagues, enjoying a joke with an older man and woman, perhaps his manager and publicity assistant. In another image, a few other hangers-on stood with them. Johnny Valentine was also present, sharing a joke with Lucas. It was strange to see Bell laughing so wildly in that stark mask, it made for a bizarre contradiction.

And then Latimer gasped in surprise.

'What is it?' Hobbes asked.

'I think I have something.' She looked at him. 'Simone has just seen Lucas Bell playing a gig in a tiny club in London, and she talked to him afterwards. It's all here: their first ever meeting. And then she writes a review of the gig for the *Melody Maker*. And a week after that she reviews his debut album.' Latimer held up a small piece of newsprint. 'It's right here. Published on the second of May, 1970. It's a great review. She absolutely loves it.'

'And?'

'And Simone gets a letter in response. Actually, it's hate mail.' Latimer showed him a small envelope and a sheet of folded paper. 'And look, a Hastings postmark.'

Hobbes took the envelope off her and checked it for himself.

Latimer started to read:

'*Dear Miss Paige, I feel that you don't fully understand the extent of Lucas Bell's genius. I take offence at your dismissal of his music.*'

Hobbes stopped her. 'You said it was a good review?'

'It was. But not in this person's eyes.'

She carried on:

'How dare you write such cretinous outpourings! You have entirely missed the point of his art. Obviously, you have no understanding of the secret meanings in his lyrics. Lucas will never be yours, Miss Paige, not ever. He belongs to a few special people only. Leave him alone! I am the first true admirer and if I see you at another gig, I will make my presence known, believe me. You are a bitch of the first order.'

Latimer stopped reading. Hobbes whistled quietly.

'But here's the best bit. The writer signs off with her name.'

'Which is?'

'Lady Minerva.'

Hobbes took the letter off Latimer and read it for himself. He said, 'When I mentioned the name Lady Minerva to Simone, she was puzzled, and thought it might mean something. But she couldn't remember the details.'

The telephone rang.

Hobbes lifted the handset: 'Who is this?'

A gruff but cultured male voice answered him. 'Is Simone there?'

'I'm afraid not.'

'Who are you?'

'I'm a police officer. Please tell me your name.'

'A police officer?'

'Yes.'

There was silence on the line, a caught breath. And then in a pained voice: 'Does this mean it's already happened?'

'Has what already happened?'

There was another pause before the caller spoke again.

'Is Simone already dead?'

The Closed Room

It was a bright, warm afternoon. Hobbes walked among the grave-stones, carved angels and mausoleums. Branches wove a canopy of leaves over the pathway, and the tombs and broken icons were covered in moss and lichen. Spots of sunlight dappled the ground.

A group of young people was standing around Lucas Bell's grave.

He stood and watched them for a moment, and then approached the man sitting on a wooden bench nearby.

'Tobias Lear?'

'Please, sit down. And it's Toby, by the way.'

He nodded towards the mourners at the graveside, who were now singing one of Bell's songs. 'More or less every day people come here to make their offerings, to say their prayers. Mostly young, far too young, and a few older ones, like myself.'

From Simone Paige's harsh description of him, Hobbes was expecting Tobias Lear to be a brash and reckless man. But the singer's former manager was small and dapper, dressed in a cream linen suit with a flowery blue-and-yellow necktie held in place by a gold pin. He was in his mid forties, with prematurely greying hair swept back neatly from his brow.

'It saddens me greatly to hear about Simone's demise. She was a gem, one of the best of the old-school writers. She was both skilful and provocative.' Lear paused and then turned towards the inspector and asked, 'She died yesterday?'

'Yes.'

Lear shook his head at this. 'She was the first journalist to support Lucas Bell's cause. I got to know her because of that. And then when she and Lucas fell in love, she was around all the time: tour bus, backstage, after-show parties, record launches.'

'And what made you suspect that she might've been killed?'

Lear gestured again to the grave. 'Watch now, they are seeking communion.'

Hobbes looked over. The four worshippers – two men and two women – had stopped singing. Their hands were joined together, forming a closed circle. Moments passed. A bird chirped from a nearby tree. And then the group broke apart and moved away down the path, leaving Hobbes and Lear alone on the bench.

'My turn.' Lear stood up and walked to the grave. He bent down and placed a single flower in the metal vase at the stone's base. Hobbes joined him there. He had seen this grave before, in the publicity photograph of Monsoon Monsoon. Here was the tombstone with its message, *Fear no more the heat of the sun*. Lear had fallen into a reverie, and Hobbes couldn't help but be affected by the mood. He closed his eyes and thought of his own son. Perhaps one day they would meet again, under better circumstances, and become close once more . . .

A dog barked, once, twice, calling Hobbes back to the world.

Lear said, 'Come with me, Inspector.'

'Where are we going?'

'If you want to know about Simone's fate, you will need to meet my lodger. And then all will be revealed.' They set off walking. 'It isn't far.'

They made their way out of Highgate Cemetery on to Swains Lane and then took a few more turnings until they reached Lear's residence. He was quiet along the way and would say no more about Paige or the murder. Hobbes did ask at one point whether he'd been Lucas Bell's manager from the very beginning, receiving the reply, 'Just me and only me, for my sins, all the way through from good times to bad.'

The house was an imposing but grotty-looking structure set back from the road and surrounded by overabundant trees. The paintwork was peeling on the window frames, and areas of missing plaster revealing the brickwork beneath. Hobbes wondered: the house must've cost a packet back in the seventies, when Lear had made his fortune, but now it was a ruined palace, its former opulence seen only in the crumbling white pillars on either side of the front door, and the old Bentley parked in the drive, one wheel missing, the axle perched on a pile of wood blocks. A map of bird shit covered the bonnet and windscreen.

'You'll have to take us as you find us, I'm afraid.'

Hobbes followed Lear into the house.

'We're surviving on royalty cheques from the good old days. Luckily, I made sure I shared a few joint songwriting credits with some of my protégés.'

But the interior of the house was spotless. The living room was cosy and old-fashioned, complete with leather armchairs and a grand marble fireplace. The scent of wood polish and pipe tobacco mixed with the light streaming through the French windows that gave out on to a large back garden.

'A terrible business,' Lear said. 'About Mr Clarke and the cuts to his face.'

Hobbes nodded. 'How did you find out about that? I kept the details from the press.'

'Neville told me. He rang me late last night.'

'Neville Briggs?'

'That's right.' Lear smiled weakly. 'Did Simone mention me, at all?'

'She did.'

'In disparaging terms, I shouldn't wonder?'

'Pretty much.'

'Um. That's understandable, given the circumstances. We were all very different people back then. The world was at our feet and this gave us the freedom to do as we pleased. Or so we thought.'

He paused, and smiled thinly. 'Only later did we realize that noth-ing is given for free. All payments will be collected.'

'We grow up?'

'Actually, I forced myself to change by sheer power of will.'

'And that works?'

'It can do. And one day, after years of effort, the original impulse to do wrong dies. And we become – well, not *good* exactly, but certainly better than we were.'

'I'm afraid I've seen too much evidence of human cruelty to believe that.'

'Oh, surely there is always a small chance of redemption?'

'I used to believe so. But these days, I'm not so certain.'

'Maybe you take after your namesake, Inspector?'

'You mean Thomas Hobbes, the philosopher?'

'He believed that men and women are essentially evil and brutish by nature, and only the power of the Law stops us from committing acts of barbarism.'

'It's one way of looking at things.'

Lear grinned, displaying teeth browned by years of pipe-smoking. 'And that makes the policeman the last defender against chaos.'

'Yes, it's like that at times. But the rational mind fights back, in all of us.'

'In some more than others, I think.' Lear smiled gently at his visitor.

Hobbes replied, 'We can't all embrace madness, otherwise . . .'

As if activated by the statement, a bell rang loudly on the wall. Lear said, 'Well then, duty calls.' He exaggerated his mild Londoner's accent into broad Cockney. 'My burden in life, my ball and chain, my trouble and strife, always wanting something or other, there's no end to it.' Then he stopped and looked directly at Hobbes. 'Inspector, you saw Mr Clarke's face, I presume?'

'I did.'

'And was it truly a copy of the King Lost mask?'

'Yes, as far as we know.'

'I see. It's just as Gavin feared, then.'

'Gavin?'

'My lodger. Gavin Roberts. He predicted that Simone Paige was in danger.'

'When did he make this prediction?'

'Only this morning, after I'd told him about Mr Clarke's face. Which is why I rang Simone, to see if she was all right. To warn her. Alas . . .'

'So your lodger has special knowledge?'

'Yes, yes he does, rather. I will take you to see him now. However, the sight may be disturbing for you. Out of his loneliness, Gavin has made another world for himself.'

'You mean like Edenville?'

Lear smiled gently and nodded his head. 'So then, you have got that far.'

'How much further is there to go?'

The bell rang again, and Lear tilted his head towards it, very like a Victorian butler responding to his master's call. He directed Hobbes out into the hallway and together they ascended the stairway.

Hobbes said, 'Simone told me that you bought Lucas the gun, is that correct?'

'To my eternal regret, it is. We went out to the woods and shot at trees and tin cans. I also supplied him with drugs, vetted his groupies, wiped the gunk from his mouth when he was down in the gutter, spewing up his day's intake. He was seeking enlightenment through excess. A common pathway favoured by Romantic poets through the ages.'

'And do you believe Lucas killed himself with that gun?'

Lear stopped as they reached the landing. He thought for a moment and then said, 'Yes and no. By which I mean, somewhere in between. If he did kill himself, then he was certainly pushed towards that outcome. And yet he could've so easily been dragged away from it, with a little love and understanding.'

'By the same person?'

'Oh yes, the person who directed him – whoever it might be – could well have saved him. I'm sure of it.'

Lear tapped on the panelling of a closed door and, receiving no reply, unlocked the door with a key.

'I met Gavin in late '69, when I first took on Lucas as a client. He was a member of the entourage. It was very much love at first sight, for both of us, I think.'

'I see.'

'Do you? I wonder . . .'

'Yet in the cemetery you called him your lodger?'

'Ah well, we haven't known each other in the biblical sense for a long time now. But we are still close friends, and, as you will see, Gavin needs to be looked after.'

Hobbes thought for a moment. Then he asked, 'Were there any other people around Lucas at the time, people he'd brought with him from Hastings?'

'Maybe. I really can't remember. There were so many hangers-on, as the years went by.'

'What about Eve Dylan?'

'Who's that?'

'You don't know the name?'

Lear shook his head. 'Only Gavin. He's the only one who mattered to me. And I don't regret a single day, despite the various difficulties.'

He opened the door and invited Hobbes to enter. The inspector was struck immediately by a simple thought – that he was walking into Edenville, or an approximation of it. Here, in this clean, sunlit room, the imagined village had been brought to a kind of life. There were posters on the walls advertising concerts and films at different Edenville venues, alongside painted portraits of Edenville celebrities. Rows of books sat in shelving units, all with handwritten, made-up titles on the spines. One wall held finely drawn maps of different areas of the village. A vast array of smaller items covered every inch of the floor, the chairs, the tables: ticket stubs, newspaper clippings, vouchers, postage stamps, sales receipts, shopping lists, football programmes, and many more.

Hobbes felt bewildered as he walked around, touching this object and that. Everything was either handcrafted, or hand-drawn. He moved to a large table in the corner of the room which was covered in a scale model of Edenville, each building represented either by houses and sheds meant for a train set, or constructed from cardboard and balsa wood. Tiny men, women and children stood around between the trees and shrubs in a miniature park.

The inspector closed his eyes for a moment of peace.

'It's impressive. Don't you think?'

Hobbes wasn't sure how to reply, not easily; not with the creator of this world sitting at its centre, his thin body arched over a tilted easel. Hobbes edged closer to the artist and watched as he worked at his latest piece, a watercolour sketch of a church, no doubt to be placed somewhere within the parish of Edenville.

Gavin Roberts was ten years younger than Lear, an entirely normal-looking man with straggles of mousy hair and a pinched expression on his face. Hobbes tried to get his attention but the man's eyes were fixed only on the point of the brush and the run of paint under the bristles.

Lear came forward and touched his friend's shoulder. 'Gavin, you rang for me?'

Only now did Gavin Roberts remove his attention from the drawing board. 'Yes, I've almost run out of burnt sienna. And I won't be able to paint the church properly without it. Do you see?'

'I do, yes. And it's very beautiful.'

'But I need the paint.'

'I will go to the art shop later today, if there's time. Why don't you make a list for me.'

Gavin nodded eagerly and then went back to work.

The two older men moved away slightly, in order to talk. 'How long has he been like this?' Hobbes found himself whispering.

'It started shortly after Lucas Bell died. That was the trigger. And it's become gradually more pronounced over the years.'

'Do you have any idea what he's trying to do here?'

'Of course I do, he's building Edenville.'

'A fantasy land?'

'Is it any different than writing a novel, or making a movie?'

Hobbes didn't reply.

'Oh, I know, it's dreadful, And some days it pains me to my core to see him like this. But then I think, well, he's happy. Gavin is creating his own world and losing himself in it, and surely that's enough.'

'Mr Lear, how long have you known about Edenville?'

'Lucas told me about it, about a year after we met. He was vague about the details, but he did explain that the place was very important to him, and to his work. In fact, he stated plainly that, without the imaginary village, he wouldn't be writing songs at all. He wouldn't be singing. Of course, I was pledged to the utmost secrecy on these matters, otherwise he would have taken his talents elsewhere.'

'And Gavin, I presume, was also one of the founders of Edenville.'

Lear nodded. 'He was indeed. Otherwise known, in the village, as Bo Dazzle. It was a nickname given to him by his mother. She used to call him her little Bobby Dazzler.' Lear's eyes blinked with happiness. 'Oh, you should've seen Gavin, back in his glory days. He was such a beautiful young man.'

'And when you first met him . . .'

'I didn't have a clue about Edenville, not back then. I knew that Gavin was artistic, right from the start. He drew the cover of Luke's first single. And I knew that he'd lived in Hastings as a child, that he was friends with Lucas from way back when. But that's all. I certainly didn't know that he was part of this crazy, made-up world. That only became evident as I said, after Lucas died.' Lear looked over at his friend and sighed. 'One day he started designing a poster for a group, a group I'd never heard of, the Plastic Flowers.

Now I pride myself on my knowledge of obscure bands, so I asked him about this, and he replied, "They only ever play in Edenville, at the Snake Pit club." And he continued with the drawing, picturing the members of the band in perfect detail, almost as though . . . well, as though they were real. And that was the beginning. The village has grown and grown since then, in his mind, and in this room.'

Lear paused. He took a deep breath and then he said, 'Poor Gavin has left this house only a few times in the last seven years.'

Hobbes found himself staring at the artist. He was, in many ways, looking at a prisoner.

'I'd like to speak with him.'

'Very well. But remember, he's not used to conversing with outsiders.'

Hobbes approached the desk. Gavin Roberts stopped working as the inspector neared. He looked ill at ease suddenly, his shoulders bunched up and his hands clenched.

'Gavin?'

The name brought a negative response. He started to rock in his seat. Hobbes looked over to Toby Lear for help, receiving an encouraging nod. He tried again:

'Or shall I call you Bo? Or Bo Dazzle?'

Now the artist looked up and smiled. 'Gavin is fine, but thank you for asking.'

Hobbes saw in this man's eyes, as though from a sudden burst of knowledge, the entire story. Something terrible had happened to him. Or else he'd taken part in some terrible event that now governed his whole being. Perhaps it was guilt, perhaps murderous intent, perhaps madness – there was no way of knowing for sure – but Gavin Roberts had nowhere left to go other than Edenville. It was his only salvation. And Hobbes knew also that this reclusive man held the truth – the truth behind the ritual killings of Lucas Bell and Brendan Clarke, and the more opportune slaying of Simone Paige.

'Gavin. I'm a police officer. I wish to talk with you. Is that all right?'

There was no response.

'I'd like to ask about the death of Lucas Bell. He didn't kill himself, is that correct?'

A single nod.

'Do you know who killed him?'

Gavin seemed to look deep within himself. And then he spoke quietly but firmly: 'It's a secret.'

Hobbes held the other man's gaze. 'You've made a promise, is that it? Not to tell?'

'More than a promise. Much more.'

'You've taken an oath?'

'Yes, on my life.'

Gavin started to tremble, and Hobbes feared that he might sink back inside himself at any moment. 'What about Brendan Clarke, and Simone Paige? Do you think they were killed by the same person?'

'Brendan, yes. Simone . . . did she wear the mask?'

'No, no, her face was clean.'

'She's different, then. But she's the cause of it all.'

'In what way?'

'She didn't love him enough.'

'She didn't love Lucas Bell, you mean?'

Gavin was suddenly lucid, his sight fully engaged on the inspector. In a clear voice he said, 'I always suspected that Simone would be taken one day.'

'Taken?' Hobbes thought of the phrase he'd learned in Hastings: *taken by the tide.*

'And now, after Mr Clarke was punished, I knew she'd be targeted.'

Hobbes concentrated. 'Gavin, can you tell me the name of the woman who killed Simone Paige?'

'I cannot.' It was a simple admittance. And with that the man's eyes darted back to the watercolour painting on the drawing board.

Hobbes sensed that Roberts kept reaching the limits of what he was allowed to say, according to the rules of the group; rules that were deeply ingrained in his psyche.

'OK. Thank you for answering. What about Brendan Clarke?'

'Brendan, he wore the mask?'

'He did. On stage.'

A sudden frenzy took hold of the artist and he cried out, 'Brendan had to die, then. Yes, he had to die!' Toby Lear moved in quickly and took hold of his friend's shoulders. It did little good; Gavin shook himself and howled from some inner pain. 'He did wrong. Brendan did wrong! Lucas did wrong. Luna Bloom did wrong. They all had to die. They did wrong!'

Lear called out to Hobbes, 'Please, leave him alone.'

But the inspector couldn't give up now. 'What did they do that was so wrong? Gavin, speak to me!'

But the spell was broken. 'My name isn't Gavin! It's Bo. I am Bo Dazzle!'

He pulled away from Lear's grip and lashed out madly, knocking the brushes and pots of paint off the drawing board. They scattered everywhere with a clatter as he smashed at the easel with his bunched fists, over and over, screaming out the whole time:

'They did wrong! They did wrong!'

And then as suddenly as he had panicked, Gavin Roberts calmed again, and he looked at Hobbes properly. The man locked away inside emerged. His eyes were bright and filled with life, and he spoke in a quiet but determined voice.

'They stole the mask. They should never have taken the mask. That's why they had to die. She killed them.'

And Hobbes knew that Roberts was telling the truth, the truth as he knew it.

The vital question remained.

'Who do you mean . . . *she*? Who killed them? Who killed Lucas and Brendan?'

Gavin's lips moved to speak but then the light darkened and he spat out in anger, 'No, it's a secret. I'm not supposed to tell.' His hands tightened and his nails dug into the cartridge paper with its depiction of a village church. The paper ripped, torn in two. He howled in abject, wordless despair.

Lear moved in from behind and pulled Hobbes away.

Gavin Roberts grew quiet at last, until only a whisper remained in his voice. 'They did wrong. The mask killed them.'

The two men moved out into the corridor. 'I told you,' Lear said. 'I did tell you.'

'Yes. I'm sorry,' Hobbes said. 'Is there any way to get some sense out of him?'

'Gavin is talking sense.'

'But only as he knows it, surely? And I need more than that. I need to know who killed Lucas Bell and the others.'

Lear stared through the open doorway. He said in a weary voice, 'I fear I may lose him completely one day. He'll return to Edenville and stay there forever.'

'Have you tried to get help for him?'

'Help? Do you really think someone, some pitiful psychiatrist, can visit the village and pull him back out?'

'I don't know.' Hobbes tried to think. 'Gavin mentioned the name Luna Bloom, just now. He said that Luna Bloom had done wrong. Does that mean that Luna Bloom is the murderer?'

Lear shook his head. 'You mean you don't know?'

'Know what?'

'Lucas told me years ago. We got stoned together one day, and he let it slip.' He smiled at the knowledge, as though finally giving up a secret after years of silence. 'When he was younger, he was known as Luna Bloom.'

Hobbes was puzzled. 'But King Lost, isn't that Lucas's nickname?'

'You really don't understand, do you?'

'Tell me.'

Lear closed the door on the world in the room and turned the key in the lock. Only then did he speak: 'Lucas Bell was never King Lost. Not to begin with. That was someone else. Someone else invented that character. Another member of Edenville.'

'So Lucas . . .'

'That's right.' Lear nodded. 'Lucas stole the king's mask.'

Names on a List

Back at the station, Hobbes rang Hastings and talked to Jan Palmer. She told him that her initial enquiries had revealed nothing of the true identities of the Minerva teens.

'But we're very busy with the Simone Paige murder. So time is short.'

'Tell your chief the cases are definitely linked.'

'Will do. The autopsy's been done, by the way. Five stab wounds, a bad one to the stomach, and one to the heart. Left ventricle. That probably finished her off.'

'I see.' Hobbes closed his eyes. Three murders, three very different locations, and each murder with its own particular mood and atmosphere, so unlike the others. Yet they all circled around Lucas Bell's music, and the King Lost mask.

Was he missing something important?

Palmer carried on. 'I did find time to look through files from the early sixties, regarding people dying, or being killed. There are the usual number of drownings, accidental deaths, and so on.'

'What about murders?'

'Very few out-and-out cases. It's mainly drunken anger or crimes of passion. Husbands killing wives, and vice versa.'

'Nothing about a group of kids killing someone?'

'No, nothing at all like that. But I'll keep looking.'

After he'd finished the conversation, Hobbes had the urge to ring Neville Briggs, to see if he'd managed to develop the negatives found in DI Jenkes's garage; but he resisted. There was work to do here. PC Barlow came into the meeting room and the three officers pooled all the data they had so far.

Hobbes began by writing the word *EDENVILLE* on the incident board.

'In the early sixties, in Hastings, five teenagers met in a literature and arts society called the Minerva Club. This club was run by a local librarian, Eve Dylan. The kids came under Miss Dylan's influence and together they created a fantasy world for themselves.'

'Do we know why they did this?' Latimer asked. 'Barlow? Any clues in the box of delights?'

'I've been through most of the contents. And this . . .' Barlow held up a sheet of paper. 'This is the most important document regarding the village's founding. It's called "Edenville: A Sanctuary for the True Heroes", and it's basically a statement of belief.'

Hobbes watched the young officer at work, and wondered at just how much confidence he'd gained in the last few days. He was no longer nervous in front of the group, and he spoke clearly.

Barlow read the statement aloud:

'Edenville will be a place of safety. A place to hide away in. A private place. A hidden place. It will not be marked on any maps. Edenville is ours, and ours alone. And whenever the world outside becomes too harsh or too dangerous, here we can hide, here we are safe. Edenville will protect us.'

Hobbes took over. 'OK, so let's assume that the five teenagers are outsiders, each in their own way. They feel let down by the normal world. The world might even be a source of pain for them.'

Latimer agreed. 'I think they've all suffered, physically, or mentally. Maybe they're gay, and don't know what to do about it. Or they're friendless. Or they've been bullied. Or maybe abused by a relative.'

'They're scared,' Barlow said.

'Yes, and because of this they feel alone, without hope. And then along comes Eve Dylan, the founder of the Minerva Club.' Saying this, Hobbes wrote the word *LADY MINERVA* on the board. 'She's the leader, or the instigator of everything that follows. And suddenly all these poor kids have a club of their own, a place where they are no longer made fun of. In fact, they're now the kings and queens of the castle. Which brings us to . . .'

He wrote the name *KING LOST* under Lady Minerva.

'King Lost. Now, we've naturally assumed that Lucas Bell was King Lost, right from the beginning, because of his career, and the character he created, or appeared to create on stage and in his songs. But we now know that some other member of Edenville was the original King Lost.'

Barlow added, 'And Lucas Bell's secret name was in fact Luna Bloom.'

'Same initials,' said Latimer. 'L.B.'

Hobbes wrote *LUNA BLOOM* below *KING LOST*, and said, 'In later life, Bell takes up the King Lost moniker for his own. Tobias Lear used the phrase "Lucas stole the king's mask". And Gavin Roberts said the same thing, when he was at his most lucid. Which might possibly give us a motive for these crimes.'

Latimer approached the board. 'Lucas Bell was punished because he stole King Lost?'

Barlow joined them. 'And Brendan Clarke did the same thing, on stage. He stole the mask, by wearing it.'

Latimer frowned. 'And he was killed for it, as well.'

'It's starting to make sense,' said Hobbes.

'Well, as much sense as it can make.'

'It makes sense in Edenville, Meg, I think that's the key. They follow different rules there. In fact, Gavin Roberts claimed that they were both killed for doing wrong, for breaking the rules.'

'So what's so special about this mask, that people have to die if they wear it?'

Nobody answered.

Hobbes continued: 'Now, there are three other founders. Miss Caliban, Bo Dazzle and Mood Indigo.'

He wrote each name on the board, and added the other information they had gathered.

LADY MINERVA – Eve Dylan (Deceased?)
KING LOST – ?
LUNA BLOOM – Lucas Bell (Deceased)
BO DAZZLE – Gavin Roberts
MISS CALIBAN – ?
MOOD INDIGO – ?

The three officers stared at the list. Barlow whistled softly. He said, 'This is crazy. We're investigating two worlds: the real one, and a fantasy realm.'

Hobbes agreed. 'As we progress, the closer we move towards Edenville.'

For a few moments they each contemplated the task ahead. It seemed impossible. Then Hobbes turned to Barlow. 'Did you have any luck with the missing names?'

'No. There's nothing in the box that gives any clue to the founders' real identities. But there was one thing I noticed.'

'Let's hear it.'

'In all the material in the box, there's only one mask depicted, the one belonging to King Lost. That's the only actual drawing of a mask, I mean.'

'And what do you think that indicates?'

'Of all the founders, the person behind the King Lost mask had the most to hide. The fantasy land isn't enough on its own, he needs to hide his real face as well. Which implies that he was suffering the most.'

Latimer asked, 'So where does this lead us?'

'Back to the story,' Hobbes said. 'That's where the truth lies.' He took command of the room. 'The group would meet in the attic of Lucas Bell's home. That was their hideaway, and the centre of operations for the creation of the imaginary village. I don't think Miss Dylan took much part in these undertakings. For some reason, in my mind I can't see her walking past Mum and Dad Bell, and climbing up into a dusty attic with a bunch of teenagers. No, I think she planted the seed, and the kids took it over and made it their own. Edenville was born.'

He paused. Latimer and Barlow were looking at him attentively. And he regretted that Fairfax was missing the meeting; they should all be here for this. But he dismissed the thought and carried on. 'This goes on for a few years, as the teens get older. Lucas comes of age and has a love affair with Miss Dylan. Or was seduced by her. We'll probably never know the exact truth of that.'

He turned to look at the list of names. 'But then something happens. Something bad.'

'But we don't know what it is,' Latimer said.

'When I talked to Nikki Hauser, she said that Lucas had admitted to a crime, something so terrible that it would damage his image, and make the fans turn against him. In fact, she claimed that the Minerva group had killed someone.'

'And the big question is . . . who's the victim?'

Hobbes turned to Barlow. 'Any clues? What the hell did the kids get up to down there on the coast?'

'Well, there's nothing in the Edenville box about any crime they committed. Some of the pieces are dated, with the last one marked February 1966. But there's nothing relating to any disaster, or tragedy, or murder, or anything like that.'

'Maybe Fairfax will bring Nikki Hauser in,' Latimer said. 'We'll get it out of her.'

Hobbes said, 'OK. Because of this mysterious event, let's say the group split up, and Edenville is stored away. The kids grow up. But the village isn't demolished. Lucas Bell gets into music. He leaves Hastings for London and starts his career. And in a very real sense he's bringing Edenville with him, in here . . .' He tapped the side of his head. 'It fuels his songs, his ambition, his imagin-ation. And Lucas isn't alone. He's brought another member of Edenville to London with him: Gavin Roberts.'

'And it may well be that other members are there as well.'

'Maybe, yes.' Hobbes's face creased in concentration. 'But then Lucas Bell reaches a crisis point; he can no longer perform on stage, or write songs. He becomes addicted to drugs. He tries to kill himself by taking an overdose, but fails. And then he falls in love with Simone Paige.'

Latimer tapped her pen against the desk. 'And she tells him to wear a mask.'

'She does. And Bell does the most extraordinary thing: right there in front of her he creates this character, King Lost; he draws the face on a napkin. Now Simone thinks he's making it up as he goes along, in the moment, but he isn't, not at all.'

Barlow took it up next. 'He's reaching back into the past, into his old memories.'

'And he copies the mask of King Lost. He throws aside his own Edenville persona, Luna Bloom, and he takes on that of another member of the group.'

Latimer laughed. 'It's incredible. That one simple act makes him world-famous.'

'And let's assume that, at this point, our murderer becomes interested. Gavin Roberts said that both Lucas and Brendan Clarke had to die, because they wore the mask.'

Latimer said, 'So you think whoever created the mask in the first place is taking revenge on them for stealing it?'

'I don't know.'

Barlow shook his head. 'It seems far-fetched, sir. As a motive, I mean.'

'Yes, yes.' Hobbes pinched the bridge of his nose between finger and thumb. 'Let's keep on. So. Lucas Bell is murdered. The killer makes it look like suicide. And then?'

'And then, nothing,' Latimer said. 'For seven years.'

'That we know of.'

'There's that. She might've killed or injured other people who wore the mask, murders we don't know about. Because nobody's made the connection.'

Barlow shook his head. 'But all those fans in Witch Haven field, they were wearing the mask as well. She can't kill all of them.'

'No, she picks out Brendan Clarke. Because . . .'

'Because he wore it on stage, in such a public manner.'

'Yes, good!' Hobbes looked again at the list of names. 'It all comes back to Edenville. And the real trouble is, the motive for these crimes exists only in a made-up world inside the heads of six people, two of whom are dead.'

'And one who's plain crazy,' Latimer added.

'And one of these remaining people is our perpetrator.' He read the names out loud. 'King Lost, Miss Caliban, Mood Indigo.'

Latimer nodded. 'Are we to assume that Eve Dylan was drowned?'

'It seems likely. I believe someone has taken over her role.'

'As the leader of the group?'

'Yes. She's the new figure of authority. And that gives her the right to kill.'

The phone rang. Latimer answered it.

Barlow said to Hobbes, 'What if we're wrong, sir?' He sounded nervous, raising the doubt. 'I mean, what if someone else entirely is to blame, someone not on the list? How can we be sure?'

'We can't be. We can't be sure.'

Latimer finished on the phone and said in an urgent voice, 'It's about Fairfax, sir.'

'What about him?'

'He's in trouble. He's been in a fight. Apparently, he's attacked someone.'

Ordinary Human Weakness

Hobbes lit a cigarette, just to get the smell of the strip club out of his mouth, and then started to walk down Berwick Street. Soho was crowded. He cut down a side alley to where the car was parked and slipped into the back seat, next to Fairfax. The young officer's carefully gelled hair was awry and his bottom lip was puffed up and marked with a trail of blood. One lapel of his jacket was torn.

'Did you sort it, Henry?'

Chief Superintendent Lockhart spoke from the driver's seat without looking round.

'I hope so,' Hobbes answered.

'DC Fairfax is playing dumb. Isn't that right, Thomas?'

The young officer didn't answer. Hobbes broke the silence. 'The club's called the Blue Moon. It's running some dodgy practices. But nothing illegal, not on the surface.'

'A back room?'

'Yeah.'

'Straight or gay?'

'Probably both.'

'Enterprising, let's give them that.'

'I had to promise them a deal.'

'A blind eye?'

'A month's amnesty.'

'Needs must. I'll sort it with Charing Cross nick.'

Hobbes turned to Fairfax. 'Do you hear that, Tommy? We're having to make deals for you, otherwise . . .'

Lockhart turned round at last. 'Otherwise you'd be up for assault. And you know what that means?'

At last Fairfax spoke, if only a single word: 'Sir.'

The superintendent frowned. 'Do you see that patch of wall over there, Detective, where the water trickles down from the broken gutter?'

Fairfax looked confused.

'Do you see it?'

'Yes, sir.'

'That's where I'd like to smash your fucking head, right there, until your nose breaks and your forehead splits open.'

Seeing the terrifed expression on Fairfax's face, Hobbes had to feel sorry for him.

Lockhart carried straight on: 'I'm this far from kicking you off the force, as it is.'

'Sir, I'm sorry, sir.' Fairfax's voice sounded thick, his damaged lip giving him trouble with the words.

'That's enough apologies. You're turning my stomach.' He glared at the miscreant for a good few seconds, to get the message across, and then looked at Hobbes. 'And you reckon Charlie Jenkes was dealing with them?'

'Yes, it's possible,' Hobbes replied. 'I saw him coming out of the place a few days before he died.'

'Fairfax, what do you reckon?'

There was no response. Hobbes said, 'Tommy, you're in the shit, waist-deep. Don't sink down further.'

The young officer's tongue licked at his broken lip as he made a decision. 'Charlie was bent,' he said. 'I know that now. He was . . .'

'Come on. Spit it out.'

'He was blackmailing someone.'

'Who?'

'I don't know. Possibly more than one person.'

'You're sure? Positive?'

'Yes, sir. I did a bit of digging and found that DI Jenkes was known at a few places in Soho. The Blue Moon was one of them.' Now that he was in confessional mode, the details came easier to him. 'I knew something was going on, words unsaid, and all that.'

'So you decided to beat it out of them,' Hobbes said.

'They got on my wick, sir. Fucking ponces.'

'And you see what happens,' Lockhart said, 'when you go in like a raging bull.'

'They started taunting me, all about DI Jenkes and his nasty habits, and his dirty little schemes, his blackmailing – it all came out, they spat it in my face, like I was to blame. They were loving it, sir! They were saying the cops were all bent, all the same. That we're all bastards, all that. And so . . .'

'And so you waded in.'

'I did what I had to do.'

Lockhart scowled. He turned back to face the windscreen. 'I'd like to know why you were looking into Jenkes. That's the mystery.'

'Because he was murdered. Well, that's the story, isn't it?'

Now Lockhart went quiet. Hobbes watched as the superintendent's head bowed down slightly. He would have to take over, try to protect Fairfax as best he could.

'The detective constable was very close to DI Jenkes, sir, when he was younger. He looked up to him, and he feels angry that his mentor might have been killed. He acted irrationally and out of character, and he knows that now.'

Lockhart's head shook from side to side. He didn't speak.

Hobbes tried again. 'He knows he's done wrong, Chief.'

Lockhart grunted. 'Get him out of my sight.'

'Right-oh. Come on, Fairfax, out you get.'

Hobbes had to lean over and open the door for him, but eventually Fairfax made it out of the car. For a moment it looked as though he was going to lean in at the driver's window and make another apology, or another justification, but he thought better of it and started off down the alleyway.

'I'm not twisting my neck any more, Henry. Not at my age.'

'No. Of course not.' Hobbes got out and climbed in the front passenger seat and waited for judgement to be passed.

'I really thought you'd keep the lid on this.'

'I tried. I don't know where the stories are coming from.'

'Well, it's too late now, too bloody late.' Lockhart pursed his lips. 'So then, is there anything in this blackmailing story?'

'There might be. I've found some negatives that DI Jenkes was hiding. I'm having them developed today. But there are other possibilities.' He decided to keep Lisa Jenkes's affair private, for now, in case it came to nothing.

Lockhart nodded his head. He laughed and said, 'He's got gumption, that Fairfax. I'll give him that. Sticking his snout in where it doesn't belong. Mind, I used to do the same thing, when I was his age.'

'What shall I do with him?'

'Why, you take him on board. Best place for him, at your side. Otherwise, he'll go off like a grenade in a tea shop.'

'And what if another copper's involved?'

Lockhart's mouth set in a hard thin line. 'The thing is, Henry, there's pressure from on high, from the gods themselves. The bad press is finally getting to them. We need to clean our dirty laundry in public.'

'No more cover-ups?'

'Spot on.'

'That might be a good thing, actually.'

Lockhart stared at him. 'Don't give me the bleeding-heart routine, please. Despite everything you might think about me, or everything you might have heard . . . if there's one thing I fucking hate, it's corrupt cops.'

'Sir.'

'So, get this sorted! Whatever the outcome.'

The conversation was over. Hobbes got out of the car and watched as Lockhart drove away. He walked back on to Berwick Street and headed over to where his own car was parked. There was a telephone box nearby. He rang Neville Briggs.

'Have you got round to those negatives yet?'

'I've only just got in. I was on a shoot—'

'Now, please. Get on it.'

Hobbes put down the handset without waiting for an answer. He couldn't move. The phone box smelt of urine and aftershave. He waited until the moment of stasis had passed, then he rummaged through his pockets until he found a slip of paper with an address written on it.

He drove back over towards Ilford.

The house was identical to all the others in the council estate but was well looked after. The front door had been freshly painted and the small garden was neat and tidy. Hobbes rang the bell and waited until a harassed-looking young black woman opened it.

'Mrs Patterson?'

'Yes.'

'Is your husband in?'

'Can I ask what it's about?' She spoke in a mixture of Cockney and Jamaican.

'A private matter.'

Her eyes narrowed, and a deep set of creases appeared on her brow. She opened her mouth to protest, but he'd already had enough by then. He showed her his warrant card.

'We need some information from him, regarding a pupil at his school.'

That seemed to settle her and she vanished down the corridor. A minute later Lloyd Patterson arrived at the door, a man of medium height, wearing spectacles and a brown check shirt with a loosely knotted woollen tie, both covered by a Fair Isle tank top. He looked every inch the old-fashioned English teacher, except for the colour of his skin.

'Yes, can I help you?'

Hobbes lowered his voice. 'I hope so. It's about your affair with Lisa Jenkes.'

Panic took over. Patterson looked nervously over his shoulder, to see if his wife was still there. She wasn't, but he stepped out on to the street anyway and part-closed the door.

'I have my car over here,' Hobbes said. 'If you'd prefer?'

'Yes, yes. Thank you.'

They walked across the road to the car and sat next to each other in the driver and passenger seat.

'I don't wish to cause you undue trouble,' Hobbes said. 'I told your wife that I need information about a pupil. You can make up any story you like.'

Patterson didn't reply. He was looking through the windscreen over towards the front door of his house, as though expecting his wife to appear and start walking towards them, but the road was empty and quiet. A slight breeze moved the branches of an elm tree growing out of the pavement, and a cat slinked by and disappeared through the gap in a fence.

Hobbes got right to it. 'I don't care what you get up to in your personal life, Mr Patterson. I just need to know one thing.'

He paused. The passenger turned to look at him, a look of utter trepidation on his face.

'Did you kill Detective Inspector Jenkes?'

A moment passed. Patterson almost laughed but then stopped himself.

'I don't understand,' he said.

'It's very simple. Did you or did you not—'

'Yes, I heard you. But I really do not understand why you're asking me this.'

'You made threats against Jenkes's life. Isn't that correct?'

'I won't conceal it, I did. I think he was a nasty piece of work, and I haven't shed a tear over his death. I doubt that any black man or woman in London has done so. But no, I didn't kill him.' He hesitated. 'In fact, I thought he'd killed himself?'

Hobbes didn't respond to this. He said, 'And you don't know of anyone who would want to hurt him? Any of your friends?'

'We're not all savages.'

Hobbes kept his cool. 'I'm talking to a number of people, most of them are white. Believe me: when it comes to villains, I'm colour blind.'

Now Patterson did laugh, and loudly. 'I'll be sure to call you, next time I get pulled over.'

They fell to silence. Hobbes said, 'Why are you still bothering Lisa Jenkes?'

'Are you friends with her?'

'I am. An old friend.'

'Would you believe me if I told you I was in love with her?'

'What about your wife?'

Patterson shook his head sadly. 'We've been having problems.'

It was all so pitiful, Hobbes thought. Such everyday passions and despairs. Is that all it was, a bored man and a frustrated woman drawn together in search of excitement? How long would it last, he wondered. If it ever came to anything, that is, given the various obstacles that would have to be overcome.

As DI Collingworth used to say: *Look for the ordinary human weakness, Henry. No matter how big the crime, simple emotions always lie at the heart.*

'Tell me. You met with Jenkes, I believe?'

'*Met with?* The man beat me up.'

Hobbes smiled. 'You were sleeping with his wife . . .'

'And that allows him to hurt me? To hit me, to kick me?'

'What would you do, if someone was sleeping with your wife?'

'I am a Christian man, Inspector.'

'Yet you commit adultery?'

Patterson made a noise with his lips. His voice changed as he quoted chapter and verse. '*Therefore do not let sin reign in your mortal body so that you obey its lusts. For sin shall not be master over you, for you are not under law, but under grace.'*

'The Bible?'

'Romans, 6:12. Of course, we are merely human, not divine.'

'What did Jenkes say to you? Anything?'

'Is this important?'

'There's a chance that he might have been murdered. We're not yet sure. But I'm looking for any possible motivation. Or any information about the state of his character.'

Patterson nodded. 'He was full of rage, I will say that. Absolute fury. He seemed to know that something would happen, in Brixton.'

'There had been trouble brewing for a while.'

'He made general threats against my race, and said that we'd get what was coming to us, one day soon.'

The inspector frowned. More and more he was seeing this other side of Jenkes. No, not another side, because the tendency had always been there. But it had been much worse than he'd ever let on. Unless Hobbes had decided to ignore it, for the sake of friendship. Again he felt the stab of guilt.

'You look like a man who's lost his way,' Patterson said. 'Are you troubled?'

Hobbes didn't give an answer. There was a pause. The cat reappeared through the gap in the fence and sauntered away, its adventure complete.

Patterson said, 'I do know who you are, Inspector Hobbes. I saw your photograph in the paper, and I read the reports about poor Michael Hennessey. And I guess I should be grateful to you, for what you did that night. I guess we should all be grateful; is that what you expect?'

'I'm not expecting anything.'

'But did you do enough, Inspector? Isn't that the question?'

'It is. Without a doubt.'

'How would you answer?'

'I don't need to answer, not to you.'

'That may be so. But to yourself?'

Hobbes stared at his passenger. And then he spoke in a quiet voice. 'No. No, I didn't do enough.'

Patterson nodded. But then he stared out through the window and saw his wife at the door of the house. She was looking up and down the street, her arms folded across her chest.

Now he spoke quickly. 'There was something said that night, when I was beaten up, it might be relevant to your search.'

Hobbes was suddenly alert. 'Yes?'

'But it's not a question of what Detective Jenkes said. It's what the other man said.'

'The other man?'

'There were two of them.'

'Another cop?'

'I don't know.'

'Do you have a name?'

'No. Not that I heard.'

'What did he look like? Did you see?'

'Not really. It was dark, and I'd never seen him before.' But Patterson made an effort to remember. 'Short hair, sports jacket. A tough-looking guy. That's all. He did most of the hitting.'

The description fit any number of the coppers Hobbes knew. 'And what did this second man say to you?'

'Not to me. To Jenkes, when I was lying on the ground. It was the last thing I heard. He said, "I hope this settles it between us." And then the final boot came in and I blacked out.'

'You didn't hear DI Jenkes's reply?'

Patterson shook his head. 'Look, I really need to get back to Ellie. There will be hell to pay, otherwise.' He made to get out of the car, but Hobbes stopped him.

'There's one more thing I need to ask . . .'

'I know. Keep away from Lisa, right?'

'She doesn't need any more hurt in her life.'

Patterson leaned in at the open door. 'Don't worry, Inspector. Two days ago I found out that my wife is pregnant. We are expecting our first child. I am fully committed to that task.'

And with that he was gone, hurrying across the street.

Hobbes watched as he drew level with his wife, who had come out into the road. The couple talked for a moment, then walked back to their house. The door closed behind them. He sat there for a while, thinking about the second man who had helped Jenkes in his attack, and the remark he'd made. Then he started the car and headed south towards Notting Hill.

Neville Briggs greeted him and invited him into the darkroom.

'They're just drying,' the photographer told him. 'I must say, they're an intriguing set of images.' He unclipped the photographs from the line strung above the workbench and showed them to Hobbes. 'I suppose the younger participant must be a rent boy.'

Hobbes remained silent. The images passed before his eyes.

'And the older gentleman, he seems to be having most of the fun. I imagine he's paid a lot for the pleasure. Do you know him?'

Hobbes did. In fact, he recognized both participants.

He left without saying another word and drove through the darkening city back towards home. The flat seemed tinier than ever. He went to make himself a cup of tea, but there was no milk in the fridge. He walked to the newsagents on the corner and bought supplies. He needed time to think, to consider what to do next. He looked over the newspapers and magazines on display in the shop, thinking how out of touch he was with the wider world. He turned towards the exit, but something made him stop in his tracks.

The sign of a cross.

And a pair of eyes.

He turned back to the shelves. Yes, there, on the cover of the *New Musical Express*, the top half of a face was visible on the folded front page.

A blue cross painted on a forehead.

He took the magazine from the rack and opened it so he could see the cover image completely. King Lost stared back at him. Another person had taken up the mask.

The headline at the top read 'Lucas Bell Special Issue'. And at the bottom in smaller letters: 'Johnny Valentine: This Time It's For Real'. And now Hobbes recognized the face partly hidden behind the painted mask. It was the washed-up singer, the friend of Nikki Hauser who had helped her escape from Witch Haven field.

He asked the newsagent when the magazine had come in.

'This morning. It's terrible, isn't it, that picture? Why would a person do that to themselves? I had to cover it up so as not to shock my customers.'

'Yes. I can see that.'

'Perhaps they think it will help them sell more copies?'

'That's probably it.'

Hobbes stared at the image. Valentine had gone further than any other wearer of the mask, further even than Lucas Bell. The photographer had actually caught the singer in the act of cutting the mask away. Hobbes thought at first it was fake blood streaming down the face, but no, it wasn't; it was real. As real as the cut in the skin was real. As real as the knife in the hand, and real as the blood on the blade of the knife. And he knew just from looking at the image that the person wearing the mask would become the next victim: Johnny Valentine was destined to die.

And more than that, now Hobbes knew why the other victims had been killed.

Lipstick Scar

The night sergeant at Kew Road told him that most of the officers were out on a warehouse break-in. Hobbes rang Fairfax but got no answer even after twenty rings. He slammed his palm on his desk. A lone WPC looked over and then went back to her work. Hobbes rummaged through the filing cabinets and through every drawer in Fairfax's desk but could find no address for Johnny Valentine. Again, he tried Fairfax, letting the telephone ring and ring, without answer. He rang Nikki Hauser's number. Her flatmate answered and told him that Nikki wasn't in, and she didn't know where she was.

'Do you need some help, sir?'

Hobbes looked up. It was the young WPC.

'You look a bit lost. Sir. If you don't mind my saying.'

Quickly he explained that he was looking for the address of a person connected to a murder case, something DC Fairfax was investigating.

'In what connection, exactly?'

'A known associate of another person, Nikki Hauser.'

As the constable started to search, Hobbes took out his copy of the *New Musical Express* and turned to the double-page spread of the interview. Here the singer was pictured in the full King Lost mask before the cutting had taken place. He was smiling, enjoying himself at this stage, happy to be back in the spotlight, even if it was someone else's spotlight he had stolen. And knowing perhaps, inside, what he would do later on, when asked the right question by the journalist. There wasn't time to read it all now, but perhaps the self-wounding was planned from the beginning – a hidden knife, a determined plan of action? Fame beckoned. Notoriety. Or perhaps the ultimate act of spiritual bonding: Bell and Valentine, joined by a wound. Hobbes remembered the freshly healed scar he had seen on Valentine's face at Witch Haven. This interview had already taken place by then, perhaps a few days before. He turned back to the cover image, with its terrible sight of flesh opened up, the blood coloured dark on the grey newsprint.

Again he thought of the reason for the murders. Of course, of course! It all seemed so obvious now.

Three deaths already. Maybe another one soon, unless he acted quickly.

The constable found Valentine's home address in a file dedicated to Nikki Hauser. Hobbes looked at the file and frowned. The name of the street and the district brought back bad memories.

'What's your name, Constable?'

'Thornhill, sir.'

'Right, you're with me.'

They drove east via the South Circular Road, skirting Clapham Common. Traffic was light at this time of night and they made good time. It was unsettling, to be travelling along Brixton Hill Road again, as he had done the night of the riot. Groups of youths were hanging around on the street corners, standing under street lamps, smoking, bursting into laughter. Loud blasts of music could be heard, the heavy treading beat of dub reggae.

'It's scary round here, sir.'

'Keep looking at the map, Thornhill.'

She had the *A–Z* of London open on her lap. 'Someone told me you were in the riot, is that true?' Her voice was a mixture of fascination and fear. 'What was that like? Were you scared? Did you smash any heads in?' The words tumbled out. 'Will we be crossing over the frontline?'

'You think it's a war zone?'

'What else can it be?'

'People live here—'

She didn't let him finish. 'I heard that officers hate patrolling the Railton Road area. That's where the black gangs rule the streets.'

Hobbes sighed. 'What's your name, Constable? Your first name?'

'Madeline. Everyone calls me Maddy.'

He'd seen her around the station but had never talked to her before now. She was a person still seeking a place in the world, at least to his eyes, and he wondered about the events and emotions that had led her towards wearing the uniform.

They took a right on to Coldharbour Lane.

'They're just people, Maddy. Sometimes they go a bit crazy, but that's what people do, black or white. And sometimes the world gets too much and we go crazier than ever, and then we regret our actions, and we try to make good.'

Actually, they could be anywhere, anywhere in the city as night cloaked the streets and the lights showed warm behind closed curtains and men and woman grew raucous and giddy outside the pub doors. Yet he knew in his heart how close he was to shutdown, if he thought about it too much. Shakespeare Road was up ahead.

Don't think about it. Keep driving, just keep driving.

Thornhill was talking non-stop. 'My boyfriend reckons we should send them all back home, but I wouldn't go that far, not as long as they stay within their limits—'

'Will you shut the fuck up!'

The car swerved slightly and a wheel hit the kerb. Hobbes brought the vehicle to a halt and he sat there staring ahead, in silence. He could feel the constable's tension, her fear of him. Her hatred, perhaps.

'There's no need to shout. Sir.'

Her voice wavered, seeking strength.

'I just need . . .' He turned to her. 'I just need to get to the address that I gave to you, as quickly as possible. A man's life is at stake.'

She held his stare for a moment and then said, 'It's the second on the left.'

'Thank you.'

They set off again and found the street. Nothing more was said, not until he asked her to keep an eye out for number 59.

'I can't see it anywhere.'

'I think it might be above one of those shops.'

He parked the car and they got out and walked along the row. Every window was covered with a grille, or else boarded up completely. The riot's aftermath. The only shop still open at this hour was an off-licence. The man behind the counter was protected by the wire mesh of a screen.

'I'm looking for number fifty-nine.'

'Directly above us. Entrance round the back.'

Outside again, Hobbes looked up at the single storey above the shop. Two windows, one dark, the other dimly lit. A flickering light. Curtains half drawn.

'This way, sir.'

Thornhill had found an alleyway further along the row. They hurried down it to the rear of the buildings and clattered up the metal stairs to a walkway above. Hobbes knocked on the door. They waited.

'Is this really where Johnny Valentine lives?' Thornhill asked. 'He's come down in the world, that's for sure.'

Hobbes banged on the door, louder this time. There was still no response. He moved to the window and peered through into an unlit kitchen. Beyond that he could see a corridor and a weak light. He went back to the door and placed his ear against the wood. Silence at first. But then he pressed closer.

'Can you hear that?'

Thornhill listened as well. Their faces were inches apart on the door panel.

'It's a voice. I think,' she said.

'A woman's voice?'

'I think so, yes. She's singing.'

Hobbes stepped back. He raised his leg and kicked as hard as he could. The door was weak, badly made, with a single mortise lock. The wood splintered at the first attempt and the door swung inwards to bang against the inner wall.

Thornhill gasped. He grabbed her by the shoulders. 'Stay here.' He stepped inside the flat.

The singing had stopped. All was quiet.

Three lighted candles marked the way forward, down a corridor. There was a kitchen, a bathroom and a bedroom, all in darkness, and one other door, open, leading to a small living room. A woman was lying on the floor of the corridor, just beyond the doorway. Her body was pushed up against the wall amid a pile of scattered shoes and boots.

It was Nikki Hauser.

Hobbes pressed his fingers against her neck, seeking life. Her skin was warm. A pulse. She stirred at his touch, and moaned. He couldn't help thinking: why had she been singing like that, from what depths had the melody arisen? It didn't make sense. He moved to the door of the living room and peered in, trying to take in the scene before him. No electric lights were on. But a candle stood on the window ledge, the flickering glow he had seen from outside. And more candles were placed on the floor, standing in saucers and ashtrays. They formed a half-circle around the armchair in the corner of the room.

Here was Johnny Valentine.

A figure slumped down, unmoving, both arms draped over the sides of the chair. He was dressed in jeans and a white T-shirt. Hobbes took a single step into the room and then stopped. He forced himself to examine the body from where he stood.

There was blood on the side of Valentine's neck. The exact same position as the fatal wound that had killed Brendan Clarke. The face was marred by hundreds of cuts, each one tiny, covering the entire range of skin in criss-cross patterns. The self-inflicted wound from the interview was even more prominent than before, the long scar coloured a vivid red with what looked to be lipstick, its bright colouring extending beyond the edges of the wound on to the skin itself. He'd been given a second mouth, a cruel and vicious sideways grin.

Valentine looked like a monster in the candlelight, an evil clown who had reached a sorry end after the last show in town has closed down.

There was a card lying on his lap, a tarot card.

The card trembled slightly.

Hobbes held his breath.

The card moved again, fell to the carpet.

Hobbes stepped closer, reached out a hand.

The body shuddered and lurched upwards, grabbing at him.

Valentine drew in one great lungful of air and cried out with all his passion, as though the word, the very sound of his lover's name, might hook itself into the flesh of life and drag him backwards from the brink, from the darkness.

'Nikki, Nikki!'

Each utterance speckled Valentine's lips with blood.

'Help me.'

Quieter now, the voice losing power, the eyes gazing upwards in the sockets. And then the body slumped once more into the chair. Hobbes shook at the full weight of the man. It did no good. Yet still he urged him to speak, to offer help.

'Valentine. Don't fall asleep.'

There was no answer. Only blood dribbling from the corner of the mouth.

Hobbes checked for signs.

A faint pulse, a wing's flutter.

There was a cry from behind him. He let go of the body and turned. It was WPC Thornhill, standing in the doorway. Her hand was covering her mouth. He shouted at her. 'We'll need an ambulance and backup. Quickly!' She turned and vanished down the corridor.

Hobbes attended to Valentine. He checked the wound in the neck: it had stopped bleeding. The killer had slightly missed her mark this time. Hobbes pressed the side of his head against the man's chest and listened for breath, but all he could hear was the distant echo of his own voice as he whispered, 'Don't worry. We're here. We're here now.'

The message went unanswered.

Valentine was dead.

Hobbes stood up straight. The room enclosed him. Two of the candles had fallen to the floor and the smell of extinguished wax drifted through the air. He moved to the corridor and looked down at Nikki Hauser. Her eyes were now fully open and she said with laboured breath, 'Johnny? Is he all right?'

Hobbes bent down to her. 'Don't move, you've been injured.'

There was blood matted in her hair.

He had a sudden fear, that Valentine's calling of her name at the end was actually an accusation. Perhaps Hauser was the killer?

He couldn't take any chances. He held her in place. Her eyes stared back at him. Her mouth moved to speak but then closed again. She looked fearful, and one of her hands came up and grabbed at his wrist for comfort, for safety. Or was it a threat?

She whispered, 'Listen.'

'Don't move, Nikki—'

Her hand tightened around his wrist. 'Listen, listen!'

And then he heard it for himself.

A noise. A woman's voice, singing.

Hobbes stood upright and looked back down the corridor, towards the kitchen.

Nikki Hauser knelt up to a sitting position and she looked over towards the open door of the bedroom; the fear sat in her eyes like twin pools of darkness.

Now Hobbes understood; the killer was still here.

He moved carefully, setting his feet down without a sound. He could see Thornhill ahead, standing at the kitchen door. He held her back with a raised hand signal.

A door on the left, open.

He looked in. The room was pitch-black.

Silent now.

His hand moved, seeking a light switch. He couldn't find it.

And then he heard the voice again, the song. Softly, softly. That familiar melody slowed almost to a crawl. The words tender, broken by the pain of memories. *Just another backstreet harlequin, lost in the Soho blues.* Hobbes stared ahead, willing his eyes to see further, to become accustomed to the dark. Until at last he saw a shape in the now greying room.

She was standing against the far wall, her arms hanging down at each side. Her hair was tousled, and shoulder-length and very dark. Her skin was painted white, with grey circles daubed around the closed eyes. There was a blemish on the chin, below the left edge of the mouth. Hobbes thought it might also be painted on. The woman's face was motionless except for the lips, which moved to form the rest of the song. *I've given just about all I can give, now there's nothing left to lose.* And then the eyes opened and glared at him. Madness. And sheer hatred. Hobbes stepped forward into the room. He couldn't make out what he was seeing; the murderer's expression puzzled him. He felt the whole case was balanced on this moment, that he needed to gather from these few passing seconds every last ounce of information. And then the killer raised a hand to show him the blood dark on her fingers and palm, a mark of pride.

'Don't move,' he said.

Her other hand came up as she stepped forward, and he had but a moment to glimpse the knife in her grip before she attacked.

Hobbes bent away and he felt her rush past him, making for the open door.

Now he was frozen, his body in shock. He cried out, 'Thornhill!'

A scream. Footsteps clattering.

Hobbes moved at last.

The corridor. Thornhill and the woman struggling together at the kitchen door.

He reached them just as the policewoman was pushed back. The woman darted through the door.

'Are you all right? Officer?'

'Go on, sir. Catch her!'

He ran out on to the walkway and looked over the balcony but could see nothing. And then a shadow moved across the yard below, vanishing down an alleyway. Hobbes made it to the stairs and rushed down. He ran to the alley. It was empty, end to end, a faulty lamp halfway down measuring his heartbeat. He ran down it anyway, and reached a junction of two roads. They were both deserted.

A police siren called to him through the night. A lonely sound.

Hobbes turned and walked back towards Valentine's flat. As he did so, a single thought worried him. Somewhere beneath the paint and colour of the killer's disguise, somewhere in her real eyes, her real features – somewhere beneath the mask was the face of a woman he had seen before.

FRIDAY

28 AUGUST 1981

The Story of a Mask

He stood at the viewing glass and looked through into the interview room. DS Latimer was sitting at the table opposite Nikki Hauser, while PC Barlow stood to attention near the door. Hauser was dabbing at her face with a handkerchief. Hobbes couldn't help thinking back to when he'd been here looking at Simone Paige. Five days ago, that's all. There was a madness at large, and he'd failed, failed to stem the flow of blood.

It had been a long night and they were still working the case at past two in the morning. His head bowed until his forehead pressed against the glass. The coldness was pleasant and he felt himself drifting away.

'So it's true?' a voice asked. 'Hauser saw it all happen?'

Hobbes came upright. Fairfax was staring at him.

'Where have you been?'

'A friend's house.'

Hobbes held his anger at bay. 'I needed you here.'

'Sir, it won't happen again.'

There wasn't a trace of irony in Fairfax's voice, and Hobbes nodded in response. He noted that the detective constable had got himself cleaned up and shaved since the last time he'd seen him, in Lockhart's car.

'What's she said?'

'Nothing. She was attacked, knocked out. That's all we know.'

'Description of the killer? Anything?'

Hobbes shook his head.

'But she knows something?'

'She does.'

Fairfax made a clicking noise with his tongue. 'About earlier . . . about the strip joint, and Superintendent Lockhart, and all that . . .'

Hobbes studied the younger man's face. 'I've made progress,' he said.

'On the Jenkes case? Really?'

'Yes, I found some evidence, photographs. Sex-related.'

'Evidence of blackmail? So I was right?'

Hobbes nodded. 'Charlie was putting the screws on someone. Another copper, I think.'

'Someone from Charing Cross?'

'Looks that way.'

'Tell me, who is it?'

Hobbes thought of Lockhart's advice, to bring Fairfax on board. But it still seemed a step too far.

'Look, Tommy, we'll get to this in a day or so. There are more urgent matters at hand.'

'Of course.'

Latimer came in. 'It's hopeless, guv. I can't get anything out of her.'

Fairfax tapped on the glass with his fingertips. 'Do you want me to have a go?'

'Not yet.'

Hobbes left the room without another word and walked downstairs to the canteen. No kitchen staff were working at this time of night, so he bought a black coffee and a Mars bar from the vending machine and sat down at a table. He thought about the latest events. About a woman he was sure he'd seen somewhere else, and quite recently.

The thin, aquiline nose. The long dark hair. Those perfectly round eyes, almost like coins: imagine them without the make-up . . .

It was no good, the thoughts slipped away.

The canteen was quiet. One other table was occupied, two constables talking quietly. They left him alone, and he was glad of that. The coffee did its best to fight against his tiredness. He'd brought his copy of the *New Musical Express* with him and he opened it now.

The journalist started off by placing Johnny Valentine's life and work in context, how he used to be a close friend and bandmate of Lucas Bell, how important they both were in the early days of glam rock. 'But I tell you this: Lucas was the best of us.' Here the journalist described Valentine pausing to drink from a whisky bottle before reminiscing: 'You could see the dreaming take hold in his eye. Lucas was gazing ahead, far off down the road.'

And then Hobbes saw the word *Eden* mentioned.

The writer was asking about the rock and roll dream, whether such a thing had ever really existed, and if so, how it had changed over the last decade or so, and Valentine answered, 'We're building a mansion. But they keep tearing it down. And the only dream left to us is chasing the dollar. Lucas said to me once, "We've been kicked out of Eden." And that's the feeling I'm talking about. Exactly that.' The writer asked what he meant by the word *Eden*. 'Paradise. It was a story he told me once, a secret story.' The writer tried to prise this secret out of him, but Valentine went off on one of his habitual tangents, and said, 'It's no bloody wonder we're all going crazy, cold and alone out here in the night. We're all destroying our masks. Even now. Now more than ever. It's just that Lucas got there first. The poor guy.'

Hobbes reread the passage. 'It was a story he told me once, a secret story.' And that one particular phrase: *Lucas said to me once, 'We've been kicked out of Eden.'* Which meant that Johnny Valentine had possessed knowledge, at least partially. He'd known something about Edenville.

Latimer joined him at the table. She said, 'Fairfax went in anyway, and had a go at Hauser.'

'How's he doing?'

'Shouting at her, red in the face.'

'Little good that will do.'

'I'm worried about Tommy, actually.'

'Oh yes. Why's that?'

'Well . . .' She sipped from a can of fizzy orange. 'Maybe he's fallen in with a bad lot. Or else . . .'

'Yes?'

'He's working another case, in secret.'

Hobbes kept his face straight. 'Any idea what it is?'

She looked at him, and grinned. 'No. But maybe you do?'

'Me?'

'Yourself. The man in charge.'

'Sorry, Meg, can't help you there.'

'You're a terrible liar, guv.' She pulled the magazine towards her. 'Silly fool.'

'Me?'

'No, this guy. Valentine.' She pointed to the cover. 'You reckon it's all about destroying the mask?'

'Yes, that's it, I'm sure. It's the connecting point, the one thing all three of the victims did: Bell, Clarke and Valentine, they all cut or pretended to cut the mask, in full public view. Either on stage, or in the press. They caused blood to run down the mask, fake or otherwise. It's a symbolic act.'

Latimer nodded. 'I've read the article. It looked to me like Valentine knew something about Edenville?'

'This is about more than killing off potential witnesses. It's about ritual. And this has been true from the very start, going back to the Minerva Club in the sixties. And I believe that's why the first two murders are so different; Bell's was made to look like a suicide, out of desperation, probably, but the intervening years have given the ritual more power. It's now an act of faith. So there was no attempt to cover up Brendan Clarke's murder: it was a statement, a public warning.'

Latimer took another sip from her can. 'It still doesn't tell us why, though. What's so bad about destroying a mask?'

'For that we need to get inside the murderer's head.'

Hobbes drained his coffee cup and put out a cigarette he couldn't remember lighting. He noticed three stubs in the ashtray, all of them his. Suddenly, he felt drained. It must've shown in his face because Latimer looked at him and said, 'Sir, you're tired. Let's start again in the morning.'

He shook his head. 'I could've saved Valentine. Just a few minutes too late.'

'You can't be sure—'

'Meg, there can't be any more, no more killings, there can't be!'

The outburst forced him into action. He pushed all thoughts of sleep aside and stood up, telling Latimer to go home.

'What about you?'

'Another shot at Hauser. I'm going to ask her about the only man she really loved.'

'Would that be Bell, or Clarke?'

'Neither.'

He walked back to the interview room, taking his time on the stairs, making sure his thoughts were in order. He took over from Fairfax, who shook his head in passing. 'It's no good. She won't budge.'

Hobbes sat down opposite Nikki Hauser. He placed the *New Musical Express* on the table, the cover image uppermost. Then he studied Nikki's face. She looked ghastly, half dead herself. Her face was whiter than ever, highlighting the old pockmarks, and her eyes were smudged all around where the tears had done their work.

A dressing had been placed over a cut high on her left-side brow.

'You were fond of this man, weren't you?' He tapped at the photograph of Valentine on the magazine's cover. 'Nikki?'

She gave a barely perceptible nod. 'He was my friend. No one else offered that to me.'

'And you loved him back. Because a friendship like that, it's all too rare.'

She stared at him. 'You wouldn't understand.'

Hobbes nodded at this. He pushed the magazine towards her. 'Did you know that Mr Valentine planned to wound himself in this way?'

Her head shook slightly and she whispered, 'No. It was a surprise to me.'

'Were you at the interview?'

Her eyes flicked down. One hand reached out across the table and adjusted the paper so she could see the cover shot more clearly.

'Johnny . . .' Her voice cracked with emotion. 'Poor, poor Johnny.'

Hobbes leaned closer. 'Take me back, Nikki. Tell me the story. What do you know about the mask?'

The question triggered something in her, a memory, or more likely a regret, and she spoke clearly for the first time. 'Wearing it is fine. But cutting into it, wounding it . . . that's wrong. It's a terrible thing to do.'

'I see.' Now he had her talking, there could be no gaps, no silences. 'And how did you know this?'

'Lucas told me.'

'It was his secret?'

'One of them, yes. He confessed to me.'

Again, Hobbes felt the need to tread carefully. 'When did Johnny's magazine interview take place?'

'Thursday. Last week.'

'Did you go along with him?'

'No. He wanted to do it alone. Just him, the interviewer, the photographer. And then afterwards, he came round to my flat and I saw his face, I saw what he'd done to himself, and I wept. I wept. I couldn't stop myself.'

'What made you weep? The fact that he'd cut himself?'

300

'No. I was used to Johnny slashing himself. But he usually did it out of sight, you know? The chest, the arms. But this was different. And I knew then, as soon as I saw him. I knew Johnny was going to die.'

'What did you do? You helped him, didn't you?'

'I cleaned him up. I put a dressing on him. The wound wasn't too deep. I could tell his hand had faltered.' Her mouth crinkled at the thought of it. 'And then I told him the truth, at least as I knew it, about the mask, and the killer. I thought Johnny would listen, and take care. But all he did was get stoned. So I rang the editor at the paper and I pleaded with him not to run the interview, or to miss out the bit about Johnny cutting himself, or at least not to use the photographs.'

'He wouldn't listen?'

'Of course not.' Her face creased with anger. 'This was a great story, something nasty for the people to stare at.'

Hobbes tried to keep to the events as they happened, one by one.

'What about your gig on Saturday, with Monsoon Monsoon? You seemed happy enough to let Brendan damage the mask—'

She exploded. 'No!' Her white face took on a flush of colour and her eyes narrowed to slits. 'No, I didn't know about that.'

'The cutting wasn't part of the plan?'

'Brendan and I talked about him dressing up for the night, and doing some songs from Luke's albums, that's all. A celebration. In fact, when we were getting ready I tried to persuade him not to wear the mask on stage. He wouldn't listen. So I told him not to do anything silly, I made him promise.' She paused to wipe at her face. 'I was as shocked as everyone else there that night, when he pulled out the knife.'

Her whole body suddenly trembled with remembered pain.

'You drove him home, after the gig?'

'I tried to make him stay with me, to come round to my place. But he was too angry at me still. And also . . .'

Hobbes completed the thought for her: 'He'd just met Simone Paige?'

'He had. He was so pleased with himself. But I did try to warn him. I really did.'

She looked away.

Hobbes considered for a moment, then he said, 'Johnny Valentine must've been angry, I imagine, when he found out about Brendan Clarke's antics on stage. Because the magazine wouldn't come out until after the gig, so he'd seem like a copycat.'

'No. Johnny didn't give a shit. He'd gone one better, hadn't he? He'd sliced the face open. For real.' She sneered. 'Rock and roll, live or die.'

'So now you had two men in danger. Two men you loved.'

Her head bowed down and she started to murmur. 'Why? Why, why, why?' That was her only question, directed entirely to herself. And she answered it almost immediately, saying, 'I was drawn to them. As they were drawn to me.'

Hobbes gave her a moment. Then he asked, 'So after Brendan was killed, you must've been scared for Johnny?'

'I was! Like I said, I pleaded with the editor to ditch the interview.'

'And then at Witch Haven . . .'

'I only went because Johnny was so determined to go. I had to keep him safe. He wanted to walk around with the scar on full view, but I made him put a sticking plaster over it.'

'Wasn't he afraid by then? After Brendan's death, I mean?'

Hauser grabbed the edge of the table. 'He didn't care. Johnny didn't care at all.'

'Nikki, tell me about today. Can you do that?'

She nodded. Her eyes blinked in the light from overhead.

'When I saw the cover on a news stand, I went round to Johnny's place straight away. But he wasn't in. Or he wasn't answering the door, I don't know. We'd had a bit . . . a bit of an argument, after Witch Haven.'

'Go on . . .'

'I kept ringing him all through the day, whenever I could. Still no answer.'

'And then you went round again?'

'He rang me in the end. He said, *Nikki, I'm in trouble, I need your help*. That was all.'

'He didn't say what the trouble was?'

'No. So I rushed round there. And this time he let me in.'

'He was alone?'

'Yes. In a terrible state. And he was scared now. He knew by then that he'd done a bad thing. And yet at the same time he was excited.'

'Why excited?'

'After Brendan was killed, Johnny realized that I was telling the truth about the King Lost mask. And he was actually looking forward to the magazine being published. He wanted to draw the killer towards him.'

'You're saying . . .'

'Johnny wanted to die. Well, a part of him did, anyway. I'm sure of it. He wanted to die as Lucas died. By the same person's hands.'

'Why would he want that?'

'He wanted to burn out.' Her voice rose. 'He wanted to follow Lucas into paradise, where only the true rock and rollers live, where they live on forever!'

Her eyes were overcome with passion as she spoke.

Hobbes urged her on. 'Nikki, keep going.'

She wiped at her eyes and said, 'There was a knock at the door. It was about ten, I think. I begged Johnny not to open it, but nothing would stop him, not now.'

'It was her? The murderer?'

Hauser nodded.

'Did you recognize her?'

'No.'

'You're sure?'

She moved back in her chair. 'Look, it all happened in a split second. All I remember is someone rushing towards me, and hitting me.' She saw the doubt on Hobbes's face. 'I'm telling you, I've never seen her before in my life.'

Hobbes felt his heart sink. But he pressed on, regardless.

'How did she attack you?'

'I don't know. She had something in her hand.'

'A knife?'

'No, I don't think so. She pushed me back against the wall. I banged my head. She was vicious. Mad-looking. You know, crazy-eyed. And then she hit me, again and again.' Nikki touched at the wound on her left temple and muttered, 'I'm so sorry.'

'You don't have to apologize.'

'No, no, that's what she said to me: *I'm sorry. I'm so sorry.*'

Her head dipped again, hiding her face.

Hobbes thought about this apology. Nikki Hauser was just somebody in the way. She wasn't a victim, and couldn't be a victim, because she hadn't taken any action that had led to the mask being damaged.

Hobbes spoke gently: 'Nikki. Look at me, please.'

It took her a while, but then she looked up. Hobbes spoke slowly, broaching the most important subject yet.

'How did you know that cutting the mask led to the person being killed?'

He could see immediately that he'd caused a problem for her.

'Nikki, if you know anything, you have to tell me.'

A fierce tremble ran through her. 'It's meant to be a secret.'

'I know that. But think of Johnny. Think of Johnny being stabbed like that. Think about the way he loved you.'

Nikki Hauser's response to this shocked Hobbes. Her gaze locked on a far distant point and she started to intone:

'I have one task only. I will protect the face and form of King Lost. His beauty shineth forth, as always.' Her hands rose up from the table and she took on the voice of a preacher. 'I will break asunder

304

all those who harm his majesty. I will preserve his spirit from all future hurt, impairment and injury. I will exult him!' And as suddenly as it came, the fever left her voice and she looked down once more. Her hands lowered to the tabletop, the fingers shaking with nerves.

Hobbes could not speak. He stared at her for a good long while.

'Nikki. Do you understand what you just said?'

She nodded.

'You were quoting something, a text of some kind?'

'It is the credo,' she answered. 'As written by Lady Minerva.'

'Lucas Bell told you this?'

She nodded. 'It was towards the end, a few weeks before he died. We were lying in bed together. The night before the Rainbow concert, his final gig.'

'What did he say?'

'He confessed to a murder. The murder of a boy, a teenager.'

'Do you know the boy's name? Nikki, did Lucas tell you the boy's name?'

She nodded.

'And?'

'It was King Lost. They killed him. All of them, all five of them. They murdered King Lost.'

Hobbes's mind raced. The strands were floating around, waiting for the final knot that would tie the web into shape.

'I'm afraid I don't understand what you're saying.'

Nikki looked at him. Her eyes were fierce with knowledge, and she spoke quickly, from the depths of a memory long fixed in place: 'Edenville was built from the mind of King Lost. He was the originator of the idea. First he created the mask, to hide his face from the world. That wasn't enough. He needed more. So he created the imagined village. It's where he lost himself, where he went to hide. Lady Minerva and the others followed him there, and built an entire city around themselves. But it was *his* place of protection. The others were merely followers.'

'And yet they killed him?'

She nodded. 'They had to.'

'Why?'

'Lucas wouldn't say. He didn't tell me.'

'What is King Lost's real name?'

'I don't know.'

Hobbes brought his clenched fist down on the tabletop.

Nikki flinched and cried out, 'I don't know. I don't! Leave me alone.'

He started to speak, but Nikki interrupted him: 'Edenville is not a peaceful place. At its heart lies great pain, and loss, and the buildings and streets and parks all radiate out from that centre. And this is why . . .'

'Why people are killed?'

'I only know what Lucas told me that night. That's all. We made love. He was wearing the mask throughout, and he told me that taking up the mask was an act of contrition, and a celebration and continuance of the spirit of poor King Lost, God rest his soul.'

Hobbes watched her every facial expression. 'So when Bell destroyed the mask on stage, the next evening?'

'He desecrated that memory, as created by the founding members. And for that he had to be punished. This is what I believe.' She paused. 'But Lucas had had enough of the mask by then. He needed to escape its confines.'

Hobbes asked. 'Is there anything else Lucas told you about the Minerva group, about the people in it?

'I've told you everything. But I do know this: the killer sees herself as a guardian. The guardian of the mask's power.'

Nikki looked at Hobbes with an intensity that scared him. He returned her stare.

There was a dark connection between them. They had both looked into the eyes of the murderer, and lived.

A Face in the Crowd

Hobbes arranged a car to take Nikki Hauser home. He walked back to the incident room and stood at the board, looking at the list of names. He was alone.

Footsteps echoed down a corridor, and then faded.

It was half past three in the morning.

A telephone rang in another part of the building, unanswered. And then silence.

If Hauser was telling the truth, then King Lost was dead, a young man or teenager killed by the other founders of Edenville back in the sixties. He also knew that Lady Minerva was not the murderer: the woman he'd seen in Valentine's flat was too young, in her thirties, he estimated. Because of this, he had to assume that Eve Dylan had drowned in the sea at Hastings. Yet the adoption of Dylan's facial blemish probably indicated that the perpetrator had taken on the identity of Lady Minerva. This tied in with the letter for Simone Paige left next to Brendan Clarke's body.

He made a few changes to the Edenville list.

LADY MINERVA – Eve Dylan (Drowned)
KING LOST – ? (Murdered?)
LUNA BLOOM – Lucas Bell (Murdered)
BO DAZZLE – Gavin Roberts
MISS CALIBAN – ?
MOOD INDIGO – ?

Which meant either Miss Caliban or Mood Indigo was the adopted name of the murderer. She killed because of an oath taken many years before, to protect the memory of the boy hiding behind the King Lost persona. A boy the members of the Minerva Club had killed. A thought came to him: perhaps these killings were punishment for the murder of the King Lost boy? Perhaps the killer was the sole member of the group who had not taken part in the murder of King Lost, who disagreed with what they'd done?

But something didn't quite gel.

The pledge that Lucas Bell had told to Nikki Hauser, and which she had quoted during the interview, seemed to be a group undertaking. They were all part of the ritual. And now one member of the group had taken it too far, believing the damage of the mask was worthy of murder. It was twisted, a horrible motive. The human mind at its worst, creating a terrible reverse morality from psychosis.

Hobbes rubbed at his eyes. He thought about going home, calling it a day, or a night, or whatever it was, and starting afresh in the morning.

The lonely rooms where he lived, the empty bed, the string tied around his ankle.

No, not yet. He would keep working.

Think it through. A young teen was so troubled that he chose to hide behind a mask, to create a persona for himself. And then to create an entire fantasy land to hide within. The other kids helped him, they supported him. Perhaps he was the weakest of them all, the most damaged? Yes, that made sense. Yet they had killed him, or so Nikki Hauser claimed. Why? Why would they do that? Had he offended them in some way, or broken the rules?

The group was everything. The rules must not be broken.

Hobbes imagined Lady Minerva saying such a thing to them, insisting on the sanctity of the group above all else. They were of an age – no longer children, and not yet adults – when a strong-willed, charismatic leader could take charge. *Impressionable*, that was the term. Easily formed. Easily controlled. He knew as much from Gavin Roberts's continued attempts to build Edenville in Tobias Lear's house. But that was a fairly benign influence, as were the songs of Lucas Bell. Yet the same circumstances had also given rise to a murderer.

It was as if they'd been members of a religion, a cult.

Hobbes thought again of the killer's face, as he'd seen it in Valentine's bedroom. That look of sheer hatred. Only belief could fuel such anger.

Anyone who damaged the mask had to be punished.

To be killed.

The mask, that bloody goddamn mask!

The one subject, the only subject. The mask. A mask so powerful someone thought it worth killing to protect it.

Now he stopped moving.

Waited.

A tingle on his neck.

He was staring at the board, but his eyes were unfocused. His thoughts elsewhere.

It's all about the mask . . .

Hobbes switched on a desk light and placed the copy of the *New Musical Express* directly under its beam. Johnny Valentine's eyes stared back at him from the mask's half-concealment. The blood ran down the singer's cheek.

Hobbes turned to the interview and reread it. He was looking for a certain passage, something that was said about the mask.

Yes, there it was. A single sentence. He read it a few more times, and was reminded of Simone Paige's journals. DS Latimer had brought them back to the station. Hobbes found the volumes on the detective sergeant's desk.

After a few minutes of searching he found the entry he wanted to read again.

Yes, the same person was mentioned, by both Valentine and Paige.

It's all the about the bloody mask, of course it is . . .

A number of photographs fell out of the journal: the snapshots taken by Paige on the night of the *King Lost* cover shoot. Hobbes studied one image in particular. Lucas Bell was there, next to his manager, Tobias Lear. But Hobbes wasn't interested in either of them, not this time. Instead his eyes focused on a young woman standing to one side. He lowered the desk lamp directly over the photograph.

He stared at it until his vision blurred.

Well, he wasn't one hundred per cent certain, because some eight or nine years had passed since the photograph had been taken. But he saw a likeness, enough to make him shiver. The same long dark hair; the same narrow nose and the rounded eyes.

She was staring directly at the camera.

Was this the murderer?

The Specialist

They met in a cafe in a passageway off Carnaby Street, a police detective with forty-four years on the clock and a young man barely out of his teens. His name was Vinny Spires. He stood up from the table and shook hands: a polite lad.

'I like it here,' Spires explained. 'It's quiet usually, and I can think. Sometimes I bring a notepad with me, to jot down ideas.' He called out to the woman behind the counter, 'Gladys, get my guest a cuppa, will yer? Cheers. Tea all right?'

Hobbes nodded. 'Thank you.'

'So this is about Johnny Valentine, yeah?'

'It is. You've made quite a splash with that cover and the interview.'

'I know, I know.' The young man's eyes sparkled. 'No one else was interested in him, but I had a hunch, don't ask me why. I thought he'd have an interesting take on the whole Lucas Bell anniversary thing.' His smiled broadened. 'You know, some of these old guys have brilliant stories to tell.'

'You don't know the half of it.'

Spires's face darkened. 'Why? Has something happened? He's not complained about me, has he?'

'It's more than that, I'm afraid.'

Hobbes was about to explain when the waitress came over and clunked down a cup of tea. He thanked her and waited until she'd gone. And even then he spoke quietly.

'Valentine's dead. Murdered. Last night.'

Hobbes studied the other man's reaction.

Spires was neatly dressed in jacket, jeans and button-down collared shirt, with carefully styled hair that was spiky on the top and gelled flat at the sides. He was stylish but not in any way a typical rock and roll figure; he might almost have a been a bank clerk except for a badge on his lapel. Now the man's eyes widened. Hobbes could see the hunger in them.

'Pissing hell,' he responded. 'Who . . . I mean, why . . . who did it?'

'That's under investigation.'

'Right, right. Absolutely . . .'

Hobbes could see the journalist's fingers twitching, already tapping at some imagined typewriter keyboard.

'Let's talk about the Johnny Valentine interview.'

'Yes, of course.'

'It took place last Thursday?'

Spires nodded. 'That's correct. The paper goes to press on Monday, so everything has to be delivered by then, words and pictures.'

'I see. And who was present for the interview?'

'Just myself, and the photographer, Jo Jo. That's er . . . Joanna Yates.'

'Do you know Joanna well?'

'Yeah, she's good, been in the game for years. Takes a nice picture. Well, you saw the cover? She totally caught the mood.'

Hobbes nodded. 'So it was just the three of you in the room?'

'Yes, Valentine was very specific about that.'

'And this took place at the magazine's offices.'

'It did. In a separate room, the door closed.'

'So, Vinny, did you have any idea at all that Mr Valentine was going to act as he did, that he was going to cut his own face?'

Spires closed his eyes momentarily, reliving the moment.

'No. It was horrible. I mean, he'd promised us some exclusive details about Lucas Bell's life, some juicy gossip. But this was incredible. There was blood! Blood all over his shirt. And you can still see the stain, on the office carpet.'

The journalist fidgeted with his empty coffee cup.

Hobbes gave him a moment, before saying, 'Did you bring the photographs I asked for?'

Spires pulled a large envelope from a shoulder bag and handed it over the table. Hobbes flipped through the shots, one by one. He saw Valentine alone, his face covered by the painted mask. He saw the knife in his hand; he saw the knife cutting into the flesh. But these didn't interest him.

'You don't have any from before, from when the mask was being painted on his face?'

'I'm sorry, no. Jo Jo turned up later, when we were ready to go.'

Hobbes took a drink of tea, to concentrate his mind. The most important questions were about to be asked.

'So you were there when the mask was painted on?'

'I was.' Spires licked his lips. 'Why, is this important?'

'Just answer the questions, please.' Hobbes consulted his notebook. 'In the article you said that Valentine insisted on getting every detail of the King Lost mask correct. He wanted his mask to be "like the original, only better". Is that a true quote?'

'He really said that. I didn't make it up.'

'Good, good. You also mention that a specialist make-up artist had been brought in, to do the mask.'

'Yes.'

'A woman?'

'That's right.'

'Did the magazine find her?'

'No, no. Valentine brought her. I don't know where he got her from.'

'How old was she?'

'Her age?'

'Yes, please.'

'Old.'

'Middle-aged, you mean?'

'I don't know, I guess so.'

'Thirties, forties?'

'I suppose so.'

'Which?'

'Thirties. Something like that. You know, getting on a bit.'

Hobbes took out his photograph of the *King Lost* cover shoot and placed it on the table. He tapped at a woman standing next to Lucas Bell and said, 'Is this the make-up artist?'

Spires studied the shot.

Hobbes helped him along: 'It was taken about nine years ago.'

'Maybe. Perhaps it is her. Yeah, it could well be.'

'And what was her name?'

Vincent Spires looked confused. 'Her name? I don't know.'

'You don't know her name?'

'She wasn't introduced to me. Valentine took her into the room and they got to work. I watched for a while, but Valentine never spoke, and neither did the make-up woman. It was like . . . like a ceremony of some kind.'

'It took place in silence?'

'In total silence.'

Hobbes thought about this. Looking again at the photograph on the tabletop, he recalled other images from the *King Lost* cover shoot, some of them showing Johnny Valentine present. That's probably where he met the make-up artist.

He turned his attention back to the journalist. 'Vinny, what happened after the mask had been applied?'

'She left.'

'So the make-up artist never saw the cutting of the face?'

'No.'

'And she wouldn't know that Valentine had sliced his own face?'

'No way. Absolutely. Andy, that's my editor, he was strict about keeping it all secret, until publication day.'

'What about the make-up artist's fee? You must have records of that, back at the office. We can go there now.'

'There was no fee. She did it for free. Andy was well pleased—'

'Damn it!'

Spires leaned back in his chair. 'Have I said something wrong?'

Hobbes stood up and threw a few coins on the table for his drink. 'Don't write about this,' he said. 'Don't talk about it, don't print anything about it, not at all. Not until I say you can. Do you hear me?'

Spires nodded. Hobbes said his goodbyes and headed back to his car. He drove over to Highgate. Tobias Lear welcomed him as an old friend.

'Still searching for El Dorado, Inspector?'

'What's that?'

'The promised land. Edenville.'

'Yes, I am.'

They were sitting in the living room. A large print of a hunting scene hung over Lear's head, the smoke from his pipe mingling with the dogs and horses in the image. There was no sign of Gavin Roberts, so Hobbes assumed he was still sitting in the room upstairs.

The summoning bell was quiet.

Hobbes got straight to it: 'Do you remember Lucas Bell's make-up artist?'

'I do, indeed. Her name was Jenny. Jenny Clough. She was with us for the *King Lost* tour, looked after Lucas every night.'

'And Miss Clough, she painted the mask on his face before every gig?'

'That she did. She was a right old laugh, as well. A good old-fashioned Northern lass. Drank the roadies under the table, and kept shagging the drummer.'

Hobbes was puzzled; this didn't correspond to his mental picture of the killer, not at all. And a Northerner? No, that didn't make sense. He took out the *King Lost* cover shoot photograph and showed it to Lear.

The ex-manager looked at the image and smiled. 'I remember that night so well; the start of a legend.'

'Can you name the people in the photograph?'

'Sure. There's me, and that's Luke. And this is Laura Townes, our publicity manager.'

'What about this woman, here . . .' Hobbes touched at the photograph. 'On the other side of Lucas, isn't she the make-up artist?'

'Oh, right. Yeah, I remember now. She was. Jenny Clough came on board later, when the album was released.'

'So who's this woman then?'

Lear handed the photograph back to the detective. 'No idea. She only did it for that one time, that first time for the cover. Lucas brought her along. That's all I know.'

Hobbes felt his grasp on an answer slipping away.

'What about the publicity manager?'

'Laura?'

'Perhaps she would know the make-up artist's name?'

'She might. But Laura left for the States some years ago. I haven't a clue where she is, to be honest.'

Hobbes sat back in his seat.

'Sorry I can't be of more help,' Lear said. 'But there is one thing . . .'

'What is it?'

'I think that make-up woman came from Hastings. She was a friend of Luke's, from the early days. Maybe she's still living there?'

'Yes, maybe.'

But without a name, what could he do? He asked, 'Did Jenny Clough ever meet with the original artist? Maybe they talked about the mask, about how to paint it?'

'I don't think so.' Lear smiled at a memory. 'We brought Jenny in months later, for the tour, and she was a real professional, worked in the theatres, the movies. But I'll tell you this, that first girl – whoever she was – she painted Luke's face better than Jenny ever did. The mask on the album cover, man, that was the business!'

And then the bell on the wall rang. Lear tapped the ashes from his pipe and stood up.

'The voice from on high is calling.'

Hobbes had an idea. He said, 'I want to ask Gavin if he knows the woman, would that be all right?'

'Sure. Why not.'

They walked up the stairs together and entered the Edenville room. Gavin Roberts sat at its centre as always, working away, gluing pieces of cardboard together to make a model building. Hobbes stepped forward and offered him the photograph.

'Gavin, do you recognize this woman?'

The reaction was instantaneous, and violent.

He cried out in pain and started to shake.

Lear came forward to try and calm him. But Gavin scrambled away from the work desk and cowered against the wall. He was muttering to himself, over and over.

Hobbes moved closer, the better to hear him.

Gavin Roberts spoke quietly, one word only, a repeated name.

'Caliban. Caliban. Caliban.'

Hobbes was insistent, almost threatening: 'What do you mean by that? What's her real name?'

But there was no more. Gavin refused to speak, or was incapable of speech.

At first Hobbes thought the old Edenville pledge of secrecy had taken over, but then he saw from the man's expression that his reaction was far more elemental, far more human.

Gavin Roberts was scared out of his mind.

A Meeting by the River

Hobbes drove back to Richmond police station, where he brought Latimer up to date. Hearing the new information, she moved to the incident board and tapped her knuckles on the Edenville list.

'So Miss Caliban is our number one suspect?' she asked.

'It's looking that way.'

'We need to find out about the young man who invented King Lost, all those years ago. We need to find out how and why he died.'

Hobbes nodded. 'And to do that, I need to go back to Hastings.'

'Give me fifteen minutes and I'll be ready.'

'Meg—'

'I'll clock you one, if you don't shut up!' She paused, and added, 'Sir.'

'OK.' Hobbes held his hands up in surrender. 'We'll set off at two, no later.'

He sat on the edge of a desk and looked again at the photograph of the *King Lost* cover shoot. It was too old, that was the trouble, people changed too much. If only he had a more recent image . . .

And that single thought caused a light to flash in his head.

A memory. Recognition.

Of course, that's where he'd seen her! It wasn't the photograph at all.

He made a quick call to DC Palmer in Hastings, asking her to pull together everything she had on local teenagers who had died in the sixties.

'I'll be paying you a visit later today, Jan.'

'Righty-oh.'

'And I want you to find someone for me.'

After he'd told Palmer what he needed, Hobbes made a second call, this time out of Latimer's hearing.

It was a surprisingly easy meeting to arrange, even though he kept the subject matter to a simple: 'It's about Charlie Jenkes. Some information has come to light.'

A pause down the line. Then: 'What's it got to do with me?'

'I can walk into Charing Cross nick and have it out with you there, if you like.'

'No. No, I'll meet you.'

Hobbes drove north towards Hammersmith, his stomach churning with nerves the closer he got to his destination. They'd agreed to meet halfway, at a pub on the embankment. He got there first. The bar was teeming with dinnertime drinkers, too crowded to even get close to the bar, so he went back outside and enjoyed a cigarette as he watched the Thames flow by. It was a fine day, the water dappled with sunlight.

Five minutes later, Detective Sergeant Mawley made his way down the path and joined Hobbes at the rail. The two men stood in silence as a party of office workers walked past. Mawley had the sort of face that belonged in a badly lit drinkers' den, or a smoke-filled incident room; in the full light of day he looked like a dead fish, his flesh mottled and flabby around the neck and cheeks.

Hobbes threw his cigarette into the river. 'Len.'

Mawley was looking angry. 'We've already had one of your lot around the station this morning, stirring up trouble.'

This worried Hobbes. 'You don't mean DC Fairfax?'

'Yeah, that's the guy. What's all this about?'

Hobbes didn't waste time. He reached into his pocket and drew out a photograph. He showed it to his former colleague, saying, 'I found this in Jenkes's garage, well hidden. There's a whole roll of them.'

Mawley stared at the image. After a moment he said, 'I'm a married man.'

'Is that an alibi? Or an excuse?'

'I've got two kids, for crying out loud!'

Hobbes pushed the photograph closer. 'Take a good look.'

The other detective did so. 'It's a bit fuzzy. It could be anyone.'

'The thing is, Len, I also know who the young man is.'

'You do?'

'I met him a few days ago. He's called Matthew. Matthew Tate.'

Mawley wiped down his face with a hand. He came to a decision. 'It was a few years back. I only knew him by a nickname.'

'Sputnik?'

'Aye, that will be it.'

'He's a good kid,' Hobbes said. 'He's come through the fire. But he told me he'd got into some bad things when he was younger. Now I know what he meant.'

Mawley looked out over the water. 'It was only a one-off. And he wasn't underage, don't start thinking that.'

'I can ask the lad himself—'

'Now look!' He spun round to face Hobbes. 'This is my private business. It's got nothing to do with you, or anyone.'

'It goes further, and you know it.'

Mawley's mouth was stretched tight. 'It's a good job we're in a crowded place.'

'Is that a threat?'

'You'd be swallowing teeth by now.'

Hobbes tried his best not to blink. 'Tell me, Len, how did you meet him?'

Mawley cursed to himself. 'There's a club, in Soho.'

'Let me guess. The Blue Moon? Off Berwick Street. Charlie was seen there as well.'

'Yeah, well . . .' Mawley hesitated. 'He introduced me to the place. Told me they cater for all tastes.'

'Is that where he got the photos of you? He set you up?'

'I guess so. I don't know. Truth is, I've got enemies all over.' He glared at Hobbes and spoke with a rasp in his voice. 'Christ, but you like digging in the shit, don't you?'

'Granted. But I haven't killed anyone.'

'What?'

'Jenkes. He was killed.'

'No, I don't believe that. I refuse to. Charlie killed himself. He strung himself up, everybody knows that. It all got too much for him and he took the easy way out.'

'The easy way?' Hobbes shook his head. 'I imagine it was quite a struggle, actually, when you wrapped that washing line around his neck and hauled him up.'

Mawley's mouth was open in protest, or shock, but only a single gasp escaped his lips.

Hobbes carried on. 'He was blackmailing you.'

'Yeah, but not for cash. Just for favours. Jobs done, here and there. Dirty work.'

'Like helping to beat up his wife's lover?'

Mawley tried to dismiss the accusation, but couldn't. 'Yeah, things like that.'

'And then what? One favour too many? And so you followed him to the garage, and—'

'No! No, no.' His voice was raised now, and some of the pub's customers were looking over. 'Look, Hobbes, can we move away a bit. Give me that, at least.'

'We're fine here.'

Mawley controlled his tone, as best he could. 'I didn't kill Charlie.'

The two men stared at each other, neither willing to give ground.

Finally, Hobbes said, 'The more I've looked into this, the more amazed I am at how easily Jenkes led me on over the years, how easily I fell for his "band of brothers" thing. Even in that cellar, I still sort of believed in him, for some stupid fucked-up reason. Like the whole thing was some kind of mistake, or a dream.'

He watched a bird skimming low over the water, searching for food.

'But now I think the man was rotten, through and through.'

'He wasn't always like that, Hobbes, and you bloody well know it. Only in the last year or so. He was having problems at home. He was in debt.'

'So that lets him off the hook?'

Mawley's head dropped. He was muttering to himself. 'Twenty-nine years.'

'What's that?'

'I was only a nipper when I joined up. That's twenty-nine god-damn years on the force. I can retire next year, full pension. And now this. Christ.'

A gang of lads left the pub and swaggered off down the riverside pathway, full of life, the brazen hope of youth. And here was this long-term enforcer of the law teetering on the edge of losing everything.

Hobbes said to him, 'I remember in the Silhouette, how Jenkes ordered you to join in. And then later on, at the inquiry, you put yourself forward to take the blame. What was that, another favour?'

Mawley nodded. 'I was hoping that would end it for good. Wipe the slate clean. But even after Charlie was dismissed, he still came after me.' He fumbled to light a cigarette, failed miserably, and then added in a pain-racked voice, 'My wife's kicked me out, did you know that?'

'No, I didn't.'

Hobbes felt a sudden compassion. He tried to imagine how it must be, to have to hide such feelings away. He thought about

Neville Briggs and Tobias Lear, how they had a much more open life, in the world of rock and roll. But Mawley was a cop. His fellow officers, his so-called friends, they would have made his life a misery. God knows what they would've done.

Hobbes said in a quiet voice, 'Len, tell me what happened.'

Some of Mawley's old bravado came back. 'Nothing happened. Nothing at all. I'm not a murderer.'

'I'm coming after you, no matter what you say.'

'Do what the hell you like.' Mawley thrust his face close. 'Charlie took his own life. And he did that because you grassed on him. That's it. End of story.'

He turned to walk away, but Hobbes grabbed his jacket sleeve.

'Get the fuck off me!'

'You won't get away with this, believe me.'

Mawley grinned. 'You're not going to find one speck of physical evidence, Hobbes. Not a fucking speck! So you can take those poxy fucking snapshots and shove 'em up your arse.'

And with that he pulled away and walked off down the pathway, elbowing his way through a knot of drinkers. One of the young men in the group fancied himself, making a remark of some kind. He'd picked the wrong victim at the wrong time. Hobbes watched as Mawley mashed the guy's lapels together in a fist. Face up close, spittle-spraying aggression: his trademark move. And then the brutal push away, shoving the young man against a table. A glass smashed on the pavement.

A second later, Mawley was lost in the riverside crowds.

Possible Kings

DC Palmer greeted Hobbes and Latimer at Hastings police station, and brought them up to speed on the Simone Paige case. The murderer had been stealing into the attic of Fair Harbour for a couple of years at least, from the physical evidence left behind: clothes, tins of food, and reading matter.

'I'd like to see that,' Hobbes said. 'What was it, newspapers, magazines?'

'A stack of them, yes. Which gave us some dates. And quite a few books. Novels, mainly.'

'What about the photographer I asked you to find?'

'He's called Jack Lyndhurst. Worked on the local rag for years. He's left the shots you asked for.'

Palmer went off and Hobbes and Latimer settled down in a side office with cups of tea and canteen sandwiches. The reading matter found in the attic was brought for them, and they tried to build up a picture of the murderer from the various titles. The newspapers and magazines dated back to 1979.

'I wonder why she never took them away, whenever she left?' Hobbes asked, as he leafed through a copy of *Amateur Photography*.

'Building a nest,' Latimer answered. 'A home from home.'

The magazines covered a range of subjects: household styling, high fashion, theatre, cinema, psychic phenomena.

Latimer said, 'Our Miss Caliban's a woman of varied tastes.'

324

Hobbes went through the paperback novels. Romances, crime fiction, and, standing out from the rest, a well-thumbed copy of James Joyce's *Ulysses*. He turned to the title page and read the inscription: *With all my dearest love to Lucas. I hope it inspires you to great heights.* It was signed *Eve X*. Not Miss Dylan, not Minerva or Lady Minerva. He showed this to Latimer for her opinion and she said, 'Perhaps she really was in love with him.' Hobbes flicked through the pages; many lines were underscored in pencil, some with comments in the margins. He recognized Lucas Bell's handwriting from the lyric sheets; the vocalist had obviously made good use of the book over the years.

Latimer asked, 'Isn't the main character in *Ulysses* called Bloom?'

'Yes. Leopold Bloom.'

'Which ties in with Lucas Bell's Edenville name, Luna Bloom.' She picked up another magazine. 'So do you reckon Bell stored this in the attic, and Miss Caliban found it here?'

'Perhaps. Or she stole it from Bell's hideaway, after she'd killed him. Along with Bell's key ring, which included the old keys to Fair Harbour.'

DC Palmer entered the room and placed a sheaf of black-and-white prints on the desk. Hobbes went through them one by one. They showed the scene outside Duffy's fish and chip restaurant three night ago, when Hobbes had watched the fans copying the cover shot of the *King Lost* album. The photographer he'd talked to, Jack Lyndhurst, had really caught the atmosphere, love mingling with desperation.

Hobbes's breath caught in his throat. He tapped at one of the shots. 'I knew I'd seen her somewhere before,' he said. 'She's the one.' It was the older female fan who'd stood behind the younger ones, goading them on to attack Simone Paige. 'She's our killer. I'm sure of it.' Latimer and Palmer leaned in. The image of the woman's face was blurry, because she never really put herself forward; she was always standing at the back of the crowd, watching. 'This woman,' Hobbes went on to explain, 'painted the original mask on Lucas Bell's face, at the photo shoot for the album cover, back in 1973 or whenever it was.'

Latimer gazed at the face. 'So she's come back to the scene?'

'Yes. I imagine she comes back every year. She's proud of her achievement. It's her moment of glory.' Hobbes turned to Palmer. 'Can you get this copied and distributed to all officers?'

'Yes, sir.'

'Ask them if they know her – her name, address, anything at all.'

Hobbes and Latimer looked at each other.

'We're closing in,' she said.

'Yes, I can feel it.'

They left the station and walked down to the Brassey Institute where they started work on the microfiches together. Jan Palmer had given them a list of the young people or teenagers of Hastings who had died accidentally or in unexplained circumstances between 1963, when Edenville was founded, and 1966, the last year mentioned in the box of files left in the attic. Soon they had narrowed it down to thirteen possibilities, eight males and five females.

'They have enough drownings down here,' Latimer noted.

Other deaths included two car accidents, a fall from a cliff, a house fire, a stabbing in a park, a choking, and one poor boy who had locked himself in a cupboard and suffocated. With Doreen the librarian's help they found local addresses for the families. A few of them had moved away, but most were still living in the area.

'People tend to stay here all their lives,' Doreen explained. 'It's that kind of town.'

Latimer checked the list a second time. 'Are we safe in assuming that King Lost is a boy? Because this Edenville crowd seem to play about with their identities a lot.'

Hobbes agreed. 'Fair point. And I'd like to check every single one of these.'

'That is going to take some time.'

'We'll do as many as we can tonight.' He checked his wristwatch. 'Most people will be home from work by now.'

'Let's split it,' Latimer said. 'I'll take the car to visit the ones who live away from the centre.'

'And I'll do all the walking?'

'You need the exercise, guv.' She scanned the list of names. 'What about Stephen Castle? He sounds a likely candidate, given the Minerva group's love of code names.'

'Because that's where kings live?'

'Exactly.' She gave a brief smile. 'But even if we find out who King Lost was, there's still Miss Caliban to identify.'

'One step at a time.'

'And Mood Indigo?'

Hobbes grimaced. 'I'll fill in every name on that list, I swear, every single one.'

They left the library and went their separate ways. The skies were beginning to darken as Hobbes made his first visit, to the household of Robert and Helena Castle, following Latimer's hunch. It was an awkward, emotionally distraught conversation.

'Your son died when he was thirteen.'

Mr Castle spoke in a monotone. 'He fell off the pier.'

'Was he alone at the time?'

'No, he had a friend with him.' Helena said. 'We think so, anyway.' She looked to her husband for support. 'It was at night, we know that.'

'I see. So he was out late?'

'He crept out. We didn't even know he'd left the house.'

Mrs Castle's face seemed to collapse inwards as she said this. Hobbes could see the blame taking over; perhaps she'd hidden it away for years.

'We can't tell you anything more,' her husband said. 'I wish we could. But we just can't.'

Hobbes spoke gently. 'A few more questions, then I'll leave you in peace.' He gave them a few moments to settle, then he asked, 'Was Stephen a member of any clubs, or societies?'

'No, I don't think so. He played football for the school team, does that count?'

Hobbes nodded. 'It might do. Did he ever make up characters, or give himself different names?'

Husband and wife glanced at each other; they looked bewildered.

'Did he ever . . . did Stephen ever wear a mask? Or draw masks?'

They still didn't know how to answer.

'Mr and Mrs Castle, did your son ever mention the name King Lost?'

'I don't understand,' Helena said at last. 'There wasn't anything strange about Stephen. Nothing at all. He was a . . . he was a normal, happy thirteen-year-old.'

Hobbes asked a few more questions, finished the interview, and made his apologies.

He visited four more households, with similar results each time. One irate mother almost attacked him in an angry exchange. He walked to the next address on the list, following the librarian's written directions. It was quite a distance and along the way he wondered how DS Latimer was getting on.

He arrived at a small end-of-terrace house. It was dark by now, and there were lights on behind the living room curtains. Hobbes looked around. This part of town was familiar to him for some reason, and he realized that Morgan Yorke lived close by. Hobbes consulted his list. A teenager called Edward Keele had once resided here with his parents, until his death in 1966. He rang the bell and waited until he heard footsteps approaching and the door opened.

A woman's face peered out at him. 'Yes? Can I help you?'

'Mrs Keele?'

'Yes.'

'I'm Detective Inspector Hobbes.' He showed her his warrant card.

The woman was suddenly worried. 'The police?'

'May I come inside?'

'Has something bad happened?'

'No, no. I'm just making enquires in the area about a crime. Do you mind?'

She looked flustered. He pressed gently forward and she was forced to open the door wider for him. He moved into the hallway.

'I'm not sure this is a good time, actually.'

'It'll only take a minute. That's all.'

They walked through into a living room. Mrs Keele turned down the sound on the television. The room was bright and neat and airy with not a speck of dust in sight, but Hobbes was conscious of an oppressive atmosphere. There wasn't a single photograph on display.

Mrs Keele stared at him. 'What do you want to ask me about?'

'It's about your son, Edward.'

She fell back into an armchair, the life taken out of her body in an instant.

Hobbes regarded the woman from where he was standing. She was around fifty years of age, with a shrunken look about her, as though the very act of living had worn her down. The weight of grief was palpable.

'I'm sorry to bring up such distressing memories,' he continued, 'but it is important to a present-day case.'

'Yes, I understand.' Mrs Keele's hands trembled in her lap.

'How old was your son when he passed away?'

'He was fourteen. One week short of his fifteenth birthday.'

'He drowned, is that correct, in 1966?'

The woman nodded.

'Could you describe Edward to me?'

'Describe him? I don't understand.'

'Did he have any hobbies, for instance? Or was he the member of a club?'

'Well . . . he was a lonely child, I guess.'

'He kept to himself?'

'He had a few friends, not many.'

'Did they ever come round to visit, these friends?'

'No. Hardly ever. They met elsewhere.'

Hobbes felt he was closing in on an elusive quarry.

'Did Edward like to read?'

Now Mrs Keele's eyes brightened. 'Oh yes, Edward loved adventure novels. Simply adored them. He was always going to the library, to renew his books.'

'Would you say he was an artistic boy?'

She looked at him strangely. 'He could certainly draw, if that's what you mean, yes.'

'What kind of things?'

'Well, faces, mainly. Made-up faces. Superhero masks, things like that.'

Hobbes must've looked surprised, because Mrs Keele noticed this and she started to tremble even further. 'Why are you asking me these things?'

Hobbes stepped forward. 'Mrs Keele, I need to—'

'Please, I want you to leave, right now.'

'Does the name King Lost mean anything to you?'

The effect was immediate. She half rose from her seat and then fell back once more. She looked exhausted.

'Please answer the question.'

'King Lost. Yes, he's . . . he was . . . he was a pop star!' This answer came as an obvious relief and she clung to it desperately. 'Yes, he was a pop star, wasn't he? A few years ago. He made an album, isn't that right?'

Hobbes pulled up a chair and sat directly in front of her. 'Does the name mean anything else to you, something to do with your son?'

She blinked rapidly, her whole face creased up in anguish.

Then she breathed out and nodded.

And with that simple act, the room seemed slightly less oppressive.

'It was a name that Edward used sometimes, when he was lonely or sad. You see, we named him Edward because it's the most

330

popular name for a king of England.' She smiled weakly. 'There have been eleven Edwards on the throne, did you know that?' Hobbes didn't answer her, so she carried straight on. 'Little Edward would often pretend to have imaginary friends, or to take on other roles for himself.'

'So King Lost was a character your son created for himself?'

'Yes. I was worried about him. Most of the time he seemed to live in a world of his own.'

There was a pause. Hobbes asked, 'Mrs Keele, is your husband still around?'

'No. No, he left home shortly after . . . after . . .'

'After Edward died?'

'Yes.'

'So you live alone?'

She nodded and her head drooped with a burden of sorrow.

The wall clock ticked on, the only sound.

Hobbes looked at her, this middle-aged woman in her plain blue dress, with her permed and tinted hair and her ringless fingers. For the first time he noticed the half-eaten plate of egg and chips at her feet; she'd been watching the television while eating her evening meal.

He leaned forward and asked, 'What's your first name, Mrs Keele?'

'Susan.'

'Susan, have you ever heard of a place called Edenville?'

She nodded. 'That's where Edward lived. He showed me a drawing once.'

'An imaginary city?'

'Yes.'

'Why did your son need to make a mask for himself, do you know? Why did he need to escape this world into a fantasy land?'

She could barely speak. 'He . . . he was frightened.' A whisper only.

'What was he frightened of?'

'Of Anthony.'

'Your husband?'

'Yes.'

'Was your husband hurting Edward in any way?'

They were sitting close together and she looked deep into Hobbes's eyes, seeking understanding. And she must've found something good in his expression, because now she started talking more freely.

'Anthony would beat him. And shout at him all the time. He was horrible to Edward, to his own son! Nothing was ever good enough, nothing, nothing at all. I tried to stop him, but it was hopeless. And he'd go on and on. Sometimes he would lock Edward away in his bedroom for hours on end, not allowing him to be fed, or to wash, or to go to the toilet, even. This was when my little boy first drew King Lost, in those hours of confinement. And then my husband would go out to the pub and I'd creep into the room and comfort him . . .' Her mind was far away by now, Hobbes could see that from the hazy look in her eyes. 'The sheets were stained. And the smell . . . it was too much to bear. Yet I *had* to bear it. I was his mother. What else could I do?'

Her eyes shifted focus. They saw Hobbes as though for the first time, and she looked suddenly ashamed.

'I'm so sorry,' she cried. 'I shouldn't have told you all this. It's very bad of me.'

'It's all right. Don't worry.'

His low, gentle voice seemed to calm her.

'Susan, I'd like to talk about Edward's death.'

She nodded. Hobbes had the impression that every single movement she made, no matter how tiny, caused her great pain.

'What do you remember of that time?'

'I really don't know how it happened. My husband had been particularly horrible to Edward that week, probably because he was having a bad time at work. Anthony often took out his anger on his son. He struck him. Again and again. But that day our

332

little boy ran off, I don't know where to. I was ever so worried. He was missing hours, and hours. And then . . .'

'Go on.'

Mrs Keele gathered her strength. 'And then a police officer called round and told us that a teenage boy's body had been found washed up on the beach. They wanted me to identify him.'

'It was Edward?'

'His face was bruised, and his skin, all over. The detective told me this had happened because his body had been buffeted by the tide, and the rocks. But I knew better.'

She fell silent.

And then her hands unclenched and she said in a weak voice, 'Oh, but I haven't offered you a cup of tea.'

'That's fine. It really is.'

'Would you like to see Edward's room?'

'His room?'

'I've kept it very much as he left it.'

'Yes, that would be useful.'

She rose from her armchair and directed him to a narrow set of stairs. 'It's the first door on the left, at the back of the house. I won't come with you, if that's all right?'

'Of course.'

'It only makes me cry, these days.'

Hobbes made his way up the stairs to the landing. He found the bedroom door, still with its ceramic *Edward's Room* nameplate. It was dark inside. He found the light switch but clicking it had no effect. There was no bulb in the socket of the ceiling lamp.

He walked into the room and allowed his eyes to adjust to the dimness.

It was a fourteen-year-old boy's room, perfectly preserved from 1966. Fifteen years had gone by. Plastic models of Spitfires and Lancaster Bombers hung down from the ceiling on pieces of thread, and a poster for the England football club adorned the wall opposite the window. The bed was neatly made, and a set of rulers,

333

compasses and pens and pencils was laid out on the desk beside a pile of exercise books. Everything was covered in a fine layer of dust. Hobbes imagined Mrs Keele attending to her son's bedroom every few weeks or so, cleaning, folding, tidying away. Yet the dust told him that she had stopped this activity at some point in the recent past and left the room to its own devices.

Hobbes turned on a desk lamp. He opened the first exercise book in the pile. It was filled with sketches and poems, all in the same handwriting. One page was filled with an early version of the King Lost mask, the split lips and painted teardrop in place but missing at this point the blue cross on the forehead. He flipped through the pages, seeing the word *Edenville* written here and there: the boy was slowly creating the fantasy world for himself, seeking protection from his father's rages.

A photograph was hidden within the pages. It showed five young people standing in a field. Hobbes guessed it was Witch Haven and that Eve Dylan had taken the shot. He recognized two of the teenagers immediately: Lucas Bell, with Gavin Roberts next to him. A boy and girl stood close together in the middle of the shot, with a second teenage girl standing slightly separate from the others. Hobbes turned the photograph over and realized immediately that he'd found the golden key. All the Edenville names had been written out on the back, corresponding to their position in the image: *Luna Bloom, Bo Dazzle, King Lost, Miss Caliban, Mood Indigo*. And beneath these fanciful names, the real Christian names of the youths were given. But no surnames, unfortunately.

He turned the photograph back over and focused first on King Lost, or Edward Keele as he now knew him. And then on the girl beside him.

Miss Caliban.

Yes, it was her, a younger version of the woman he had seen at the fans' recreation of the album cover, and in the photograph from the original shoot.

She was called Natasha. He still didn't have a surname for her.

He shifted his focus on to the second girl, the one standing at the edge of the group. This was Mood Indigo. She looked to be eighteen years old or so. He stared at her face, and the shape of her body, and he checked again the name given on the back.

He couldn't quite work out what this meant. It was a mystery to be puzzled over.

But he didn't have time for that now. He had to find out the real identity of Miss Caliban. He searched through the exercise books, finding nothing more. He opened the desk drawers and found in one a silver picture frame lying face down. He lifted this up and saw that it held a photograph, this one showing just two people. Looking at it, Hobbes started to get an inkling of the truth.

A floorboard creaked behind him.

Without turning he asked, 'Mrs Keele, do you have a telephone?'

There was no answer.

A shadow crossed the walls.

Suddenly, the room blurred around him. He couldn't work out why.

Now the yellow beam from the table lamp seemed to swing across the ceiling. He was falling, his hands flailing about but finding nothing to hold on to, nothing at all.

Confused, he writhed on the carpet, seeking purchase.

Then the second blow came down. It glanced off his shoulder. His eyes closed. Now he realized and he tried to struggle. It was too late. A third blow caught him on the brow.

At the last moment he forced his eyes open.

He saw a model fighter plane spinning, spinning, and a glimpse of a woman's face looming over him.

The plane started to spin in the opposite direction, faster and faster.

And then darkness.

A Doorway to Paradise

The world arrived slowly, sound by sound, item by item. Indistinct noises, shapes. Somebody moving close by, a figure in black.

He tasted powder on his tongue, his mouth filled with dust. Then water, then foam.

And once more, he slept.

A woman's perfume.

Somebody kissing him, or touching his face.

It felt like a dream, or a memory. Or a story someone was telling him.

A bedtime story.

Music was playing. Inside his body, or outside? He could not tell.

In sleep he moved beneath the stage lights. He was looking out through the mask even as it tightened on his face, the crowd staring at him, yet he couldn't remember the lyrics, no words, no music, only silence, and the audience turned against him. His hand came up holding the knife. He would do anything, anything at all to get the crowd back on his side, even this act of pressing the blade against his own skin, cutting in, peeling the flesh back.

Now he woke up, in pain, in panic.

And his hand came to his face, searching.

Yes, the cut was there, he felt at it. Already half scabbed over, the crust forming.

A smear of dark blood on his fingertips when he looked, and other colours: pancake white, lipstick red. His face stung. Hobbes traced the wound, from below his left eye, down to the corner of his mouth almost, and relived it again, the knife that had reached into his dream and sliced him open.

The sound of a bell woke him. An alarm clock going off, yet all was quiet when his eyes opened.

This time he was fully conscious.

His body was lit by a single lamp directly overhead, its shade directing the glow into a cone. Beyond this the room was dimly lit and shadowed, and then dark.

There was less pain now, but the left-hand side of his face still ached. He tried to bring his hands up, to check on the wound, to see if it was still real, still there . . .

He could not move.

His hands were tied at the wrists to a chair, his legs also, wrapped with twine at the ankles and tightly bound to the struts of the chair.

He howled and pulled at his bonds and cried out for help, for a response, anything, a sign of life, for a fellow soul here in the cold, lonely dark of the room.

The twine cut into his wrists, digging fresh wounds.

His own voice echoing.

Then silence.

He could feel the greasepaint on his skin, his pores clogged, a mask covering his face.

The smell of animal fat, up close, the cheap make-up.

He could hardly breathe.

He wondered vaguely about DS Latimer, about Meg. Whether she had reported him missing yet, whether they were tracing his steps from house to house. It seemed impossible.

Where was he?

He looked around, stretching his neck as far as he could.

He was in a cellar, he saw that now.

337

Concrete walls, no windows. Stacks of tea crates, a workbench with rusty tools just out of reach: spanners, chisels, screwdrivers, a claw hammer. Instruments of torture.

The smell of damp, mildew. Spiderwebs on every joist and beam.

Cracks across the ceiling and down the walls, the overhead lamp with its tattered shade.

A moth batting against the bulb.

He had to let his eyes close. One moment of rest, that's all. Yet his head slumped down with the effort of merely staying awake.

He felt heavy and sluggish inside his skull, with too many thoughts. Something moved within his veins, that was it, a drug, a narcotic of some kind.

He was fading away. Sleep reached out for him . . .

A light flashed and burned and its glow penetrated his eyes and pulled him awake with its yellow flare.

Now a large, full-length mirror had been placed in front of him, directly in his sight.

He sat there, tied to the chair, this pitiful man with his pitiful mask, his sliced cheek, his hair matted with blood where he had been attacked in Edward Keele's bedroom.

It was coming back to him, the whole passage of time, the events that had dragged him to this place, this chair, this cone of light, this mirrored image.

He was King Lost.

The red lips extended upwards at the edges as though cut through; the blue cross on the forehead; the white skin, the black teardrop painted below his left eye.

And the wound on the other side of his face, the sheer ugliness of it.

And seeing it now, he remembered his own hand holding the knife in a dream, cutting himself. No, not in the dream, but for real. The self-inflicted wound. Someone guiding his own hand as it pressed the knife into the flesh.

He was being prepared, another sacrifice.

Above him, the moth continued with its endless back-and-forth journey between bulb and shade.

Hobbes stared at himself in the glass.

He could see the fear in his own eyes. As though a part of him had already departed the confines of the skin.

He licked at his lips, tasting the paint.

It would be so easy to give in, to let it all slip away . . .

He pulled his head upwards. Stay awake! He had to stay awake.

The light flared once more, brightly, off to one side. It was a camera, taking pictures of him. His sight blurred with it, as a figure moved, a nebulous shape.

And he struggled once more with the chair, desperate to escape, only to scrape the chair across the floor, the legs teetering, almost falling. He fought against gravity, just managing to stay upright.

If he fell over, it would be even more painful, and more desperate.

He had to stay calm.

To breathe, that was it, to breathe easily. To close his eyes and hold the body still. To find a place for himself where he could crawl and curl up and wait out this pain, this loss, this terrible piercing sense of doubt.

Hobbes allowed the world to settle around him.

Now he opened his eyes, and he listened.

The music was playing.

He knew it well, this song.

Just another backstreet harlequin, lost in the Soho blues.

It was his own song, his own journey through life.

I've given just about all I can give.

That time when he had roamed the streets of London, a new arrival from the North, lost and alone; and then with new pals, sometimes drunk and rowdy as all hell; and then in the force, first as a copper walking the beat and learning the ropes, and then later on as a detective, working cases. Friends, colleagues, victims and criminals. Jenkes. Dead. Hobbes's wife, his child, all gone, drifting away.

Now there's nothing left to lose . . .

Where had it taken him, all that effort, all the years? What did he have to show for it?

A few lives saved. The line of duty.

Yes, he could say that. He could put that on the scales and see how much it weighed against the loss of love, of friendship, of hope. He pictured the balance as it tipped this way and that, and then settled at last.

He turned his head and held his own stare in the dusty mirror, and he smiled.

'Show yourself, Caliban. Let me see you.'

The camera clicked again, another flashbulb popping.

A blossom of light.

The figure moved on, circling, taking picture after picture, and then retreating into the further darkness.

'Caliban! I know it's you.'

He shouted as loud as he could. Now the room became still once more, with only the music playing in accompaniment. Hobbes screamed into the blackness.

'Caliban!'

In answer, two hands appeared, one on each side of the mirror, two black-gloved hands. The mirror was wheeled away.

Hobbes fought against the last effects of the drug. He was still drowsy, and his eyes were heavy. The room shifted in his sight. He fell forward in his chair, only the bindings at his feet and hands keeping him in place.

A figure stepped forward, positioning herself at the edge of the circle of light.

It was a woman dressed entirely in black, with long dark hair hanging down on each side of her whitened face; her eyes were black within smudged circles of grey make-up, and they glistened in the lamplight. A single mark adorned the chin below the edge of the mouth. It was Lady Minerva's identifying mark, a symbol of Edenville's empress, and probably a mark of respect.

Hobbes held the woman's gaze.

'Natasha? Is that correct? Or Miss Caliban, shall we say?'

'Miss Caliban has retired. I have taken over the role of Lady Minerva.'

'I see.'

'Do you? I very much doubt that.'

Her voice was fake, affected, another woman's tone and timbre. Something copied. She stepped closer and glared at him. Hobbes tried to keep his heart steady, his breathing level. His eyes locked on hers.

'I found a photograph in Edward Keele's bedroom,' he said. 'It showed the two of you standing together. Edward was smiling. You were frowning, and staring off to the side. How old were you at the time?'

She didn't answer. Her eyes studied his face, every square inch of it.

Hobbes continued, pulling together rare strands of logic in his half-drugged brain. 'How old were you at the time? Eleven or twelve? Edward was younger, the baby of the group. There was a family resemblance between the two of you. Brother and sister.'

Her eyes carried on searching his features.

'The photograph was captioned, telling me the names of the children: *Edward and Natasha*. I thought it strange: your mother never mentioned having a daughter. Why was that?'

Now her eyes met his once again. They seemed to look deep inside him.

Hobbes could hear his voice trembling. 'Your arm was draped over Edward's shoulder. More than a loving embrace, or even a friendly one. It was protective. So the question is this – what were you protecting him from?'

For the first time the woman's eyes blinked.

'From your father's wrath, I presume.'

Her eyes closed completely for a second or two. When she opened them again, there was a light in them, and she spoke in a calm and loving voice: 'Many's the time I stood before my brother and painted his face for him, according to his wishes, following his design. Each element, like so, and like so . . .' Her hands worked at an imagined face, as though applying make-up. 'The whiteness of his skin, the cruel broken mouth that could never dare speak in public, his brow marked with the cross of our Lord, tilted to the side. Just so. Finally, the teardrop on his cheek, the tears that could never dry. Now at last he was complete.' She smiled deeply. 'Now my brother was safe. He was strong! King Lost, arise! You shall never be defeated.'

Hobbes watched her, fascinated. The remembered actions were utterly embedded in her soul.

And then the darkness returned to her eyes. In a cold, cruel voice she said, 'You have brought injury to the sacred image and spirit of King Lost.'

'You did that yourself, Natasha. You know that! You carved my face.'

'Your hand held the knife that dug into the mask, and through the mask into the flesh itself. I see the mark of blood upon you.' Her gloved hand traced at his face, pressing into the wound. 'For this act, you must be punished.'

She pressed deeper, and Hobbes felt pain shoot through his nerves. He jerked back in the chair and cried out. From the depths of the pain, he found the words needed: 'Your brother wasn't murdered, was he?' Her own wound, exposed and pressed at.

The hand hesitated in its progress.

'He killed himself. Or rather, you did it for him. You helped him.'

'We helped him.'

Hobbes tried to guide her along the memory. 'All five of you?'

'Four. Myself, Luna, Indigo and Bo. With Lady Minerva standing close by, overseeing our progress. Edward was wearing his painted mask, as only he could, so beautifully. We walked out under the moonlight, into the shallows. The water lapped about our waists. And there we held him, dear King Lost, we held him in our arms outstretched, beneath the incoming tide, so the water came over him, gently now, gently.'

She laid her hand on Hobbes's face, the fingers outstretched to cover his features. He felt the pressure on his skin increasing as, in her mind, she held King Lost under the water. But Hobbes didn't push back. His mind was working. He had to keep her talking for as long as possible, in the hope that Latimer had taken action and was at this minute on her way.

So now he asked, 'Did your brother struggle?'

Keele lifted her hand from his face. 'He struggled. Yes, at first. But he wanted this. He persuaded us, all of us. He pleaded with us. It was his only way out. And he wanted the group, his only true friends, to help him into the darkness.'

Her voice was now entirely her own.

Hobbes made a statement. 'The pain was too great for him. The pain of life.'

She smiled at his understanding. 'It was far too great. He had taken too many blows, too much hurt over the years. Too many wounds, inside and out, and too many scars. The mask would no longer protect him, Edenville would no longer keep him safe.'

'So you held him under the water. For how long?'

'Minutes. Minutes on end. Three, four, five. Until the tide took him as its own.'

Hobbes breathed more easily as Natasha Keele moved away. She seemed to be lost to the world, entirely at home elsewhere, in some other realm.

'And then you made your pledge, is that correct?'

'Yes. Some of them didn't want to do it, they were weakening. Death had caressed their faces. But I held them to their faith.'

'They were scared of you.'

'There is no room for weakness, not in Edenville. King Lost had shown his courage, now I needed them all to show theirs. To be as brave as my brother! And so we gathered in the dark and held hands, all five of us, and we spoke in a whisper as one, the words that Lady Minerva had written for us.'

Her voice changed, taking on a soft, lyrical tone.

'I have one task only. I will protect the face and form of King Lost. His beauty shineth forth, as always. I will break asunder all those who harm his majesty. I will preserve his spirit from all future hurt, impairment and injury. I will exult him!'

Now Hobbes understood. He saw the whole thing clearly, the hurt that had led to this moment, to this woman's intense desire to protect her brother's image, even to the point of death. For only by perpetuating the image, the mask, the face of King Lost, could she maintain the depth, courage and meaning of her brother's passing.

King Lost had to live on, so her brother could live, in spirit, in memory.

Nothing else mattered, only that.

It was madness, yet it held within itself a terrible kind of beauty. He saw it in her eyes, in her stance, her movements; he heard it in her voice, in the song that she returned to, over and over again.

'You must've loved Lucas Bell very much, when he took up the King Lost mask for himself, when he made it famous around the world.'

Natasha smiled. She spoke from the very centre of her being: 'My brother's spirit travelled the land, indeed the whole world, taking root whenever Lucas played and sang, taking root in people's hearts. In such manner, Edward lived on, bringing joy wherever his song took flight!'

Hobbes gave her no time to think of anything else, only the story. 'And it hurt you, when Lucas killed the mask live on stage?'

Her eyes narrowed. 'I was crazed with fever, with injury.' The white paint on her face cracked into many tiny lines. 'My brother was dying again, in such a public manner! No, it was wrong, dreadfully wrong.'

'So you punished him. You murdered Lucas Bell.'

Her expression changed and she spoke in a distressed tone. 'He deserved all that was coming to him, yes, for what he had done.'

'You found him that night, didn't you? In Hastings.'

'Lucas rested in the dark. He hid himself away, and trembled in the dark for what he had done, for the pain he had brought the world.'

'You killed him!'

She made no answer, and Hobbes felt his anger rising. He spat to clear his mouth and said, 'And you think it's fair, and just, to kill a man? To kill him merely for going against a promise he made, when he was a teenager? He was barely out of childhood!'

She glared back at him. 'I didn't kill him. I was called to his side.'

'You mean he did it himself, Lucas Bell killed himself?'

She smiled again. 'He needed persuading.'

'You held the gun for him, you made him do it—'

The room spun and flashed with sudden colour. Without warning, Natasha Keele had swung her arm back through the air and brought it forward at speed, to slap him hard with the flat of her hand. Hobbes toppled back, the chair almost falling to the floor. But Keele grabbed him by his shirt front and held him suspended at an angle.

The pain of the blow broke through the shock and reached his cheek, where the knife wound lay, and he gritted his teeth against it, as Keele sneered at him, her face close to his now.

'I have punished where necessary, according to the oath taken, at the homes of Brendan Clarke and Johnny Valentine. Both of them were quite enamoured of me, of what I was, of what I stood for, my relationships to Lucas and to King Lost. Brendan especially was tender in my arms.' Hobbes could feel her breath on his face as she spoke. 'Now the message is spread far and wide. The mask is safe. People will not dare to sully its contours, they will not dare to bring injury to my brother.' Her voice reached its topmost pitch. 'They will not dare!'

She let go of him. For a second he could feel himself falling, bound to the chair, his heart leaping with fear, but she grabbed him at the last second and dragged him back upright. She laughed in his face.

'And what about Simone Paige?' he cried. 'Did she really need to die?'

A quiver of doubt crossed Natasha Keele's features.

'I killed her because she discovered the secret dwelling place, where the first stones of Edenville were laid, and because she caused Lucas to remove the mask from his face. She is to blame, and for this I struck out wildly at her body.'

'I don't think Simone was to blame,' Hobbes said. 'I believe Lucas made his decision on his own. He'd had enough—'

'No!'

'He'd had enough of King Lost—'

'No, no!'

'King Lost was strangling him. He was killing him.'

'NO!'

She cried and shrieked.

The wordless howl of her voice. A blur of movement.

And suddenly Hobbes could no longer breathe.

Something was covering his head, his face, his eyes, his mouth.

Opaque, sticky.

He struggled to escape.

It was a plastic bag. Miss Caliban's face was barely seen through the covering, a dark mask. That's how he saw her now: Caliban, a demonic, half-human creature. Her hands tight around his neck, holding the bag in place as the plastic moulded itself to his features, clogging his mouth and nostrils. He sucked in air where there was none, and felt himself choking, his throat and chest filled with fire, his eyes flickering with dots of light. He rocked back on the chair and, more from instinct than will, he applied his whole force into the act of escaping this torment. He pushed back further with all his strength until at last the chair toppled over under his and Keele's weight combined, and they fell together to the hard floor. The old chair hit the concrete and crumpled and smashed and suddenly his left arm was free or partially free – he couldn't see because of the bag that still clung to his face.

He rolled over and took Miss Caliban with him.

Still her hands were clasped around his throat. Still she clung on, holding the bag in place, tighter now, even as he smashed the wooden arm of the chair against her shoulders, her neck, wherever he could hit by blind chance as the darkness closed in around his eyes, the final lights popping out, red, then yellow, now blue, dying, fading . . .

No, it would not happen, not here, not in this damp, stinking hole in the ground, he would fight this, he would struggle on, his entire being set to a single purpose: he would live, he would hold on, he would hold on to life.

It was an empty promise that he made to himself as the darkness cloaked him entirely and his lungs drew in their last few breaths.

Yet a light still flickered behind his eyes.

A tiny light. A spark.

Enough to trigger his body into one last movement, and he roared with anger that he should be this close to the void. His entire body jerked and thrust forward, his free hand grabbed at Miss Caliban, his fingers clutching randomly at a fold of flesh and he closed upon it, squeezing, digging his fingernails in, deep, deep, until they ran with warmth, a fluid, he could only think it was blood, and he dug in further until he could hear her screaming and her hands came loose from his neck.

It was all he needed. A moment. *A chance.* And he grabbed at it, this single chance, binding himself to it, and rolled away as far as he could, as the chair crunched beneath him, jabbing at his back and his other arm, but now he was ripping the plastic bag free of his face. He tore it loose and stood up, kicking the remains of the chair away from him.

One arm was still attached to a broken strut, the other was free.

He tottered on his feet from his ordeal and he peered through a haze of redness: Miss Caliban and another person, a woman, he thought. He spat out the words, her name . . .

'Meg! Meg, Meg!'

She was standing over Miss Caliban, who lay on the floor, supine, her face covered in blood.

The mist began to clear from his eyes, and he saw it wasn't DS Latimer at all.

His body swayed, he was losing his balance.

The woman stepped forward, a spanner in her hands, dripping with blood.

Was it the mother of the household, Mrs Keele? Her face shimmered under the hanging bulb. She was speaking to him, the words muffled, heard from many miles away.

No, it wasn't Mrs Keele.

He saw that now.

She stepped close, reaching out.

His eyes started to close and he fell and hit the concrete floor and lay there, wanting nothing more than to be home again, in a place of safety, at last.

The woman leant over him, and murmured, and cried.

A Faraway Night

Detective Inspector Hobbes sat up on the ambulance's bed, brushed off the medic's help, and walked unsteadily to the open door. The street was filled with squad cars, police officers, and a gathering of spectators beyond the cordon. He could see DS Latimer coming out of the front door of the Keele household. The sky was clear overhead, and the moon was full. The sight of it filled him with a tender, brittle joy. He stepped down from the ambulance and took a few careful steps. He'd been given pain-killers, and his head was bandaged. The wound on his face would need stitches, but for now he'd insisted on just a dressing. There were more important things than his own well-being. He looked round, searching the crowd, the bustle and the noise and lights. He saw Natasha Keele being guided unsteadily into a patrol car. The blue light on the roof of the vehicle pulsed to a beat Hobbes could barely comprehend. A stray thought was calling to him – the idea that he'd made a mistake, that he was still missing a piece of the puzzle. He turned in a daze and saw Susan Keele being led away by another officer – her eyes were dead to the night around her and they passed over Hobbes without seeing him.

'Should you be walking, guv?'

It was Latimer, her face showing concern.

He nodded and said wearily, 'Where is she?'

'Who? You mean Natasha Keele? She's being taken in—'

He grabbed Latimer's arms. 'No. The woman who saved me? Where is she?'

'She's at home. DC Palmer's with her.'

He was already walking away from the scene. Latimer followed, taking his arm and steering him in the right direction. The address was only a street away and they were there in minutes. The door was open.

'Apparently, she saw you entering the Keeles's house, and was worried. The family has a bad reputation around here.'

'That's not it,' Hobbes said.

'How do you mean?'

'The colours of the rainbow.'

Latimer gave the inspector a quizzical look. But Hobbes had already entered the house. He paused on the threshold of the living room.

DC Palmer was sitting at the table, holding the hand of Violet Yorke. The daughter of the house, Morgan, was resting in an armchair in the corner of the room. The girl's face was free of the King Lost mask, and Hobbes saw her clearly for the first time.

He could see in her features exactly what he expected to see.

The connection.

He turned his attention to Violet Yorke, who immediately broke contact with Palmer. Her eyes would not meet his.

Hobbes stepped into the room and said, 'I want to thank you, Violet. For saving my life.'

Mrs Yorke nodded, still without looking up.

Palmer stood up and offered him her seat at the table, and he took it gratefully. He was suddenly tired, but he needed to say what he had to say, and that was all that mattered. He reached out and touched Violet's shoulder, urging her to look up at him, and she did so, and he saw the tears in her eyes.

'Perhaps your daughter should leave us?' he asked.

Her head shook and trembled, and she answered, 'No. She needs to know.'

'What are you talking about?' Morgan asked.

Violet looked over at her daughter and smiled weakly. 'I love you,' she said.

'I know that, Mother.'

The line was repeated, even more quietly – *I love you* – and then Mrs Yorke turned back to the inspector and waited for his questions.

Hobbes began by saying, 'Violet, when you were young, you came under the influence of a very powerful woman, someone who changed your life, and the lives of other young people, for both good and for ill. In fact, mainly for ill.'

'Yes, I know.'

'I saw a photograph of you and your friends. But I didn't recognize you at first.'

'I have changed, I know that.' This was said with an air of despondency.

'But then I turned the photograph over,' Hobbes continued, 'and your code name was given, along with the other five residents of Edenville. And I saw that your name was Mood Indigo.'

She smiled broadly, hearing this. 'Yes. That was me. The name was given to me by—'

'I don't understand. Who is Mood Indigo?'

It was Morgan speaking, interrupting her mother's speech. Violet Yorke looked at her daughter and said, quite simply, 'I am Mood Indigo. The name was given to me by Lucas Bell.'

Morgan smiled. 'You're saying that you knew Lucas?'

'I did, yes.' Violet Yorke was speaking calmly. Hobbes could see the physical effort she was making, holding her body still and upright in the chair, keeping her hands out of sight, maintaining eye contact with her daughter. She continued now, 'I've never told you before, my love, but I was quite friendly with him, when I was younger.'

'I know you've always liked his music,' Morgan said, 'but I never realized . . .'

'Well, there it is. A true story.' And with that she turned back to Detective Hobbes and said, 'Did you work out the reason for the name?'

Hobbes nodded. 'I thought of Violet and Indigo being next to each other in the rainbow. And I recalled the phrase I learned at school to learn the correct order of the colours: *Richard of York Gave Battle In Vain*. And I realized that your surname was included in the line.'

'Lucas was always clever, that way. Playing word games, leaving clues all over the place.'

Morgan was staring at the detective and her mother. She was alert, and yet anxious at the same time.

Hobbes continued, 'You were eighteen or nineteen at the time?'

'Eighteen,' Violet answered.

'And you were pregnant. I saw that from the photograph.'

'Yes, I was. I was pregnant with Morgan.'

Her daughter made a noise, a gasp of surprise, but Violet held up a hand, and said, 'Please, darling. Let me explain everything.'

Quickly, Hobbes carried on. 'So you were young, and unmarried. And I'm guessing that you moved in a tiny circle of people, namely the members of the Minerva Club?'

'They were my only friends.'

'There were three boys in the group, Lucas, Gavin and Edward, but I can't imagine Edward Keele or Gavin Roberts were the type, really.'

'That's correct.'

'So Lucas Bell is the father of Morgan?'

'Yes.'

Morgan stood up from her chair. She was going to move forward, but it got no further than a thought, a shiver of fear. To Hobbes's eyes, her features had now taken on the ghost of her father's face. Her mother turned to her and said, 'Morgan, I told you your father was a man who had moved away from the town. That was a lie.'

The girl managed a single word: 'Why?'

The question silenced her mother.

Hobbes said to Morgan, 'Please sit down.'

The girl did so immediately, glad to be given a task.

The detective turned back to the table. 'Violet, why don't you tell us what happened. From the beginning.'

She looked at Hobbes and then at her daughter. The look in her eyes, the utter yearning that she held, spilt over into tears. She wiped these away with the back of her hand and then visibly steeled herself for the story.

'I was very much in love with Lucas,' she began. 'It was a teenage crush, I know that now, but at the time it felt as though nothing else mattered in the whole world, nothing at all. I gave myself to him, completely. And I found myself with child.'

Here she paused and took a few deep breaths.

'Did Lucas love you back?' Hobbes asked.

'No. Not really. Well, a little perhaps. But his family absolutely hated mine; they thought we were awful and very working class, and that it was all my fault, that I'd tempted their son into mischief. My parents were Catholics and they were adamant that I have the child, but then insisted that I give the baby up for adoption. Of course, I would not do that.' She glanced over at Morgan, with a sudden brave, defiant look in her eyes. 'I loved my child more than anything else.'

'And then Lucas left Hastings?'

'Yes. He stuck around for a few more years, until Edward Keele died, which ended the whole Edenville dream, and then he left for London.'

Mother and daughter stared at each other. Hobbes saw the look that passed between them, the fierce determination they shared: they weren't that different, really.

'I watched from a distance as Lucas became a pop star, adored around the world, and I looked after Morgan, and played her his records from an early age, which was my way, I suppose, of allowing her father to remain an influence on her.'

'Did Lucas ever try to get in touch?'

'No. Occasionally, in the early days of his career, a cheque would arrive through the post. But as his fame increased, the money stopped entirely. And by that time, Morgan and I were settled into our life together.'

Hobbes said, 'It must've been strange to see him take up the King Lost mask?'

'It was. But I was happy that poor Edward's creation had been given this new lease of life.'

'How did you feel when Bell destroyed the mask?'

'It seemed to me inevitable that such a thing would happen. Of course, Natasha was livid, beyond any kind of measure.'

'You were friends with Natasha Keele?'

Violet flinched. 'Hardly that. But she was the only one of the Minerva group that I still saw. She was quite horrible, easily the worst of us all. She carried the most pain, shall we say. But we spoke now and then. Natasha was always so full of regret, and bitterness.'

'And then Lucas came back to Hastings, after his final gig?'

Violet Yorke licked at her dry lips and closed her eyes momentarily.

'Yes, he came back. He waited until I had left the house one day, and he came up to me in the street. He wore a hat, and a jacket with a high collar which he had turned up to protect his face. It was an ineffectual sort of disguise. But he actually looked quite ordinary out of his stage clothes and his make-up, a very ordinary man. And he was drunk, and I believe he had taken a drug of some kind. I don't know, I'm not an expert on such things.'

'Did he want to see Morgan?'

'No. My daughter was ten years old at the time, and was staying the night at a friend's house, a sleepover. That simple fact embold-ened me. Lucas and I sat on a bench in Alexandra Park, and we talked of many things – well, of his life and his problems, mainly. He was very depressed, I think. Lost. A helpless soul, burdened by the weight of the world.'

'Did you feel sorry for him?'

She met his gaze for the first time with a fully directed look. 'Yes. It was strange, I thought I would feel anger, but I couldn't find it inside me. It just wasn't possible, because he looked so very, very pitiful. He told me a story, that he'd sent a letter that morning to an old girlfriend of his. He thought that by promising her his future love, he would somehow escape the present day, and its troubles. But sadly, he told me, it was not to be.'

'What happened then?'

'Dusk was falling, and the park was being closed for the night. He walked me back to his car, his lovely blue car, and he offered to drive me out to the countryside, to the cottage he'd rented in Westfield, a village to the north of the town.'

'And you agreed to this?'

'I did.'

'Why?'

'Well, I was curious, I suppose. And more than that, I could see he was in no fit state to drive, and I was fearful of him being in an accident, or even killing someone on the roads. So I drove him home.'

'Did you see a tarot card on the dashboard?'

'No. Natasha placed that there, later.'

'Why?'

'She told me it was a marker, a symbol of King Lost's eternal soul. You see, Lady Minerva introduced us to such things, and she gave each of us a card that represented us. For instance, Edward was the Emperor, I was the High Priestess, and Lucas was the Fool. And he really didn't resent such a term – in his youth he revelled in the blind promise of adventures to come. He was very close to Minerva, when he was young. Yes, very close.'

A tinge of jealously took over her features.

'Did you go straight to the cottage?'

'Not quite. Lucas wanted a drink. I told him the pubs were closed, but he wouldn't listen. He told me to stop the car. I was quite scared, he was thrashing around, shouting, and so on. So I stopped, and he staggered out and walked towards the nearest pub. I remember a man standing there on the pavement, staring at him. Lucas had taken his hat off and his dyed, streaky hair was on view. He must've been recognized. I pleaded with him to get back in the car, and he did. I think the fact that he'd been recognized sobered him up a bit.'

'So you drove out to his cottage?' Hobbes asked.

'We did.'

'Was there any sign of Natasha Keele?'

'No. Not yet. She came along later.'

'But this was the last night of Lucas Bell's life?'

'It was.'

At this simple statement of the truth, Morgan spoke up for the first time in a while. 'Mother, did you see Lucas Bell kill himself?'

Violet Yorke nodded.

Morgan wanted to ask another question, but Hobbes interrupted her. He needed to keep the interview on track.

'What took place when you reached the cottage?'

'It was an isolated place, which suited his need to escape. Inside, the place was filthy, smelly, with lots of unwashed plates and piles of dirty laundry. I could see that for the last three weeks, since he'd killed off King Lost, he'd just about given up on life. And there were pages and pages of lyrics on the floor and the table. I looked at some of them; they were songs from long ago, tunes I'd heard him play for the Minerva Club. Songs about Edenville.' She paused and then said, 'I thought he was looking for clues.'

'Clues to what?'

'A reason to live. He had also been reading the tarot, I saw the cards set out in the Celtic cross layout. Seeking help, I guess. Clarity.'

'So Lucas Bell had decided to kill himself, at this point?'

'I know that to be true.'

'Because?'

'Because he told me so. He poured himself the remains of a bottle of whisky and he sat there in the middle of all this mess with his head in his hands and he told me the truth. That his life was over. He told me this, and once he'd started talking, he couldn't stop. It all came out. That fame was destroying him, that his guilt over Edward Keele's death was too much to bear. He had worn the King Lost mask for a while, hoping that would relieve the guilt, but it was no longer working. He felt that his success was built on a stolen crown. That was his exact phrase. *A stolen crown.*'

Violet Yorke stopped talking, overwhelmed by the emotions she was bringing back to life.

Fearful of stemming the flow, Hobbes prompted: 'So you helped him?'

She nodded. 'He asked me to drive out to Witch Haven. It wasn't that far away, and we could've walked, quite easily. But we took the car. It was a clear warm night, the moon almost full. I can bring it all to mind quite easily.'

'What time was it?'

'Nearly midnight, I imagine. Ours was the only car on the road. We stopped at the crest of the hill and Lucas got out and opened the farm gate. He asked me to park the car in the field. Which I did. We sat there with only the car's interior light to shine on us. And that's when I saw the gun.'

Hobbes could hear Morgan draw a breath.

'You weren't expecting that, I imagine?'

'I don't know what I was expecting, to be honest. Sleeping pills, perhaps. Washed down with more alcohol. I thought I might be watching over something peaceful, a slow fading away. And of course I was drawn back to the night of Edward's drowning.'

'Go on, if you can.'

Violet nodded. 'He took the gun from the glove compartment. I wasn't scared. I mean, I wasn't expecting him to turn it on me. I could see from the look in his eyes that the desire to end it all was in him. He placed the gun against his temple. And then . . .'

'He hesitated?'

Her voice broke. She wiped more tears from her eyes. 'He faltered. It was terrible – why, why did he do that? If only he hadn't, if only he'd gone through with it, as he intended.'

'What did you do, Violet?'

Again, Violet Yorke looked at Hobbes directly. 'I thought I might yet save Lucas.' She stopped and glanced over at her daughter. 'So I asked him a question.'

'What did you ask?'

'You see, in all our talk in the park and on the journey to Witch Haven, and in the cottage, not once had he mentioned Morgan, not by name or anything. So I asked him about her. I said, *What about Morgan? Surely, you would like to see her. If you lived, that would be possible.* The gun was still in his hand when he answered me.'

'What did he say?'

'*Nothing matters. Nothing at all. Nothing.* And that was it. That was all I needed. The anger rose up in me from nowhere and I reached out and grabbed his wrist to hold the gun in place against his head. He was trembling now. Sweating. I could see the fear in his eyes, as though he wanted to pull away, but I closed my hands around his wrist and I held the gun. A spell enclosed us both. One of my fingers crept forward and squeezed itself inside the trigger guard, on top of his.' Her voice wavered. 'I wasn't thinking. It just happened, one action after another.'

Her eyes were staring ahead, far away from this living room, as far away as yesterday – she was back in that car, parked in Witch Haven field on that night with the moon clear and the hills rolling away into the darkness.

'I pulled the trigger.'

There was a dreadful moment of silence in the room.

It stretched out. No one spoke.

Not until a terrible scream split the silence in two. Morgan Yorke stood up and lurched towards her mother. DC Palmer intercepted her, wrapping her arms around the girl's body and holding her back. Morgan struggled and reached for her mother, straining against Palmer's hold.

Hobbes kept his eyes on Violet Yorke. She would not look at her daughter, not at all; her sight had returned to the room, to the present day, but only to focus on the patterned tablecloth in front of her.

Morgan fell quiet at last and stopped her struggling. And when Hobbes nodded, and Palmer let the girl go, Morgan collapsed to the floor.

Hobbes stood up. With Palmer's help, he took hold of Morgan and lifted her to her feet. She was led through the doorway by Palmer, and he waited until he heard their footsteps fade before turning his attention once more to Violet Yorke.

'How did Natasha Keele get involved?'

She answered in a voice drained of feeling. 'I walked in a daze back to Luke's cottage. I honestly can't remember how I managed it, but once I was there I rang Natasha from his telephone and told her I was in trouble. All I could think about was Morgan being taken away from me, because of what I'd done.'

'Did you tell Natasha what had happened?'

'No. Not then. Just that I'd committed a terrible act. My tone must've given me away. She drove straight out there to help me. Apparently, she found me huddled in a corner of the room, crying to myself. I told her what had happened, and she took immediate charge of the situation; she was always very good like that. She gathered some things from the house. I remember she tore a sheet of paper in two, I couldn't think why. I couldn't imagine what she was planning. But together we drove back to Witch Haven, and I was glad that someone else was now in charge. I remember being scared that we might meet someone on the way, but it was even quieter than before, and darker. The moon had clouded over.'

'What happened when you got there?'

'We walked down to the parked car. Natasha had brought a torch with her and I could see that she was excited by what she saw, the state of Lucas, his wounds, the blood. Her eyes were wild. She smiled, and it was horrible to look at, but I was grateful for her help. I watched as she placed a slip of paper in the glove compartment. And she had a tarot card with her – she must've picked this up from the cottage. She lodged it on the dashboard, in front of Luke's body, and she made some comment about it, but I'm afraid I can't remember what she said.'

'That's fine, Violet. Just carry on.'

'And then we walked back to her car and we drove down the hill towards Hastings. It must've been two o'clock, by then. There was music playing on the radio. I was suddenly tired, but when I looked over at Natasha, I could see the excitement still in her eyes. I had done her a service by killing Lucas, or helping him to kill himself. Whichever it was.'

Violet Yorke looked at Hobbes as she finished her story.

'In her mind, I had punished Lucas for the crime of destroying King Lost. And now I know that I set Natasha on a course that night, a course that led her to kill again, and again. I must take some blame for those further actions. I have to . . .'

She could say no more, and her head bowed down.

DC Palmer came back into the room. Hobbes left her with Violet Yorke and walked back out on to the street. Many of the spectators had returned to their homes. He saw Latimer chatting to a uniformed officer and he walked over towards her. As he did so, he reflected on the fantasy village called Edenville and the six people who had lived there, over fifteen years ago. Each name now had a face, each face a name.

Latimer saw him, and smiled.

Hobbes touched at the dressing on his face and thought of the wound he had received. He stopped where he was, halfway across the road. The shock was setting in and he started to shiver as a sudden cold ran through him.

He couldn't move, not one step.

Edenville

Bo Dazzle – Gavin Roberts
King Lost – Edward Keele
Lady Minerva – Eve Dylan
Luna Bloom – Lucas Bell
Miss Caliban – Natasha Keele
Mood Indigo – Violet Yorke

MONDAY
31 AUGUST 1981

The Call-Out

Hobbes struggled to pull the plastic bag from his face, but the more he tried, the closer it clung to him, to his skin and his mouth, and he woke up gasping for breath and wondering what the noise was, the noise that still rang in his ears, piercing the gloom.

He groaned aloud and sat up in the bed.

The doorbell continued to sound.

He bent down to slip the loop of string from around his ankle and cursed as he did so: the dull throb in his head suddenly spiked into a sharp red-hot pain. Well, at least he hadn't been sleepwalking; perhaps he was free of all that, at last.

He stumbled into the hallway and called out, 'Yes, who is it?'

'It's PC Barlow, sir.'

'Barlow?'

'Yes, sir.'

Hobbes opened the door. The constable stared at him. Hobbes blinked a few times and then pulled his pyjamas tighter around himself.

'What the hell do you want?'

'You're needed, sir.'

For a moment, Hobbes could make no sense of what was being said.

'What time is it?' he asked, rubbing at his eyes.

'It's almost five.'

'Five o'clock! Jesus.'

'We've been calling you, but we couldn't get through.'

'I took the phone off the hook.'

'Right. Shall I wait while you get ready, sir?'

'What's the problem?' An awful thought struck him. 'It's not Martin, is it? My son?'

'It's Fairfax.'

'Fairfax? He's not . . .'

'I don't know what the trouble is, sir.'

'OK. Give me a minute.'

Hobbes went into the bathroom and splashed cold water on his face. Then he dragged on the first clothes he could find and hurried outside. Barlow was at the wheel of an unmarked car. Hobbes got in the passenger seat and saw DS Latimer sitting in the back.

'Guv.'

'What's going on, Meg?'

'Tommy rang the station. He sounded desperate.'

'He's been attacked?'

Worry took over her face. 'I don't know. He asked for you, specifically.'

They set off. Hobbes probed around his mouth with his tongue and wished that he'd taken the time to clean his teeth. He felt terrible. He'd been in bed for most of the weekend, nursing his wounds and running a careful finger over the stitches in his cheek. And having the strangest dreams.

He realized that they weren't heading for the station. 'Where are we going, Barlow?'

'Putney, sir. DC Fairfax gave us the address.'

Nobody seemed to want to talk, which suited Hobbes. He settled back into the seat and watched as the early morning streets of South London passed by. Some people were already up and about: taxi drivers, bakers, market traders, a street-cleaning vehicle.

Latimer tapped him on the shoulder.

'We're almost there.'

'Right.'

Barlow was steering the car down a side street. The area looked run-down: a place you ended up in, rather than aspired to.

'This is it,' Barlow said as he brought the car to a halt. 'Number seventeen.'

Latimer looked out through the window. 'Looks like a boarding house, or a hostel.'

It did, and a grotty one at that.

Barlow stayed in the car. Hobbes and Latimer got out and walked up to the front door of the building. It was opened immediately by the night manager, a middle-aged man who fretted about them both, saying, 'I'm glad you're here, I really am.'

'What's going on?' Hobbes asked.

'The visitor used the payphone in the hall, just here. Then he went back up to the room. Do you see what he's done to my property?'

Latimer examined the handset. It was covered in blood.

Hobbes looked up the stairs. 'Which room are we talking about?'

'Number nine, top floor.'

'And who lives there?'

The manager frowned. 'A police officer. Name of Mawley.'

Hobbes cursed.

They climbed two flights of stairs. The place stank of damp and rot. So this was where DS Mawley had ended up after his wife had thrown him out.

At the very top of the house, the manager pointed to a door. 'That's the one.'

Hobbes tried it. It wouldn't budge. He tapped on the panelling.

'Fairfax? You in there?'

There was no answer.

'It's Hobbes. I've got Latimer with me. Meg's here.'

Latimer stepped forward. 'Tommy, it's me. Come on, love. Let us in.'

There was still no response. The manager produced a bunch of keys. He indicated the correct one to Hobbes, who used it to turn the lock. Carefully, a fraction at a time, he pushed open the door. Then he nodded at Latimer, gesturing for her to stay on the landing. He stepped inside and closed the door behind him.

The room was neat and tidy, with the occupant's few possessions set out in their proper places. A man's shirt was drying over the back of a chair. This, a single bed, a cabinet, and a tilted wardrobe were the only pieces of furniture. A lamp had fallen to the floor.

Detective Sergeant Leonard Mawley was sitting against the wall, his legs folded under him on the carpet and his hands attached to a radiator pipe with a pair of police-issue handcuffs. The wounds on his chest and shoulders were visible above the white vest he was wearing. There was blood all over the vest, and spots of it on the surrounding floor and walls. Mawley's face was a pulpy mess, the nose busted and one eye puffy and forced shut. He'd probably lost some teeth, judging from the state of his jawline, but it was difficult to tell for sure because of the dirty tea towel that had been stuffed in his mouth. The one good eye tried to focus on Hobbes. Whatever portion of life remained was gathered in that blackened pupil.

Tom Fairfax stood nearby, a tyre iron held in both hands.

Hobbes didn't move, not until he'd taken in the whole scene and his pulse had slowed. Then he took a step closer. Fairfax raised the weapon.

The inspector tried to speak calmly. 'OK. Let's take this easy, shall we?'

'Stay back, I'm warning you.'

Hobbes raised his hands. 'OK, Tommy. Look, I'm not moving.'

'I'll do him! I'm going to sort him out once and for all. I'll finish the job.'

'I know you will.'

Fairfax wiped a smear of blood from his mouth. There had been some kind of scuffle, before he'd got Mawley under control. He must have been fiercely driven, to have overpowered Mawley, a bigger, more experienced man, a man with viciousness in his soul.

Hobbes breathed steadily. He tried a different tack. 'DC Fairfax, you called for me, isn't that right?' A nod in response. 'You wanted to talk.'

'Yes.'

'Well, here I am. Let's have it out.'

Fairfax turned to look at Mawley. His face held scorn. 'I got him, the dirty fucker. I worked it all out, bit by bit.'

'Aye, you did a good job. You might well get a promotion for this . . .'

It was a mistake. Hobbes knew that even before the words had left his lips. The tyre iron came down with a crash on to the rickety bedside cabinet, smashing it in two. Wood splintered and an alarm clock fell to the floor. Mawley jerked back and pressed himself against the radiator. His wrists pulled at the handcuffs.

Fairfax screamed. 'This is about Charlie Jenkes, and who killed him. Nothing more!'

Hobbes risked another step. 'How did you find out? I'd like to know.'

'You gave it away, Hobbes. Sir. You told me about the photos, and the blackmail, and another cop being involved.'

'But how do you know it was Mawley?'

'A process of elimination.' He was proud of his work. 'Who else could you take the pictures to, to get them developed, but someone you knew, someone away the force. I tried a few places.'

'And then you went to see Neville Briggs?'

Fairfax grinned. 'I had it out of him, no trouble. A little pressure. He showed me the prints.' Now his face creased into utter disgust. 'It made me sick, just looking at them.'

'Tommy, I don't think you rang for me just to show off. There's something more, isn't there?'

Fairfax shook his head vigorously. 'It was a mistake calling you.'

Hobbes kept his nerve. 'I think you want me to help you. That's why you called. So I'd stop you from going any further.'

Fairfax made a threatening gesture with the tyre iron, and Mawley struggled on the floor, his mouth gagging on the towel. Fairfax reached down and tore the gag loose. Immediately the bound man started to cry out.

'Get him off me, Hobbes – he's a fuckin' psycho!'

Hobbes didn't move.

'One more blow should do it.' Fairfax's expression lacked all feeling. 'One hard blow to the head. And he's gone.'

Hobbes kept his cool. He looked down at Mawley. 'Len, is this true? Did you do it?'

'He's already confessed.' Fairfax was ready to attack.

'I know that. But I need to hear it for myself.'

Mawley raised himself up as best he could, his body curved and straining at his bonds. 'Get me out of here, Hobbes! I need a hospital. I need you to do the right thing.'

The right thing . . .

Yes, that seemed like a good idea.

'Did you do it?'

It was a cold question; and it got a cold answer.

'Damn right.' The one visible eye closed. 'Yeah, I strung him up. As he deserved.' Mawley spat out blood, one gobful for each phrase of the confession. 'He was a bastard, through and through. You both know that!'

'You see?' Fairfax's eyes blazed. 'I want you to watch, Hobbes. While I kill him.'

Hobbes walked up close. 'Wait. Think about it, Tommy.'

'If you had an ounce of guts, you'd join in.'

'Perhaps. But that would make me no better than Mawley. And he's as bad a cop as I've ever seen.'

The younger man hesitated. Doubt flickered in his eyes. Hobbes reached out. 'Come on, it's over. We've got our man.'

But then the door opened and Latimer stepped inside the room. Fairfax didn't like this. Shame painted his face red, and he gave Hobbes a push, hard enough to make him stumble back and hit the wall.

Fairfax shuddered. He cried out, 'Meg, get out of here!'

Hobbes said to her, 'Best do as he says.'

But Latimer disobeyed his command. Instead she walked up close to Fairfax, and said, 'You stupid prick. I mean, look at the fucking state of you.'

Fairfax withered under her gaze.

'Meg,' he said, his voice trembling. 'Meg. I'm sorry. Don't look at me like that. Don't look at me.'

But Latimer kept her eyes right on him. 'I'm not turning away, not until you put that stupid thing down.'

Fairfax blinked the sweat from his eyes.

Hobbes looked on. The situation could turn in a second and he tried to ready himself to deal with any eventuality.

Mawley buried his face in the crook of his arm.

The tyre iron trembled.

Latimer touched Fairfax on the arm. 'Tommy. I'm on your side. We both are.'

And that was it. That's all it took. Those words. Fairfax made a whimpering sound and his hand opened, and the weapon fell to the carpet. And then he collapsed. He folded into Latimer's arms, sobbing.

Hobbes remained where he was, taking in the sight of his two fellow officers, and his former colleague huddled up against the radiator. He saw the broken furniture, the blood in splatters, and his own damaged face in a mirror above the bed. This little room. Latimer, Fairfax, Mawley. For the first time in months, in years even, he was a part of something. It was strange and barely understandable, but right here in the midst of love and hate, right at the fracture, the balancing point, this was his place in the world.

Acknowledgements

Warmest thanks to:

Susanna Jones, for the seeds of Witch Haven field.

William Shaw, who told me a story about the very early days of a world-famous rock band. From that conversation, the concept of the imaginary village grew. He also gave me expert advice on writing for the crime genre.

Vana, Michelle, Alex and Russell, who read the manuscript at different stages and offered invaluable help and guidance.

Everyone at Transworld for their amazing work in bringing the book to life, and especially to my editor, Bill Scott-Kerr, for seeing the potential of both the story and Detective Hobbes.

I received financial help from the Society of Authors and the Royal Literary Fund during the writing of *Slow Motion Ghosts*, and I wish to thank both institutions for their dedication and support.

About the Author

Jeff Noon trained in the visual arts and drama and was active on the post-punk music scene before becoming a playwright, and then a novelist. His novels include *Vurt*, *Pollen*, *Automated Alice*, *Nymphomation*, *Needle in the Groove*, *Falling Out of Cars*, *A Man of Shadows* and *The Body Library*. He has published two collections of short fiction, *Pixel Juice* and *Cobralingus*, and is the crime reviewer for *The Spectator*.